HOSTS OF REBECCA

In the light of the Corpse Candle I saw his face, eyes bulging, jaw dropped for the scream.

Flat on my belly now, wriggling towards him, grasping the tuft-grasses, the hair of the peat bog, and I reached him in pistol shots of cracking ice.

'Granfer!' I cried, but he gave no answer. Not a sound he made standing there to his waist in bog, with one hand gripping a bottle and the other hand pointing to Tarn. The fingers I clutched were frozen solid. Preserved all right was Grandfer but not in hops as he'd planned it.
Preserved by peat for Cae White's generations. As I snatched at his belt he slipped from my sight and his soul flew up to Bronwen, his lover.
And the peat bog sighed and sucked in hunger.

Hosts of Rebecca

Alexander Cordell

CORONET BOOKS
Hodder and Stoughton

Copyright © G. A. Graber 1960

First published in Great Britain 1960 by
Victor Gollancz Limited

Coronet edition 1976
Third impression 1984

―――――――――――――――――――――――――――――――――

Set, printed and bound in Great Britain for
Hodder and Stoughton Paperbacks, a
division of Hodder and Stoughton Ltd.,
Mill Road, Dunton Green, Sevenoaks,
Kent (Editorial Office: 47 Bedford
Square, London, WC1 3DP) by
Cox & Wyman Ltd, Reading

ISBN 0 340 20509 1

For Georgina

... I retain my belief in the nobility and excellence of the human. I believe that spiritual sweetness and unselfishness will conquer the gross gluttony of today. And last of all, my faith is in the working class. As some Frenchman has said, 'The stairway of time is ever echoing with the wooden shoe going up, the polished boot descending.'

Jack London

CHAPTER 1

1839

A PEBBLE HIT the window, bringing me upright.
  In the sea of Grandfer's fourposter bed I sat, staring into the nothingness between sleeping and waking, shivering in the pindrop silence.

A handful of gravel at the glass now, spraying as thunder. Out of bed head-first then, scrambling over the boards. Night-shirt billowing, I raised the sash.

"Hush you for God's sake," I said. "You will have Morfydd out."

"Then move your backside," said Joey in the frost below. "It is damned near midnight."

Twelve years old, this one – a year and a bit younger than me, with corn-coloured hair and the face of a churchyard ghost, starved at that. A criminal was Tramping Boy Joey, the son of a Shropshire sin-eater; raised in a poorhouse, thumped by life into skin and bone, but the best poaching man in the county of Carmarthenshire. Our bailiff had fits with his legs up when Joey was loose, for he poached every meal. You keep from that Joey, said Morfydd, my sister – you can always stoop to pick up trash.

I dressed like a madman in the stinging silence of December with the window throwing icicles into the room, for it was a winter to freeze dewdrops, and the moon was shivering in the sky that night, rolling over the rim of the mountain. Ice hung from down-spouts, water butts creaked solid and the white plains were hammered into silence. Black was the river where the hen coots were skating, and the whole rolling country from Narberth to Carmarthen city was dying for the warmth and tumble of spring.

"You got a woman up there or something?" whispered Joey, blowing on his fingers and steaming.

I flapped him into silence.

A house of ghosts, this one; ruined and turreted, where the creak of a board was clatter. I listened. No sound but Grandfer's hop-reeking snores from the kitchen below. A hell of a Grandfer I had – back teeth awash every night regular, head sunk on his chest and bellowing in the place like a man demented, legs thrust out before the fire. Had to get past him somehow. A peep and a listen at the bedroom door and I crept back. Under the bed now, fish out the china, wrap it in a bedsheet and lay it snug, with a pillow below it for the curve of the body. Enemies right and left when you are thirteen. Back to the window with me like lightning.

"Right, you," I said.

"About time, too," said Joey, stroking his ferret.

With my boots in my hand I crept down the stairs, pausing outside Morfydd's door, for she was the true enemy. Thunderbolts could fall and nobody stir but Morfydd, my sister, for when my mam hit the bed she died. But Morfydd's sleep was the sleep of a conscience, breathing as something embalmed but one eye open for saints. And the step of a mouse would bring her out with hatchets, a wraith on tiptoe that peeped round doors and bent over beds.

Down to the kitchen now with its smells of last night's supper. A shadow moved from under the table, a crescent of whining joy that encircled my legs. Ever wakeful was Tara, like all Welsh terriers, and already hearing the stamp of the rabbit.

"Quiet!" I breathed, gathering her up. With my hand over her muzzle I tiptoed past Grandfer. Flat out in the armchair was Grandfer, his snores spouting up from his belted belly, his goat beard trembling in the thunder of his dreaming. The big lock grated its betrayal, but I got out somehow and clicked the door shut.

"Look!" whispered Joey, pointing. "Rebecca is at it again," and the name snatched at my breath. For bonfires were simmering and flashing on the white hills and a rocket arced in a trail of fire and drooped, spluttering into stars.

"Rebecca rioters, is it?" I whispered.

8

"Come," said Joey. "While Waldo Bailiff is out chasing rioters he is not trapping poachers. You got the towser?"

"Under my arm," I said.

"You scared of mantraps, Jethro Mortymer?"

Just looked at him, and spat.

"Right, us. Away!" whispered Joey. "We will give him Waldo."

As ragged heathens we ran down to Tarn, to the white-bouldered world of skulls and skinny sheep – to the burrows of the rabbits that riddled Squire's Reach, leaping frozen streams, plunging through undergrowth and wallowing in the marsh track till we came to the fence of Waldo Bailiff. Gasping, we rested here, steaming, flat on our backs. Tara and the ferret were running in circles about us, playing as children in bounds and squeaks, working up a joy for the coming hunt.

"Easy now," said Joey, sitting up. "Under the fence and follow me, and watch for mantraps."

This was Joey's world and he knew it backwards. Wild as a gipsy, this one, his bed under the moon in summer, seeking warmth on the rim of the limekiln fires in winter. He had lived alone since Cassie, his mam, hoofed it out of the county two years back – wanted by the military for caravan stealing. Joey baked his hedgehogs in balls of clay; was a better cook than Morfydd when it came to a rabbit, roasting them on spits or stirring them in stews.

"Mantraps are against the law," I said.

"O, aye?" said he, old-fashioned. "And who do say so?"

"My grandfer."

Joey jerked up the wire for me to crawl through. "Mantraps with spikes is against the law," said he. "Waldo's are legal, for they only break the leg. You watch for spikes, though – the spikes I fear for they rip and tear – like little Dai Shenkins down at New Inn – you heard about Dai?"

"No," I replied.

"Night before last, it was. Addled was Dai, poaching without a moon, for the moon shows mantraps, never mind bailiffs. Over at Simmons place he caught it, did Dai."

"Bad?"

"Rest another minute," said he. "Jethro Mortymer, d'you think much of me?"

"Pretty tidy." Strange was his face turned up to the moon. "What about Dai Shenkins, then?"

"Never mind him, you think about me." He sighed. "Look, these old nights are shivery, and you got a henhouse back home at your grandfer's. Hens are warm old things in nights of frost. Could you get me in?"

"A booting, mind, if Grandfer do find you."

"Aye, a stinkifying grandfer that one," said he, vicious.

"Could try, if you sleep quiet. You slept with hens before?"

"O, eh! Often," and deep he sighed, his face pale and shadowed in the blue light and his eyes all mystery and brightness. "You ever stopped to think, Jethro Mortymer, hens are better'n humans. Humans be thumpers and hens gentle old women. Sorry I am for hens, too, being done down for eggs all their lives and finishing up between knees. But I do not love cockerels, mind – there's lust in them cockerels, says Cassie, my mam – always leapfrogging and crowing to tell the neighbourhood. You eat a cockerel every Christmas for the rest of your life and you will eat more sin than me eventually."

"You eaten sin?"

"Aye, and why not? Folks got to eat something, says Cassie, my mam, so we did the funerals – swallowing the sins of the dear departed, taking the blackness off the poor soul going down, or up – case may be."

"Good God."

"You know Clun?"

I shook my head.

"Eight years old, me, when we did Clungunford – first time at sin-eating, for me. We knew we were into something pretty shocking when we got a spring chicken and wine to wash it down. And us that hungry we'd have stained our souls with child-killing for a piece of poorhouse bread, said Cassie. And the dear departed a clergy, at that."

"Chapel?"

"Church of England, but we sent him up clean as a washday. Eh, dear me, I reckon I be loaded black. Who started all this?"

"Hens," I said.

"Right, then – you fix me in your henhouse?"

"Out at first light, is it?"

"And not an egg missing. God bless you, Jethro Mortymer." He rose and stretched. "Right you, Waldo," he said. "Just look out."

"Come easy or she'll spring."

On tiptoe I came, peering.

"Throw me that stick. Watch the towser," said Joey.

I saw the steel jaws of the mantrap, gaping, smothered in leaves, and the spring steel curved tight and ready for the footstep.

"Eh, Waldo, you swine of a bailiff," said Joey, and swung the stick and the jaws leaped and slammed shut. "But not as bad as some – all legal. You seen Dai's leg?"

"Dai Shenkins?"

"Neither has Dai. Spikes, see? Took it off neat at the knee. And the Simmons bailiff found it next morning and followed the blood right up to New Inn. They'd have had little Dai, but he died. Died to spite them, his old mam said – hopping his way to his Maker for a rabbit, you can keep your old Botany Bay – she's a regular cheek is Dai's old mam. You got the towser?"

"Aye."

"Right," said Joey, and fished in his rags for his ferret, parted bushes and stuffed it down a hole. "Put the towser by the hole near that tree. Ready?"

I nodded, and set Tara down. And out came the rabbits in a stream.

I have seen dogs at rabbits but never one like Tara, my little bitch, for she threw them up as soon as they showed their eyes – two in the air at a time, hitting the frost as dead as doornails.

"Some terrier!" cried Joey, delighted.

Five rabbits came from the burrow and then came Joey's ferret, nose up, sniffing for more, and Tara got him square, for the light was bad that minute. Six feet up went that ferret, dying in flight, and Tara ran round him, sniffing delighted.

Good God.

"You black-faced bitch!" yelled Joey, and aimed his boot, but I caught his ankle and brought him down flat. With the mantrap between us we faced each other, sitting, and the silence grew in the shivering yard between us with Tara going round us in circles of joy, counting the dead.

"Here, Tara!" I said, and she leaped into my arms, licking and grinning.

He wept then, did Joey, with the tears leaving tracks on his grimed face.

"I am sorry," I said.

No sound he made in that sobbing, and he reached for the ferret and put it against his face; just sitting there with the wind stirring the branches above him, wisping up his bright hair.

Minutes I stood there kicking at leaves, for words are useless things in the presence of injured friendship, then I gathered up the rabbits and put them tidy at his feet, but he made no sign that he noticed.

"Rebecca is about," I said. "You heard they carried Sam Williams on the pole for blowing up that serving-maid down in Plasy? And the hayricks of the gentry are blazing something beautiful. Look, Joey boy, you can see them from here."

But he just went on weeping and kissing the ferret.

"Look, now," I said, short. "There is more than one ferret. That old thing was a rabbit-feeder, anyway. I will buy you another and train him rigid. Heisht you, is it?"

"Go to hell," he said, and his eyes were as fire.

"It is only a ferret, Joey – let us be friends."

Up with him then and blazing. "Out you get, Mortymer – you and that black-faced towser!" he shrieked. "You be bastards the pair of you, you and the bitch!"

With Tara held against me I watched as he turned and climbed the fence, bending to the hill on his way to his lime-kiln sleep.

"I will slip up the catch in the henhouse, Joey!" I called.

Not even a look. Just me left, and moonlight.

Nothing to do but go back home, taking the short cut this

time along the road to Carmarthen, but I dived into a ditch pretty sharp as the cavalry came galloping. Helmeted, spurred, they rounded the bend, thundering hooves, jingling and clanking, flashing to the moon, their big mares sweating and snorting smoke. Trouble in St Clears by the look of it; twelve dragoons this time of night.

I stopped near the shippon of home and unlatched the henhouse to give Joey a welcome, and the feathered old things grumbled, fearing the fox. In the back now, put Tara under the table; tiptoe past Grandfer who was snoring in shouts, up the stairs as a wraith and I got to my room. Up to the bed, throwing off my clothes. Shivering in the nightshirt I reached for the china; touched Morfydd's face and nearly hit the ceiling.

"Right, you," said she, rising up like the Day of Reckoning. "Poaching again with Tramping Boy Joey. Account for yourself, and quick."

Black hair over her shoulders, eyes narrowed with sleep, face as a madonna and looks like daggers. Beautiful, she was, to anyone but a brother.

"Quick," she said, thumping the blanket. "And no lies!"

A saint of a mother I had, but a tidy old bitch of a sister.

CHAPTER 2

JUST A couple of months me and my women had been at Cae White, Grandfer's house – Morfydd, my sister; my mother, and Mari my sister-in-law – running to Carmarthenshire from Monmouthshire iron; from the flash and glare of the Top Town furnaces where my father had died to the pasturelands of the west. Quiet and sweet it was here, a change from starving and sweating; far from the bellowing industry, as the opening of a Bible after a bedlam of labour.

Hitting it up for fourteen I was at this time, and coming a little hot with me about women. There are women and women, said Morfydd my sister, who was no better than she ought to be, but my mam, as I say, was a saint. Even the neighbours admitted she was a cut above the rest of them, with Good morning to you, Mr Waldo Bailiff, and Good afternoon to you, Mr Tom Griffiths, and God help even a seller of coloured Bibles who put his foot in the door without her permission.

"Rebecca was burning the hayricks last night," I said at breakfast, aware of slanting eyes.

"And how do you know when you were in bed and asleep?" asked Grandfer.

Five feet exactly, this one – every inch of him pickled in hops. The villagers said he was Quaker blood that had slipped off the black shine of the Book, though some said he was gipsy. But whatever his blood he soused himself regular five nights a week on the profits of the farm – ten jugs on a Tuesday when the drovers came down; with a crag for a settle and the moon for a blanket, snoring in icicles out in the mist, singing his bawdies in the company of goblins. Reckon Mari, my sister-in-law, was ashamed of her Grandfer Zephaniah.

"Big fires, though," said my mam. "Looked like tollgates – saw them myself."

"Read your history," said Grandfer. "Hayricks. Rebecca rioters – eight barns went up last night – and the dragoons came out from Carmarthen. I would give them rioters if I got my hands on them."

I chewed the black bread, watching Morfydd. Flushed and angry she looked, spooning up the oatmeal broth.

"Eh," sighed Mam. "We run from Monmouthshire iron for a bit of peace and we bump into riots all over again. Isn't just, is it?"

"You will always have riots while we bear such injustices," said Morfydd, eyes snapping up.

"Now, now!" said Mam, finger up. "Not our house, remember."

"I would burn the damned gentry, never mind their ricks," said Morfydd, and she swept back her hair. Excellent at rebellion and speeches, this one, especially when it came to hanging the Queen. Beautiful, but a woman of fire; an agitator in the Top Towns, married to an agitator once but no ring to prove it, and God knows where she would land us if she started tricks here, for we got out of Monmouthshire by the skin of our teeth.

"Let her speak," said Grandfer. "Let her be. Does she also write poetry?"

"Aye," said Morfydd, and fixed him with her eyes. "The centuries of Time echo to the tread of the clog going up the stairs and the buckle coming down. Burning hayricks – chopping down tollgates? A barrel of gunpowder would bring this county alive."

I looked at my mother. Her face was agonized. For this was the old Morfydd sparring for a fight, and we were here by the grace of Grandfer. But he smiled, to his credit, and stirred his tea.

"Speak, child, speak," said he. "You know your Bible? Genesis twenty-four, verse sixty. Let us draw your teeth." And Morfydd raised her dark eyes to his, saying, " 'And they blessed Rebekah, and said unto her, thou art our sister. Be thou the mother of thousands of millions, and let thy seed possess the gate of those which hate them.' "

"Amen," said Grandfer, eyes closed, and turned to my mother. "God help me, woman. Retired, I am, and I have opened the house to a nest of Welsh agitators." He swung to Morfydd. "The first tollgate burned, young woman?"

"Efail-wen, just this year," said she.

"When?"

"May the thirteenth – by Thomas Rees of Carnabwth. Burned twice since, thank God – June the sixth and July the seventeenth. Tollgates!" Morfydd sniffed. "Back home in my county we fought it out with redcoats."

"Remarkable," said Grandfer, quizzy.

"Aye, remarkable," said Morfydd. "If your people had half the spunk of the Welsh I come from you'd have taken to arms and marched on Carmarthen. Look at the place! The people are either starving or pinched to the bone, your workhouses are filling up daily – they transport you here for poaching rabbits," and here she looked at me, "and all you can do is burn a tollgate when you ought to be hauling up cannon. Good God!"

Sweating now, the beads bright on her face, and she sighed and wiped it into her hair.

"You see what I have to put up with?" asked Mam, hands empty to Grandfer. "She lost her own man to the riots in Monmouthshire, and I lost mine to the iron. You see what I have for a daughter?"

"I see that you are harbouring a vixen," said Grandfer. "But the goals are the same north or west." Down came his fist and he thumped the table. "Keep a grip on that tongue, young woman – I have no use for it here."

And Morfydd rose, shaking off crumbs. "And I have no use for yours. Thank God for starving, thank God for kicks. If the damned house burned down you'd be too frit to fetch water," and she slammed back her chair, looking knives. As she reached the door her son came through it – Richard, her beloved, aged three, and she stooped and snatched him up and held him against her. "Come, boy," said she. "There is no place for us here."

That is what it was like in those early days at Cae White Farm; my mam the sandwich between Grandfer's dislike and my sister's fire, but it settled down after a bit, thank God. To hell with Morfydd, I used to think; to heaven with my mother, she being all gentleness in the face of rebellion. Eh, did I love my mam! If I had to die on the breast of a woman I would die on my mother's – Morfydd's next, though hers was mainly occupied. But where my mother went, I went; touching the things she touched, smoothing her place at table. Sometimes I wondered who was the more beautiful, Morfydd or Mam, who could give her twenty years, for Morfydd was lifting up the latch for thirty. Smooth in the face was my mother, carrying herself with dignity; pretty with her bonnet streamers tied under her chin, five feet of black mourning that turned every set in whiskers in the county. The basses went a semitone flat in the Horeb when she was present, but there beside me, singing like an angel, she didn't spare the men a look. A smile for everyone, her contralto greeting, she was alive and dancing outside. Inside she was dead, in the same grave as my father. My father had joined the Man in the Big Pew over twelve months now but he still lived with us, I reckoned. For sometimes, when the house was sleeping, I would hear my mam talking to him in a voice of tears. And next morning at breakfast the redness was in her eyes and her mouth was trembling to her smile, as if it had just been kissed.

"Somebody slept in the henhouse last night," said Grandfer now.

I got some more barley bread and packed it well in.

"Not rioters?" whispered Mam.

"Boys," said he, eyeing me. "Same thing. And anyone this applies to can listen. If Tramping Boy Joey shows his backside round Cae White I will kick the thing over to St Clears, understand? Poachers and thieves, stinking of the gutter – I will not have him near!"

Chewing, me, eyes on the ceiling.

"Did you see anything of that Joey last night, Jethro?" asked Mam.

"How could he have seen him?" asked Morfydd from the door with Richard in her arms. "He was in well before dark and he slept with me. Come, Jethro, *bach*, it is cleaner outside."

A bitch one moment, sister the next.

Two months of hell, it was, living with Grandfer.

Yet I remember with joy the early spring days in the new county, especially the Sundays in the pews of the Horeb. Mam one side of me, Morfydd on the other, she with an eye for every pair of trews in sight, until she caught my mother's glance which set her back miles. Proud I felt, the only man in the family now; well soaped up and my hair combed to a quiff, singing quiet according to instructions, because my voice was breaking, but dying to let things rip. Little Meg Benyon was hitting it up on the harmonium, eyes on sticks, feet going, tongue peeping out between her white teeth, one missing; with Dai Alltwen Preacher beating time and the tenors soaring and basses grovelling. Deep and beautiful was Mam's voice in the descant, and Morfydd with her elbow in my ribs.

" 'All hail the power of Jesu's name . . .!' " Tenor, me,

threatening to crack, hanging on to Mam's contralto. Double bass now, with the crack turning heads and bringing me out into a sweat. And the hymn of Shrubsole flooded over us in glory and Dai Preacher lifted his eyes to the vaults of Heaven.

" 'Crown Him, Crown Him, *Crown Him . . .*!' " Top E, and me hitting soprano.

"For God's sake!" whispered Morfydd as I hung on the note.

"Leave him be," said Mam with her soft, sad smile.

"I will be doing some crowning when I get you back home," and I get the elbow.

"Mam," I said, "look at this Morfydd!"

"*Hush!*"

Aye, good it was, those spring Sundays, with the smell of Sunday clothes and lavender about us, and peacock feathers waving and watch chains drooping over stomachs begging for Sunday dinner, and the farmers had twenty quart ones in this county. There is Hettie Winetree in front of me done up in white silk and black stockings, all peeps and wriggles around her little black hymn book – second prize for missing a Sunday School attendance, presented by Tom the Faith – fancies herself, does Hettie Winetree. Behind me sits Dilly Morgan, tall, cool, and fair for Welsh, her tonic-solfa beating hot on my neck. Down comes Meg Benyon's little fat behind as she thumps the keyboard for the Amen and Dai Alltwen Preacher is up in the pulpit before you can say Carmarthen, leaping around the mahogany, working up his *hwyl*, handing hell to sinners from Genesis to Jonah. Motionless, we Mortymers, though other eyes may roam and other throats may clear. For a speck of dust do show like a whitewash stain on strangers wearing the black, says Mam.

Sunlit were those mornings after Chapel and the fields were alight with greenness and river-flash from the estuary where the Tywi ran. This was the time for talking, and the women lost no chance, giving birth to some, burying others while the men, in funeral black, talked bass about ploughing and harvest. Waldo Bailiff was always to the front, the devil, handsome and bearded, little hands folded on his silver-topped cane and his nose a dewdrop. Very sanctimonious was Waldo, loving his neighbour, and a hit over the backside for anyone breathing near Squire's salmon steps, never mind poaching. A big fish in a little puddle, said Morfydd, and when his dewdrop falls Waldo will fall like the leaning tree of Carmarthen. I never got the hang of how that dewdrop stayed with him; stitched on, I reckon, for when a gale took every other dewdrop in the county Waldo's was still present. But Welsh to his fingertips, give him credit, as Welsh as Owain Glyndwr but no credit to Wales, and more Sunday quarts died in Waldo than Glyndwr could boast dead English. But he drew me as a magnet because of Tessa, the daughter of Squire Lloyd Parry.

A lonely half hour, this, waiting for Sunday dinner, and grown-ups chattering. Lean against the chapel gate and watch them. Crows are shouting in the tops of the elms for you, half boy, half man. Yellow beaks gape in the scarecrowed pattern of branches. And you think of the lichened bark of Tessa's tree as being velvet to the touch, and the cowslip path to the river that is crumpled gold. There we would stand in my dreams, me and Tessa Lloyd Parry, watching the river, eyes drooping to brightness while the reed music of spring flooded over us.

"You dreaming, Jethro Mortymer?"

Do you see her framed by leaves, wide-eyed, restless always – as leaf-movement and the foaming roar of the river under wind; never still was Tessa – all life and quickness with words, snatching at every precious second. Small and dark was she, with the face of a child and the body of a woman, and often I would dream of kissing her. A week next Sunday if I plucked up courage. But Tessa flies in the movement of men. Waldo wipes his whiskers in expectation of a quart in Black Boar tavern. The men drift away, the women chatter on.

Here comes Polly Scandal now, black beads and crepe, donkey ears wagging in her fluffy tufts of hair. Straighten now, hands from pockets. Buzzing around the women, she is, getting a word from here, a word from there, and saving it up for weekdays. She will have them over the county by Monday with a death before the croak and a pain before conception. My turn now. Flouncing, hips swaying, she comes to the gate; three sets of teeth.

"Good morning, Jethro Mortymer."

Nod.

"Very happy you are looking, if I may say. Courting, is it?"

"No."

"Tessa Lloyd Parry, eh? And her the daughter of Squire! There is gentry you are now, boy."

"O, aye?"

"Aye, good grief! Marrying you will be before long, I vow. Whee, terrible, you new Mortymers, and such beautiful women! True your big sister Morfydd's moonlighting with Osian Hughes Bayleaves?"

"First I've heard of it," I answered, rumbling for dinner.

"Couldn't do better, mind. Prospects has Osian Hughes with fifty acres in the family and his dada starting death rattles. Eh, close you are, but Polly do know, mind – can't deceive Polly. And that mam of yours too pretty for singles, too. Waldo Bailiff off his ale because of her and Tom the Faith laying a shilling to nothing he has her altared before summer. You heard?" Up with her skirts then. "Eh, got to go. Goodbye, Jethro Mortymer, give my love to Tessa."

And here comes Hettie Winetree with her little black hymn book, brown hair drooping, a hole in each heel of her mam's black stockings.

"Good morning, Jethro Mortymer," flushing to a strawberry.

The trees wave in perpendicular light, the wind sighs.

"Enjoy the service, Mr Mortymer?" Screwing the back from her hymn book now, eyes peeping, dying inside at the shame of her harlotry. Anxious was Hettie for the facts of life, according to her mam, said Morfydd.

"No," I said.

"O, God forgive you," says she, pale. "Hell and Damnation for you if Dai Alltwen do hear you, mind."

"And to hell with Dai Alltwen via Carmarthen," I said.

This sets her scampering and I mooched over to Morfydd, digging her. "Damned starved, I am," I said. "You coming?"

But she, like the rest, are into it proper now. Nineteen to the dozen they go it after Chapel; hands waving, tongues wagging; dear me's and good grief's left and right, shocked and shamed and shrieking in chorus; the crescent jaw of the crone with her champing, the double chin creases of the matron and the quick, shadowed cheek of the maiden, all lifting in bedlam to a chorus of harmony, hitting Top C. And God put Eve under the belly of the serpent.

"Good God," whispered Morfydd. "Look what is coming!"

Osian Hughes Bayleaves, six-foot-six of him, with a waist like Hettie's and a chest as Hercules, white teeth shining in the leather of his face. Low he bows, jerked into beetroot by his high, starched collar.

"Good morning, Miss Mortymer," he murmurs.

Down they go, all eight of them. Pretty it looks, mind.

"My mam have sent me to ask you to tea, Miss Mortymer."

"Eh, there's a pity," says Morfydd to me. "Today of all days, and we have company, eh, Jethro?"

"First I've heard of it." Gave her a wink. For beauty as Morfydd's must duck its own trouble.

"Damned swine," she whispers, smiling innocently. "Some other time, Mr Hughes, and thank your mam kindly." And away she goes in a swirl of skirts, giving honey to Osian and daggers to me.

"But Osian Hughes has prospects, remember," says Mam on the way home.

"You are not bedding me with prospects," says Morfydd. "Give me a man a foot lower and fire in him, not milky rice pudding. Pathetic is that one," and she sniffed. "A body made for throwing bullocks pumped into passion by the heart of a rabbit."

"Time you was settled, nevertheless," and Mam sighs.

"I don't do so bad, mind," said Morfydd, and I saw Mam's dig.

We had put up with all this before, of course. I wandered beside them kicking at stones in visions of the lips of Tessa Lloyd Parry, dying for manhood that I might honour her. The wind whispered as we laboured up the hill, and it was perfumed.

"You cannot live in the past," said Mam to Morfydd.

No answer from Morfydd, but her eyes were bright.

"You must think of your Richard. Soon he will ask for a dada."

Out came a handkerchief.

"Now, now!" said my mother, sharp.

"O, God," said Morfydd.

It was the Richard that did it, the name of her son and the lover who sired him three years back.

"Hush, love her," whispered Mam, holding her. "Jethro, walk on." But a bit of sniffing and wiping and we were back to normal and Cae White grew before us ruined and turreted, blazing in the sun, with Mari, my sister-in-law, waiting in the doorway with Jonathon, her baby, asleep in her shawl.

O, this Mari!

CHAPTER 3

STRANGE THAT I knew Cae White was mine the moment I set foot in it; that I would shoulder the burden that Mari's grandfather had carried for life, and mate with it, and bring it to flower. Beautiful was this old Welsh gentry place gone to ruin, standing in its thirty acres with pride of nobility, shunning lesser neighbours. No time for it, said Morfydd – too damned proud – and how the hell Grandfer got hold of it I will never understand. Cheap, mind, at a pound a week rent, land included. Fishy. For places half the size Squire Lloyd Parry was charging double and he was not a man to lose sight of a pound. Most of the villagers worked for Squire, but not Grandfer, and Cae White was stuck in the middle of Squire's acres as a ship in full sail. Left and right the little farmers were being pushed out by rising rents and the gentry were forcing out their land enclosures faster than a wizard mouths spells, but nobody shifted Grandfer who had the power of the Devil in him, some said. Others said that Squire was pixilated and had never set eyes on Cae White though he passed it most days of the week. And I had seen him and Grandfer walk within feet and neither offer the other a glance while grown men were tugging out forelocks and their wives draping the ground. Indecent, said Morfydd, there are secrets at Cae White.

Things were happening in Carmarthenshire just now. The gentry were forming Trusts for road repairs and setting up toll-gates to pay for the labour, but drawing fat profits for the money invested by charging the earth for tolls. Left and right the gates were going up now, placed to trap the small farmers. Graft, too, as usual, for some gentlemen's carriages passed the tollgates free and bridges were being built to serve the needs of big houses. Men were flocking away from the land, queueing for the workhouses, and at the beginning of spring whole families were starving. And I was starving for Tessa Lloyd Parry.

"You keep from that one," said Morfydd. "Hobnails mating with lace."

"Leave him be," said Mam, sewing up to the light, squint-ing.

"To make a fool of the lot of us? Listen, you!" And Morfydd peered at me. "Gentry are running this county same as back home. You heard of Regan Killarney?"

"South of Ireland," I said to shift her.

"Transportation for twenty salmon – dished out by a clergy-man magistrate yesterday – getting his protection for the water he owned. While men like Killarney stink in the hulks for Botany Bay you'd best keep away from gentry Welsh lest the working Welsh call you traitor. You listening?"

"Half the county's listening," said Mam, stitching, sighing.

"Too damned young to be courting, anyway," said Morfydd, pale.

"Too damned old, you," I said, ducking her swipe.

Wandering about now, hands pressed together. Gunpowder, this one, dangerous to a flame. "The Devil take me," said she. "When I was his age I was spinning six days a week and hymning in Sunday School the seventh. . . ."

"O, aye?" said Mam, pins in her mouth.

"And here he is cooing and sweeting on gentry lawns with the people who starve us!" Dead and buried, me, with her looks.

"Not much starved you look from here, mind," said Mam.

"Not yet," said Morfydd. "But give them time. A tollgate went up on Flannigan's road last week and another's going up on the road to Kidwelly. Wait till lime-carting time – cost more for the tolls than the lime."

"Eh, agitators," said Mam. "God save me."

"And it is long past time somebody agitated. For where does the money go? On road repairs? Aye, on road repairs after it has paid a nice fat profit – on the backs of gentry or buying new plate for Church." She jerked her thumb at me. "And here is a worker playing silk purses and sows' ears and snobbing with people who are bleeding the county."

"Please do not refer to Jethro as sows' ears or I will be having a hand in it," said Mam.

"Trouble is coming," whispered Morfydd, tightlipped.

"If it doesn't you'll soon fetch some," I whispered, but Mam did not hear. She lowered the new backside she was putting on to Richard.

"Too old I am for fighting, Morfydd, too tired to get hot. Been flogged enough, I reckon. I have a man in a grave and a son in transportation. The gentry have the whip and they use it. Leave it, there's a good girl."

"This county is a bitch to nothing," said Morfydd, rising again. "My brother gets seven years transportation for a rebellion against Queen and State but Killarney is joining him for poaching."

"Hush you when Grandfer gets in, mind," said Mam. "And the rivers are owned by the gentry."

"The rivers are owned by God," shouted Morfydd, swinging to her. "And by God we will have our share. Salmon are so thick at the Reach that Lloyd Parry can't cast a fly in season, and the children of Killarney will grow legs like beansticks."

"Do not remind me," whispered Mam.

"O, Morfydd, shut it," I said.

"Shut it, eh?" She leaned, peering. "You ever seen a child die of hunger?"

"Saw them back home," said Mam. "No need to travel for that."

"With their bellies as balloons and the bread whooping up as fast as you push it down?" Morfydd straightened, and I saw tears in her eyes. "God, I have seen them – six died the week I came here and another three at Whitland a week after that – on the poor rate, mind – two shillings a week, with reverend fathers rooting round the sty for the last little chicken and hauling down the last scratch of bacon to pay Church tithes." Colder now, her voice breaking. "God, I would give them God if I were God Almighty. Too much jolting on the knees has driven the Church loopy, the ministers in the pay of the gentry and the gentry in the prayers of the ministers – walking into the City of Judah seven days a week while helpless children starve. Eh!" Deep she sighed. "The trouble with hassock-bumpers is that they forget the poor and needy, but God's people will remember them. Wait and see."

"Talking about chickens and bacon you'd better get the potato soup back on," said my mother. "Grandfer and Mari will be in directly."

"God forgive you, Mam," said Morfydd, eyes closed.

"God grant me peace," said my mother. "I cannot feed the county, I can only cast it from my mind." Rising, she kissed my sister. "O," she said, "afire was my womb when it brought forth you. Please God you find peace, like me."

And the door came open and Mari came in.

"There is a miserable set of old faces," she cried, smiling. "Tollgates again, is it?" And she danced in with her basket.

"It is Jethro courting little Tessa and Morfydd handing hell to hassock-bumpers in the name of the poor and needy," said Mam. "Come you in, girl – got anything decent?"

And she looked at me and smiled, did Mari, bringing low my eyes.

This was my sister-in-law, wife to Iestyn my brother in seven years transportation. Months he had been gone now, leaving her with Jonathon, her son. To this day I cannot explain the sweetness her presence brought me. Church of England, was Mari, from hooded bishops to gilded altars, and Christian. She blunted the edge of Morfydd's fire, forgiving trespasses in her every word and glance. Four years the younger, I had once shared her kisses, till I grew a head the taller and too high for her lips. Now she winked.

"At last we know why the boy's off his food." Eyes dancing, with her baby cradled against her now, and Mam reached up, taking him on her knee.

"No laughing matter, Mari," said Morfydd at the window.

"O, come," said Mari, hooking the door shut. "Do a little boy's courting put the house untidy when there's three grown women by here and not a man in sight save Grandfer?"

"Daughter of a squire," said Morfydd, gentle. In love with Mari, like me.

"And crumbs on her mouth from her tea. O, girl, they are children!"

"And not so much of the children," said Morfydd. "Nigh twelve stone is that thing and hair on its chest. Before we know it we'll be washing gentry napkins and I'm full to the stomach with gentry."

"And my stomach is empty and howling for supper," said Mari. "Where's my Grandfer?"

"Black Boar tavern, as usual," said Morfydd. "Drowning his sorrows – the house is plagued with drunkards and lovers."

"Morfydd!" said Mam sharp, but Mari only smiled.

"Strange he should drink at a time like this," said she.

"He drinks because of a time like this," answered Morfydd. "The man has lived alone for over half a century and we hit him up with six women and kids," and she turned from the window as a shadow went by it. "God, here it comes."

Loaded was Grandfer, with only his staff to keep him upright; as a leathery little goat complete with beard and his little pot of a waistcoat tearing at its seams above his bandy, gaitered legs. Bald as an egg, toothless, he had been good in his time, said Waldo Bailiff, but cooled after sixty, and the more virgins he had around him now the holier he felt, something we were short of at Cae White.

"Grandfer!" cried Mari, ducking his stick.

Belching, drooling, the senility blundered in, taking breath to keep its quarts down, glazed in the eye, dragging its feet. Hobnails clattering it leaned on the table, wagging its head in grief.

"Knowest thou the biblical? Ah, me!" said he. "Woe is Grandfer! The house is filled to the brim with suckling children and female Nonconformists." He belched deep, begging our pardons. "Knowest thou the murmurings of the Israelites through the speeches of Moses? 'Have I conceived all these people – have I begotten them that thou should sayest unto me, carry them in thy bosom as a nursing father beareth a suckling child?' Eh, dear me! 'I am not able to bear all these people alone because it is too heavy for me. Kill me, I pray you, out of hand, let me not see my wretchedness.' "

"Amen," said Morfydd.

"A fine one to talk of the biblical!" said Mari, shocked. "He is not himself today, forgive him."

"Old and feeble, he is," whispered Mam. "Do not take it hard, girl. A smell of the Black Boar pints and he is standing on his head."

"Not true," I said. "He can sink twenty without breathing."

"You will speak when you are spoken to," said Mam, eyes wide and flashing.

"Leave Grandfer to me," said Morfydd, taking his arm. "I can handle grandfers."

"Twenty years back you wouldn't," said he, leering into her smile. "Look upon her now, this vision of beauty!" Swinging wide, he fell into Morfydd's arms. "The only woman among you with the spunk of a man. Rebecca and Chartist, a fighter for the rights of men – Venus reborn! Clear the house of infidels and varmints, especially God-forsaken poachers – may they soil themselves in their pits of iniquity, but save me Morfydd. Still got an eye for a pretty woman, mind, and I like them rebellious."

"Take him up to bed," said Mari in disgust.

"Will you take me up to bed, Morfydd Mortymer?" Evil was his eye.

"As far as the landing," said she. "You are not as old as I thought. Come, Grandfer."

Bride and groom left for the bedchamber.

"O, he is disgraceful," whispered Mari, red and ashamed.

"When the ale is in the wits are out," said Mam, soothing. "But I know the truth of it, we should not be here. Too much to ask," and she followed Morfydd to see fair play, leaving me and Mari alone.

Tragic is the one who is meat in the sandwich. Oblivious of me she paced the room, her teeth on her lips, holding back tears. But more tragic still is the one to whom love flies and the longing to give comfort, but words are useless things between boy and married woman. I sat and longed and found no words. At the window now she picked up her baby Jonathon, hugging him against her.

"I am sorry, Mari," I said.

A brush at her eyes, a flash of a smile.

"With his tongue submerged he can still use it," she said. "O, God, if only my Iestyn were here."

"He will come back," I said.

As stabbed she stopped pacing and swung to me. "O, do not take on so, Jethro!" Fingers at her wedding ring now, twisting. She did this when the talk was of Iestyn. "I see him in your face, your smile. Jethro!" She wept, turning.

Up like lightning and she was in my arms. No ring, no Iestyn. Back even quicker to Morfydd's clatter on the stairs. Strange the guilt.

"Now, that is over," said Morfydd, coming in. "A cup of decent tea, for God's sake. Fought like a demon when I put him in his nightshirt – like the rest of the men, he is – all promises. Supper, is it?" She kissed Mari in passing.

Nothing like a table for taking away gloom. And I think a house is happy with its table dressed in its white, starched apron and its spoons tinkling as people go past. Come from a gentry house, Grandfer's table, serving rye bread and butter-milk now, but dreaming its past of silver plate and feasts; of crinoline gowns and fingers touching secretly in its curtained darkness. And pretty was the kitchen at Cae White with its great Welsh dresser standing in polished dignity on the flag-stones, heavy with its scores of jugs and their sighs of a thousand cows. My women were beggars for the polishing, like most – flicking the dust from one corner to another, burnishing the brass trinkets for shaving in. The low ships' timbers bore down upon us, the sea murmuring in their splits; faded wall-paper where the bed-warming pan flashed copper light; a painting called *Lost* was above the mantel, where a man of icicles groped in a blizzard. *God Bless Our Home* hung in laurel leaves next to the portrait of Victoria whom Morfydd had managed to crack. But best of all was that table made for a company of Guards. Grandfer, now absent, always sat at the top with Mari on his right and Mam and Morfydd on his left, with Richard aged three beside me and Jonathon in Mari's lap. And at the end sat the ghosts – four empty places that my mother always laid – for my father and sister who had died up in Monmouthshire; Richard, Morfydd's man who was shot by redcoats, and Iestyn my brother who was in Botany Bay. Only Morfydd railed at this palaver – let the dead lie in peace, she said, but Mam still laid the places. Strange are women who treasure the dust of memories, eating at table with dead men, sleeping with them in the beds. Strange was Cae White with its three longing women, their make-believe love-making, their intercourse of ghosts. And upstairs was Grandfer, hop-soaked to drown other memories, it seemed, puggled with his past.

Me of the lot of them the only one normal.

CHAPTER 4

VERY STITCHED up are the Welsh when it comes to neigh-bours, till they know you. Most prim was everyone, bowing very formal when we went out for Chapel or market, and, being strangers, we were doing our best to make a good impression, though we were at a disadvantage with my sister Morfydd in the house. For it was not only rebellion that stirred in Morfydd's breast, said Mam; at thirty she is old enough to know better. Most fanciful for the men, was Morfydd, with the lips and eyes that drove the chaps demented. I know that the loss of her man was unstitched within her but she still had an eye for trews. And it soon got round the village about the beautiful women at Cae White, one prim, the other improper. Very alike were Mari and Morfydd – could be taken for sisters being both dark and curled, lithe in the step and with dignity. Long-waisted, high-breasted, they swirled around Cae White, and the men were hanging on the gate like string beans for a sight of them, which shocked my mam, put Mari dull, and painted up Morfydd's cheeks with expectation.

"Willie O'Hara again," said she, lifting the curtain. "Must be keen, see, in four degrees of frost."

"Shameful," said Mam. "Down with that curtain this minute."

"And Elias the Shop all the way from Kidwelly. There's a compliment. Did you invite him, Mam?"

"No fool like an old fool," Mam replied. "If my Hywel was alive he'd soon clear them."

"O, look now!" cried Morfydd. "Old Uncle Silas from the Burrows – coming very jaunty, too – life in the old dog yet."

"Let's have a look, girl," I said, getting up.

"Back you," cried Mam. "Objectionable, it is."

Pretty wrinkled was Uncle Silas; buried two wives and looking for a third, said Grandfer, and his eye was on Morfydd, strange enough. Every Sunday regular after Chapel he was pacing the end of our shippon with his starched collar round his ears and his bunch of winter flowers. Queer are old men looking for wives, for ten minutes with Morfydd my sister and anything under five-foot-ten went out boots first, I had heard. But Willie O'Hara, now here was a difference. Topped six feet, did Willie, big in the shoulders and sinewy, with mop-gold hair on him, strange for Welsh Irish. Come down from the industries, it was said, but not long enough in iron to be branded. And he leaned on the gate now, broad back turned, settling for a fortnight's wait by the look of him.

Lucky for me having my woman inside.

The old log fire flamed red and cosy in the kitchen that night near Christmas. Sitting crosslegged before it I would watch Mari's hands; long, tapering fingers white against the black braid of her dress, with her needle flashing through my dreams.

"There now, that's you," and she flung me the socks.

They landed in my lap but I did not really notice, for her eyes were staring past me into the fire and she took a breath and sighed, telling of her longing for my brother.

"Irish potatoes, is it?" said she. "I know some good round Welsh ones. Easy on the socks, Jethro, you will wear me out." She smiled at the window where Morfydd was standing. "Still at it, are they? Do not blame me, Mam, I do not give them the eye."

"No need to tell me who does that," said Mam, treadling at the wheel. "Damned criminal, it is, when you have no intentions, and Dai Alltwen Preacher swimming the river Jordan every night down in the Horeb. God help you, Morfydd, if Dai finds out."

"Can't let Willie starve," said Morfydd, lifting her bonnet. "Solid ice he will be in another ten minutes. I will not be late, Mam."

"At this time of night? Morfydd, it is indecent!"

"Now what is indecent in a bit of a walk?"

"Nothing," said Mam. It was the way she looked.

"I am thirty years old," said Morfydd, eyes lighting up. "Do I have to account to you for every minute?"

"Every second while you live here," replied Mam, sleeves going up.

"At thirty I am past those damned silly capers!"

"Count yourself lucky," said Mam. "When I was thirty I wasn't."

"Don't do as I do but do as I say, is it?"

"Morfydd, hush!" whispered Mari.

"Do not be rude to our mam," I said.

"Quiet, you, or I'll clip that damned ear," said Morfydd, swinging to me.

"And I will clip the other one," said Mam. "But a boy, you are, and you will keep from this conversation. You will be back at eight o'clock, Morfydd, understand? Nine o'clock otherwise, but I do not stand for rudeness."

"Yes, Mother."

"And you keep walking with that Willie O'Hara, understand?"

"O, Mam," said Mari. "She would not breathe on Willie O'Hara."

Under judgement stands Morfydd and I gave her a wink.

"You may kiss me," said my mother, taking the wish for granted.

Kisses all round except for me, and off Morfydd went under her black poke bonnet. I waited till she had gone then stretched and sighed.

"And where are you off to, pray?" asked Mam.

"Not in front of Mari, please," I said.

"I am sorry," said my mother. "But do not bait your sister, remember."

Cold round the back with the stars all Venuses and the Milky Way dripping with cream in the frost. I whistled, and Morfydd paused, a black witch against the stars, and came back.

"And what do you want, little pig?"

"Back home at eight, remember," I said. "Eh, there's delightful, and Mam don't know. Do not make a meal of it – tin drawers it is with Willie O'Hara, so watch it or he'll have you."

"One word from you . . ." she whispered, her finger going over her throat.

"Get on, get on," I said. "He'll be no good to you freezing."

She laughed then, head back, and ran to the gate. I stood there as she took Willie's hand and he swung her down the road to Ferry.

The wildness of her made me afraid, but I would not have changed her for any woman in Carmarthen, save perhaps one.

Never in my life will I forget that first Christmas at Cae White; the service at Chapel with Dai Alltwen roasting the Devil up in the front pews, then back home, Grandfer leading, for he always reckoned on Chapel for Christmas Day. Back home now and I hit out a poor little chicken from the henhouse and plucked him and handed him to Mari who was cook at Cae White, and the smell of him was all over the house, with Jonathon crowing and Richard toddling around the kitchen for peeps at him on the spit. Blistering and browning he turns above the fire and the fat drips and flares. Up at Squire's Reach they had a little dog to do it, says Morfydd; climbing the circle of the stepped wheel, panting in the heat, tongue hanging out, coat singed, shrinking to a prune for the lusts of humans. Wonder what the baby Jesus would say if he saw that little dog, I wondered, for I was sweating for two in the glow, with Mari dashing around with her spoons and pans, working herself to death for that Christmas dinner, our first meat since we came to Carmarthenshire. Boiled potatoes and cabbage and gallons of gravy, and she always made pints because she knew I loved it. If a woman can make gravy it is enough to ask of a wife, I think, and anything she has after that is only grist to the mill. The seven of us at table now, Grandfer going at the chicken and tongues wagging and the boys banging spoons, with Mari scooping up the vegetables and handing down the plates, me last, though she fixed me with a leg while nobody was looking. Into it now, smiles all round, and isn't it delicious and thank God for Grandfer who was enjoying himself for once. And there is nothing like a plate when a dinner is finished, I think, and you get the bread in a putty and wipe it round, making the old thing shine. Polished is a plate by the time I have finished with it, saving the washing-up if I had my way, but doing it under the eagle eye for I always sat next to Morfydd.

"O, look, Mam," said she. "Tell him to behave."

"Leave him be," said Mari. "He is enjoying it."

"I will not have beastly eating," said Mam, her fork up. "There's plenty of room for that in sties. Jethro!"

Another bit of bread, with your eye on Morfydd's gravy, she being finished and glaring. Couldn't get enough those days – eat her, too, if she slipped on the plate.

"O, God," says she, disgusted.

33

"Stop it this minute!" shouted Mam, hitting the table and bouncing forks.

"You have raised it, woman," said Grandfer. "It is you who should stop it."

Eyes cast down at this.

"More?" whispers Mari from the top of the table.

"There now, you can start again," says Mam. "And knife and fork like the rest of us, no need for piglets."

So I gave the thing to Morfydd to pass up.

"I am off," says she. "I can get this in barnyards, no point in coming to table."

"You stay till the rest of us are finished, Morfydd!"

Grandfer at the top, whiskers drooping, getting well into it, and everyone else pretty busy, so I gave Morfydd one with the hobnails as she passed the plate down with looks to kill at me.

"Eh, you bloody little devil!"

"*Morfydd!*" Mam now, pale and shocked, glancing at Grandfer who didn't bat an eyelid.

Everything in the county from bishops to lay preachers, cassocks flying, up and rushing.

"I beg your pardon," said Mam.

"Mam, he booted me."

"Never touched her," I said. "Hell and Damnation she will have for that, mind, straight to Hell's sulphur."

"And hush you, too!" Mam shouting now, flushed and ashamed, for a bloody or two could be mortal sin on a Sunday, never mind Christmas Day. I gave Morfydd a glance in the pinging silence, for even Grandfer had raised his head now. In disgrace, poor soul. Head low she sat, face pale, sending me threats from the corners of her eyes.

"And where did you learn such language, pray?" asked Mam, solid ice. "Not in this house, I vow. Thirty years old, is it? Old enough to give an example, especially to the children. You will keep a clean mouth, do you understand?"

"Bloody, bloody, bloody," cried Richard, hitting his plate.

"Do you hear that?" asked Mam, and Mari clouted Richard and he opened his mouth and howled.

"Go to your room this minute," said Mam. "Christmas dinner or not I will make an example of you."

No reply from Morfydd and I was into the gravy again.

"Do you hear me! Stop eating this minute, Jethro – leave the table!"

"Me?" I asked.

"Away this minute, and do not come down till I tell you."

"She did the swearing, mind."

"And you the booting to make her swear. Up this instant or I will take a stick to you, big as you are."

"Go quick, Jethro," whispered Mari, agitated.

Left the plate with half an inch of gravy, and Morfydd jerking her thumb at me under cover of the tablecloth. Could have killed her. One word from me about her and Willie O'Hara and Mam would have roped her for razors. I got up and went to the door.

"Now you," said Mam, and Morfydd rose, which sent me a bit faster for the lock on my bedroom door. Twelve months back she got into me and I wasn't having it again, for she swung and hooked like a man and I couldn't hit back because of the chest.

"I apologize for my children," said Mam sorrowful as I climbed the stairs with Morfydd following. "God knows I have done my best to bring them up decent. A grown woman, but she acts like a child, and the other. *Well . . .*"

Into the bedroom now, swing the key, and the handle goes round as Morfydd tries it. Nothing but the black of her dress the other side of the keyhole.

Silence, then:

"Jethro," she croons.

"Aye, girl?"

"I will have you, mind. If I wait six months I will have you for that."

But I know she will not because of Willie O'Hara.

CHAPTER 5

CHRISTMAS NIGHT!

The family circle now, all trespasses forgiven, sitting round the fire with the lamp turned low, the windows rimed with frost and the snow falling vertically as big as rose petals against the white dresses of the mountain. All was silent save for Mari's voice as she shivered us to the marrow with ghost stories from way back in history, then a bit of a prayer for the Christmas dinner and a Reading from Grandfer, all very holy. Must have been nine o'clock, for Richard and Jonathon were abed, I remember, and I was thinking of Tessa and spring when the tap on the door brought us all upright.

"For Heaven's sake," said Mam. "This time of night?"

And then it began!

Sanctus. Full harmony from the back. In glorious song came the old Welsh hymn flung by soaring sopranos, blasted by bass, with the tenors doing a descant over the top, and the sudden glory of the sound froze us into wonder and we got to our feet as with cramp and stared at the back door.

> 'Round the Lord in glory seated, Cherubim and Seraphim
> Filled His temple, and repeated each to each the alternate
> hymn . . .!
> Lord, Thy glory fills the heaven, earth is with its fullness
> stored;
> Unto Thee be glory given, Holy, Holy, Holy Lord!'

And my mother cried out in joy and flung open the door to the great choir of neighbours and we formed up before them and joined in the hymn that breathes of my country. Last verse now, with my mother's rich contralto in my ears, Grandfer's squeaky tenor and Mari and Morfydd going like angels. O, good it was to be accepted by neighbours at last with this, their seal of friendship. Biddy Flannigan front rank with her son Abel a foot above her; Tom the Faith grunting and growling and Dilly Morgan and Hettie Winetree holding hands and singing to the stars. Pleased to see Dilly there for she was heading for a haystack midsummer though she didn't know it. Osian Hughes and his mam back row; Toby Benyon and missus, Dai Alltwen Preacher, Adam Funeral, gaunt and black, come for measuring up; Willie O'Hara, his eye on Morfydd; Justin Slaughterer with his eye on Mari, and I hated him. Thick and strong and handsome, this one – cutting throats spare time to labouring and enjoying every minute, and he'd had his peeps on Mari from the second we'd come to Cae White. Cut a throat or two myself if this continued: waylaying her from Chapel and happy I am to know you, girl – Mari first name, isn't it? Justin be mine. Permission to call would be very tidy, Mari Mortymer, me being friends with Grandfer. Thank God she sent him about his business, her a decent married woman. He could even sing well, the swine, booming bass, and I closed my hand as he winked at her now. Last chord to strip the whitewash, and the crowd suddenly parted, cowering back in mock horror, for the terrifying *Mari Lwyd* was shoving a path through them. Now it stood on the threshold, its lower jaw champing, glass eyes flashing. This, the horrifying *Mari Lwyd* – a man clad in a white bedsheet wearing the skeleton of a horse's head where his own head should be.

"God save us," whispered Mam.

Glass eyeballs on this one, its skeleton head covered with gay rosettes, and its coloured rein streamers were flying in the wind. Jawbone champing like the bell of doom, it surveyed us, gaze sweeping right and left – fixing on Morfydd now, bringing her hands to her face. Then, in a shrill falsetto, the horse began to sing, though I knew it was Waldo Bailiff by the size of its boots. Enough to frighten decent folk to death.

"O, *Mari Lwyd* so jolly has come all the way from Kidwelly," sang he. "So will you invite us to sing, good people. And if we are not welcome then please let us know with your singing," and he flung up his skeleton head and neighed like a soul in torment. "O, please let us know with some singing."

Dead silence.

"For God's sake give it a penny and shift it," whispered

Morfydd, but Grandfer, grinning, faced the apparition, flung his arms wide to it and replied in his squeaky tenor:

"O, *Mari Lwyd* so jolly, come all the way from Kidwelly to visit friendly neighbours. If you are friendly too, then welcome to this house."

"Friends and neighbours indeed!" bawled the *Mari Lwyd*, tossing and neighing. "And we beg entry, mam – is it in or out?"

And Grandfer bowed low and touched Mam's arm, leaving it to her. Would have died scalded for Grandfer at that moment.

"Open to friends and neighbours!" cried Mam, going damp, and she flung her arms wide. "Come in, people, do not starve to death in the cold!"

A hell of a thing it is to be accepted, mind.

And in they came, the *Mari Lwyd* leading, snapping and snarling left and right at the men and bowing to the women. Waldo Bailiff in his element, holding the stage, and Mari and Morfydd were dashing round shouting for cups and plates and digging out the larder for the Christmas cake which was damned near finished. But they need not have worried for the neighbours brought things with them, specially cooked for the surprise, they said, and soon the table was groaning.

"Greetings to the Mortymers!" cried Waldo through bared teeth. "Welcome to the county, I say – the prettiest women in Wales, not counting fat little Biddy Flannigan by here!"

"O, go on with you, Waldo," said Biddy, all creases and blushes. "There's terrible he is, now, and in front of strangers."

"Strangers no more!" roared Abel her brawny son. "For I have a little barrel of good stuff from Betsi Ramrod's place but I am needing a woman to roll it in, doing the custom. Any volunteers?"

"I will go," said Morfydd, rolling her sleeves, and the look she gave Abel Flannigan sent up my blood, never mind his.

"A kiss from the beer-roller, remember," called Mari. "Mind what you are taking on, Morfydd!"

"Dark out there!" I cried, while everyone roared.

"Darker the better," shouted Morfydd. "Bring him back in one piece, is it?"

"Morfydd, behave!" called Mam, looking worried. Cheers and shrieks as Morfydd rolled the little barrel in and Abel came staggering after her on rubber legs, and I saw Osian Hughes Bayleaves send Abel a filthy look from his corner where he sat with his mam. Ring-dancing now, singing and laughing, back-slapping and a bit of spare kissing going on, with the young men rushing round with jugs of the foaming ale and Mari dashed past me for the boys who were bellowing upstairs. Caught the eye of Dilly Morgan through the surge of the crowd.

"*Phist!*" I said.

Ambitions for this one, me, for Tessa was up at Squire's Reach and every woman has a separate appeal.

"Me?" she mouthed back, eyebrows up, thumbing herself.

I jerked my head and went through the door of the back and I heard the rustle of her behind me.

"What you want, Jethro Mortymer?" Knew damned well what I wanted.

"Plenty of old kissing going on, Dilly Morgan," I said. "You fancy kissing me?"

"And me fourteen? Eh, there's indecent!"

"Got to start some time," I said. "Look up by there, girl – you seen Venus?" and I got my arm around her waist.

"Don't you start tricks, now. I have heard about you, Jethro Mortymer. Sixpenny Jane down at Betsi's place do say you're a grown man the way you're behaving. Loose me this moment."

But I had her, though she was thrusting, and her lips were as wine in the frosted air. Pushed me off and caught me square, the bitch. "Tell my mam, I will," said she, and up with her skirts and away through the door.

Not much doing when you are fourteen, but I waited a bit for I knew Hettie would come. Beggars are women when they think they are missing something. Pretty she looked, though, in the light from the door, skirt held up between fingers and thumbs, and she bowed with a nod.

"Happy Christmas," said she. "Didn't expect to find you

out here, Jethro Mortymer," and she nearly fainted for the shame of it.

"Same to you," I said. "You come for kissing?"

"Just passing," said she. "Looking for Dilly."

No slaps from this one. Soft were her lips, unprotesting; been at it all her life on this performance. Got a future, Hettie, but I'd much rather had Dilly. Just getting her set up again and the door came open and Morfydd peered.

"What is happening out there?" she asked.

"Looking at Venus," I said.

"O, aye? You can see it through glass, then. Want your head read sharing darkness with that thing of a brother, Hettie Winetree. In, in!" And she whirled behind us and brushed us in with her skirts. Probably for the good for I was coming a little hot with me, and I saw a few guests give us the eye as we came into the light. Betsi Ramrod followed us in, five-feet-ten of ramrod mourning, and Gipsy May her assistant from Black Boar tavern followed her rolling a barrel, and I heard Dai Alltwen Preacher give them a sigh, for their tavern had a name in the county. Waldo up on a barrel now, hoofs beating time to a roar of singing, and then, quite suddenly, the bedlam died. People were turning towards the door, and Mari shrieked in joy.

Black-frocked, enormous, he stood in the doorway, hands clasped on his stomach, beaming down. As a sentinel of Fate Tomos Traherne stood there, smiling around the room; full twenty stone of him, spade beard snowflecked, his broad felt hat under his arm. And my mother turned from the table and saw him.

"Tomos!" And she ran straight into his arms.

There's awkward.

Half a dozen possible suitors in here already and in comes a stranger and she greets him like a lover; a fine one for examples, said Morfydd after.

But it was better than that, though the locals did not know it.

Everyone going formal now, backing to the wall, trying to look uninterested – very interested in boots, nudging their neighbours, and when Mam's handkerchief came out the women started whispering. Didn't blame them. Couldn't expect them to understand.

For this was our Tomos from back home in Monmouthshire; the giant of the Faith; fearful to the iniquitous, the persecutor of harlots, but a broth of a man when it came to the hungry. Fat, ungainly, his belly belt was worn bright on the backsides of children late for Sunday School, and he could hit wickedness from South Wales to North in a single swipe. Friend of my dead father, this; the protector of my mother in the agony of her grief. Mari at him now, hanging on to the other arm. A foot the taller, he stood quite still, then turned to face the room. A bit of sniffing from my mother, and then she spoke.

"Dai Alltwen and friends," said she, taking local preacher first. "This is our friend, my husband's beloved friend, come down from Monmouthshire Top Towns to visit us. I ask all here to give him a welcome."

This didn't do Dai Alltwen much good but he bowed proper and the man-mountain bowed back, catching my eye and winking as he came upright.

"Any news of Iestyn, Tomos?" asked Mari, and I saw the pain fly into her face as he pressed her hand for answer. Round he went in the circle now, bowing to the women, breaking the hands of the men, until he came to Morfydd. With her illegitimate son held against her she faced him and her voice was cold and clear.

"Good evening, Mr Traherne."

History here. Cast out from Chapel by Tomos when she brought forth Richard.

But not as easy as that, for Tomos bent and kissed her face, and then her son, and took him from her arms and carried him round the circle, and Morfydd lowered her arms, her eyes cast down. But nobody really noticed Morfydd for all eyes were on the gigantic minister. The introductions completed he raised his hand and roars and cheers as it hit the ceiling, and his voice as thunder boomed around the room.

"Good people, God's people," said he, double bass. "You of this county are as the Welsh of my county – faithful in labour, generous to neighbours – true Welsh, I see, by all the saints!

As a Welshman I greet you and bring you God's blessing. As the adopted father of this beloved family I give you thanks from the bottom of my heart that you should show them such kindness. And here I vow . . .!" and he raised his fist, "that whatever trust you put in them they will not be found wanting. Look the world over and you will find no better neighbours with whom to share this Christmas. And may the good Lord, Whose eternal Spirit guides the hearts and minds of decent men and women, cover you with the mantle of His blessing, and keep you pure and free from harm. Amen."

And we stood in respectful silence, conscious of his greatness, trembling to his *hwyl*. Vibrant, fervent, his voice rolled on:

"And listen! Do not mistake the kiss of this lady, for she has kissed me often when her man was alive, and he never raised an eye! Shall I tell you of this family, of its father who stood for the things that are good and clean in life? Shall I tell you of the son who languishes in far off Van Diemen's Land because he fought, prepared to die, for the things that are decent – against the tyranny of foreign masters in a revolt against the State? Let there be no sin in opposing evil wherever it is found. And Richard Bennet, Morfydd's man, do you know that he died in this fight and left her alone to raise her son? I can see that you do not know these things, for the Mortymers were never ones for speeches, so I tell you now with pride. Let there be no secrets between such neighbours as you. Let it be known that the Mortymers, too, have their place among you, that they have earned the respect you pay them, with their lives."

Clapping and cheers at this, and I must admit I felt a thrill of pride that brought the water stinging to my eyes as I thought of my father and Iestyn, my brother. My women were standing rigid, their heads low, and my mother was weeping, her face wet, with no attempt to wipe the tears. I looked hard at Mari. White faced, she stood by Tomos, and I pitied her. For I had heard in her first shriek of joy at the sight of him that she was hoping for news of my brother. Nothing for her save confirmation of Botany Bay, with visions of the chained labourers and the blood-soaked ground of the triangles. But Tomos was speaking on:

42

"And as I laboured along the road from Carmarthen town I rested by the wayside to catch my breath. There, in the frost, I listened to *Sanctus* – to the sound of your voices, and beautiful it was to the weary traveller who has walked nigh eighty miles. The sound of your hymn ennobled me, and I knelt in the snow and gave prayers for you, receiving in turn renewed strength for the journey." His voice rose higher. "And so now, before I take leave of you to find rest – last verse of *Sanctus* again. Lift the roof with it – ring it out to Monmouthshire. Full chorus now, full harmony, to the beautiful words of your Richard Mant. Ready, ready . . . ?" And his arm swept up and down, and we sang. God, how we sang! Deafening to the ears, this time, rising to such beauty and power that it caught at my soul and snatched it upwards in the last, glorious line.

"Holy, Holy, Holy Lord!"

And in the ringing silence Tomos caught my eye again.

"Jethro!"

"Tomos!"

I ran into his arms.

CHAPTER 6

BITTER OLD winter, this first one at Cae White, with the coots slipping on their backsides well into March and the hedges iced like gentry wedding cakes. The trees rattled as moody skeletons in the salt-tang of the estuary and the peat bogs rammed themselves into glass. No longer the otters barked along the banks of the Tywi, with the curlews too nipped to shout at dawn. Gaunt and forbidding was the country still, biting at fingers, twisting at noses, and the whole rolling country of mountains and pastures from Llandeilo to Haverfordwest was hammered into frost by the thumps of winter.

Out at first light, me, back with the curtains. I dressed quickly with mist billowing against the window, trying to get down before Morfydd for once. Snatching my towel I went on the landing and Mari stood there, her eyes dazed through the loss of another night.

"You all right, girl?"

She nodded, smiling faintly.

"Heard you last night, tossing and turning," I said.

"Too tired for sleep," she said. "It will pass."

"Do not come down," I said. "Morfydd and me will get ourselves off."

Morfydd at the bottom of the stairs then, peering up. "Mari," she whispered. "Go back to bed – do you think we need nursing?"

"But you must have some breakfast," she replied.

"God alive, woman, can't we get that ourselves? Back and try to sleep, there's a good girl. Mam says she will have Jonathon and Richard."

Haggard in the eyes, Mari turned without a word.

Slower now, thoughtful, I went down to the kitchen. Morfydd was already boiling the oatmeal broth. Nearly retched. Sick of the name of it, the smell of it, stomach-heaving at the taste of it, for things were coming shrimpy with us now our savings were gone. And though Grandfer gave us house room he couldn't be expected to feed us, though most of what Cae White brought in was put against the walls of the taverns. Rye bread, oatmeal broth, potato soup, a bit of fried bread, no meat, a cabbage or two and buttermilk when we could get it. Reckon I could have eaten a mattress of fat bacon. In the Monmouthshire iron they laboured us to death, but at least we fed except in strike times. I joined Morfydd at the hob in the kitchen.

"That girl's going under," said she.

Haggard in the eyes and sleepless, was Mari, since Tomos Traherne had visited three months back. Pleased enough to see him, true, but God knows what he had brought with him that Christmas, for Mari was a different girl since. No tears, no sadness one could see; just sleepless and wandering as if dazed.

"Happy enough until Tomos came," I said. "You noticed?"

She shook her head. "I wondered that, but I doubt it. Only just occurred to her, I think, that she'll wait years for Iestyn.

You be gentle to her, Jethro, you could not have a better relation, and she needs a boy like you – you being his brother."

"Now what have I done wrong now, for God's sake?"

This turned her, spoon up. "Nothing, or you'd never hear the end of it. Just be gentle, that's all. Poor little Mari."

Nothing angered me more than this sister-in-law stuff that Morfydd was always turning out. Indecent to have a relative nigh a head shorter but only four years older than you. Facing Morfydd I got the bread down somehow and spooned up the dirty old oatmeal.

"We will try Ponty," said she.

I just sighed.

"Well, don't look so ghostly – something's got to be done. We will work the only way we know – in coal."

"It is spring, damned near. I could try my hand at farming, for the place is going to the dogs under Grandfer."

"Grandfer's privilege – his farm. Best stick to what you know." She sighed herself then. "Queer, isn't it – just as Mam says – we run from iron for a bit of peace and land in dirty old coal. *Diawch!*"

I had worked coal in Nanty, like Morfydd, the rest of my family being in iron, except Mari, who had taken her share of hauling trams one time. I hated coal – sixteen hour shifts six days a week, a shilling a day if the seam held out, nothing if it ceased. Black trash were colliers, these days. I had seen the battered heads of the Top Town colliers, the smashed hands of the hewing poor. Furnace work I do like if you can keep clear of the scald, but coal is a trap with no back door out. I cannot stand the galleries and the creak of the splintering prop. Drop the pick, go sideways, watch the slow lengthening of the wane of the pole. Upward it spreads to the pitch, widening: ten million tons of mountain moving, perched on the tip of a four inch prop, and you hold your breath in the seconds of eternity while the county yawns and stretches in sunlight. For you, the microbe, work in the belly, raking at entrails, tunnelling in bowels, and the mountain groans as a child with an ache and its guts rumble thunder. It howls then as the wind breaks and seeks relief by changing position, then bucks to a bright

45

explosion of pain, seeking the balm of its underground rivers. A hit in the stomach as its floor comes up; you squirm for protection as the roof comes down; grip, wait, ready for the crush. Dai Skewen caught it in Number Five, two others walled up.

"What is wrong with you, now?" asked Morfydd.

"Nothing, but I would like iron."

"Who wouldn't. Is this Ponty pit a winder?"

"Ladder. And the foreman Job Gower is blessed double with bastards, I heard say, but he is dying for labour."

"Hush your bad language," said she. "But I will give him, bastards if he proves a thumper. We go on Top Town rates mind." Rising, she swung off the kettle and screamed the teapot. "Skilled rates or nothing, or I will tell him what he does with his Ponty – ladders and all."

I sipped the tea, blowing steam. "We look like staying, then, for he don't like barristers."

"Skilled labour," said she. "Different." She chewed at the window.

"Skilled or unskilled, all the same rate. Sixpence a pound for a dead pig – shilling a week for a live serving-maid."

"There is a dainty expression – where did you learn it?"

"Tramping Boy Joey – he had it off his mam. Two-pounds-ten a year she drew as a scrubbing-girl, all in, keep included."

"O, aye," said she. "Everything counts."

"But happy enough was Cassie Scarlet, mind, while she was scrubbing."

"Pity," said Morfydd. "If the two-pounds-ten includes being bedded you might as well enjoy it."

Bitter, she was, and I chanced a look at her. Grey streaks at the temples now, the high bones of her face flinging shadow into her cheeks. Black-eyed, gipsy-slanted; and beautiful was her mouth so full and red when not twisted as now. Dress her in lace and she'd rock the county.

"Morfydd."

She didn't hear three feet away.

"Morfydd, listen," I said.

She sighed, eyes closed, her lashes spread wide on her cheeks.

"No lectures, Jethro."

"Just this, then," and I took her hand. "Treat Ponty respectful and bring home money, is it? Just for a little while. In a month or two I'll be into farming, then no more coal."

"Yes," she said.

She gripped my hand then and my fingers cracked, and in the ringing silence between us came the grumble of the bed as Mam turned over and the dribbling tune of Richard at the china and his call to Mari to waken and help. Morfydd rose and kicked back her chair. "I will work," she said. "But no lash will drive me now, for I am past those damned capers. Labour, nothing more, for I have heard of this Job Gower, too – women's language that you do not understand. Sixpence a pound for dead pigs, is it? Twopence a stone for a dead Ponty foreman if he tries his tricks on me. There's advantage in being born with the looks of a sow." She pointed. "And you keep clear. I take care of myself."

Got up and kissed her, couldn't think why, and the look she gave me froze me standing.

The windows winked with light from the blackness as we took the road to coal.

It was a two mile walk along the river to Ponty and the mountain behind us frowned blue with the promise of dawn. Over Fox Brow we went, leaping the puddled places, tiptoeing over the iced peat with our hair riming in the frost and the wind from the estuary tearing into us. Near Treforris the track narrowed and the woods of the hollow rose up sharp and clear as the sun ripped at the veil of night with a hatchet of fire. As scarecrows stood the trees, their boles gleaming white with frost, branches flaring and all over dripping as long suddy fingers from the weekly wash. An eye out for corpse candles, me, though Morfydd seemed at peace, whistling quietly under her shawl. I have never been afraid of things on four legs or two, but Will o' the Wisps and Buggy Bo Goblins do give me the creeps when trees are standing as tombstones and the thick pile of a thousand autumns sigh beneath the feet. Grandfer reckoned he saw a corpse candle once; red and evil, it was,

47

topped with yellow and dancing over the peat – sure sign of death for someone, and God knows what is happening fifty feet down where Buggy Bo lives with his blistered victims. Sweating, me; nearly died when Morfydd gripped me and drew me behind a tree.

"Down!" she hissed.

She pulled me closer and I saw the sudden white of her face smudged with shadows.

"Look," she breathed.

"Buggy Bo," I whispered.

"Buggy Bo to hell," said she. "Look, *Rebecca!*"

A Rebeccaite was standing in a clearing before us, dressed in white from head to feet and the wind caught at his gown, billowing the hem as he raised his hands as if in a signal. Leaves rustled, branches snapped. A company of men came from the woods and made a ring in the clearing, all dressed in women's petticoats, their faces blackened. A horseman came next. Tall and broad in the saddle was this Rebecca, his petticoat streaming over the horse's flanks, and he entered the ring of his daughters and the horse reared, forelegs pawing as he checked on the rein. On his head was a turban as of silk, bejewelled and flashing in the shafts of dawn and the golden locks of his wig reached to his waist.

"Bring Luke Talog!" he cried.

"A judgement," Morfydd whispered. "Look, a prisoner."

"Heisht!" I whispered back, "or they will have us, too."

Two men came from the tree-fringe, dragging between them a naked man, and I saw his face upturned in terror as he drooped before the horseman.

"Luke Talog, is this your name?"

And the naked man sank to his knees, biting at his hands.

"Luke Talog," cried Rebecca, "by us will you be judged. For you have crossed a serving-maid in the house of your wife, and filled her, and cast her out into hunger, which is against the law of God. Dost know the Word, Luke Talog – Deuteronomy twenty-two, which saith, 'If a man finds a damsel that is a virgin, which is not betrothed, and lay hold on her, and lie with her, and they shall be found . . . then the man that lay with her

48

shall give unto the damsel's father fifty shekels of silver, and she shall be his wife: because he hath humbled her, he may not put her away all his days.' Right now, Luke, will you marry the damsel?"

And the prisoner trembled and shook his head.

"Aye, Luke boy, that is the trouble, eh? Already married, isn't it?"

The palaver that followed raised me a foot. A weeping of mock tears at this news, and a beating of breasts, with the tormentors in white gowns sobbing on each other's shoulders in grief. Rebecca rose up in his stirrups, shouting:

"See the grief you are causing my daughters, Luke Talog – what about the poor bloody damsel's. Ashamed you should be. Now bring forth the father of the poor girl who was wronged!"

A stooping, white-haired old labourer was pushed into the clearing.

"Thou art the father of the maid," said Rebecca. "Take thou these fifty shekels of silver that have been wrung from the pockets of Luke Talog, being the payment exacted under the law of God," and the shillings were counted into the old man's hands.

"The law of God has been fulfilled, O, Mother!" called a follower. "But what of the law of Rebecca. What is the price of virginity?"

"Can you prove it?" shouted another, and laughter echoed.

"Was she worth it, Luke?"

"Should he not be cast into a pit?"

"A pit of spikes?"

"Or be hanged by the neck?"

"For Luke Talog has worshipped the phallus, and the price of that is death!"

The naked man screamed as they laid hands on him and dragged him upright for the judgement, and the man Rebecca raised his hand as if in blessing, bringing all to silence.

"*Listen!*" whispered Morfydd.

"Hearken ye, my daughters!" Rebecca cried. "The judgement is given. A man who worships his body and defiles that of a child must endure the shame of his own obscenity. Luke

49

Talog shall have his obscenity exposed by the shame of the *ceffyl pren*."

"The wooden horse," Morfydd whispered. "O, God!"

Hustle, bustle now, with white gowns dashing demented, tripping in leaves, scrambling, and where the hell is the pole of shame and who had it last, for God's sake. This, the miming, part of the punishment. Couldn't find it. Up came a wraith and bowed low to the leader.

"A little pole or a big pole, Mother?"

"Was it a big pole or a little pole he used on the maid?"

"A little stick or a big stick to quieten her?"

"He is not being judged for thrashings," cried Rebecca. "Hasten! The dawn is up and the dragoons are out from St Clears – do you think we have all day?"

Comedy now, the sentence given. They jostled each other, measuring poles for length, testing them for strength while Luke Talog on his knees stared at them in terror.

"What will his poor wife say when we carry him through the parish?"

"What will the neighbours say when Luke goes through on the pole?"

"With his backside turned to the sky and the wind taking a whistle at his poor little troubles."

"Chair him," said Rebecca. "He can put on his coat. Up on the wooden horse. Up, up!"

And I could not drag away my eyes.

To business now, the fun over. Up with him, down with him flat in leaves; squirming, screaming, mudstained – bloodstained when they hit him quiet. Pitiless these men of Rebecca, as their own oppressors. And they roped Luke Talog across two poles and hoisted him up, with the ends of the poles resting on two horses. Head lolling, he drooped, pot-bellied, obscene, cradled.

"Pretty brisky for spring, mind. The poor soul will catch his death. O, Mother, have pity – it is a four mile march to his parish."

Rebecca wheeled his horse, bridle chinking, white shroud streaming.

"Down to his parish with him," he cried. "Spare your pity. From magistrates to adulterers we will carry them on poles – clergy, even, if the crime deserves it, and show them the fury of the people. For the bars of Hell are crammed with Luke Talogs and the gates of Heaven are thronged with the helpless. Time it was changed and by God we will change it, and cleanse the fair name of our beloved county. Away!"

In single file they went, Rebecca leading, the wooden horse next, and then the Daughters, as ghosts of silence till the clearing was empty.

CHAPTER 7

WE SPOKE little the rest of the way, shocked into silence by the punishment of Luke Talog. The wooden horse was everywhere these days, although only one tollgate had so far been burned. Rebecca, more powerful every minute, was now fighting to put right the social wrongs, setting herself up as judge of social morals. Horsewhipping for the minor crimes, burning in effigy most nights now, threatening letters to magistrates for unfair sentences, rumours of attacks on the workhouses which were springing up like mushrooms under the new Poor Law. Rebecca was everywhere, especially in Pembrokeshire, but our county was getting its share. Daren't kiss your girl without a glance over your shoulder, and thinking of girls brought me back to Mari. Sweet, sad Mari.

Strange it was Mari who was sending me back to coal. . . .

The lights of Gower's mine winked through the mist as we climbed the last hillock to Ponty. This, a green land ten years back, was now outraged. For the new industry of coal was treading on the skirts of iron and the black diamond wealth of my country was making fortunes for men who had never set foot in Wales. When a shaft struck a black seam the merchants were killed in the rush for profit. Ironmasters, greedy for better investment, came running, and their capital was doubled by our cheap Welsh labour, for taxes and tithes and tolls were lowering our power of bargaining. Slave-owners, fresh from their auctions of the Black Trash of Africa, came surging in shoulder to shoulder with the new Welsh gentry who hated their brothers for the sin of their poverty. These, our great benefactors, came flying – from the slave buying of Bristol to the counting houses of Mother London – to negotiate and quarrel on the body of my country, and the scars of their greed will stand for everlasting.

Across the blackened tips went Morfydd and me to the rag-tailed, heaving labourers staggering under their baskets of coal and mine – women and children, mostly, cheaper labour than men. Little ones bent under loads, their stoops a perpetual deformity that jackknifed them over the eating tables and doubled them in their beds; black-faced, white-teethed; spewed from the womb of a deeper world, chanting to the labour of the stamping trot; a tuneless breath of a song that kept them to the rhythm, this, the night shift ending in exhaustion. Eyes peeped at the strangers, heads turned under baskets, but the labour never faltered, and the shale trembled to hobnail stamping. And we stood in the misted air, me and Morfydd, and watched the ants; watched them building the anthill; chanting, scurrying, one eye wide for Foreman – building up the monuments that future generations will despise, sweating and dying for their ninepence a day.

"Worse than bloody Nanty this," I said, and fisted Foreman's door.

Never seen the like of this Job Gower for size. Ducking under the frame he grinned at Morfydd, ham-hands on hips, stripped to the waist in frost. Deep-chested, hairy, the bull of his family; out of a Welsh womb by a Donegal slaughterer, according to Grandfer; tore his mam to pieces, sixteen pounds.

"You wanting labour?" asked Morfydd, hands on hips, too.

"*Well*, now!" Double bass, flat as that.

"Good labour. Skilled," I said, but he never even heard; just strolling around Morfydd inspecting fresh cattle.

"Brecon coal, Top Town iron," said she at nothing, "and we work on rates."

He rubbed his bristled chin, grinning.

"Monmouthshire rates for skilled labour," I said. "Trams or basketing, ladders or winding – towing if you like."

"Coal face hewing and he works to chalk," said Morfydd.

The bedlam rose to a shout about us, the tempo surging at the sight of Foreman. The pigmies scurried, these the brothers; brother to the black-skinned slave of the cotton lands, the earnicked trash of the branding iron, whip-scarred, mutilated.

"There is a beauty," said Job.

"Till you put a hand on her," said Morfydd. "Then she's a bitch."

Didn't stop grinning, to his credit.

"Bargaining, eh?" He turned to me. "Coal face, you – with Liam Muldooney on Number Two. He's driving me to hell, let's see what he'll do for you. The woman goes towing, no skilled women."

"Monmouthshire rates. Penny a basket," said Morfydd.

"Trams, too – halfpenny a basket – twenty a day," he replied.

"Ladders thrown in?" I asked, innocent.

He grunted.

"And what height is this pit?" asked Morfydd.

"A hundred feet – you can damned near jump it."

"Then jump," said she. "A penny a basket is Top Town rates and we weren't born yesterday."

"I can see that," said he, looking her over. "Take it or leave it."

"Come, Jethro," said Morfydd. "Work to death by all means, but not starving too. Come."

"Penny a basket," said Job Gower. "But keep it to yourself."

"Thank God for the Unions," said Morfydd.

"Plenty of tongue for strangers," said he. "We will see how you do. If not, you're out, the two of you."

Twenty shillings a week between us, six day week. Not bad, I thought, but I was afraid of the ladders for Morfydd.

A hundred feet down is a platform of light and the two

ladders are snakes that reach to the bottom, baskets coming up one side, baskets going down the other.

"You first," said Morfydd, and I saw the sweat suddenly bright on her face, for she had never done ladders before, and I wondered at her head for heights. Job Gower was behind us as I swung myself into space and gripped the rungs, and I saw the shadow of Morfydd's leg come over above me as I went down hand over hand. Twenty feet down I stopped, for a woman was climbing against the platform of light, and her gasps were preceding her on the swaying rungs.

"Down with you," roared Job from the top. "Don't mind old Towey, plenty of room to pass."

Down, down, hand over hand, with the ladder bucking and the coal dust flying up, sucked upwards by the draught. Looked up at the light above me and the morning clouds and saw Morfydd coming after me, her fingers peaked white on the rungs, skirts and petticoats billowing indecent, and I knew she was fearing the drop. Began to wonder how I could break her if she came, hang on and elbow her against the shaft, foot against the up-ladder, but I knew she'd take me if she came from a height. So I waited a bit till her feet were above me.

Down fifty feet and I met Mrs Towey. Swing over to the right as she comes labouring up, for her basket is lopsided and her body is swaying.

"Good morning, Mrs Towey," I said to cheer her.

"O, Christ," said she. "Do you give me a hand."

Sixty if she's a day, this one, eyes upturned, breathing in gasps; sweat-streamed, shuddering, clinging to the rungs, with the coal from her basket spilling down and dancing as gnats against the square of light. Thank God nobody was following her.

"O, God," said Towey.

"Shift you over, woman," I said. "I will come on your ladder," and steadied her basket.

"O, man," said she. "Let me keep my coal."

"Easy with it, then," and I jacked the thing up with my knee. "Rest," I said, gripping her skirts. The two of us there with Morfydd above me, and I looked up past her to the sky and

Gower's face was peering down with clouds doing halos above his head.

"What the hell is happening down there, Towey?" he roared.

"Come down and see," I roared back. "Little old Towey it is, and I am giving her a spell. Damned scandal, it is."

"Aye? She'll have you basketing for her before you are finished."

"Strangers, is it?" asked Towey, eyes closed, forehead sweating against a rung.

"Aye," I said. "Rest yourself, girl."

"Kind, you are, boy. This old ladder will be the death of me, mind. Twenty times I have been up it since last night. Is it light up by Job, or darkness?"

"Morning," I said. "The end of the shift."

"Thank God for His mercies," said she. "For there is fire in my chest and I couldn't climb again" and she opened her eyes and looked at me with a wrinkled grandmother of a smile. "Eh, now, young you are, man. But a baby."

"Nigh fourteen," I replied. "Do not talk."

So we rested, Towey and me, with Job shouting his head off at the top till Morfydd started some lip and he went off disgusted.

"Will you climb now, old woman?" I asked.

"Eh, aye! Got my breath back now. Mind, fit as a horse I am most times, see, but poorly lately, not up to standard. You Chapel?"

"For God's sake," I said, heaving back to my ladder.

"O, a curse on the first woman who ever climbed this ladder," said she, "and rot her soul in everlasting Hell. Dying this, not living, and I have a husband to keep – you heard about Tom Towey?"

"For grief's sake," said Morfydd above us. "Are we serving up tea?"

"Go now, Towey," I said. "It is only fifty feet."

Up with her then, basket creaking and her coal spilling down, clouting on the head and naked shoulders of a woman coming after her. Irish by the sound of her, sending up Irish curses. Legs as sticks has Mrs Towey, the rags about them fluttering, and Morfydd gave her an elbow as she went up past her to Job hands on hips at the top.

Welsh and Irish waiting at the bottom; waiting for their turn with their baskets at their feet. Waiting for Towey to get clear being the truth of it, for a six inch coal nut takes some heading.

"Good morning," they said in chorus. "Who you after, man?"

"Liam Muldooney."

"Down on Number Two, girl."

"Eh, there's lucky. Biblical, mind, but a dear little man, old Liam."

"Hewing, then?" asks one, stumps of teeth champing – Towey's mam by the look of this one.

"Hewing for him," said Morfydd. "I am for towing."

"You got the pads, girl? 'Tis terrible rocky. Plays the devil with your poor old knees."

"I have pads," says another, and Morfydd catches them.

"Strangers, is it?"

"Aye."

"Brother and sister?"

"Don't be daft, girl – look, spit and image."

"Dear God, anna she pretty!"

"Church of England, is it?"

"Chapel," I said.

"Eh, Chapel! Oi, Meg Benyon by there – strangers are Chapel, you heard? Nothing like Chapel, mind, real Christian, and a fine little minister we have in our Horeb, very good to the children, bless him, too."

"We are Horeb," I said to please her.

"Speak for yourself," whispered Morfydd.

"Now, where's that Meg Benyon? Anyone seen Meg Benyon?"

"Passed just now, Crid – gone back to Muldooney."

"Well, there's a pity, for she is with Muldooney. Horeb, eh? What a coincidence. Where you from, boyo?"

"Nantyglo."

"Where the hell's that, man?"

Morfydd told her.

"Other end of the earth, eh? O, well, got to get going."

"Is that old Towey up?" She looked Towey's grandmer till she bent to the basket and it flew up under her hands. Must have been forty, no more.

"Shake your legs, woman."

"Up a dando, then – give a bunk on this old basket. Take care of the strangers, mind. Liam Muldooney they are after, see?"

On.

Hand in hand now, me and Morfydd; along the galleries where the trams are thundering, with the tallow lamps flaring in crevices of rock, on to the switch road where the nightshift lies hewing, naked as babies, these men, flat on their backs. And the tallow lamps flash on their postures of love-making, rolling, frowning up to the black seam, picking, chinking as they head the new gallery. A snake of women now, bending to their baskets, headed by a Welsh girl, broad as a man, stripped to the waist and shining with sweat.

"Right for Number Two, Liam Muldooney?" I asked her.

"Next gallery, boy. You just come down?"

"Aye," said Morfydd.

"The props are going on Six – has Gower heard?"

"Never mentioned it," said I.

"Give it an hour and the roof will be in." She turned, cupping her hands, shouting above the picks. "Gower don't know, Mark. Send Foreman down, is it?"

"Head first if you can, followed by the owner," came a whisper from darkness.

The Welsh girl nudged me sideways.

"That your sister, man?"

"Aye."

"Watch, then. A swine for a face as pretty as that, is Job Gower. Eh, *hark* at that Bronwen!"

Bronwen is howling by the draught door of the gallery that heads Number Six. Important is Bronwen, shilling a week;

opening and closing the draught doors so men can breathe.

"Now, now," said Morfydd, kneeling. "What you crying for, you pretty little thing?"

Cats.

"Cats, is it?" asks Morfydd, cooing.

"Took the bread from my fingers," says Bron, and her arms went out, but Morfydd folded them back. Frowning up, she said, "Bait bag, Jethro," and I gave it to her. "There now," says Morfydd, "we will give you more bread. Damned old thievers, them cats. You have this, Bron."

"Stand clear," cries a voice, and Bron opens the draught door.

Meg Benyon, this time, the Meg we missed farther back. On all fours is Meg Benyon, shod as a donkey, kneepads, handpads, with a belt round her middle and a chain over her flanks, and up on her haunches she goes, smoothing her black hair from her face.

"Well now, good morning. Just come to see Bronwen I have, and bump into strangers. Welsh, is it?"

I gave her some and she slapped her thigh, joyful. "Well, there's a pleasure – all in the family. Two in three are foreigners these days, undercutting wages. Chapel, too, is it?"

"Horeb," I said, getting used to it.

"Well! And I called you strangers! O, hush your moaning, Bronwen, *fach*. You still weeping? Still the old cats, is it? Now you leave them to Benyon, I will give them a belting." She looked as us, eyes flat. "A scandal, isn't it?"

I nodded.

"No child of mine would come down the pits. Die first. You towing, girl?"

"Over with Muldooney."

"And I am hewing there," I said.

"Same face as me. There's fine. A caution is Liam, mind – good job you're Chapel, though he's Irish as the shamrock. Lay preacher spare time, too – very kind to my mam, Mrs Towey – taking her from ladders a week next Monday. Never been the same since she lost our dad. You see her coming down?"

"Saw her going up," I said.

"Six at home she had, see? Me being eldest, and I am going up soon, says Muldooney, being in child. Three months more, have it in summer. You be gentry, says old Liam Muldooney, you have it in comfort up in daylight, leave the pit-births to donkeys though they carried our Lord. Eh, God bless our Liam – second saviour, I reckon, treats you respectful, not like that Gower. Ah, well, got to get going. Straight down, now, follow your noses."

Mane flying in the draught, hooves scraping, harness chinking, Mrs Benyon goes through with the coal tram after her, ducking her head to the two foot roof – the tunnel that leads to the waiting carts.

Liam Muldooney is fetching out coal, trews on, thank heavens, lying in the pit props. Long and gaunt, with the face of a grandfather, was Liam, though I guessed him right at under fifty. Away with his pick and he scrambled out.

"Be damned," said he. "There's a neat little woman for me – Irish, is it?"

"Welsh," I said. "Are you Liam Muldooney?"

"Sure as I'm Irish – you sent by Gower?"

We told him. "Trams and hewing, when do we start?"

"God be praised for a spirit, now," said he, and down on a rock with him and out with a pipe. "It's a rest I am needing and you have come the right time, for I have a few minutes to give praise to my Lord." From a little box beside him he pulled out a Bible. "Do you know this little Book, now, me darlin's?"

"We are Welsh," I said.

"Eh, and I forgot. The harder they hit us the deeper we go, isn't it, and there's fine feathers up in London town who'd have difficulty spelling the great name Samuel, and you and me know it off by heart. Lucky you are, mind, best face in the county, this – best vein and easiest pickings since shamrock land, or I'm not Liam Muldooney, though me real name's foreign, now! Settle you down the pair of you for a talk with Liam," and he patted the rock. I looked at Morfydd and saw pity in her face.

And I looked at Muldooney; at the battered head bumped by

coal, the red-rimmed eyes of the lifelong collier. Men like Muldooney were as thousands in the upland counties, most with the look of the mountain fighter, though many had not seen a fist closed in anger. Flattened noses; screwball ears, as little bits of brain battered out of their skulls, by falls and clouts, not fists, and their speech came slow.

"Have you heard of the man of Kabzeel who did the fine acts, now?"

"Kabzeel," I said, searching Samuel.

"Make it short, Benaiah," said Morfydd.

"Well, there's a woman – got me right first time, for sure. Just giving a little test, I am, for your knowledge of the Scriptures – necessary for people like us working within three foot of the Devil. And no offence, little maiden. Benaiah is my name, speak now."

Morfydd was smiling, ever a soft spot for the Irish.

"Samuel twenty-three," said she, "but you've hit me for the verse. Book two."

"Good enough. I am working with christian brother and sister – I can see that a mile. Verse twenty, for your information. Jchoiada was me dad, you see; slaughtering up the men of Moab – hitting up the Philistines right and left in spare time as I do every Sunday from pulpits in the name of Jesus the Lord. And down into a pit comes Benaiah to slay a lion in time of snow. You see the connection?"

"No," I said.

"And you in a pit a hundred feet down?"

"Go on," said Morfydd, happy with him.

"And in the depth of winter, and all!" He flared his pipe and the flame lit the forest of props about us and the tram line shimmering down the tunnel. Strange place to find a man with a Bible, least of all a prowling lion.

"Ah, me, little lady," said Liam, and took Morfydd's hand and kissed it. "No offence, you understand, for being shamrock I always kiss me friends, and I will not ask more, alone or not. Fallen among thieves, the pair of you, taking work with that pig Job Gower, but you will work at peace with Liam Muldooney who is a slayer when it comes to women-snatching

60

foremen. And now it is winter and a time of snow, so hip and bloody thigh I will strike him if he pesters my women, begging the pardon of the Lord for the language, for with Jchoiada for a dad I couldn't do otherwise. You listening?"

"God bless you, Mr Muldooney," said Morfydd.

"So you come hewing, little man, and you go towing, little woman, with never a backward look for Gower, and I prefer my women covered in the breast, you understand?"

"Yes," said Morfydd.

"And my men with trews, you see."

"Of course," I said.

"Now then, you seen my little Meg Benyon go by just now?"

"We passed her coming in," I said.

"Aye, well I sent her up the switch to see to my Bronwen, for the tears of a child is the grief of angels. Right now, do not sit around. Kneepads, handpads, pick – down and get towing, girl, or we will not enjoy the Sundays."

Stripping to the waist I joined him in the props. Morfydd waited till Meg Benyon got back with her empty tram, and she harnessed up to the one I was filling. Down on all fours she went between the rails, heaving.

"Good little tower, though," said Liam, eyeing her. "She done it before?"

"Yes," I said.

"She conceived?"

"She is single," I said.

"Safe she will be on Muldooney's shift though, and she is safer on towing than them dirty old ladders, so shift you over and do not be fidgety. Would you hear again about my dad?"

So we started in coal, Morfydd and me, at Ponty.

CHAPTER 8

FOR A year me and Morfydd had laboured with Muldooney for the first summer had been drenching and most harvests failing, and Grandfer was not keen to have me in the farming, though he did precious little of it himself.

But this spring had been glorious, with the countryside melting early in the quickening sun, and even the weeping willows on the banks of the Tywi were laughing and the lanes from Cae White fluttering white with blossom. Hedgehog Grandfer, yawning and stretching from his hop-winter sleep, rose up in April, and belted and buckled he fair bounced round the place. Even Mam came from mourning, dainty with lace from the money coming in. Mari had grown new smiles again, singing and tickling her baby Jonathon, growing lovelier with every day's passing, and I was fishing for kissing terms with Tessa Lloyd Parry.

Eh, were I a poet I would write a song to Tessa up at Squire's Reach, telling of the beauty of the daughters of the gentry. Seeing quite a bit of her lately, though I kept it secret, and sharp after Sunday dinners I would go through Waldo's preserves to Squire's Reach and a once-a-week loving. Held her hand Sunday before last. Kissing this week if I plucked up the courage.

There is kissing and kissing, of course. You can have one for a penny from Sixpenny Jane, though I'd never tried it, and I could have had one a minute from Hettie Winetree, though Dilly Morgan was sharp with backhanders, her dad being strict. But the kissing of gentry is a very different thing, and practice is needed to get the thing perfect.

Morfydd's mirror. Into her bedroom for a good clean parting, polished up and pulled in, hair flat with water.

"Tessa!"

I would have given my soul to be gentry just then; cool, calm, sure of myself. And then I remembered a painting Mam had once, of a poor chap grovelling, all wigs and laces, beseeching a bone from a lady disdainful.

"*Tessa!*"

Try one knee, for both looks like begging, giving it to her with a voice like a tombstone, and Morfydd comes in. Took one look, the bitch, and sat down rocking. Just sat there holding her stays, beetroot in the face to burst blood vessels, making no sound.

Up scalded me.

"A damned sneak you are!" I shouted.

"Aye? Then whose damned mirror, whose damned bedroom? Cross my palm with silver or it is going over the county," and she reeled away to the bed and went flat on it, thumping.

"What is the trouble, what is the commotion?" Mam now, feathers waving, just come from Chapel. "And bad language, too – I will not stand for it, Sunday at that!"

But Morfydd just shrieked, thumping the pillow.

Away, me. Downstairs like a bullet, skidded through the kitchen and out the back, upending Grandfer coming in for dinner.

Sunday afternoon.

Along the spring lanes, me; full of beef undercut and Mari's plum pudding, for we were eating better these days; whistling to lose my front ones, hands in pockets, special combed and fluffed up like a hen coming broody. Quite determined, now. One day, I knew, I would marry Tessa Lloyd Parry and bring some gentry into the Mortymer blood and knock some of the pugilism out of it. One day from Tessa I would bring forth my kind, though just then I couldn't imagine her bringing anything forth save a little silver slipper. Dainty, she was; Welsh dark, only up to my shoulder, but educated. Fifteen today, too, with Greek verses and Homers on her table at tea: raised in a hammock between two cherry trees, eating honeybread to pass the time while I was into oatmeal soup and crawling under the county. Queer old pair we made, come to think of it.

Some nights, when we first came to Cae White, I would walk in the darkness of her home at Squire's Reach and watch the comings and goings behind the lace-covered windows. There, dying for a peep at Tessa, I would see the gentry; the men, elegant in their frock coats bowing to carpets; slim men, tall, the pick of the English officers, some billeted there to put down Rebecca. And lovely were the women, with waists for dog-collars and their high-pushed breasts curved white under the chandeliers. Minuet now, the hand-drooping dances, with harpists brought in for the price of a dinner. I am partial to music myself, being Welsh; preferring a good solid choir with plenty of brass under it to a milky minuet. And colour and dignity I like, too, seeing them sometimes in a woman off to Chapel or the sight of a big man hewing in strength. But the bowing and scraping of lords and ladies I could never bear, especially in the men. For the fingers of Man were made for clenching and handclasp, not for waving lace, and I would rather stink of honest cow muck than despoil my manhood with perfume.

Beautiful was Squire's mansion up on the Reach, with the flowering clematis and creeper of centuries drooping in profusion over its entrance, while behind the marble columns all the pride and wealth of the county danced and curtseyed to the bowed good evenings. And sometimes, in the glitter of the room, I would see my Tessa staying up late for a special occasion, being delicate. In her high cane chair she would sit with the beaux of the county dancing her attention. About my own age, some of these, and I longed to get among them three at a time. Bitter, unequal, I would watch from the shadows of the drive, born the wrong side of the blanket, listening for the gardener and his get to hell out of it. But sustained within by the truth of it – that Tessa Lloyd Parry didn't give a damn for the gentry sons while I was loose – me, Jethro Mortymer, torn coat and hobnails.

We met first on Waldo Bailiff's afternoon off. Up on the Reach I was, looking for suicide salmon, Mam being partial to it, though it damned near choked her with the speed she got it down. But a salmon has a right to die as anyone else, I reckon, being sick of the parasites and weary of the journeyings. So down on the bank you go, slip in a stick with a wire noose on the end. For hours you might lie till the poor creature comes, jaded, unhappy, seeking an end to it. In goes his head, pull the noose tight, out on the bank with him and a crack with a boulder, and you slip him back in the river to float past Cae White where Morfydd, by chance, happens to be waiting. Salmon, I think, are much like humans. Like Jess Williams, Grandfer's neighbour about thirty years back – dying to meet his Maker, was Jess, and down he comes in his nightshirt, a rope in one hand, a bucket in the other, with Moc, his twin brother, waiting in their barn. Up on the bucket went Jess with the rope over a beam, and Moc kicked the bucket away at a given signal. Helpful, I call that; brotherly love. Murder they called it in Carmarthen, and they hanged Moc in public.

"Die hard, Moc Williams," called his mam from the crowd. "Die hard like our Jess," and Moc did so, for he loved his mam.

Wrong, this, for if a man is begging for St Peter he should be assisted.

I helped my first salmon out of it soon after arriving. This summer I was waiting for my fifteenth; dozing on the banks of the Reach in the bee-loud silence, watching the waving of the water-lilies and the caress of bindweed where the quicksilver fins flashed bright in the depths. Ring-doves were shouting from the fringes of Cae White, rising as diamonds in the windless air. Sweating, I dozed, but a splash brought me upright. More fishermen – splashing along in a welter of foam, mam leading, dad following and three babies after him swimming demented. Whiskered noses swept the river, black eyes gleamed in sunlight – throwing a live trout from snout to snout, an arc of silver, wriggling, diving. Whistling, plunging, the otters played, and I never heard a footstep.

"Good afternoon," said Tessa.

Up like lightning, fists clenched, looking for a bailiff's chin, and the stick and noose slipped into the river and drifted down to Cae White. Through a pattern of branches Tessa made shape.

Am I supposed to tell of her with only words to use?

Pale was her face, lips stained red; thin and dark, a hand would have snapped her. Her long, summer dress was white and dainty with lace, her long hair black against it. And she held aside her pink parasol and smiled, her eyes coming alive in her face. Always known her behind glass before, never met officially.

"How are you?" I said. Just sat, awaiting sentence. Caught poaching on her dada's river, and in daylight. And how the hell she got there was anyone's guess just then.

"Jethro Mortymer, is it?"

65

Amazing what gentry know. Hooking at my collar, me.

"How is your mother, Jethro Mortymer?"

"Very pleasant."

"Did you see the otters?"

"O, aye."

"Beggars for the poaching, though. Listen to that, now," said she, for the belly-flops of a salmon pursued came up the river and the otters were whistling and plunging as madmen. "O, that sound drives Waldo Bailiff demented. Do you come here often?"

"First time."

"To poach salmon?"

"Upon my soul!" I said, shocked.

She laughed then, face turned up.

"There's a pity, for one salmon more or less don't make much difference," which is not the way she said it but the only way I can tell it. "Especially when the otters kill for sport. You heard them at night?"

Nearer she leaned, her voice coming secret. "O, there is a wildness and freedom about otters, I do think, and a good full moon will always start them capering. Some nights, when the vapours are billowing, I pull back the curtains and listen till dawn. And old Grandfer Badger down in Bully Hole Bottom grunting and singing at the moon. Killed four fox hounds last fall – you seen him?"

"Never," I answered, for he had his hole in Waldo's preserves and I had sprung four gins to save him last spring. "Never seen a badger in my life."

"You seen herons down on the estuary?"

"No," I said, for the estuary was near the rabbit warren.

"Old Bill Stork on the mere?"

I knew him like a brother; shook my head.

"Backward, you, for a farming boy," said she, peeved. "Hen coots you know of, I expect?"

"O, aye, seen tons of coots."

"And heard the Reach curlews calling at dawn?"

"Then I be sleeping."

"Good grief," said she, and straightened herself tidy.

"Reckon if Grandfer Zephaniah wants Cae White ploughing this year he must do it himself again."

"Ploughed," I said.

"But not by you, I vow."

"Indeed?" I said, cool.

"Indeed," said she, cooler, and we sat there just looking, knives chiefly.

I glanced at the sky for the sun had pulled up his trews again and the air of the river blew sudden cold, though a mite warmer than Tessa who had one shoulder turned.

"How old are you, Jethro Mortymer?" Duchess now.

"Hitting it up for fourteen."

She eyed me sideways. "Is it true you've got a brother?"

I nodded, coming warmer, for this was Iestyn my god.

"In transportation, isn't he?"

"Seven years he got at Monmouth," I replied.

Her chin an inch higher now, untouchable.

"A criminal he is, says Waldo Bailiff. That true?"

"Seven years," I said, hot. "For fighting against gentry like you and scum like Waldo Bailiff, to make things decent for people starving. And we are waiting for him, me and the family, keeping Cae White until he comes back."

Eyes like saucers now with me standing over her.

"And when he comes back he will build the place up," I said, hotter. "He'll build Cae White as big as Squire's Reach, and we will buy up the river and fish our own salmon, for he'd dust any ten round here with Waldo Bailiff to fill in time, so tell him watch out."

Pretty worked up. Always the same when I spoke of Iestyn. She was staring at me, her eyes ringed with their sleepless nights of shadow, and as we were looking it rained.

No warning, just pelted; hitting the river into life in a sudden sweep of the wind.

"O, dear!" said Tessa, and up with her parasol. "Ben, Ben!"

"Who's Ben?" I asked, standing over her with the flaps of my coat trying to keep her dry.

"My servant. Ben!"

Squinted through the trees, but no sign of him.

"O, my dress – just *look* at my dress!" She turned her face to mine, rain-splashed, appealing, and I thought she would cry.

"Up a dando," I said, and knelt, lifting her, running like a demon to the veranda of the big house. There I set her in a cane chair, and turned, skidding down the steps from the holy portals of Squire to the teeming white of the river. Awkward questions to be answered if I hung round there. Away then, back to Cae White, reaching home just as Morfydd was fishing the stick and noose from the river and yelling to Mam that Jethro was drowned.

Damned near it.

I leaned against the shed at the back and looked up the Reach, thinking of Tessa. Wet was my face, and not all the wetness rain. For the cripples of Carmarthen city are as Tessa Lloyd Parry, I thought; knobbled knees on their winter pavements, the drumstick wavings of their starving children, the ragged droop of their twisted crones.

From a lopsided womb had come Tessa, spewed, not delivered, and she had not walked since birth. Strange you can pass the cripples of the poor without a second look while the sight of crippled gentry brings you to tears. Strange is Man's pity. The cripple in rags is revolting but pity is flung at the cripple in silk.

Cutting hearts in oak trees now, entwined, pierced, dripping with blood.

We met in secret, of course, with a tongue-pie for Tessa and a belting for me if her dad, the Squire, got hold of it, and if old Ben, the servant, knew of our meetings he kept it pretty well buttoned. Special, this Sunday – Tessa's birthday, being June, and a cameo brooch for presentation from me – thieved by moonlight from Morfydd's room. Death by fire for the thief if she found him.

O, that Sunday!

Larks were singing in the unbroken blue and just enough heat in the air to evaporate Waldo's dewdrop. White-sailed schooners ploughed the estuary and the mountains were fleeced with the splashing brooks as the bath plug came out of spring. Bedsheet clouds were billowing round Gabriel who was sorting them out for weddings and shrouds, and the old sun, catching alight to the flame of summer, flung golden swords over the bright green country. O, wonderful is summer! Crescent wing on bubbling air, the eaves-chattering sparrows, with a million hearts leaping to the wooing every square mile, including me. Singing, face turned up to the sun, my heart was pounding with every step nearer to Tessa. Down from Cae White to the woods of the Reach, leaping the gates, diving over the hedges to Tessa's red lips and a once-a-week loving – through Waldo's game preserves now, into Squire's field where his rams were grazing. Clovenhooved swines, these, with the faces of Satan and enough lust in their matings to satisfy Nick himself. Never took to rams much, preferring their wives and their children with their thumb-sucking daintiness. So over the gate with me and I landed on one's back, gripping his horns, heeling his sides, and away across the field we went as things insane with the other ram following and baa-ing blue murder. Nothing like a ride on a ram, says Joey; an art in itself, says he, for if you can stay on a ram in June you'll ride most things. Through the lambs we went and over his backside went me, with his mate catching me square as I presented the target, the devil, bowling me somersaults. I fled with rams after me and belly-dived the fence into Bully Hole Bottom. Duck Waldo's fence again and the mantrap faces you; try it with your toe for the fun of it, risking your foot for the joy of it, and the game birds rise to the shattering crash. Wait, steady. Stand stock still, for the woods have eyes, one pair especially. Over by there, a bit to the left. Motionless he stands, old Grandfer Badger, carved in stone, every nerve trembling, for he knows what is coming if I get within reach of him. Nose down to leaves he stands, hoping to be missed in the forest stillness of branch and leaf. Hands in pockets, I started whistling, wandering towards him, kicking at stones, not the least bit interested in badgers. Then leap the last yards. Shoulders screwing he dives for his earth, frantic, for the earth is a fox hole and not designed for badgers. In! Kneeling, I stared into darkness, then cursed his

69

soul, for he kicked with his hind feet and shot out pebbles to blind me. Down flat for revenge then, one arm down the hole. Legs waving, I reached for him, fingers prodding till I touched his backside, then walked my fingers to the stump of his tail, gripped it and heaved; and the earth is rumbling to the thunder of his indignity. Red in the face, he is, bracing his forelegs, scraping his hindlegs, for that swine Jethro Mortymer's got hold of my tail. Heave. Grandfer heaves back. Seen and unseen we grunt and strain, but he is a grandfer and I am younger, and out he comes bellowing. Roaring, he comes, stumps of teeth bared, wheeling for the conflict, snapping, snarling. Away, me, followed by Grandfer, leaping the boulders, putting up pheasants. But wait!

Little Mam Pheasant is lying in leaves, and her beak is red and her chest is heaving, for Waldo and his gun have passed her in flight, and she turns up her head to the tickle of my finger. Dad Pheasant now, head on one side, inquiring; cannot make out why she's broody in June. Soft was her neck in the twist of my fingers and the wind did a sigh as her little soul flew upward. Up in a branch with her, for Mam has a fancy for pheasants; up beyond the reach of thieving badgers, and on to the river. Running now, hobnails thumping for the last quarter mile. Breasting a rise I raced down the hollow and along the bank where Tessa sits waiting.

"Tessa!"

Sitting as I left her last Sunday. But different this time, sweetened by the year of our parting. Breathless, I reached her, and knelt.

"Tessa," I said, gasping.

The way she looked, perhaps, the narrowing of eyes. No need for mirrors. I kissed her. And I heard the quick inrush of her breath as I put my arms about her and kissed her again and her yellow straw hat fell off to her shoulders and her hair tumbled down to the force and fire. Great was the strength in me, sudden, unpitying, and she turned away her face and twisted in my arms, and there was a trembling within her that leaped to my fingers. Soft was her breast. . . .

"Jethro!" she said, sharp. "*Jethro!*"

Didn't mean to do it, sorry now; but I'd do it again if she so much as looked. Sat back then and watched her in profile, seeing the flash of the river behind her, and her eyes were all mystery and brightness. Gave me a glance then, the glance of a woman, and I reckoned she knew what I had in mind, for she put on her straw hat and set it tidy, very prim, tying the bows again, looking away.

"If you don't mind," she said.

"Many happy returns," I said.

"Thank you," said she. "But my birthday. Not yours, remember."

O, beautiful, she looked just then.

"I am sorry," I said.

Silence, save for the wind and the splash-plops of the river, and gurgling.

"But a child you are, Jethro," she said then. "Do not make it hard."

Poor Tessa. Just wanted to hold her then and soothe and kiss her, but I did not dare. Had to say something.

"Look," I said. "Old Grandfer Badger is down in Bully Hole Bottom, girl. Roaring and raging, he is, for I've just had him out by the tail. You ever seen Grandfer?"

"No," she said. Eyes low now, threatening tears, fingers ripping at her little lace handkerchief.

"Not interested?"

She shook her head, lips trembling.

"O, Jethro," she whispered, and wept.

I held her. All the heat gone, I held her, and her old hat fell off again and her hair went down again. Just the two of us in the world then.

"Thought I'd forgotten?" I asked, holding her away. "See now, here is a valuable. Your birthday, and I've been saving up for months. Tessa, don't cry. Look, look!" and I fished out the brooch. Wonderful was her face as she blinked away tears and her eyes opened wide at the sight of it. God knows what would happen if Morfydd saw it on her.

"Jethro, you shouldn't have done it!"

"Cost a small fortune," I said, but I know it cost twopence

71

for I watched Morfydd buy it from the tinker. "Got it down in Whitland," I said. "Fair day."

"O, it is lovely!"

"Shall I pin it on, girl?"

Eyes up at this. "I can manage myself, thank you."

"Tessa!"

"Eh?"

"Will you be my girl now and stick to me, is it?"

"Not much chance of me running," she answered. "Look, boy – is it tidy?"

"There's an old wacko you are," I said. "Pretty it do look on you," and I leaned forward as she reached for my lips.

"Pretty for you," she said.

"Till death do us part and down in wooden suits," I said. "You are my girl now, you promise?"

"Yes."

"Dry up, then," I said. "Do not look so mournful. Down to Bully Hole Bottom with us, is it?"

"How can I walk to Bully Hole Bottom? Jethro, have sense!"

"On my back," I cried. "I could carry an elephant. Look, if we hurry grandfer will still be there and I will fetch him out again for you. Come on!"

"O, stay!" she replied, and just looked. And the way she looked.

"To the devil with badgers," she said. "Jethro!"

The lips so curved are dying for kisses, and her eyes closed to the sun as I drew her against me, and saw, in a rift of her hair the distant roof of the mansion and the poplars of the Big Field misted in sunlight and the silver ribbon river winding to the hills.

Cool is the kiss at the beginning, then growing to warmth as the kiss is longer, steaming dry to fire as the breaths come quicker, till the kissed is a quarry that seeks escape from the circling iron of the capturing arm and she sighs and faints in the greater strength. O, mad is that strength!

"Jethro!"

I did not answer and she clung to me, and I saw the faint

72

white scratches of my chin on her face, that would later turn red.

"Jethro, do not touch me, not again!"

"Tessa," I said, and was ashamed.

"Just . . . kiss me. So I can remember?"

CHAPTER 9

Now I stood in a universe of nights and days boiling in the inch between boyhood and manhood, and listened to the call of the scythe. The wind sighed through the grasses and the corn of Grandfer's acres were as gold. Coo-doves called from the woods, herons from the Tywi where the salmon swirled up for their act of creation and Tessa's otters barked in moonlight.

Waking early that morning I pulled on my boots and went down to the kitchen to the back, listening to the tinkling splashes from the mere as the hencoots got busy among beaks where the bulrushes stood in shimmering silence. There came to me a song then, not the song of Ponty, sweating and grimed, but the windy sighing of corn falling obliquely to the scythe, its razor edge flashing and stained with clover flowers that clung to the wetted shine of boots. I saw, in my sleep-gummed eyes, the line of the reapers, waist-deep in the corn, their naked backs sweating in midday heat, and the swing of their blades made sunfire in the gold. Earth smells came; the scent of burned pine; sour stinks from the rotted dumps of kale, the perfumed wind of overflowing barns. Great was Cae White then, as a ship at sea with billowing mists sailing in her turrets.

The women were stirring in the bedrooms now, curtains swishing to let in sunlight; pot-clanking, bed-squeaks as Morfydd got out and her son's thin protest at the sudden bedlam. She awoke like a man, this one, with all the palaver of a man, and what damned time do you call this and get to hell out of it. She washed as a man, too, stripped to the waist in frost.

"*Diawl!*" she said at the door now. "Somebody's got a conscience. Have you put her in trouble?"

Venus, complete with arms, towel dangling, hair on her shoulders.

"Don't worry about me," I said. "Just come naked."

She smiled at this and came to the water butt beside me and flung back her hair and tied it with red ribbon, and I turned away as she hit the tub with all the corkings and bubblings of a man from shift.

"Well, now," said she, rubbing for a glow. "And what is it thinking?"

"My business."

"O, aye? Then it do happen to be mine also. D'you know what time Grandfer got in last night?"

"I go to bed to sleep," I said.

"Not much option round these parts, mind," and she winked and held the towel against her. "Coo-dove time, an hour or so back. Belted with quarts, he was, climbing up one stair and belly-sliding ten – making enough commotion to raise the damned rent. Reckon you must die if you didn't hear Grandfer. Drunk? Three nights running now." She jerked her head at the standing corn. "The place won't get a shave this side of Christmas the way he's going. Time those fields was down."

"Where he gets the money from puzzles me," I said.

"Grandfer's business – not yours, or mine. Neither is scything my business. What I know about farming can be written on a toenail, but I reckon to eat next winter."

"And I know less than you," I said.

"Time somebody learned, then, time somebody moved. I'm a different shape in the chest to you but I'd have a try if there wasn't a man around."

"What about Ponty? Do I hew with Muldooney and farm, too?"

"I'll handle Ponty."

"Twenty acres of corn," I said. "Abel Flannigan might help."

She was tapping her foot now, eyes narrowed.

74

"Or Osian Hughes," I said.

I had made a note of Osian. With Morfydd's suitors tip-toeing around Cae White thicker than fleas in workhouse bedding, Osian was the handiest. She had only to wink her eye and he'd have lowered our corn in fifteen minutes.

"Listen, you," said she. "If we take scissors to these fields we will cut them alone, for our men have never gone crying yet. Grandfer's finished, understood? Give him six months and he'll be boxed in cedar and brass handles. When a man slips on quarts he slides to the devil. Do you want your Squire Parry to take the place over? For he'll damned soon do it if the corn isn't lowered."

"He will not do that," I said.

"Gratifying. Influence, is it? You'll get some influence if he catches you with Tessa." She turned to the door. "You heard what happened at the Reach last night?"

I nodded.

"And how your Parry is roaring and threatening to put out his tenants?"

With good reason, I thought.

For his river had been emptied between Tarn and the Reach; near four hundred salmon littering the banks, brought out by the poachers and left to rot. This was Rebecca again, dishing out punishment because Squire had lent money to a turnpike trust. By night she visited the Tywi with flares and cudgels and the fish were harpooned and dragged out to die; scores being spitted on the railings of the mansion, flung over his steps and lawns, thrown through his windows, tied to his knockers. There is no law to say that Squire is sole owner, of roads or salmon, said Rebecca in her note. With hungry men in gaol for poaching the temptation must be removed, said Rebecca, and Squire Lloyd Parry must have the lot. As his gates will be burned when he puts them up.

"And tonight we are eating like fighting cocks," said Morfydd, "for I fetched in a fresh one at midnight."

"That is asking for trouble," I replied sharp. "Waldo Bailiff has a nose for boiling salmon."

"Boiled," said she. "And if he shows his dewdrop in here he

will breathe his last. I will handle Waldo – you handle that corn. I am going alone to Ponty."

Cups and saucers were tinkling from the kitchen as I came in from the tub. Smoke curled from the twisted chimney, chairs scraped on flagstones, and I thought of the days when we first came to Cae White. Grandfer was in charge then. Seven of us down to supper at night and not a whisper while we fed; just belches and pardons from Grandfer at the top and wallowings from Richard and Jonathon, while the big black clock on the mantel ticked time to the pork crackling, with hands reaching for bread or grasping pewter for cider gulps. Money in plenty those days, too, and Grandfer was a giant of a man for five feet odd, very much in charge; beating his breast with one little hand, thumbing up the Testaments with the other, and every Grace was the same – a whine about some poor soul at a feast who was told to get shifting and who up and said that even curs were due for crumbs, Amen, and slap went the Book and into things went Grandfer, for the head of the house had to be fed with a regiment of in-laws to keep. Different now. Grandfer was finished with Cae White. So with my first harvest waiting I went into the kitchen, and the table, I saw, was laid for one. Husbandman first, said Mari, smiling. Farming stock for generations and proud of it.

I sat down, watching her as she sweated over the hob.

"Men first, Jethro, women later," she said, smiling wider, and I knew then that the women had been planning, with Morfydd having the first go at me and Mam coming after. Fat bacon was sizzling in the pan, God knows where they got it; the kettle singing his lovesong to the pot; buttermilk, bread whiter than usual, and the cloth was as snow. Most important now, Jethro Mortymer, with the head man gone lazy and pickled in hops.

"Sit you down, *bach*," said Mari, smoothing and patting, and I looked at her.

Expectation was in her, evident in her trembling hands, and I saw the ring of gold that bound her to my brother, and smelled the lavender sweetness that was Mari's from the day

Iestyn brought her home to Blaenafon. Bright were her eyes, meeting mine but once, flicking away with the colour reddening her cheeks. Jonathon, Mari's baby, was two years old now, but she still had him on the breast. We saved the easy work for her for she was still making up for her breech-birth labour; couldn't pull round on oatmeal soup, said Mam. But satisfying Jonathon was harder than kitchen work with his cooings and bubblings and reaching for her breast. Strange that I was jealous of Jonathon. His whimpering offended me because she was slave to him, leaping to serve his first strangled cry. His pear-shaped bottom was vulgarity to me – something that was smoothed with oils in public, reflected in mirrors, even kissed. The body of a girl child to me is a thing of beauty, and the body of a baby boy atrocious. For one paints its picture of the fountain of life, and is fruitful. But the body of a boy is all cherubs and cupids, the lie to manhood with its belly-rolls and wrist bangles.

Sometimes, from my chair in the corner, I would watch Mari with Jonathon; one eye on the *Cambrian*, the other on his suspended animation, frenzied in his fight for freedom while she gripped his fat ankles between fingers and thumb. Head dangling, upside down, he would catch my eye and bubble his smiles, exposing his nakedness without a blush and his shocking maleness with pride. And Mari, pins in mouth, would be ardent to do best by him in sweating concentration; wiping stray hairs from her eyes, forearm on his chest, tiptoeing her knees up in case he rolled off. And fighting to get the rag round him he streams his indecency down to her ankles.

"O, Duw! O, there's a horrid boy, Jonathon. O, Jethro, look now, drenched, I am drenched!"

Up with the newspaper, pretend not to look, and he crows his delight in shouts and gurgles. Hand up, she threatens, but never brings it down.

"I will smack you next time, mind, or call Uncle Jethro, for he is handy with smackings. Dirty old boy!"

"Taking after his uncle, though," says Morfydd, sewing, needle held up to the light. "Remember, Mam – a soaking baby if ever there was one, that Jethro."

"Whoever was nearest, girl. You, me or the Bishop of Bangor."

Up with the *Cambrian*.

"And the time he drowned old Tomos back home, remember?" Morfydd again. In her element, the bitch. "And Tomos dressed for speechifying. Aye, aye, and the Sunday trews his speciality, too." She winks at Mari. "But take a tip, girl – contented was Jethro. Two and a half and still on the breast – never got a fork into solids till he was nigh on three, and what we lost in the soakings we saved on the stomach gripe, eh, Mam?"

"And the belly band – remember the belly band." Mam now, treadling away.

"O, aye, girl. Never without it. It do cut the wind for certain do the belly band."

And there was Mari's eyes sober serious, meeting mine over the top of the *Cambrian* with her sweet, sad smile; not knowing of the torment, pure in heart.

Too pure in heart to realize that the inch of her breast was curved in whiteness, switching my eyes.

Eh, this business of growing to manhood.

Now she stood beside me to serve my plate in the kitchen, with something of love in her face.

"Jethro," she said.

"Aye?" I turned away, breaking bread.

"Jethro, you will reap the corn for me? Never mind the old coaling down in Ponty – it can wait, and with Morfydd labouring it is enough for a family. Ashamed, I am, with Grandfer sleeping drunk, but already the fields are turning. For a field of blackened corn is as sad as a funeral cloth, and everyone has their barns stacked save us." Back at the hob now, she turned. "I will cook and mend for you, as I did for my Iestyn. O, but a boy you are, but there is life in Cae White and you must not let it die."

"I am a furnace man and collier," I said. "I know nothing of farming."

"But you will try?"

Just went on chewing, wanting to hear her voice.

"Mam and me will work, too, and Richard will come for the gleanings. To build Cae White for Iestyn, Jethro – for when he comes back."

"Long years yet, Mari."

"But they will pass. O, I have been waiting, waiting, and you have made no move."

"All right, all right," I said.

Her face was radiant. "Today ?"

Strange the glory in seeing her pleading.

"Yes," I said. "Now send Mam in, it is her turn now."

"I am here," said Mam. "Do not worry."

"Jethro," said Morfydd from behind her. "Mam do want to speak to you, official."

"Away the lot of you," I answered. "I am entitled to breakfast."

"He is reaping, he is reaping!" cried Mari, dancing.

"Should be worth seeing," said Morfydd, in now. "Two feet shorter by the time he comes in tonight. And the point of a scythe can get into funny old places, so mind."

I just ignored it, feeling superior. Never before was I so wanted; walked out and left them, in search of the scythe.

I have seen white beards waving over the snathes of sythes, and arms no thicker than my wrist that have swung from dawn to dusk; the sinewy bodies of grandfathers too old to die, the pendulum bellies of drunkards that have swayed to the sigh of the whetted ground. Spitting on my hands I gripped the splits, and swung, and sunfire flashed on the edge of the blade as it hissed for my ankles. Leaping high, I fell, with the thing pitchforking as something alive.

Gently, this time, the point held low, I cut a few stalks at a time, feeling for the balance, for the touch of a gorse-fly's wing is enough to send the point diving. An hour of practice and I was revelling in the singing cut of the steel, though I knew it would take a lifetime of learning; left foot forward swing, and the corn lies down; the backward swing, then forward in the rhythm of Nature. The sun, flushing after his heavy meal of summer, was strickening in brilliance. Left foot forward, swing

79

and back. I smelled the mowing smells of bruised corn, a dryness crept to my throat, but the song of the scythe was an exultation within me, and I disdained the pain of my already blistered hands. On, on, the blade flatter now, a bow of steel encircling my legs. The ache of my loins crept to my back, spreading fingers of fire to my shoulders, but still I worked on. Sweat ran in streams over my face. On, on, left foot forward, swing, and back. Sickening now, but I was still at it strongly, scything in a fashion, getting the damned stuff down. Great I felt then, tied at the knees and belted. Above me in the inciner- ating blue a lark nicked and dived, his body a diamond of light, and his joy drove me on, eyes narrowed to midday glare now, teeth gritted to the cramping agony in a world of gold that shim- mered and swayed. An hour later the sun was hottest, the poplars of Cae White alight and glittering. Heat reflected on my naked shoulders, but I plunged on blindly. Gasping now, longing for the cold draughts of the colliery shafts, the pain was a ring of steel about me, and the last swing came with an indrawn breath. The point hit a stone. The sky somersaulted as the scythe heeled again. I fell, seeking oblivion in the earth and the waving ears above me. Panting, I opened my hands. Claws for fingers, cramped and red, and the sudden gush of tears splashed and stung them, running in salt veins, mingling with blood. Knew I was beaten. Shutting my eyes to the sun- glare I let the fire and sweat run over me.

An ant was crawling on the snathe of the scythe, just an inch from my nose. Brushing away tears, I watched; the posturing daintiness, the nibbling, acrobatic dancing, seeking everything, finding nothing in a world of exploration. Up the handle with you, down again in whiskered concentration; wipe your face, clean your teeth, then round you go in a circle, bright you flash in sunlight. I watched and dreamed. Sleep lazed my eyes again in the metallic burnishing of the sun. Reed-music whis- pered to the scent of bruised corn, and I awoke again with visions dancing and the stalks above me rippled in an oven of heat, for steepled ears had risen beside me; a harelip snitched not a foot from mine. Face to face, we were, the beaten and the hunted, and the wheat went flat to the brown streak's passing.

Next came the stoat, black, relentless, lithe body swerving in the jungle of corn, but I clenched my hand and hit him flat. Smooth was his coat to the touch of my fingers and the corn stalks waved to the terror of the rabbit. The corn hummed into silence. Nothing remained but the molten pour of the sun. In nothingness, with the stoat in my hand, I slept.

Give me a pick and a colliery face if I have to labour. Leave the scything to grandfers.

CHAPTER 10

IN BED for two days, with Morfydd and Mari dashing round with flannels, giving me hell.

Eight days it took me, but I scythed Cae White, with Morfydd on her knees spare time swiping with a reaping hook and Mam, Mari and Richard coming for the gleanings, and we stacked the barn high. If Grandfer saw it happen he did not make mention. Didn't see much of him these days at all, with him lying in bed all the morning and teetering bowlegged down to Black Boar tavern on his ploughing corns and not a glance for anyone. Going to the devil fast, was Grandfer, not even an eye for Randy, his horse.

A black-faced towser of a horse, this one, and he'd seen better times, having once served apprenticeship as a travelling stallion, and he couldn't forget his past. Grandfer loved him as life itself, but he didn't work him often, and now I had him in the shafts for the harvest. Very pugnacious, this one, with the kick of an elephant, and every ploughing regular he sent Grandfer ears over backside along the shippon, but I was used to four legs, having worked them in iron. I let him belt the plough to bits and then I belted him, but he never forgave me for it, I knew. Along the ruts with a load we would go with the old traces slapping in a jingle of harness and horse and man friendship, but I knew he was watching by the roll of his eye. Cruel, I suppose, being a horse when you have once been a stallion – a hell of a time with the women one moment and cut off without an option the next, but he came pretty useful later, did Randy.

Tired to death that night, I sat in a chair with Richard on my knee. Four years old was Morfydd's boy now, light-faced and fair, with gold curls to his neck and as pretty as a girl, save for the square of his jaw and his deepset eyes – a throw-back from the dark Mortymers.

"The white line is in us," Mam used to say. "As a white-breasted blackbird, he is, as my little girl Edwina."

For Edwina, my sister who died up in Monmouthshire, was albino, and the strain had come out in Morfydd's son, though her lover, like Morfydd, was as dark as a gipsy. A dear little boy, this Richard; quiet about the house in his comings and goings, busy with his labour of tying stooks now harvest had come, and lessons in English from Mari when she had spare time. There was no school near save the keeper of the new tollgate near Flannigan's farm, and he is not being taught by traitors, said Morfydd.

"You joining Rebecca, Uncle Jethro?" said he now.

"Not while he lives in this house," said Mam, pottering. "Just farming for us now, no need to look for trouble."

"That right, Uncle Jethro?"

I was giving a bit of thought to tollgates and Rebecca about this time, for big Trusts were being formed by the gentry who were investing money in them for the erection of tollgates which were supposed to earn money for the road repairs, and the gates were going up like mushrooms. Rebecca who burned gates once was now sending threatening letters to Trusts and tollgate keepers. Humble men and women, these keepers – the Welsh bleeding the Welsh, said Morfydd. The levying of the tolls was unjust, too, for some gentlemen's carriages passed free, because they were gentlemen; the charge for a horse and cart with broad wheels was fourpence while a cart with narrow wheels cost sixpence, so the richer the farmer the cheaper the toll. Time was when the Kidwelly Turnpike Trust let lime through free, but new gates were springing up round the kilns now. Osian Hughes Bayleaves was a business man, though Morfydd gave him no credit for gumption. Thought nothing of a five mile detour, did Osian, to avoid a tollgate, some-times ending in gentry fields. When building his new barn he brought in his bricks under a layer of manure, which passed through free. Aye, no fool was Osian till we all started trying it, and then he got caught and fined three pounds, enough to set him back weeks. Every night, lying in bed, I could hear the tollgate carpenters knocking them up, and the noise made me sweat with seven people to keep and a harvest to sell, for to try to get into Carmarthen or St Clears was like trying to enter a besieged city.

I could see us starving at the height of winter. Sweated blood at the thought of it.

"We will work it out," said Mari.

The house was quiet that night for Morfydd, exhausted by a late Ponty day shift, had gone to bed with Richard and Jona-thon. Grandfer was drowning his back teeth down at Black Boar tavern, but Mari and me were not alone, Mam saw to that. Sitting in Grandfer's rocking-chair she was dozing and waking in snuffles. Keeping things decent, she said, you understand, you two, no offence meant, mind, she said.

"None taken," replied Mari, but I saw the hurt in her eyes.

"Gone dark, see," said Mam. "A young married woman ought to be escorted after nine o'clock at night, never know who might be looking through a window."

"My sister-in-law," I said.

"Never mind," said Mam.

"Iestyn's wife, then."

Fingers up now. "Look," said she. "I am not accusing any-one of capers. It is only the custom, and customs die hard. Old fashioned, perhaps, but I think it safer."

"You are making too much of it, Mam," I said.

"Jethro, I am only thinking of Iestyn. So hush!"

"I am doing that night and day," said Mari, and I saw her eyes go bright.

"Fetch the accounts," I said. "We will see how we stand. And enter a sixpence for Mam standing guard."

Up with her then. "No cheek, Jethro, I will not stand for it. Still your mam, I am, and I will take a stick to you, big as you are. Now then."

Gave her a sigh, fluttered an eye at Mari. So we had Mam's company when we worked the accounts, adding up rent and church tithes, coal rates and toll payment, with Mam going soprano in snoring, keeping it decent. Full length on the mat and she wouldn't have known it.

"Rent, rates and tithes," said Mari. "Eighty pounds outlay, and wear and tear."

"And with decent harvests like this last one, a hundred and thirty pounds income – fifty to live on and seven to keep."

"Pretty shrimpy," I said, thinking of the tolls.

"But that is not counting Morfydd, mind – ten shillings a week, remember. How much is that a year?"

"Take us all night to work it out," I said. "And she will not earn it for ever. You noticed Morfydd lately?"

"Time she came from coal."

"Long past," I said. "Nothing for it. I will have to go back to Ponty and part-time farming." Sick, I went to the door.

"Where you going, Jethro?"

"Black Boar tavern."

"Got money?"

I rattled it, grinning. "Enough for a quart."

"At this time of night?"

I shrugged. "Early for Betsi. She don't close at all these days."

I pulled on my coat and Tara, my terrier, came wriggling to my heels.

"Jethro."

"Aye?"

Pale was her face. "We will manage, mind. A bit shrimpy it will be, but we will manage. You keep from Betsi's place, boy."

"Listen. If Grandfer can souse himself on his savings every night the least I am entitled to is a quart."

After me now, her hand on mine. "It is not the old drinking, Jethro, it is where you drink that matters. Drink quarts, if you like, but at the Miner's Arms, is it – somewhere decent."

Over her shoulder I saw Mam's eyes open, watching. Give her a broomstick just then and she'd have been round chimneys.

"Jethro," said Mari, begging, "you keep from Rebecca. For me, boy? Wicked, it is, carrying poor men on the *ceffyl pren* and slaughtering salmon and burning ricks."

"More wicked to build the gates that cripple us."

"Then leave it to others – remember my Iestyn."

This turned me. "I am doing that. There will be no Cae White for my brother to come back to unless the gates come down."

"O, God," she said, empty.

"Go to bed, Mari. Here, Tara!" and the terrier scrambled into my arms.

But Mari did not move. It was as if I had struck her. Motionless, she stood, shocked pale; always the same these days when her husband's name was mentioned, and I pitied her. Helpless, I touched her hand. "Bed," I said.

"What is happening out by there?" Mam now, peering, spectacles on the end of her nose.

"Me and Mari kissing," I said, hot. "For God's sake go back to your snoring."

I heard Mam's voice raised in protest as I slammed the door to show her my anger. Getting sick of things at Cae White lately, with Morfydd coming snappy with overwork, Mari mooning about Iestyn and Grandfer stupified. Enough to think of without having to put up with guardians of virginities, and it infuriated me that Mam, of all people, should go under skirts with thoughts of Mari who was pure and beautiful, for a thought like that brings canker into a house and we had given her no reason for it. But with every day's passing now Mari was more substantial, less of a relation. This working together, the sweet intimacy of her presence, had brought me joy, obliterating something of Tessa, the girl. I loved her, of course.

Cursed myself for it under the stars.

The moon was hanging doomed in a friendless sky as I went down to Tarn.

The sheep track from Cae White leads to Black Boar tavern, a track that carries the refuse of the north; the Midland drovers with their stinks, ghosts of the transportation hulks and prison, the fire-scarred puddlers of the Monmouthshire iron – not a pint of good Welsh blood in a thousand; all come flocking to the coal industry of Carmarthenshire and to Betsi's place, the strongest ale in the county. Light and smoke hit me as I shouldered the door.

Betsi Ramrod is serving the jugs, dark eyes flashing in her hatchet of a face, swabbing up her counter now, scooping up her pennies. Irish as Killarney is Betsi Ramrod – the Welsh had a name for her – man-hating, man-loving but fearful of conceiving, straighter than a fir tree and twice as prickly. She hoofed it out of Ireland ten years back, it was said, her black shawl scragging her domed head, her stockinged sticks of legs plastered with the mud of her barren country – running from the rumbling bellies of a potato famine, one hand gripping her twopenny fare, the other waving the last crust in Ireland: running for Rosslare Wharf and Freedom's schooner, a walking ballast journey of no return alive. A hundred thousand Irish crossed the sea about then, most to neat Welsh graves, but Betsi was one who did well out of it. From the ballooning stomachs of her country to the best cellar in Carmarthen county via the bed of a travelling tinker, she gave short change over the counter if you dared to bat an eye.

A few of my neighbours were drinking when I got in there – Osian Hughes Bayleaves for one, shivering in his corner to draw my attention, mortifying for Morfydd still, scared of her reception, for she'd split his skull with the nearest thing handy if he tried it on, and he knew it. Hairy Abel Flannigan sat opposite him, one hand gripping a jug, the other a bottle, stupefied, trying to forget tollgates, and God help him if Biddy his mam finds out, for she is still serving him beltings. Job Gower, of all people, Morfydd's Ponty boss; up at the counter, dwarfing every man in sight, his eyes still black-ringed from the day shift and roving for good labour. And the sawdust was jammed with farmers and drovers, with the foreigners of iron quarrelling and bellowing, spilling out their wages; ragged men, beggars, hoydens and hags, two per cent Welsh, thank God. A cock-fight in a corner now, bloodstained, wine-stained, elegant with dandies; a man-fight in another – two north country drovers, their blue chins jutting with lip from Lancashire, fists bristling, eyes glaring, dying for each other and the meaty thuds of the slug it out, with dark Gipsy May thrusting between them to take the first thump, hands spread on their chests, her white teeth shining as she laughs at the lamp.

"Trouble, Betsi, trouble! Grandfer Zephaniah, up by here and give me a hand with some muscle!"

"Settle your own business," says Grandfer, steering up his quart.

Not seen me yet.

"Oi! Osian Hughes Bayleaves – six-foot-six of you for God's sake. Part these two pugilists for your poor little gipsy, eh?"

And Osian trembles and goes deeper into his mug. From the table rises Abel Flannigan and shoulders through the crowd, undoing his coat: a north country drover every week for supper, this one.

"Now, now!" shrieks Betsi Ramrod, and up on the counter she goes, landing in the sawdust with a flurry of drawers. "Sit you down, Abel boy, Betsi will handle it." She shoves the drovers out of it. "This is a respectable establishment, me boyo, anyone fighting will pay for the damages, a penny for every mug broken, twopence for a jug. By all the saints suffering, God what a life. Fighting, fighting! Good evening, Jethro Mortymer, most unhappy you are looking for somebody courting the gentry. How is Tessa Lloyd Parry?"

"She does not come in here," I answered, and shouldered drovers aside for the counter.

"No offence, mind, only asking. Heard she was poorly again, that's all."

"Right poorly," said Gipsy May, joining me. Strange about this gipsy. Coffee-coloured, blowsy, half a yard of breast showing and bangle-earrings, was Gipsy, the daughter of Liza Heron of a Cardigan tribe; a woman in love with things that screeched and as tame as a meat-fed tiger, but mother-gentle when it came to Tessa. I lifted the mug and blew off the froth

87

with Grandfer's eyes boring holes in my shoulders. First time we had shared Black Boar.

"You heard what ails her, Jethro Mortymer?"

I had heard but I would not say in there. Weak in the chest, was Tessa, and coughing with her the last time I saw her, eyes as bright as stones in her fever, and I had called old Ben, her servant, and he had carried her back to the house in tears. Three Sundays running I had walked to the Reach, letting Grandfer Badger off with a caution, feeling dull, and Tessa had not been there. Called at the house once and fished out old Ben, but he had turned up his nose at the garbage.

Sixpenny Jane in the corner by there, buxom, dark, pretty as a picture, giggling, posturing, her head flung back, kissing the air with her lips at a drover, driving him daft. Down on the Burrows lives Jane with her dad; a terror for the men, the curse of the women, but as clean as a new pin, and quiet. Strange how she resembled Mari with her inborn daintiness; cast in the same mould, the woman and the harlot. I cursed her soul as I saw her coming over for Grandfer's little eyes were peeping over his quart.

"You loose tonight, Jethro Mortymer?"

I looked at her, at the smoothness of her, the whiteness of her throat, and she smiled then and her lips were red and curved above the shine of her teeth.

"Don't judge by yourself," I said.

"O, hoity toity, eh? Respectable, is it? Gentry, is it?" Eyes closed to the light, she laughed, tinkling above the bedlam. Saw the curve of her waist, the dress taut across the upward sweep of her breasts. Pity I felt, and longing. But up leaped Flannigan, and shouldered her out of it.

"Leave her," he said. "There's quicker ways of dying," and he grinned and back-handed his bristling chin. "You heard, Mortymer? I've got a gate."

"You're lucky," I said. "Tom Rhayader's got two."

"Bullin's men. Sassenachs, not even Welsh. God, what a country. Another's going up in front of the kilns – that will catch the lot of us."

I drank, watching him. Dangerous, this one. I reckoned I

could take most there that night, including Gower, but not Abel Flannigan. Deep-chested, he topped six feet, and his hobby was bull-taming. When bulls went mad they always called for Abel. "Bull gone mad down at Morgan's place, Abel me son," Biddy would shout, "slip down and see to him, there's a good boy," and Abel would kill a quart or two to liven him up and cut a yew branch for the taming. Slippery on his feet for a big man, he would vault the gate and get the bull's tail and hang on relentless to the kicking and bucking, and every time the thing turned its head Abel would cut him on the nose with the yew. Bulls around our parts tossed and turned in their dreams of Abel.

"Something's got to be done, hear me? I'm burning ricks now but I'm heading for tollgates."

I jerked my head and lifted my mug as Osian Hughes got to his feet. Towering above us, he was biting at his fingers, his looks girlish, his face as white as a fish belly.

"O, God," said Abel. "Don't tell me," and turned.

"I've got a gate," said Osian, soprano.

"And what are you doing about it?"

Osian wrung his fingers.

"Look what we're up against," said Abel. "No guts, no fight, no nothing. Go to hell, girl, find yourself a drover."

"My mam says pay," whispered Osian. "We can't fight the Trusts."

"We can't fight with the likes of you to fight with," said Flannigan. "Thank God I was born with an Irish surname if yours is Welsh. But my mam Biddy is proper Welsh, and Biddy says fight. Look, Mortymer," he turned to me. "I have reckoned it up. If I take a cart to the kilns for a three-and-six-penny load it'll cost me one-and-a-penny to get it through. Three gates stand between me and the lime now, and full price tolls, mind, not halves."

"That's the gatekeepers," I said. "More fool you."

"But the notice is up there – full price tolls!"

"And you can't read and they know it."

"By heaven, I will have those keepers," he whispered, fist in his hand.

"And they are planning for another – Kidwelly to St Clears," said Osian.

I nodded. I had heard, but did not say, not with Flannigan in this mood.

"Bastards," said Flannigan. "You thought how many of us will use that one?"

"Nigh twenty," replied Osian, "counting me."

"Nobody's counting you," said Flannigan. His eyes narrowed and he prodded me. "More like fifty, I say – counting the upland people – folks like Tom Rhayader, and the upland boys like a fight for the fun of it. What you say?"

The cockfight grew to a shriek about us and feathers flew in a flash of spurs. Blood spattered the boards where a cock lay dying and money chinked from hand to hand. Men were shouting, shoving to the counter but giving the three of us a wide berth, eyeing Flannigan.

"Rebecca, eh?" I grinned at him.

"O, dear God!" whispered Osian, sweating.

"You get to hell out of it," said Flannigan. "Get yourself weaned," and brought up his elbow. He frowned around the room then, his eyes on Gower.

"Mind your tongue," he said soft. "There is more than one Judas."

"Just counted another," I replied, for Grandfer's eyes were unwinking from his corner, his little nose shining over the top of his quart. "And leave Gower be," I added.

"Just thinking," said he. "Best treat him respectable. Six months of this and we will all be at Ponty. How's that Morfydd of yours sticking it?"

"Don't mention her in here," I said.

"Outside, then. We will stick to Rebecca." He looked at me. "Bloody fool to talk in front of Osian. If they closed a fist at him he'd blab to the devil."

The June night was warm and alive with candle-flame stars, with a fat, kind moon. We leaned against Betsi's fence.

"You in with us or out, boy?"

"In," I replied. "Those gates come down."

"Which gates?"

"Kidwelly to St Clears."

"Give me strength, but a kid you are for all your size. The bloody things aren't up yet. Gates in general, I mean – round these parts."

"I'm with you."

"Right, you." He fisted my chin, knocking me sideways. "It's fixed. We are meeting next Wednesday, midnight. Up on the mountain in Tom Rhayader's barn."

"First meeting, Rebecca? Damned near Squire's Reach, mind."

"Poetic justice, boy. It was Squire Lloyd Parry who started the Trust and he is taking his profits from Lewis, the toll-contractor. Have his mansion next, like we had his salmon."

"You?" I had suspected it was Flannigan.

"Me and six others – Tom Rhayader leading. You heard about this Rhayader?"

"Seen him, that's all."

"We couldn't have a better Rebecca. He was there at Efailwen with Twm Carnabwth when they burned the gate. Chapel pugilist. I wouldn't tangle with him."

"Some man," I said.

"And a brain. Dangerous, mind – he will not stand nonsense."

"I will be there," I said.

"God help us," said he. "Goodnight."

I watched the stars for a bit, thinking of Mari, not knowing why, and turned to go back into Betsi's tavern and found myself facing Grandfer.

"Nice night, Jethro."

I nodded, sick of him.

"You mind your company, boy."

"You mind your business."

He chuckled then, tapping with his stick, his bald head scarcely up to my shoulder.

"How old are you, Jethro?"

"Hitting sixteen."

"Big boy – you look like gone twenty. And you mate with Abel Flannigan near twice your age?"

"I mate with whom I like," I said.

"Take you to the Devil, mind."

"Then I'll be in good company."

He looked up then and I saw the pouches of his red-rimmed eyes, his pickled walnut of a face, his jagged smile.

"Pretty stinky you think me, is it?"

I did not reply. Half a man is better than nothing and with this one living on ale and sawdust for no good reason I had worked myself stupid to harvest Cae White. Time was I owed him something. Not now.

"You make no allowance for age?"

"Uncle Silas is damned near eighty and still farming." I turned away.

"You know how old I be?"

"No more'n seventy."

And he grunted and cackled and stamped with his stick on my boot. "Don't know my age myself," said he. "Old enough to be born twice, I reckon," and he sighed deep and gripped my arm. "I've fought and drunk with most round here, young lusties – last fifty year – and they've all been called by St Peter 'cept me. You know my christian name. Zephaniah. Zephaniah, there's a mouthful. You know something more? Could be that a man with a name like that comes at the end of the cloud alphabet – could be St Peter's got his thumb on my name when he turns the pages of Paradise. Keeps passing me over, see? Me, poor old Grandfer, longing to die. You like the women, Jethro?"

"Old devil, you are, worrying Mari to death," I said.

"I asked you a question – you fancy the women?"

"Sick of women," I said. "Got too many back home."

"And poor little Sixpenny Jane back in there coming fidgety for turfing – there's a waste." He tapped with his stick and rocked with laughter. "Bless me, she'd get what she wanted from Grandfer forty years back – most did, forgive me soul." He belched and pardoned, staggering against me and I held him off, for there is nothing so vulgar as age and its conquests.

"Aye," he added, "a century back, it do seem. All honey and fire, I was chasing the skirts. But I've worn pretty well, mind, everything considered."

"For God's sake come home," I said, but he set back his shoulders and pulled up his shirt and his chest was white in its parchment of age. "Look now," he cried. "There's beautiful for eighty and some – very gratifying, life in the old dog yet, and I've laid my mark on the women of this county, don't you worry; many being privileged to say nothing of thankful. Now, that Morfydd sister of yours, there is a woman for favours to keep a man awake – with the face of an Irish and hair from Spain, and a temper on her like a boar coming frisky. You like my Mari?"

This turned me. Wicked was his eye, mouth grinning, beard trembling, knowing of the shaft. I sighed, bored.

"Oi, oi! Strikes a chord, do it? But no offence intended, mind – it was the same for me when I was your age."

"I am going home," I said, but he hooked me with his stick and looked up at the moon.

"Hush, you," he said. "Give me a minute, Jethro. All for your good."

I waited, disquieted, and listened as his voice came low and sad.

"A long time ago I knew a woman like our Mari. Bronwen was her name. In a shroud of night is our Mari, dark, dark, but this Bronwen girl came opposite – a white, blossomy piece as a hawthorn bush in spring blow and the face of a madonna – never seen the like of her since for beautifying." He looked at me and his eyes were different. "And gentry, too – remember that – gentry. All crinoline and ribbons, she was, and with perfume, and riding habit regular, she being keen on the hunt. She lived up by Laugharne with her dad, Sir Robert, her mam being dead. And I was her stable boy – ostler, you gather me?"

I nodded.

"And every evening on Sundays she would gallop her mare along the banks of the Taf River to Milton – to the long grasses where I lay waiting." He sucked his teeth, eyes narrowed to the memory. "And up she would come with her mare fairly lathered, wild as a gipsy, dying for me – me, Zephaniah, the ostler."

He looked at me. "You want more because you won't bloody like it."

"Go on," I said.

"Well, we met first when harvest was on us and the barn hay flying all golden and windy – in secret, remember, because of her dad. Eh, beautiful in summer are the crags and whirlpools of the Taf, with the herons crying doleful over the marshes, but terrible it is in winter when the snows are melting and the river is rushing in anger, spraying arms. But even in winter she came to me – for lovering."

"How old were you this time?"

"Stripling – same age as you, thereabouts, dying for garters. And after the lovering we would part pretty formal – Bron going back to her gentry feathers and me to my stable straw. 'Yes, ma'am, and no, ma'am,' it was, of course, with her folks growing ears, but every Sunday regular we would make love red-headed, my Bron and me, with naked bathing in the Taf pools and frolics on the river bank after with nobody watching but herons. You get much practice at that, boy?"

He was coming to a point now. I did not trust him. "I am going," I said, but he barred the way.

"Wait, you," he said. "Nothing personal, mind, lest you run a conscience."

"Wicked old devil," I said.

"Ah, so! But so was this Bronwen, remember – showed me the way, she did – near twice as wicked as me. You know Dai Education, the new tollkeeper up at the kilns near the Reach?"

"What's he to do with it?"

"Just wondered. Reckon little Dai might give us the answer, him being a scholar – as to why a beauty like Bron was interested in a chap like me. You fancy a quart, Jethro? Your Grandfer's gone dry."

"Just had a quart."

"But you want the rest of it, eh?"

I had to know the rest of it.

"Well, well! A wicked old tale it is for a chit of a boy like

94

you," and he gave a long shroud of a sigh. "Listen, then. Welsh gentry was my Bronwen – Welsh to her fingertips, as her name do tell, and Welsh-speaking, like me – which is proper Welshness, none of the foreign old English stuff you bring down here. County's changed, boy. Fifty years back you'd be straining your ears for an English damn, but the place is going to the bloodies just now. Mind, Dai Education do say it's the industry, these furnace men and collier chaps coming in, staining the land with their foreign ideas . . ."

"For God's sake," I said. "What about this woman?"

"And me with a throat like the bottom of a bird cage – parrots at that."

"Just one, then we're back out."

"Sharper than billhooks, boy – promise."

So we went back into Black Boar tavern.

I passed over the twopence and Grandfer went up for the quarts, slapping down the money, bawling for attention, helloing to strangers – one in particular, a tiny wizened shrew of a man who was cranked and blue. Jackknifed, hobbling on his ploughing corns, he was carrying and slopping his ale to a table. Back came Grandfer wobbling the quarts and we sat down opposite.

Grandfer jerked his head. "You notice Ezekiel?"

I nodded. Bald as an egg was this Ezekiel, whiskers drooping, and his face and hands were as blue as a blackberry, and I pitied him.

"Reckoned Ezekiel would be in just now. That's why I came back."

"Why?" I asked.

Grandfer drank deep and wiped with his cuff. "Powerful is the Man in the Big Pew, and fearful when He is denied. Terrible is He to His misbehaving children." He waved his mug at the room. "And there's one or two in by here due for His wrath pretty soon, boy. You mind you don't join them. Have a look at Ezekiel."

"What about your Bronwen?"

"Bronwen can wait. You see Ezekiel there? You know how

he got so cranked? Well, thirty years back it would be when Ezekiel was courting Biddy Flannigan, Abel's mam. Down in the Big Wheatfield, it was, all of a summer's day. Tall and straight was Ezekiel then, forking a harvest as high as the next. You listening?"

I sighed.

"Well, coming pretty hot with him was Ezekiel, and poor little Biddy was all legs and petticoats and hollering for her mam, for the boy was that determined. Not a cloud in the sky, remember – harvest time, remember. But the Big Man was watching and His sky came dark – nobody near to give Biddy a hand. So down came the lightning and caught Ezekiel square – smack in the middle of the back, and Biddy Flannigan not even singed."

"O, aye?" I cocked an eye at him.

"The truth. Just for fulfilling a normal function. And that is the first example. Now for the second, the lesson of wrath." He lowered his mug and stared at nothing. "In child, was Bronwen. In child by me, you understand?"

The bellowing of the room died between us.

"And the child was born, Jethro. The child was Mari's mother, which makes our Mari gentry blood." He turned to me, eyes fixed to mine. "Down from Laugharne came her dad with his whip, and I had it. God, I had it naked – damned near killed me. But he left me Bronwen – cast her out as the gentry do a wayward hound. He left me Bronwen and Cae White to go with her for a pound a week rent for the rest of my life. Now listen," and he gripped my wrist. "Payable on his death to his son, Squire Lloyd Parry. You following me?"

I was gaping now, knowing the secrets of Cae White, knowing of Mari.

"Aye, Cae White is mine, and Parry can't turn me out of it, and it is Mari's after I am gone. . . ."

"And your Bronwen?" I whispered in a lull.

"If I go on the hops it is because of my Bronwen, boy. For she bore my child and then she vanished, went down to the river for the shame of it, in the place where we loved. And they found her three weeks later on the reaches of Laugharne – on the night of Whitland Fair, it was, with mud in her mouth and her eyes taken by gulls. Reckon she walks Cae White by night. You heard her?"

Terrible was his face in that grief.

"God help you, Grandfer," I said, and he raised his face, his eyes swimming.

"God help me, is it?" he said. "God help you for mating with gentry, Mortymer, d'you hear me?"

I rose, staring down at him. "You cranked little devil," I whispered. "Me and Tessa Lloyd Parry's been nothing but decent!"

"Sit down!" and he got me sharp with his stick. "Do I fear the wrath of the likes of you when I have faced the wrath of God? Who's talking about Tessa Lloyd Parry? The girl is a cripple and couldn't mate with a butterfly, her body dead from the waist down. Is she the only gentry girl who is taking the rove of your eye?"

I clenched my hands.

"Be warned, Mortymer," said he. "Grandfer has been watching. With Cae White as your Eden and your brother's wife for a lover, the fingers of Cain shall reach up from the dust, and seek you. Be gone!"

Light chopped the hedge as I opened the door. The gables of Kidwelly were gaunt in the distance, a steeple a pine-needle of silver in moonlight. With Tara against me I walked back home. Sick, sick I felt, of life.

CHAPTER 11

September!

I AWOKE ON the Feast Day Sunday to a dazzling, jewel-blue morning, and the air through my window was sparkling and heady with its scents of coming autumn and the fields below me swam in vivid light, every bough tipped with hoar frost and dripping diamonds as the sun kicked Jack Frost out of it. Rebecca meetings, threats of action, notes to magistrates, but not a suggestion from Tom Rhayader that we should get down to the business of tollgates, and I was getting sick of it. To hell with Rebecca, I said, and to hell with Grandfer, too, including his gentry Bronwen.

To hell with farming, too, for this was the Feast Day.

Plenty of activity downstairs, with women up and rushing with pots and pans clattering, everyone singing and laughing in anticipation of the joys to come.

Up and doing, me – dashing down the stairs with the towel waving, gave Morfydd one with it as I skidded through the kitchen, and out to the water butt to plunge my head down. Splashing, ducking, I didn't hear them come up behind me, and Mari got one leg and Morfydd the other and I was in head first and drowning till Mam ran out swiping with a dishcloth and hauling me out while the boys were leaping around as things possessed. O, great was the joy of that September morning, all cares forgotten, the house tinkling with laughter, and even Grandfer allowed himself a chuckle, his warnings washed away in the Black Boar jugs. Best clothes, me; smarming my hair down with Mari's goose fat which she used for chests; getting the hair flat to the head; clean shirt, belted up to strangle; nip into Grandfer's room for his funeral stock, and I stood before Morfydd's mirror all shines and creases, a sight fit to turn the head of a countess. Downstairs to make an impression, for a man who is handsome and six feet is a fool not to make the best of it, but everyone seemed too busy to take notice, for Mam and Morfydd were dressed for prize bantams and Mari came down all ribbons and lace, slim and willowy in the new black dress she had made. Richard, too, very smart in the suit Mam had stitched for him, and Jonathon with an old one of Richard's cut down. Eh, there's handsome are little boys dressed for Feast Days, all curls and podges, their little faces alight with teary excitement.

"Precious baby!" cried Morfydd, throwing up Jonathon and kissing him and Richard climbed up me with Tara trying to nip him out of it, and in the middle of the commotion in comes Grandfer.

"*Whee*, there's an old wacko!" cried Morfydd. "Look, Mam, look! O, love him!"

Funeral suit for Grandfer; bald head polished for glass; breeches and knee gaiters, frock coat and buttonholes either side and a gold-knobbed cane, proper gentry. And the women got him in a ring and danced around him shrieking and laughing, with Mam soothing and patting him, telling what a good boy he was not to let the family down, and Morfydd even kissed his cheek. No damned notice of me, anyone. Set the room tidy, a last brush of clothes, looking for stray hairs on the black dresses and Mam saying her stays were killing her, and then the form up. Hushing for quiet then, fingers to lips, behave to the children, and out of the front we went very sedate and along the road to Osian Hughes Bayleaves' field where the Fair was set; Mam and Grandfer leading, Morfydd and Mari next, then the boys, and me at the behind to keep them in order. And my heart thumped with pride as we entered the field. Not a glance right or left, keeping our dignity, for there is nothing neighbours like better than a good impression, so we gave them proud Mortymers. Knew their places, too, for the women were dropping curtseys and the men thumbing their hats. Can't beat the Welsh for politeness in the morning, mind, even if it comes to free fights at night. O, that Fair Day! We came a bit late, of course, which we thought proper, and hundreds were there lining the field, all green and sunshine and colour, with scarves waving and skirts swirling, and some of the couples pairing off already. Saw Sixpenny Jane as we walked in, very pretty, very swelling above the waist, thank God, and the look of adoration she gave me lasted a lifetime. Biddy Flannigan next, wheezing and panting, with Abel, her son, beside her, his brow dark with his plans for burnings.

"Good morning, Mam Mortymer and family. Good morning, Grandfer!"

"Good morning, Mrs Flannigan," said Mam, inclining her hat, though any other time she'd have gone rings round Biddy. But stepping it out on Grandfer's arm now – taking the obeisance like a French aristocrat. Saw Osian Hughes by the gate, too, fish face lighting up at the sight of Morfydd.

"A very handsome family, if I might say, Mrs Mortymer," said Mrs Toby Maudlin scarecrowed in black, her stays creaking for ship's timbers as she made her bow, hitting her Toby with an elbow till he lifted his hat. On, on, to the middle of the field, turning every head in the place, with the labourers pausing at the field ovens for eyefuls of Mari and Morfydd, easy the loveliest women in the place. Saw Hettie Winetree near the cider barrels with something under her apron, feet itching, hands screwing for a sight of me, then found she was looking at some other chap, could have killed him. Nobody taking a blind bit of notice of me so far, except Sixpenny, and she was man-mad. And then, O, joy! I saw Tessa watching me from Squire's party in the middle of the field. Pale and thin she sat in her wheelchair, scarfed and rugged against the wind while old Ben, her servant, bowed and grey, stood behind her, watching every move. On, the procession – straight up to Squire Lloyd Parry, and full marks to Squire despite his Trusts. Surrounded by gentry on all sides, he came out and waited – didn't give Grandfer a glance, but he bowed back low to Mam as she stepped aside and held her skirt wide to her headdown curtsy. Don't like scraping, mind, but I like good manners between man and maid, and so pretty it looks when they bow to one's mother. Morfydd next after Mari went down. Stipped naked she would have faced tigers before lowering a knee to a man, least of all Squire, but she inclined her head, and I saw a few gentry ladies whispering behind fans. Ten thousand pounds for a face like Morfydd's, this, the hauler of gentry trams. Harps and singers were rolling up now, Irish fiddles being tuned, drums beaten, horses neighing and a roar from the crowd as a dead pig was hauled up. Could have wept, for I thought of poor Dai Two back home in Nanty going to his ancestors like a saint. Did it myself, too, God forgive me, had to eat something. A little sucking pig came next, first prize by Squire for the wrestling contest, and I saw Justin Slaughterer smack his backside to send him screaming and then wipe the spit from his chops in anticipation, for he was reckoning to win it.

"Is he getting away with that?" asked Morfydd after the reception.

"Who, now?"

"That Justin Carver, wrestling."

"Never wrestled in my life," I said.

"O, aye? What was that look from Sixpenny Jane, then?"

"*Heisht!*" I said, for Mari was in earshot.

"Big and stupid enough, mind," said Morfydd. "All backside he is. If you fetch him low enough he'd never get up, and I would like that pig. You see to him later or you'll never hear the end of it."

"Justin would cripple me," I said, weighing him.

"Doesn't matter what he does to you, just get me that pig. Hey, look now!"

"Where by?"

"Over by there, man, you are getting the eye. Mind you don't waste it."

"And what is this about wrestling and sucking pigs?" asked Mam, tapping.

Asses ears, this one, whispers being shouts to her.

"Eh, nothing," said Morfydd.

"And you the instigator? Being watched today, so I will not have violence. Wrestling, indeed!"

"Do you think I would throw him to Justin Slaughterer?" asked Morfydd. "For the sake of a sucking-pig? And me in love with the family?"

"I am happy I misheard, then," said Mam. "Sorry."

"You get me that pig, mind," said Morfydd, moving away, "or I might drop a word out of place."

"A lady is waving to you, Jethro," said Mam, coming back, and her face was flushed with pleasure.

"Tessa!" I whispered, straightening my stock.

Gentry now, a rise in social standards, with the ladies and gentlemen all looking our way and Mam nodding and bowing and he won't be a minute he's just coming over.

"Squire is asking for you, Jethro," said Mari, running breathless.

"Away," said Morfydd, "and don't make a pig of yourself."

"Mind your manners, mind," said Mam, flushing with

pleasure. "Pleases and thank you's if you are offered anything, remember."

"And straight back, too," whispered Morfydd. "None of your Sixpenny Janes."

"There's a good boy," said Mari, brushing at me. "Try to make a good impression. O, there's an honour for the Mortymers, that proud I am!"

Over the fifty yards or so to where the gentry were standing, with glasses going up and fans coming down and look at that fine young man, good God. As a man to gallows, me, with me going one way and my suit another and my feet all hobnails, red as a lobster, for a hell of a thing it is to be called over to gentry. Nearer they came, grouped and dignified, the ladies on one side of Tessa, gentlemen on the other, all polished bellies and chins and gold-topped canes, and lovely were their women haughty and drooping under their lace-fringed parasoles, sweeping the grass with their long, white dresses. Heard Morfydd's giggle as I stopped short, and I put my hand to my breast and bowed to Tessa, and the men bowed back.

"Good day, young Mortymer." Squire now, his voice bass music.

"Good day, sir," I said.

O, what is it that bites and tears in the breast when you feel unequal? I fought it down in Tessa's radiant smile, and then my world was made.

"Handsome boy," whispered Squire to a lady. "And from a handsome line, I would say. Have you noticed his sister? Most respectable people, also."

"And Tessa appears interested, I can see," and the fan came up to hide the kind smile.

"Jethro!" Hand out, was Tessa, her eyes burning in her thin, grey face.

"Good day, Miss Lloyd Parry," I said, going down again. Up and down like a bloody ninepin me, that Fair Day, but it had its compensations, for every eye in the field was on me and Mam coming a bit damp with her and dabbing with pride, no doubt.

"Well mannered, most collected, d'you notice?" whispered a man.

If I looked collected I didn't feel it for my belt had stopped my breathing minutes back and my new oiled boots were killing me.

"How is your mother, Jethro?" Poor Tessa, a whisper for a voice.

"Most pleasant, I may say, Miss Lloyd Parry. I trust you are better?"

This put a couple of them sideways. Give hobnails a chance and they soon match gentry.

"I have never felt better," Tessa replied, clutching at her handkerchief. "O, Jethro, what a beautiful day!"

Searing is the sadness that hits you in the face of such courage; when words are empty, useless things. Sick to death she looked at that moment, but with a spirit that would have taken her twenty rounds and stripped to the waist with Justin Slaughterer. She smiled then, her red lips fevered against the paper whiteness of her cheeks and her fingers brushed old Ben's knee. He drifted away, as did the gentry. Saw Squire move then, pressing his fingers to his forehead, his face turned down.

"There now!" I said, and sat down beside her.

Her hand sought for mine and found it, gripping, unashamed.

"Jethro, when are you coming again to the Reach?"

"Been up six times," I said. "No sign of you, girl."

This sat her up. "God bless you," she said. "O, Jethro, I do love you so. I have been off colour a bit lately, but I will be there again now, for they say I am better."

"Truly better?"

"And this is the best day of all. Wonderful I feel today, every scent, every breath . . ."

God help her.

"Jethro."

"Yes, girl?"

"You . . . will come to me again?"

"Every Sunday. I promise."

"And you will wait for me there – no other girls?"

"Just you," I said.

"O, I am terrible," she whispered. "Jethro, I am ashamed!"

I thought she was going to cry and longed to hold her.

"Tessa, people are watching."

"I do not care. Jethro, you are still my boy? There is nobody else? Sometimes when a girl is away . . ."

"Still for you, Tessa," I said.

She laughed then, and I saw her father give us a queer old look and a smile.

Strange are gentry. Boiling oil for me twelve months back.

"Before the autumn goes I will meet you," she said. "I will come down to the river again with Ben, and you will kiss me again as you did in summer?"

"Hush, you are making me wicked," I said. The woman leaped into her face at this and she clutched at my fingers and closed her eyes, gusty in breathing.

"Jethro."

"Yes?"

She turned away her face.

"Nothing," she said, but I knew what she was thinking. Then:

"One day I will love you, Jethro. Truly. One day . . ."

"Aye," I replied. People were watching us now. Didn't give a damn for them, except for Tessa. Gentry eyes were switching, hats coming round.

"One day you will touch me, I promise," she whispered.

"Tessa, I must go."

"Yes. Goodbye, my darling."

I do not remember going back to my family, but I know I went without pride, and Morfydd touched my hand when I got back, and smiled.

"Good boy, you are," she said. "He can have his old pig. Poor little Tessa."

Dancing now, in the midst of joy, for the wind had blown up sudden and cold and Tessa went home with a waved goodbye. Just couldn't have danced with Tessa there.

Dancing to the Irish fiddles now, with the bright red stockings going up in a thrill of lace petticoats, Biddy Flannigan in the middle beating the time, and the leather-jacketed men turning in circles, hands on hips, poaching caps at jaunty angles, linking arms with the maidens, breathless, singing.

"Come on in!" cried Morfydd, whirling me into it, dragging at Mari, and the three of us went into the *Gower Reel*, taking partners, backwards and forwards, and I noticed Justin Slaughterer prancing away opposite Mari and Abel Flannigan bowing to Morfydd and handing her round. Fiddles were soaring, harps twanging and the drums beating in a medley of joy and movement. The crowd surged round us, laughing and clapping to time. Little Meg Benyon, up with her skirts, handing on to Osian Hughes; Toby and Mrs Maudlin, Gipsy May and Betsi, even Grandfer and Mam now, skirts swirling, boots tapping, O, joyful is the dance! The longer it runs to the rhythmic beat the wilder and wilder it comes, throbbing at the heart, swinging at the senses, and the last, breathless chord comes when you kiss your partner. Biddy Flannigan nearest, so I grabbed her, fighting another man off, and a good old smacker I gave Biddy, bringing down her bun and making her scream, and then I saw Mari. Justin had her – kissed her once and pulling at her again while she fought him off, shrieking and laughing. But her laughter died in the crush of his lips as he hooked her against him when everyone had finished. As a bear he had her then, laughing, his hair ragged while she pushed at his chest and yelled for Morfydd. Fun, of course.

"Oi, Oi, Oi!" shouted Morfydd, coming up, tapping him.

"Oi, Oi," said Justin over his shoulder and bent to Mari again.

Fun no longer. In a stride I was at him and yanked him away from her.

"No, Jethro, no!" screamed Mari. Too late, for I had him; seeing the swing of his hands as he turned to face me and the square of his jaw. He fell against me, scraping down the front of me, landing at my feet. Just stood there, aware of eyes, and silence, and the searing pain of my hand, for Justin was cast iron. Whispers now. Men bending to pull him off; lay him out tidy, snoring happily. Strange how a man unconscious snores. Stranger his face, alive one moment, lifeless the next. Caught him right – everything right for me, a three inch hook and him running on to it. Didn't know what hit him, just dropped. Then Mam came up and swung me round, her face blazing, her arm pointing.

"Home," she said. "Home this minute!"

"Mam," said Morfydd, her hands out, and I saw Mari weeping.

"Home!" My mother brushed Morfydd aside; tongue-tied, white with fury.

"Mrs Mortymer," said Biddy Flannigan. "You cannot blame the boy."

"That is no kind of kissing," said another. "And she a young married woman. Isn't decent."

"And it is not decent to resort to fists. Jethro, I said *home*!"

"Count me, then," said Morfydd. "I go with him."

"Go, then. O, I am ashamed, ashamed," whispered Mam.

People crowding round her now, sympathizing, women chiefly, but Dai Alltwen gave me a look to kill, though out of the corner of my eye I saw Abel Flannigan nodding and smiling as he bent above Justin who was coming round now, and Abel winked. Soon fixed the Feast Day, put an end to the dancing. Everyone very dull now and thank God Squire had left, might have frightened little Tessa to death, poor soul, and isn't it a shame having to mix with pugilists, battering each others brains out, you heard about these Mortymers – the same up in Monmouthshire, you heard? The father being the worst, and what can you expect of people not Church, to say nothing of Horeb.

"Pretty good hook that, though," said Morfydd, going home.

"Shut it," I said.

"He'd have got worse, mind, if I'd been three feet nearer, the beast."

Too ashamed to talk, me. Grandfer was standing at the gate, I noticed.

"It'll be a day or two before he gets his chops into beef," said Morfydd. "Justin Slaughterer, is it? Justin just slaughtered. Eh, pretty good that. Look out, here is trouble."

Grandfer barring the way from the field, smiling, his hand up to stop us.

"Do not take it badly, Jethro," said he. "Your mam will come round."

"You on our side, Grandfer?" asked Morfydd.

"Who else, girl? Does he stand and watch her ravished?"

"The filthy swine," I said, trembling. "It will teach him to keep his dirty hands off her. Filthy, filthy . . .!" The anger was coming to me now, strangely, and I saw Morfydd's glance.

"Just what her husband would have done, Jethro," said Grandfer, leering. "Rest you in peace, do not have a conscience."

But I did not really hear his words until I got home. I knew what he meant, and hated him.

"Better go up," said Morfydd. "You know what Mam is."

"She wouldn't dare!" I said.

"I have had it, remember – she can hand out beltings, little as she is. And she don't know her strength with a three foot willow."

"I am not being thrashed like a child!"

Morfydd jerked her thumb. "Up, boy, you've got to bloody have it. Thumpers and pugilists have got to be brought into line – reckon you'd better fold up the *Cambrian*. She raised lumps on me last time she belted, and you'll be lucky with trews on and good sound packing, I was drawers off."

Fussy walk coming down the path now, Mam meaning business, with Mari running beside her dragging at her and the boys tearing after them for a look at the slaughter.

"Up," said Morfydd, "lest you have it down by here."

"Jethro!" Mari at the bottom of the stairs now, weeping, clutching her dress. "O, Jethro, I am sorry."

I winked, grinning at her. "What Mam gives me now I will give back to Justin, do not worry, girl."

Mam now, just found the stick after rummaging, working herself into a fury, blocked at the bottom of the stairs with Morfydd and Mari pushing and shoving her and begging her to be reasonable. Don't know what hit me then but I had to laugh. I threw back my head and rocked with laughter, ran to my room and went full length on the bed. Just hit out flat a fifteen stone slaughterer and running from a five foot mam with a stick. I laughed till I cried and the first stroke hit me. Round the room we went, Mam swinging, me ducking, but she cornered me at last.

She should have been in the Navy with her mainmast floggings.

CHAPTER 12

TROUBLE WAS coming.

The wooden horse was stalking the Carmarthenshire hills most nights now, catching the spots from Pembrokeshire. In every town Rebecca was springing up, and this, a movement that began with the small farmers, was now bringing in farm labourers and even quite rich farmers – both ends of the social scale. No gates were burned since Efail-wen, but hayricks were going up nightly, fewer threatening letters sent to the magistrates, more action instead. Floggings were frequent for those who dished out floggings, but Rebecca was best with the moral wrongs. Chiefly a Nonconformist movement, the laws of God were invoked as reason for the punishments. A man could not even beat his wife without a warning or worse; flog a child and be flogged; bastard babies were delivered at night to callous fathers who had cast off their mothers. A guardian of public morals was Rebecca, thank God, said Morfydd, who was a fine one to talk, said Mam, the way she had carried on in Monmouthshire and now trying the same antics here.

September died into the mists of late autumn. Prices were going up, the cost of living leaping weekly, but the price of corn was coming down – blame the damned speculators, said Flannigan, though he couldn't spell the name – blame the rapacious men of industry who were discharging labour in order to keep their bulbous profits. Blame the swindlers who were jacking up food prices without official control at a time when people were starving and prepared to work for a loaf. One thing to grow your corn these days, quite another thing to sell it, and what slender profit you managed to get was swallowed by the iniquitous road tolls. So I threshed our corn that year, paid in kind to the miller for its grinding, and used the flour for our bread – living off the land in every sense, but I knew this would not last for long. I was paying the pound a week rent now, not Grandfer, and our savings were again nearly gone; Morfydd alone kept us from the workhouse, and I knew I would have to join her at Ponty soon again, although I had grown to love farming.

"Potatoes, potatoes," said Morfydd, "that is the county's trouble.

"The county would starve without them, though," said Mam.

"Work it out," replied Morfydd, hot as usual. "Potatoes and biddings are the root of starvation, and this is how it works. A couple in love want to marry, and can't – they can't because they haven't twopence to bless themselves with. So they have a bidding and their friends subscribe, and they rake up a few pounds to start a home. Then come the kids, one every year, with the couple forking out their shilling a week for their friends who want to marry – returning the bidding money. This brings them low, so they drop to potatoes – once a day for a start – three times a day later, and that is starvation."

"Nothing wrong with a mess of potatoes, though," said Mam. "God knows what we'd do without the old spud."

"God knows," I said, "until you eat them every meal."

"And if the crop fails, you starve," said Morfydd, "like Ireland. Potatoes, undernourishment; more potatoes, illness; no potatoes, death. And if you doubt me ask them in Dublin. Same with this country. A north country farm labourer is cheaper to employ at fifteen shillings a week than a Welsh labourer on half the money, for the Welshman has been reared on your precious spuds and his output is a third of the man from the north. If you flog him to work, he dies – worked out at thirty – open your church registers."

"Happy little soul, you are," said Mam. "Talking about death. Do you think we could talk about living for a change."

"Give me something to live for and I'll try," replied Morfydd.

I chanced a look at her. Still beautiful, still vital, I could see her changing with every month at Ponty. For a tram-tower she was living on borrowed time; should have passed on years back.

"Something will have to be done," continued Morfydd. "Wherever you look the coffins are out and doing, but few bishops die, except from overeating, arriving at the throne room with a chicken leg in each hand, side by side with the workhouse poor. One consolation, questions will be asked. The gentry the same – go to Carmarthen for the gilded carriages with their damned postillions whipping for a path. Eh, God alive! Banquets and feasts on the smallest excuse while we get by on oatmeal broth. Few gentry die, except from port."

"How is Tessa these days?" asked Mari.

This as always, the discreet, the gentle; changing the subject, blunting the edge of Morfydd's knife; God, I loved her, and flung my thoughts back to Tessa.

"I have not heard," I said.

"Do you think it would be too much trouble to find out?" asked Morfydd.

"I have been to the Reach waiting every Sunday for months."

"If I loved a man who was dying I would not knock at the door. I would be in there quick, and hook him out. You could have called, Jethro." She looked at me.

"Leave it," said Mam, frowning.

"Seconds back you were shouting about gentry," I said, bitter.

Morfydd glanced up. "Gentry living and gentry dying are two different things. Poor little soul."

"You cannot expect him to knock at the door," said Mari. "Morfydd, they would only throw him out."

"He is a Mortymer," said Morfydd. "He does the throwing."

"Better go up, boy," said Mam. "For once Morfydd is right."

Morfydd rose and went to the fire, hands spread to the peat blaze. "You don't have to worry, they are sending for you tonight."

"Who?" I asked.

"Squire. Don't ask me more, I don't know any more – heard it in the village. Tessa is nearing the end. . . ."

"God," I said, and got up, wandering, gripping things.

"And Squire is sending down for Jethro?" whispered Mari.

There was a meeting that night up on the mountain, but I could not go now. Rising, I went out the back and looked at the sky. I was watching for rain about then, having in mind an early ploughing. Leaned against the back, dreaming. The fields were coming ghostly under the moon and he was as big as a cheese with him and rolling over the mountains. A nip of frost was in the air and a scent of peat fires, and I saw for the first time quite clearly the mud and wattle houses squatting on the foothills as little bullfrogs, their blind windows glinting for eyes. Went back into the house, cold away from the fire. And Mari was reading from the Book.

" 'By night on my bed I sought him whom my soul loveth: I sought him, but I found him not. I will rise now, and go about the city in the streets, and in the broad ways. I will seek him whom my soul loveth: I sought him, but found him not. The watchmen that go about the city found me; to whom I said, Saw ye him whom my soul loveth . . .?' "

Sitting down, I watched Mari's face. No grief there, save for the brightness of her eyes, which could have been because of the beauty, then I looked at my mother. Stitching away like mad, she was, too busy for innocence, and Morfydd nodded at them a queer old look and a sigh. I knew what she was thinking.

"Can't you find something happier, Mari?" I asked, sitting down.

"It is what Mam wants," said Mari.

"Great is the Lord and with humour," said Morfydd. "Heaven knows why we clad Him in sackcloth and misery, as if He never smiled."

"My Reading," said Mam. "There are other rooms in the house. Go on, Mari."

And Mari read:

" 'It was but a little while that I passed from them, but I found him whom my soul loveth; I held him, and would not let him go, until I had brought him into my mother's house, and into the chamber of her that conceived me . . .' "

My mother was weeping softly, stitching away.

"Mam, for God's sake," I said, and she raised her eyes at me, lowering them with a gesture of helplessness.

"No good hunting for tears, Mam," said Morfydd. "There is enough to go round for the lot of us."

Something was into me that night. I said, "A damned grave this is, not a house. Is it right to bleed yourself about Dada one minute and sing the glories of meeting in Heaven the next?"

"Jethro," Mam whispered, helpless.

"You mind, now!" said Morfydd in panic.

"Weepings and Readings will not bring him back!" I said. "God, if he could see you sometimes. Ghosts walk this house, not people – Richard; my father, and Iestyn – even Grandfer has his own pet ghost. Is it courage, is it living?"

"One day you will lose somebody, Jethro," said Mari.

"I am losing somebody now. And when once she is gone nothing will be gained by weeping and moaning."

It is bitter to see someone you care for making no fight of it. My mother had courage once, when she fought Nanty; when she scraped night and day to keep her family alive. Arrogant was her grief when she lost Edwina, as if she had made a fist of sorrow and brandished it in faces. No patience in me for this milksop weeping, singing the Song of Solomon, twisting herself to tears.

"You finished?" asked Morfydd, cold.

I turned away.

"Good," said she, "now let me have a say. It do so happen that I have lost a man, too, and though I may not show it his loss turns like a knife, and we do not need the likes of you to tell us how to bear it lest you tell us with your fist in the fire till the sinews stretch and snap. Women have tears and men mind their business. Damned cruel, you are, to our little mam."

"I am going," I said, and got up.

"And damned good riddance, forgive me, Mam."

"Wait," said Mari. "Somebody is coming."

"Hearing things," I said.

I was not heartless, just bitter that my mother should torture herself, and I knew why. The visions of my father returned with greater power, she had said, since Morfydd had started coaling in Ponty; as if the grime of the washing-sink had re-stained her; the galleries of Nantyglo making echo in the dust of Morfydd's hair and her coal-rimmed eyes. *Bitter*. I could have taken the name of my father just then and hurled it over towns, over the smoke-grimed roofs of Nanty where he died, battered it on the walls of mansions. Bitter, bitter, and I spit at grief. I got up, swinging on my coat, knowing a morgue better than this one, Black Boar tavern.

"I said somebody was coming," said Mari. "Listen," and a footstep scraped on the flags outside and a fist came on the door. I opened it.

Ben, Tessa's servant, come down from the Reach.

"You Jethro Mortymer?"

"Know damned well I am."

"Squire wants you up there, it's important," and he wept.

I closed my eyes and turned, looking into the room, and there came to me a song that was mine, the song of Tessa.

Left them alone with their Song of Solomon.

Queer is life and its sweet, sad music.

Never been up to the mansion before save for kisses and poaching, strange going up as a guest. And I went in the front way to Lloyd Parry's credit, old Ben standing aside. Parry was awaiting me in the hall, the hall I had seen so often through windows. Narrow waisted, six feet odd, handsome in his black frock coat and cravat, he was waiting.

"Tessa is calling for you, Mortymer," he said, and gripped my shoulder.

This was the ogre of the Trusts, a man broken, grey with grief. This was the one they had over every night in the taverns now, roasting him alive, drawing his name in ale. A fine as soon as he looks at you, they said, six months gaol for the leg of a rabbit. If his mantraps don't get you Squire Parry will. Land in prison for sure if you stand before his bench; enter his Reach and you don't come out alive.

"O, Jethro," he said, and gripped me, sobbing against me. Just two men now. I held him, giving the nod to Ben over his shoulder.

"All I've got," he said.

Just held him, nothing more I could do. Then he straightened, bracing himself and his head went up, bringing out the breeding.

"Tessa is dying," he said.

Words come like fists swung in anger and you cannot ride or duck them, but stand square to the smack, as rooted.

He ran his fingers through his hair, lost, and I pitied him.

"For some time she has been asking, it seems, but we could not make it out till old Ben listened."

"Yes," I said.

"You will see her?"

"Yes, sir."

"You will be good to her."

I nodded, screwing at my hat.

"Come," he said, "I will take you up," and turned to the great white staircase and its thick, crimson carpet. I followed him up the stairs to the landing where peak-faced servants rustled to a great white door as the gateway of Heaven. Silently, he opened it.

"I will leave you alone with her," he whispered.

The room was musty, every window shut tight against the chance of draught, with a smell of burned tallow. A great log fire burned in the hearth, leaping, spluttering. An ocean of a bed with a silk panelled head and blue counterpane, and the ship of its sea was Tessa's face; stark white that face, her black hair flung over the pillows. Tiptoed in and stood beside her, looking down. Beautiful. Her skin was transparent in the light of the bedside candles; one hand on the silk, as wax; and the long, slim fingers were moving, seeking. Kneeling, I pressed them.

"Tessa," I said, but she made no sign.

Just knelt there beside her, watching, remembering summer, and I bowed my head. When I looked again her eyes were open and she smiled, but not with her lips.

"Tessa." I bent nearer. "Jethro, it is. You asking, girl?"

An otter barked down on the Reach and its mate replied with a whistle and I saw her eyes move to the window.

"You hear the otters, Tess?"

She nodded. No sound then but the sparking of the candles and her gusty breathing. The barking came again and she moved her eyes, listening. I leaned closer.

"You hear them?" I whispered. "Them old poachers still at it – going like demons for the salmon near the steps. God, there is big ones this year, coming up for spawning. Thirty pounds or more, I reckon, you should see them leaping!"

It breathed new life into her and she gripped my hand.

"And Bill Stork is still on one leg, down on the estuary – old Grandfer Badger's rooting round Bully Hole Bottom – remember Grandfer? Had him out by the tail again last Sunday when I come up. And the curlews are crying from here to Kidwelly – you heard them?"

She smiled then, her eyes coming alive. Excited, I drove on.

"And the hayricks are burning right down to Tarn – remember Rebecca? Rockets most nights, too, but beautiful are the fires, as glow-worms, just as you said. Rebecca like I told you, done up in petticoats, looking for bad men to carry on poles. O, Tess, when you get better I will take you down to the Taf, and I will kiss you and you will weave a rush hat for me just like you did last spring, remember?"

But she was not really listening now, though her eyes were full on my face.

"O, God," I said, and wept.

Just once she spoke, scarcely heard it:

"Jethro," and she took my hand and held it against her breast.

Wearing the birthday brooch, too, just seen it.

Soft her breast on the tips of my fingers, cold her lips in that autumn of fire.

I kissed her.

Dear little woman.

CHAPTER 13

THE TIME for lovering is spring but they do things different round our way. The blood heats up in November, it seems, and thins itself down for May, though Morfydd reckoned the sport was all the year round.

One or two going daft in our village. Tom the Faith for one – dying for our mam, pitiful to see him, and Waldo Rees Bailiff likewise, the pair of them losing weight. Very rarely apart, these two, which is strange for chalk and cheese, with only one thing in common – the Black Boar tavern ale, though Tom the Faith went there for pints and Waldo for Gipsy May.

A maligned man was Tom Griffiths the Faith, with a wedded-all-over look since my mother came to Cae White. He lived on the banks of the Tywi in a cottage old enough for savages. Grandfer's height but big in the stomach, Tom's pipe was his only friend; his music the clatter of his dead wife's teacups, his memories the swish of her shuttle when spinning. Sitting by his winter fires with the rushes of the river tapping his window, Tom's short life with Martha was the past, present and future in the hands of the Lord. For Tom the Faith knew it all, from Genesis to Revelation and back return journey, and every Sunday at dawn he would stand up to his neck in the river for an hour to atone for the sins of the village. Cherubim and Seraphim mated, was Tom, till he sighed at our mam and went on the hops.

Different was Waldo Rees Bailiff; most sure of himself, this one, with the spiked moustache and fob watch and all the things that go to make up gentry save gentility. Virgin pure, too, saving himself for the right lady, he said, though Morfydd reckoned she was safer with Grandfer's stallion than trusting herself to Waldo, who spent a shilling a week on Gipsy May.

Tom Griffiths first. Did things properly, give him credit; very spruced up and collared was Tom, fortified well by the

116

smell of his breath. And he stood at the door in splendour, did Tom, bowing double, his hat sweeping the doorstep.

"What the hell does he want?" asked Grandfer, peeping over the top of the *Cambrian*.

"It is only a social visit, mind," said Tom, and the heels of his boots were hitting like clappers.

"Wants our mam," said Morfydd.

"Good God," said Grandfer. "Honey and Hornets. Grant me release. This is a house of virgins, Tom Griffiths, and I will not have it otherwise. I know you biblicals."

"Never mind Grandfer," said Morfydd, "come you in, Tom Griffiths," she having a sneaking regard for Tom because he worked among the poor.

"I will not come in, never mind," said Tom, crimson. "Just passing, I was, and hoping for an appointment with Mrs Mortymer, no offence, she being a widow lady."

"God help us," said Grandfer. "I will be sheltering four generations. Make no mistake, Tom Griffiths, you are not living here."

"O, Tom!" cried Mari coming in, and she hooked Morfydd out of it. "In with you, *bach*, and welcome. Is it Mrs Mortymer you are after, man?"

"Just passing, I was, and . . ."

"For an appointment, is it? O, yes, now." Finger under her chin, working things out. "Let me see. She is out tomorrow, down at Chapel. Thursday she is visiting Dai Alltwen Preacher, being he has people coming. Friday she is down with Mrs Tom Rhayader, the baby expected, you understand . . ."

"Eh, grief," said Tom, "she is a very busy woman. Saturday, is it?"

"Saturday she is bathing me," said Grandfer.

"Do not notice him," said Mari. "Saturday would be convenient, say half past seven?"

" 'Tis private, you understand," said he, mystic.

Private all right now Grandfer had it.

"And . . . and you will tell her I visited, mind. Expect you guess the reason?"

"Got a fair idea, Tom Griffiths, you leave her to me."

"God bless you, Mari, girl. Goodnight, now."

And Morfydd exploded as the door closed.

"Enough of that," said Mari, severe. "The man is entitled to a hearing."

"About all he will get," I said.

"Mam's business, please. A good little man is Tom Griffiths. I could think of a few worse, I expect," and she shot Grandfer a look that brought up his *Cambrian*.

"Hey, you know about this!" said Morfydd, giggling. "Matchmaking, is it?"

"Ask your mother. I am nothing to do with it," replied Mari.

I had often wondered if my mother would marry again, too good a woman to stay single with decent men in loneliness. And I was partial to Tom the Faith. Barge poles would not have touched her when she first came to Cae White, but time and tears were making her mellow and she had come from black some time now, looking lovely in her lace and dainty little hats. She may not have forgiven me for protesting about her grief, but at least she had listened, being different lately.

The house was close and silent that night, with nothing but the rustle of Grandfer's newspaper, and I wished him to the devil with his champings and grunts. Tessa was with me, too; strange I could not lose Tessa. Every bark of an otter brought me her face. About then I was losing myself with the mountain meetings where the talk was now growing like a flame to the burning of gates. A gate that would catch me square was going up on the road to Kidwelly, so I got up and left Grandfer to it.

Spring air is like wine, autumn air as old casked ale, with a smell of centuries about it. Night birds were doing themselves proud in the elms that night, late for November, and I stood for a bit on the road outside Cae White and listened to their chirping; their beaks uplifted against the moon and the saliva bubbles from their throats sailing upward in the windless air. Screeches came from Waldo's woods where things were dying, for owls were hunting with beak and claw. A screech time is late autumn, I think; of round eyes glowing from shadows, as if the winged things have starved themselves with song-making all summer and now squaring up their stomachs for the torrent of winter. But I do like autumn and her glories; the blood-stained edges of the beech leaves, the boles of the alders painted silver. Aye, autumn to me is best, as a perfumed gentle old matron, while winter I think of as a crone, toothless, shivering, nose-jewelled and with frost on her lashes. Summer could be Mari swinging out on the road for Chapel; spring is like Tessa dancing naked on lawns.

Drinking pretty hard these days, Squire; fist to his head, legs thrust out, hammering for bottles according to reports. Never been outside the Reach since Tessa died, grief being as sharp for beggar or gentry. I gave him a thought as I passed the mansion, muffled against the wind. Thought of Tessa then, for the stars were as little moons above Kidwelly and the wind had promises to freeze in his shrieks, buffeting down on the foaming river. Heard the door of Cae White come open in a lull and a sword of light shafted the shippon far below me, with Grandfer stumbling in the hilt of it. This moved me faster and I turned by the bend of Osian's place and bumped into Waldo Rees Bailiff.

"Well, good evening. Jethro Mortymer, is it." He peered up into my face.

"Good evening, Waldo Bailiff," I said.

Carrying twins by the look of him, most expansive, thumbs in his waistcoat holes, fingers wagging.

"Is it well with you, Mortymer?"

"Not since that gate went up."

"Gate, gate? O, come now, do not be so peevish. You use the roads you must face the tolls, is it? And a trifling amount is sixpence a load."

"My sister hauls trams for a shilling a day," I said.

"Mind you," and he looked at the moon, going secret, dew-drop swinging. "It do seem unjust for some, those just starting. But there is plenty of fair men in the county, remember – and many have influence. So how is your dear little mam?"

"Very clever," I replied. "You know the tollkeeper?"

"A word in the right place, boy – leave it to Waldo. Come from black, I notice?"

"Who, the tollkeeper?"

"No, you bloody fool, your mam. Setting them alight in Chapel last Sunday, did you hear? Pretty as a picture, too, laughing and chattering, quite at home with Waldo. Mind you, I am choosey about the women, not like some I could mention. Respectability do count every time."

"Whiskers, too – I give you the tip," I said.

"Aye?" And he twirled them delighted, sharp as rose thorns, hooked at the end.

Gripped my arm. "Do you think I have a chance, boy?"

"Same as any other," I said. "You seen Tom the Faith lately?"

"Great God, why mention him? Would she choose a worn-out widower before a man in his prime and lusty?" And he thumped his chest as a barrel. "Three in a bed, it would be, with his dead wife Martha in shrouds down the middle. At least I have never been wedded – single as the day, I am, and free for loving!"

"And never been bedded, counts a lot, for virginity comes uppermost with a lady as my mam. You fix that gatekeeper and I will put in a word for you, but watch that Tom the Faith for he has a deceitful nature. Goodnight, Waldo Bailiff."

"But wait, wait!"

"Go to hell," I said, and was away along the road and singing, happy in my soul at the knowledge of his misery, for he knew he had no chance. And round the corner now in the floodlight of the moon I thought of my father, the giant of strength; fervent in love, demanding in purpose, with Waldo Rees in one hand and Tom Griffiths in the other, holding them high to Mam, shaking them in a thunder of laughter, that they should presume to desire her, she whom his body had worshipped and given his kisses of gentleness. I saw my father on that walk in the moonlight. Wide of the shoulders, he was, lithe of step, bright-eyed, quick with words, noble in features, sullen in anger. And these, the dead fish of a county's manhood were quarrelling and whining over her body. Tom the Faith; well, not so bad. Waldo Rees Bailiff . . . ?

Standing in the road, I listened to his galloping. Waldo of the mantraps, the virgin of the bedposts, running to the arms of Gipsy May; tearing her skirt in the hayloft, despoiling her womanhood, degrading his manhood. Obese, despicable, soiled, *obscene*.

See my mam dead first.

CHAPTER 14

MEMORIES FADE on most things with the passage of the years, but never will I forget the day Tom the Faith called to ask for Mam's hand, bringing references with him ranging from Squire Lloyd Parry, who thought he was honest to his marriage lines, and his Martha's death certificate entered as natural causes.

"It is what Dada would have wanted, Mam," I said.

"Perhaps," said she, "but I do not intend to be rushed."

"Rushed?" said Morfydd. "The chap has been at you two years."

"And another two if I will it," replied my mother. "Taking a bit for granted, he is, coming a bit previous," and she bustled about the kitchen.

"Look," said Morfydd. "It is all right starting that business now, but you must have given him the eye, Mam."

"And I did no such thing. Heaven forgive me if I have given any man just reason . . ."

"Do not heed her, Mam," I said. "A lonely old life it is being a widow and you are entitled to company, so give it careful thought – a nice little man is Tom Griffiths, as long as it isn't that Waldo Bailiff."

"Eh, that thing? Wouldn't be seen dead with that."

Morfydd said, eyes slanting, "But still rivers run deep, girl – not such a fool as he looks, old Tom – might expect more than your company, mind."

"O, Morfydd, hush!" whispered Mari.

Blushes and looks at boots at this. Devil, that Morfydd.

"Are you raising them in singles, Mam, or settling for twins?" said she.

"Not very considerate the way you are behaving, I must say, Morfydd."

Had to giggle myself with Mam trying not to laugh. In front of the mirror now, pushing and patting her hair, straightening her neck lace. "Indeed, I do not know what the present generation is coming to – no respect for parents, is there? Only just turned fifty I am, remember. In oak and brass knobs you would have me half a chance."

"And very beautiful you are, too," said Mari, kissing her. "Do not mind old Morfydd, Mam. An old torment, she is, and jealous. Can't find a man for herself and determined you won't have one," and she clipped at Morfydd's ear going past.

"Two minutes to go," I said.

"Lace on the head, is it?" asked Mari.

"I will stick to my bonnet," said Mam. "Now listen, listen all of you. This proposal of marriage do not mean I am going to accept Tom Griffiths, understand? I am giving him a hearing out of politeness, but nobody is sewing me in bridal sheets before I am ready, so I want no interference, especially from you, Morfydd Mortymer."

"Heaven forbid!"

"Aye, well don't look so damned innocent. Very embarrassing it will be for Mr Griffiths with me pushing him out and you pushing him in, and you will have me to contend with afterwards, remember. Get the old pot on the go, Mari girl, parched I am at the thought of it."

"Half a minute late," I said, looking at the clock.

"Left at the altar, Mam – probably changed his mind. Quick now, first impressions count most. Line up, all of us, quick. I can hear him coming."

And the door burst open and through it came Grandfer, a bunch of flowers held high, whooping and cackling.

"A damned fine proposal of marriage this will be," cried Mam. "Mari, get the old varmint out of it."

This even shifted me and the four of us were pushing and flapping at him but he rose up like a dog hackled and threw us off. "Am I not the head of the house?" he roared. "Am I to be rushed to bed because of a chit of a man coming courting?"

"Grandfer," begged Mari. "It is not decent. Away now!"

"Now rest your hearts my pretties," said he. "Just a little seat at the back to watch the capers, I promise to sit quiet. Tom the Faith, is it? God, there's a selection."

"He is coming," I said. "Quick, the tableau," and we all formed up opposite the door to give good impressions to the suitor.

Tap tap at the door like the brush of a butterfly's wing.

"Come on in," called Mari, and in came Tom the Faith, all five feet of him with a stook of flowers up to his ears and his little bald head shining above his high starched collar; funeral black proposal clothes, very gallant, and down with him, then, bald head gleaming, very elegant, and Grandfer lifted a knee and swung his face to the wall, slapping it and howling.

"O, God," said Tom, white as a bedsheet. "Not Grandfer!"

"Do not mind him, Tom Griffiths," said Morfydd. "In with you now and welcome, he is just off to bed, anyway," and she took the flowers and swept him in.

"Most welcome, if I might say," said Mam, looking rosy. Young and happy she looked standing there with the flowers now. Pleasant to know she was wanted, I expect. Official introductions then, though everybody knew everybody else, and the chairs were brought up to the fire while Mari dragged Grandfer to bed shrieking. We all sat down when Mari came back; backs like ramrods, most formal, expectant, for it was up to Tom to make the first move, he being suitor. And never in my life have I seen an Adam's apple like Tom's for travelling, creeping up under his chin one moment then diving out of sight, but to his credit he rose and spoke.

"Mam Mortymer," said he. "Nigh sixty years I am, living the last ten of them alone, and the loneliness is upon me, having lost my Martha. God-fearing I have always been, strict Chapel, and if I take a couple at times it is only for the company, you understand. Childless I am, too, with no fine children like yours to bring me company. I have little money, but I am industrious and will work for you and keep you in gentleness if you decide to treat this offer kindly. Mam Mortymer, I do come to offer you marriage, making the offer in the company of your children, according to custom, you being widowed, that they may advise you after I am left here."

And down he went, Adam's apple leaping.

Damned good, I thought. Must have rehearsed it for months, word perfect.

Up got Morfydd then, she being eldest. At Sunday School she was, fingers entwined, eyes cast up, shoulders rocking.

"Mr Tom Griffiths," said she. "Me being eldest it is up to me to reply. Of all the men of this village I do like you most. Industrious you are, for I have been inside your house and seen it. Clean as a new pin, if I may say," and here she bowed to him, "although there is no woman about yet," and she smiled down at Mam who was coming pretty hot, I noticed. "And when you are left here, Tom Griffiths, I will advise my mother that she do think of you kindly, and more, because you are good to the needy and speak the true word of God."

Down with Morfydd and I noticed Mari was a bit bright in the eye with a secret sniffing and wiping, for it is touching when older people present themselves in this fashion, I think; being sincere and humble, with little thoughts of marriage beds and the breathless kisses of midnight. So we sat in silence now and there was no awkwardness in us, no shame at this counselling, for the purity of it had filled us, and made us at peace.

But that was all he had coming just then, of course, for a woman cannot make up her mind on the spot, so we just sat a few minutes in quiet with the wind doing his falsetto in the eaves and buffeting in the chimney, till Mam gave Mari the eye.

"I will read from the Book," said Mari, and rose, drifting across the room, her black skirts held between fingers and thumbs, and she sat down in rustles and opened the Book of the King, and read:

" 'I am come into my garden, my sister, my spouse: I have gathered my myrrh with my spices; I have eaten my honeycomb with my honey: I have drunk my wine with my milk: eat, O friends; drink, yea, drink abundantly, O beloved. I sleep, but my heart waketh: it is the voice of my beloved that knocketh, saying, Open to me, my sister, my love, my dove, my undefiled: for my head is filled with dew, and my locks with the drops of the night . . .' " and she closed the Book.

"Amen," we all said.

Usually made me pretty hungry, this one, but the others found it touching, with handkerchiefs turning out and dabbings from the women and a good strong trumpet from Tom.

"Now to food," said Morfydd, recovering. "Starved, I am, and the body must be fortified as well as the soul. A good little man you are, Tom Griffiths, with speeches like that last one you ought to be in the Parliament."

Out with the cups and saucers then, cups of tea and bread and a two pound cheese that had set me back a fortnight, and we chattered and feasted, and Mari fetched Grandfer down in his nightshirt for his supper and congratulations all round. Well after ten o'clock before Tom left, jaunty and confident, bowing himself out, but I didn't give a lot for his chances by the look in Mam's eyes. Bit of a comedown, mind, when you've been used to two yards of a man and drop overnight to a bald five feet. Morfydd and me got into the crockery. The house was quiet save for Grandfer's snoring, and there was a silence in Morfydd as she handed them from the sink. I knew she had something under her apron.

She handed me a cup.

"Jethro, boy, you keep from Abel Flannigan."

I grunted, wiping.

"This county's going on fire soon, and Abel is doing the kindling in this part of the world – he will lead you to trouble, mark me."

"Do you think Mam will take Tom Griffiths?" I asked.

"Not for a moment; we were talking about Flannigan."

"So what do we do – sit down and whine?"

This turned her. "The Mortymers haven't whined yet, Jethro, and not likely to start now, but this Rebecca business fair stinks of danger."

125

Unlike Morfydd this. Even six months back it was go to the foot of the scaffold rather than bow to injustice. Now she was swilling the cups and saucers and smacking them down on the board. We did not speak for a bit, then:

"You keep out of it – leave it to the county men, it is their county. I do not like this Rebecca movement."

"Six months from now you won't get a cart to Carmarthen market," I said. "County people or not, we still have to live here. Move or starve, just as you like."

"Who builds the gates, Jethro?"

"Gentry – landowners, squires, squireens."

"Who else?"

"I do not know what you mean," I said.

"I will tell you – magistrates. The people who build the gates fork out the sentences to those who burn them. So expect no mercy if you are caught in white petticoats and happen to be a foreigner – they will make an example of the foreigners because of the bad blood coming in." She looked at me. "Special, you are, so watch it. And talking of petticoats, I have missed one. When did you take it?"

Worn out, ragged old thing. God, she didn't miss much.

"Night before last," I said.

"My property, Jethro. I will have it back, if you please."

"Slit over the shoulders now," I said. "The thing wouldn't fit me."

She flung the rag into the sink, dried her hands and turned to the dying fire. The lamp was low, flinging soot into her eyes as she sat down. "Eh, Jethro, come to me."

I went, standing before her.

"Down by here, boy," and she patted. "Now, listen. Time was when I was as you – full of the injustices, mixing gunpowder, and where has it landed me? Alone with my son and not a thing gained, save bitterness. Where did it land the Chartists – even your brother Iestyn?" She shook her head. "They are too big for us, too many. Power is always slipping from the many to the few because the few are more vigilant. In my time I have fought to raise the poor, but do they want to be raised? Nothing but defeat on the end of this Rebecca business, boy, believe me – the poor are the mass but they are not behind you – too afraid to help, and too weak."

"You are a fine one to talk," I replied. "Fight and be damned, it was, less than six months back."

"We are doing all right!" said she, thumping the chair. "We are making a living, What else do you want?"

"What living we have you are making. If you came from Ponty we would start starving tomorrow for there is nothing in farming. Every yard I move now swallows the profits."

"Then let the farm rot – come back to Ponty."

"Any day now," I said, "but there is more to it than that now. You may be beaten, but I am not. Whole families are starving between here and Pembroke, bled to death by grasping landlords. The magistrates are corrupt, the workhouses spilling from the windows – whole families are queueing at the doors – children torn from parents, husbands from wives, living like animals on scraps, working their fingers to blood on the oakum. Is it decent for men to sit down under this?"

"And you will fight for them, is it?"

She looked at me steady. The fire blazed suddenly, lighting her face, and she never moved her eyes from mine.

"Are you sure you are fighting for the poor?"

"For the lot of us – for you, Mam, the children – even for Grandfer."

"But not for Mari?"

Still those eyes. Uncertain, I moved away. She was watching me. The clock ticked in the sudden silence.

"A bitch of a sister, isn't it?" she said.

"For . . . Mari, too," I said, sullen.

"Thank God she's mentioned. You love her, don't you?"

"Not in the way you think."

Damned women. They take a lever to the soul and prise and peep.

"Think again, Jethro."

This swung me. "I do not love her as you call love!"

"All right, all right. You are not selling pigs. I only asked."

A moth flapped over the lamp, creeping from his rot-corner,

thinking it was summer, and the shadow of him was as big as a bat on the wall as he pecked at the glass.

"Singe your wings," said Morfydd.

"I do not love Mari!"

"Half dead if you didn't. If I were a man I would want her lying. Couldn't help myself. I would want all of her, soul and body."

"You and me think different," I said to wound her.

"Much obliged. We think the same, but I am more honest."

"She is Iestyn's wife!"

"Thanks for reminding me." Very smooth now, possessed, smiling. She rose. "Listen, you. You are hitting seventeen now – big enough for double your age – big enough to be talked to straight. The way you love Mari is the way you love me, Jethro. And any other kind of love you can save for Sixpenny Jane down at Betsi's place, though the way she looked at you Fair Day I reckon you could get her free."

"You don't understand," I said, furious.

"About men?" She laughed soft and low. "*Duw!* If you know of one wild enough you can send him down to Morfydd for taming, just to keep my hand in. If you throw enough buckets you quench the fire but the sister still burns bright, thank God. Aye, I know most about men and you in particular, including the birth mark somewhere special . . ."

"Please don't be vulgar."

"Right, then, but hear this, Jethro. To love Mari wrong is to love her vulgar, and I will not have it, not while Iestyn breathes."

Gave her a glance and wandered about. Witch-black she sat, hands folded in her lap, her eyes following my every move.

"You do her no credit, Morfydd," I said, but I could have struck her.

"And I do you less, boy, but I know I am right. Poor Jethro." She cornered me by the fire and her arms went round me. "Do not be ashamed," she whispered. "To love her is dangerous. It will grow and grow inside lest you knife it quick. O, the little shrew, she is, being so beautiful, being Mari.

Jethro, come back to Ponty. I will help you, I will make it easy."

"I . . . I would not touch her, you understand?"

"Yes," she said.

"Not . . . not even give her a look."

She nodded, kissing me although I twisted away. She caught my hand then and we stood together. Strange the heaping love I felt for her then.

"If you must fight for Mari, then do it careful, Jethro. Look now, there is soot on your collar." She ringed it with her finger showing the black.

"Those are the mistakes," she whispered, "sometimes the difference between life and death. When you blacken your face for the night meetings tuck a rag round your collar first. Has Flannigan mentioned that?"

I shook my head.

"Saw it last night," she said. "Now look at the fire. Do you see the grooves of your fingers scratching on the chimney? Take it with your palm, boy, not the tips of the fingers, for the first thing they looked for in Twm Carnabwth's house was the marks of his fingers on the back of the fire. None there, and as white as snow was his collar. They knew who broke the Efail-wen gate, but no one could prove it. Another thing."

I listened.

"Watch for informers – the prissy men like Osian Hughes, the evil men like Waldo Rees Bailiff, though he will never join Rebecca. But a man like Hughes would not stand for two minutes with his hands tied behind him and a dragoon booting him in the belly. You can trust your Flannigans for all their Irish names – real Welshmen, see. But men like Osian are an abomination – with a name as Welsh as Mynydd Sylen but ashamed of his ancestry." She narrowed her eyes at the fire, sitting down. "Strange is my country – the people are either afire – harp-Welsh people and dying to prove it, or Welsh to their toes and dying to forget it; slipping and sliding and whispering about being English – Irish, Scottish – anything will do. Lucky those people are few, but we've got them. And

God knows what Wales has done to have to put up with them."

Never seen her in this mood before. Leaning against the wall, I listened.

"And people write books – wish I could write. For I would write a book that would stand for a century – a book telling of my people and how they fought to live; telling of their music, their courage, their forbearance, their love of things beautiful, their fire, their God. And I would write of the money-beggars who suck them, the magistrates, squireens, the gentry who live on them, the gaols, the transportations, the unfair trials, and of those who spit on our language." Her voice rose. "And what the hell am I talking English for now? With centuries of Welsh behind me I am speaking in a foreign tongue, which shows the job we are making of it." Empty, she looked, fingers spread. "And if my book was printed they would call it fairy tales, revolutionary, a pack of damned lies, for people believe only what they are told to believe, and anything contrary to the preachings of Church and State is rejected. People are strange – no intelligence, no compassion. Aye, muckraking they would call it in a hundred years time, because they did not know my generation that died for the things they will enjoy." She sighed, and the blaze in her died with her sad, sweet smile. "Well, fight if you must, but fight for Wales, nothing else, remember, for the land of your fathers. Your blood is of Wales, every drop – your heart is of Wales, for she created you – the breath you draw is of the mountains of my country. O, God, to be part of this country, to love her as I do! And listen. Make it vicious – no half measures – for the people who oppose you are clever and vicious. Hit the big man, easy with the small man, do not take advantage. Burn your gates not singly but in hundreds, and when they go up again burn them down again. Fire your hayricks, massacre your salmon, walk with the *ceffyl pren* against the moral injustices – put the wrongs right! 'Woe of the bloody city! it is full of lies and robbery; the prey departeth not; the noise of the whip . . . the horseman lifteth up the bright sword and the glittering spear . . . and there is none end of their corpses . . . Nineveh is laid waste!' " She put her hands over her face, whispering now. "Fight to the death if needs be, for the land is despoiled. Better to destroy the Wales we love than stand to see her degraded."

I nodded, commanded by her, unable to reply. She rose, trembling.

"Got to be up early tomorrow," she said. "Dawn; deep shift with Liam Muldooney, bless him. God, there is Welsh Irish, good little man. Agitators, is it? Crawling round on all fours harnessed like a bloody donkey, fine job we've made of it." She came and kissed me. "Fight, but be careful – remember Iestyn. I will not stand idle if I lose you, too."

"I am not afraid," I said.

"Aye, of course not." She shrugged, looking helpless. "Do not mind old Morfydd – an old frump she is getting. All embers now, no fire. Goodnight."

"Goodnight," I said.

CHAPTER 15

As A MOTH on a pin Tom the Faith fluttered, and a month went by and my mother made no move to stem the bleeding heart. Then Waldo Rees Bailiff tried her, and Morfydd slipped with a bucket of water, half drowning him, though what she was doing with a bucket on a window sill was anyone's guess. Terrible to see poor Tom, though – mooning around the lanes, hand-wringing on the doorstep, never within yards of Black Boar tavern, hangdog, drooping with lovelight in December.

These were the mornings of the frozen water butt; of ice-cold water freezing teeth in their sockets when you washed every morning in the grip of the frosted land. The snows came in beauty and the flaring bare arms of winter were all over dripping with icicles. The rivers were shouting again after the drought of summer, their music a thunder that bellowed at Cae White, and with Christmas upon us I thought of Him Who was born for us. I am not much one for religion but I believe in the Man, though I could never accept Him from the brushes of painters; soft-faced, doe-eyed, gentle as a baby. For great are His works, and wonderful. So the God I see is a man of strength, with a chest as a ship's prow and ten feet tall. Seaweed for hair has He, seven fathoms deep are His eyes as green as the waves in anger, with a voice as the thunder.

I gave Him more thought as I went up to Tom Rhayader's place that night for my third proper Rebecca meeting. The sky was lanterned over the crest of the hill where Toby Maudlin lived. Not very bright, was little Toby, but a good man with a vixen of a wife from Cardie, sharp as a needle and a tongue as a razor, and she raised lumps on Toby every Monday night regular when he went to Black Boar for his weekly pint. Light kissed the snow from his door as I passed, and I saw him creep out with his boots in his hand.

"Good evening, Toby Maudlin."

"Good evening, Jethro Mortymer. Where you bound for?"

"Same place as you by the look of it. You joining?"

"Got a gate," said Toby, lacing his boots.

"Damned lucky. I've got three and more every week."

"Same up at Tom Rhayader's place – you heard? Four if he works to St Clears. But he can still work to Carmarthen if he adds six miles though he'll be paying out more for boots. Eh, these Trusts! The county's gone mad."

"Not as mad as you think, Toby. Speculation is the same whatever road it takes. They know what they're doing."

"There's a queer old word. Speculation, is it? New words cropping up every minute. Is the toll money likely to go on road repairs, for instance – I've got Moses' tablets on mine."

"That is the excuse," I answered. "But most of the money is for paying out the investors and we don't get a pothole filled till the rich get their cut, and there isn't much left after Bullin takes his share and we build new bridges near the houses of the gentry."

"Good God," said he, "there's education for you. Speculation and investors, is it, bridges and Bullins and gentry. Explain it, please."

"The money is being stolen, or just about."

"Good enough for me," said Toby. "Thieves and vagabonds, is it. Count me in, man – you know the password?"

"Genesis for us. You brought a petticoat, and soot?"

"The soot I have here," replied Toby. "Got me old girl's nightshirt under me waistcoat. Hunted high and low for it, she did, then hopped in naked. Hope she bloody freezes. You know what she hit me with a week last Monday?"

"Hush, you," I said. "Rhayader don't like bellowing."

"Better get garmented, lad. We're here."

Ghostly he looked in the moonlight with his little round face blackened and shrouded in white, nightdress trailing, for his wife was a head the taller. I raised my fist to hit the barn door.

"Wait, you," said Toby. "Somebody's coming."

A lanky wraith now, mooching against the snow.

Tramping Boy Joey.

I had not seen Joey for months. Last time I heard of him he was cowman over at Kidwelly with a Cardie farmer and I'd heard he had done a stretch in Carmarthen workhouse in between. Now he was poaching Waldo again, sleeping at the lime kilns where we went for our lime. Not much time for me, Joey – couldn't forget his ferret, though he must have had fifty through the passage of the years. Strange, I thought, that Joey should stand for Rebecca when a labourer, for the movement was backed mostly by farmers.

"There's a stranger," I said.

"That makes two of us," said Joey, looking evil.

Abel Flannigan opened the door.

Fifty or so Rebecca's daughters were squatting in Rhayader's barn, mostly smocked, but some dressed normal like me. Powder-guns, I noticed, were stacked near the door; axes, hatchets, scythes were piled in a corner. Looked like business. The place reeked with smoke, pipes glowed in the darkness.

"Right, Jethro," said Flannigan, and I was in. "Who's this?"

"I've got a gate, mind," chirped Toby.

"Through," said Flannigan. "And watch that tongue. Who's this one?"

"Joey Scarlet," said Joey, eyes shining in Flannigan's lamp.

"You a farmer?"

"Workhouse boy, mind," said a voice. Got a shock when I saw the speaker – Tom the Faith. "He's entitled."

"To what?" grunted Flannigan.

"More to it than gates," said another. "The first thing Rebecca did, damned near, was to burn Narberth workhouse. What workhouse, son?"

"Carmarthen," said Joey.

"In," said Flannigan. "And get here on time – midnight. The Sunday school's next door, not here." He turned and hung the lamp. "Two new members, eh? Let me make something clear. Rebecca has a knife and a fancy for tongues, so we brought in Justin Slaughterer to oblige. You can take the oath afterwards. Right, Rhayader."

And Tom Rhayader rose from his box in the corner; small, lithe, nothing like a leader save for his eyes. On fire were those eyes, bright in his strong, square face. He had kept to himself till now, coming down from the north with his wife and daughter a year or so back, and Mam had delivered his second. He had never seen the counter of Black Boar tavern; was a bit of a lay preacher and three times to Chapel every Sunday, Baptist. Easy was Rhayader, fists on hips, an inch higher than Flannigan's shoulder, but he had the thin scars of fighting over his eyes. I would have backed him against Flannigan there on the spot.

"First," he began, "I have a message from Rebecca who governs West Wales, our leader. Listen," and he read from a paper, " 'The masses to a man throughout the three counties of Carmarthen, Cardigan and Pembroke are with me. O, yes, they are all my children. When I meet the lime-men on the road covered with sweat and dust, I know they are Rebeccaites. When I see the coalmen coming to town clothed in rags, hard worked and hard fed, I know they are mine, these are Rebecca's children. When I see the farmers' wives carrying loaded baskets to market, bending under the weight, I know well that these are my daughters. If I turn into a farmer's house and see them eating barley bread and drinking whey, surely, say I, these are the members of my family, these are the oppressed sons and daughters of Rebecca.' "

134

Rhayader lowered the letter. "The message is unsigned," said he. "And if the message were signed it would rock the magistrates of the county, for we are led by a man of high birth and responsibility. May his name never be mentioned lest someone die for it. May he be respected and shown honour by all the daughters of Rebecca, this man who works for justice and against the oppressions that bring us together this night."

Very cool, very calm, and the men nudged each other and murmured. I glanced at Joey. Mushrooms for eyes had Joey, staring hypnotized, and Justin Slaughterer beside him, his broad chin cupped in his hairy hands, intent.

"So let us pray that we are together tonight," went on Rhayader, "for this is a meeting of war. The time has come for this village, too, to take its part in the fight against oppression and we are the better equipped because we are men of God. Yes, we will burn the tollgates, we will smash tollhouses, and carry the fight to the very seat of authority, but have this clear in your minds. Do not encompass your minds with mere bars and chains, for the barred road that exacts the unfair toll is only the symbol of the resentment we suffer. The mud-walled cottages must be razed to the ground, the rat-infested hovels of the starving poor swept away and new dwellings built to house a fair people. Our men and women must be fed well, not on rye bread and potato soup; be clothed in wool, not in rags. Our women must come from the fields and carry their children with dignity, not labour as oxen at the plough from dawn to darkness, barefooted, ill-fed, treated as animals. Skeleton children must be fattened and taken from straw when in fever. North and west of us the gentry are merging their farms into holdings, their rents going higher to turn small farmers out. From Llandovery to Pembroke the workhouses are crowded by people who have lived in dread of the workhouses which are leaping up under the new Poor Law, dividing whole families, making it a sin for a man to honour his wife." Rhayader paused, his dark eyes drifting over us. Powerful in oratory, this one, with the *hwyl* of the good minister. No need to raise his voice.

"With the gates flying up and the tolls going higher the price of producing is rocketing. The Corn Law levy is ruining us.

Wheat at sixty-two shillings, is dropping; barley at six shillings a bushel, is plunging lower. Butter, which we cannot afford for our hungry children is at sevenpence a pound, half its price. The upland farmers like me are throwing away their stock, too dear to feed them, for we must raise corn to live. But worse lies ahead, for the country is being invaded by the colliers and iron-workers of Monmouthshire, where pits are being closed and furnaces blown out since the fall of the Chartists. And where are the authorities who guide our destinies? I will tell you – roystering in the London taverns!" His voice rose to a shout of sudden anger. "The squireen landlords are bleeding the counties to death – drawing incomes of thousands in rents for farms they see once a year, if that. But they depute their responsibilities, mind, O, yes, they depute – to the crooked little Napoleons you find in every corner of Wales – and not only English, remember – Welsh, too – by God, we've got them, for easy pickings bring up the dregs of a country. So we are dominated by the little landowners who have the power of life and death over us – the crooked little magistrates. Heaven help you speaking Welsh at the hands of their interpreters – pleading guilty before you go in. God help you more if you have deducted a single penny from their profits. And some are Church clergy! Is it the function of men of God to send their neighbours to prison or transportation, even death?" His fist came down on the box and he glared around us. Pretty worked up now. He stopped for breath.

"Listen," he ended. "We cannot burn investments or bonds or tithes or Corn Laws or Poor Laws, but we can burn the things that stand as other injustices – the gates! We cannot feed the starving in their thousands or succour our poor, but we can fight the moral wrongs, break down the workhouses that shame our country and carry the transgressors on the wooden horse – from squireen to clergy we will carry them and bring them to ridicule, because they dishonour us and the law of God. 'And they blessed Rebekah, and said unto her, Thou art our sister, be thou the mother of thousands of millions, and let thy seed possess the gate of those which hate them.' Amen."

"Amen," came the grumble of voices.

He spoke again.

"Flannigan – the first gate?"

"Two, sir – the bar and gate, Kidwelly to Carmarthen. And while we are in that district I know a couple of ricks for tinder – the Reverend John Jenkins, for unfair gathering of tithes."

"His crime?" asked Rhayader.

"Sold a labourer's Bible, being a shilling short of his tithe."

"Good God, forgive him," said Rhayader. "We will not. Have his ricks, then, every one in sight. Give the labourer a Bible, present from Rebecca."

"I will see to that, sir," came a voice from the back. "My old Gran's got two and she's pretty well blind."

"Good. Enough for one night," said Rhayader. "Back here in half an hour, every man. Bring horses those who have them, for the way is long – hooves covered with grain sacks, reins tied against chinking. The dragoons are out near Kidwelly, remember."

"Dragoons moved to St Clears, maister – night 'fore last."

"Good."

"What about snow, Tom Rhayader? Making fair tracks, mind!"

"God will smooth us out."

"Isn't the dragoons scaring me, mind. Case my old woman do follow us!"

Roars at this, with Flannigan hushing at us for silence. Rhayader said:

"Those who have powder-guns, carry them, but God help the man I find with shot. Bring hatchets, axes, pikes and levers – saws and scythes. And hearken. We do not fight unless cornered. We drift back into the night where we came from. If we become divided then make your way home separately, not in parties. The man who returns to this barn gets my gun – with shot." Laughter at this. "If you are taken tie up your tongue – you cannot even spell Rebecca – or Justin Slaughterer will have it out the day you are loosed. No man knows his brother, his Rebecca sister, his daughters, and, by God, no man knows me. The informer dies. Right, away! Fifty-three strong we start from here for the march on Kidwelly. But we

137

will gather them from the villages in hundreds. God bless us as God-fearing men. And may God help us. Back in half an hour. Away!"

Flannigan doused the lamp and we filed out into the snow.

Back home I went for Randy, for it was some way to the gates beyond Kidwelly and I did not fancy the walk. Besides, he was always looking for trouble and here was his chance for some; so far spent the winter eating his head off and dreaming of straw and women. Cae White was iced as I crept into the shippon and slipped up the peg on the stable door, and the smoke from the kitchen chimney was standing as a bar in the still, frosty air. Randy wagged at me as I went round his hind legs, snorting and looking ugly as I hooked up the saddle, so I gave him one in the chops to quieten him and he lifted up his hooves as a lamb while I tied them with corn sacks. Strap down the reins now to stop them jingling and Tara was whining at the kitchen door, knowing I was there. Crept to the door and opened it and she came out sideways with wriggling, then leaped into my arms. Had to laugh at the thought of it – it would have shortened Grandfer's span had he seen me just then – a shrouded ghost with a blackened face, creeping over the shippon with Tara in its arms. I thought I'd got away with it but a window grated as I led Randy out.

Morfydd was standing by the landing window, face white, diamonds for eyes, and her hair black against the crusted sill.

"Jethro, for God's sake take care!"

I nodded and climbed into the saddle, leaned down and hooked up Tara. And together we went up to Rhayader's barn.

I didn't look back, but I knew she was there.

CHAPTER 16

OVER FIFTY strong, we started, about thirteen horses between us, some two up, but most on foot. But we gathered them in scores on the road to Kidwelly where groups of the daughters were standing in the woods. Powder-guns shouldered, pikes swaying as a forest, we moved through the woods single file just short of the town; Tom Rhayader leading, sitting proud on his mare. Excitement mingled with awe within me as we drifted on in the misted silence; could not drag my eyes from Rhayader, my first Rebecca. His head was turbanned with silk, the back-knot flowing over his long, white shroud. Erect he sat as born to a horse, peacock feathers waving high, glass earrings flashing in moonlight. In his right hand he held a sword, wielding it for direction. Behind the magnificent leader came the gigantic Abel Flannigan. Drooping in the saddle was Flannigan, long legs trailing the snowladen undergrowth, confident, dark with anger. Good to have Flannigan about for he was spawned in these parts and knew every track as the hairs of his hands, every escape road home. Behind him came Justin Slaughterer, a barrel with legs, bowing his horse to the weight of him, bareheaded, his new-grown spade beard flecked with snow. Tramping Boy Joey was walking alongside Justin, gripping his stirrup. This disturbed me. Just plain mischief had brought Joey Scarlet, for he had no gates, and there was a roll in his eye I distrusted. Joey hated people; magistrates, bailiffs and Rebecca alike; come to destroy, nothing else. Only an inch of tongue was needed to send us all to the hulks, and Joey had yards of it, and I could not make out why Flannigan had sworn him. On, on, silent, dozing to the muffled clops and the stuttering crunch of boots in snow. A curse here and there as a man slipped flat and the crack of a twig was enough to send Rhayader swinging in the saddle. Keep clear of the roads now; whispered consultation as we lost direction in the depths of the woods with Joey whipping up from Flannigan to point out the way. A hand gripped my stirrup and I gave him a glance. Stranger to me, this one, with a sallow, pinched face and the big dull eyes of hunger. Just a boy by his looks, and he brushed snow from his wheat-coloured hair and smiled, his face coming alive.

"You weary, boy?"

"After my bedtime," said he.

"Kidwelly you belong, is it?"

"Pembrey."

"What is your name?" I asked.

"Matthew Luke John, last being the surname – the whole New Testament."

"Heavens," I said. "You got gates down in Pembrey?"

"Not me personal but my dada has plenty, back home in bed."

"Then rake him out of it. Anyone can lie in bed."

"Different, man. The old bull got him," he answered. "Last spring, it was – ripped him something cruel. And there's only me working – me and my mam. Five kids to keep, see, the youngest six weeks. O, it's a bastard. You got kids?" He wiped snow from his eyes, peering up.

"Sort of," I answered.

"And these damned old gates, see – cannot get moving. Couldn't bring in the lime last carting season, hadn't got the toll money. Poor harvest this year because of it."

"Aye," I said.

It was snowing harder now, riming his lashes, painting up his hair, changing his sex. Lovely he looked just then but he grinned of a sudden and spat like a man.

"Eh," he said, "my mam's an old witch. Comes pretty hard on her – working her fingers to the bone with the old man lying stitched – and one on the breast, did I tell you? Our Glyn – rare little savage, he is, always at her, but you don't make milk on potato soup. You get those gates down, Matthew Luke John, says she, being Welsh. You Welsh?"

I gave him some, pretty rough, and he answered me back, delighted, though I thought his accent was Cardie.

"Up here in the saddle, boy," I said. "We'll give you a spell."

"Whee, bloody jakes!" he said and took hold of Tara while I dragged him, and Randy turned with hate in his eye. "Easy on the cloth, Rebecca," he added. "Sackcloth and ashes if I tear the old girl's petticoat. Eh, there's delightful!" and he fingered the lace of Morfydd's nightshirt. "That come from a real woman, never mind my mam, is she better with it off?"

"Hush, you," I said, for Flannigan was trotting towards us, face thunderous.

"What the hell is this?" he demanded – "a Rebecca burning or an Irish Wedding? Shut your chops or I'll damned soon shut them, the pair of you!"

"God, he's a brute. Who's he, then, the Spanish torturer?" said Matthew Luke John. "Send him back home for a week with my mam, she'd damned soon settle him."

"Abel is right," I said. "Hush."

On, on, plodding, drooping; feeling like death at that time of the morning after a hard day of it farming. The boy drooped on Randy and I drooped on him; eyes wide open I caught myself snoring.

Big country now, rolling and jagged, the limestone outcrops of a shattered world painted into artistry with the hand of snow. The woods stood loaded in sombre silence and the stars were as fire above the stark outline of Kidwelly; dear little town, this, hit sideways by the Trusts. Dead and gaunt it looked now to my drooping eyes; flat and dreary, strangled into silence by the garrot of the moon. A dog barked, yelping, as frightened by its shadow, for nothing moved in Kidwelly save the sick, denied sleep by weariness; and babies seeking food and fisting at ribbons for the sleeping breast, for one cried plaintive. We straggled past, and I thought of the town and its low, thatched roofs quilting the sleepers; the sharp-nosed widow lying flat on her back; jaw-sunk, eye-sunk, snoring for a grampus with widow weeds behind the door, the high-laced boots with their toe-kissing postures, laces dangling beneath the iron bed. Brass knobs on this one, with clover-leaf railings, romantic one time, holding up lovers, now creaking its sadness at feather-bedding widows. Grey-haired, she sleeps, hands entwined on stomach, third finger left hand being ringed with gold. Sam Lent was his name, girl, thirty years dead, girl, what a waste of loving – knew he was for it the moment they brought him in, girl; knew he was past it when they laid him on the bed. Half past two from the house, girl – knew it the second I saw him – never strong in the ticker, mind, just like his dad, God rest him. Went the same way, girl, didn't know what hit him, expired without a word. Looked lovely in his box, mind – did him a world of good that week down at Tenby, bless him.

Had him done in medium oak, him being in the timber business. God grant him peace, girl, he is happier dead.

Creep on, drooping, snuffling, plodding.

Silent he sleeps, smooth-faced, and mottled, his blood-pressure up with that little tot of brandy, hands as if in prayer flat beneath his head. Smiling, he sleeps, and with every breath exhaling the little bit of pillow-down leans over gracefully, struggling upright as he draws back in. Shiny black coat is hanging on the hanger, trews with seat to shave in are under the bed – creases, see – sharper for pulpit next Sunday, for the matron in the front row gets the best view. Black Book, black cassock, me – very Church of England; John chapter eleven for my sermon next Sunday, got to get it off by heart, the raising of the dead. For Lazarus is my name, and that is my sermon. O, there's a lovely story of our Jesus of Nazareth! Parson of Kidwelly, me; trying to be decent, but would to Heaven people would give more love to neighbours. Nothing wrong with this town, mind, O, grant the world be like it! Welsh as me this town, but full of Nonconformists – like that little serving-maid living down the way – will have to win her round one way or the other. O, God, she is pretty, that little Rhiannon – not a patch on her is that front pew matron. Wonder if she'd have me if I tried her quiet – married to a maiden as sweet as my Rhiannon! Ten years older, but I still keep my figure . . . a bit flabby in places though she doesn't seem to notice. In a little ring of gold I circle my Rhiannon . . . and Jesus my Master and His raising of Lazarus.

On, on, harness creaking, on . . .

Parson Lazarus Frolic is lying on my pillow. Dear little man, he is, gentle as a baby. Wonder if he'll speak to me a week next Sunday? Strange how he's always strolling past the old chapel. . . .

Smiling, she lies, arms by her sides, eyes half open in her dreaming sleep, and her nightie is sideways and her breast is mother-of-pearl in moonlight, the leaded lights are prison bars black on her face. Red lips half open, she pouts and dreams: little serving-maid, second parlourmaid; Cook is a bitch, mind, but Butler most considerate. Black cotton dress is hanging on the wardrobe, wrist-lace on the marble slab gravestone to the china, hairpins on the floor, stays on the window sill crumpled at the waist – nineteen inches round, and the laces are swinging in the draught from the window. Bright red garters on the handle of the door. That old black suit he wears, now there is a scandal! I think he sleeps on it the way it is creased. Rhiannon and her flat iron would do something about it; little Parson Frolic, will you never bring it down? And that chap down at hotel stables coming very hot for winter . . . find it most upsetting. O, dear little parson, won't you save my soul for Heaven? For the boys of the village are wicked and the men are even worse, save in Kidwelly where they come pretty tidy. . . .

Think I'll turn over, and she pouts and dreams.

And that Church of England matron who eyes you every Sunday, smiling at your sermon with her ear inclined – you'd be shocked about that matron if I cared to open my mouth. Too mean for words, she is, lived next door for life, she has, and nothing on her washing-line in nineteen years. Mam says it isn't decent – not even a pair of drawers, mind – perhaps she doesn't wear them, shouldn't be surprised. . . . O, why was my dad born an old Nonconformist when you know the path that will carry me to Heaven? And talking of trews, boy, yours are quite indecent – spit on that iron, girl, send up steam. O, little Parson Lazarus Frolic, don't you ever dream . . . ?

And the first slashing finger of dawn rose up behind Kidwelly and the cocks yelled like demons as we hit the tollgate.

I awoke from the swaying slush of my visions as Tom Rhayader hit the tollhouse, and the top window came open and out came a face; terrified that face above its nightshirt, sleeping-cap slipping sideways, bobble swinging.

"What the hell is happening, have you all gone raving?"

"Out, out!" and Rhayader's sword was slashing, ripping at the tollhouse door. "Out this minute or we burn you alive. Out!"

"And me with wife and children, man? Six children, last one hardly weaned?"

"*Out!*" cried Rebecca, his horse wheeling. Sword lowered, he clattered about while men and horses pressed about him.

"For God's sake, pity!" yelled the face.

Flannigan said, "A tinder to that thatch would damned soon shift him, Tom."

"He has two minutes," said Rhayader.

"Two minutes could cost us our lives," grumbled Justin.

"The chance we take. I am not burning people."

The door burst open and the wife came out, hair in curlers, eyes stuck with sleep. One look at the wraiths and back she went, hand to her heart, moaning. A tot at the door now, barefooted, terrified. A girl was screaming inside; grunts and cries now as the keeper booted them awake.

"You, you," said Rhayader, pointing. "Inside quick and give him a hand. Bring out his blankets, clothes, furniture – everything you can save and work like devils, every second counts," and two men leaped to his command.

"But where will we go?" The woman now, recovering; down on her knees pleading, pulling at Rhayader's gown. "For God's sake, man, have mercy! Six children in here and the depth of winter – where will we lie?"

"You should have thought of that before," said Flannigan, pushing her off. "You damned keepers are the scum of the Welsh!"

"But my daughter – sixteen years old? O, God!" Her wild eyes looked round our blackened faces.

"She is safe with us, woman – go fetch her out. Mortymer, where the hell's Mortymer?" he turned in the saddle.

"Here," I said.

"Bring out the girl, Mortymer, you've got a good handsome eye, and treat her as a sister or I bring you to account." Damned fool, I thought, for mentioning my name, but I flung a man aside and entered the tollhouse.

"There's a farm down the road!" roared Flannigan then. "Two of you fetch a cart."

Bedlam inside the tollhouse; children wailing, the baby screaming and the girl in a corner screeching with fear. Ducking the furniture I slipped along the wall beside her.

Tables were going up, bedding being dragged out, china from the dresser smashing on the floor as I reached her.

"Hush," I said, "nobody will harm you, hush!"

You can see a man's fist coming but women strike like cats. Caught me square, the bitch; uncovering her eyes and striking with talons, ripping me from forehead to chin. I gripped her wrists.

"For God's sake, girl, you only have to walk. Would you rather stay to fry?"

The blood of my face seemed to quieten her. Hands lowered, she stared, then rolled her eyes and slipped down at my feet. Sickened, I stooped and gathered her up. I had not bargained on war against children. Her head lolling, hair streaming down, I kicked my way through the room, giving a special boot to Joey Scarlet who was already into it, swinging an axe like a man seeking freedom, roaring with triumph.

"First blood to the tollgates," said Rhayader as I got to the door. "Next time you search them for bread knives, Jethro."

"Fainted," I said.

"Right, find a blanket and cover her. Get her on the cart when the boys come back." He wheeled. "Where the devil's that cart, are they building it?"

"Are you going to burn us, sir?" A blue-eyed youngster of six eyed Flannigan.

"Not you, son, but your house. To the ground, and the gate with it – you can warm yourself to the blaze." Flannigan cupped his hands. "Out everybody, out!"

"I'm the last one," cried Tramping Boy Joey at the door, and he swung his axe at the window, shattering it. "Where's the tinder?"

"The gate first," said Rebecca. He raised his hand. "Silence, silence!"

And the roars and cheering died. This, our first gate, was due for the opening ceremony. Tom Rhayader dismounted and walked towards it, hands groping blindly, eyes closed, touching it, feeling it; wandering along it seeking to pass.

Dead silence now save for the weeping of the keeper's wife

and the chattering of the children. Strange how a mob is silenced by ceremony.

"My daughters," said Rhayader, turning. "I can go no further. There is something here that impedes me and I cannot pass. What is it, my daughters?"

"Why, there's a strange thing, Mother," boomed Flannigan, touching it. "'Tis an old wooden gate across the road. *Well!*"

"But what is it doing here, my daughters?" asked Rhayader, groping. "My old eyes are not too good, see – the thing wasn't here last time I went to Carmarthen."

"O, aye, Mother," said Flannigan. "Just remembered. It is one of them old tollgate things built by the Trusts. Hundreds and hundreds are going up in the county." He turned to us. "That right, sisters?"

"Hundreds and hundreds," we cried.

"But the gate must come down, my daughters," said Rhayader. "We cannot have gates on the roads of Wales – for how will we get to the city of Carmarthen? How will I take my goods to market?" And he turned then and faced us. "This is the first, my daughters. Smash it to matchwood, burn it to ashes – the tollhouse, too. By God, we will give them tollgates – down with it, down with it! Hatchets! Tinder! Down, down!"

A roar of cheering now. The powder-guns were going, pinning the moonlight with shafts of fire. Tarred brushwood was lit for flares and flung through the windows, tossed on the thatch. Flames billowed and swept along the eaves. The thatch caught, spluttering, flashing. Flannigan and Justin, Joey and a dozen others were chopping at the gate, their axes rising and falling and glinting red in the flames. Guns were exploding, men cheering as demons, dancing against the fire, drunk with success. Kneeling beside the unconscious girl, I watched. Pretty little thing she looked with the redness on her face and her black hair down. Opened her eyes then and the fear sprang back.

"Easy," I said. "It is only the old tollgate, easy," and turned. "Mam Keeper," I cried. "Your girl's come round. Mam Keeper!"

"Here comes the cart," someone bellowed. It came galloping, skidding, scattering the men. Bending, I raised the girl.

"Can you walk now?"

And she spat in my face.

"Get the family into it," said Rhayader. "Eh, there's a sight, boy," and he grinned at me. "A cat you've got there, spitting and scratching – give her one on the backside if she doesn't behave. Come on, come on! Pile them in – the children first, then the furniture – blankets, bedding, throw it all in, and watch this vixen of a girl by here if you fancy your eyes. Hurry, hurry!"

The bile was rising to my throat. I spat, turning away, wiping blood from my face. She had done me pretty well for her age; nails like cut-throat razors by the feel of my face. Felt sick as they flung the belongings into the cart and hustled the people in after them: thought of my mother and what she would say. The gate was flat now. Joey was flinging the smashed timbers on to the tollhouse blaze which was going like Hades and setting the night alight, with flames roaring up and ammunition exploding inside. I looked towards the cart again. It was ready for off, with the keeper's family hunched among the furniture. The girl was sitting motionless in her blanket, watching me, I noticed, with her great brown eyes.

"Rhayader," I said. "What happens to these people?"

And Justin Slaughterer shouldered his axe and turned from the fire.

"Aw, shut it, man! Rebecca, is it? Your petticoats suit you," and he spat. "Dancing and dabbing at women and kids – get back to your gentry!"

Suddenly enraged, I leaped and hooked him but he ducked and brought up the axe and Rhayader was instantly between us, one fist for Justin and the other for me, like lightning, and I staggered against the cart, tripped and rolled between its wheels.

"Abel Flannigan, my hearty!" laughed Rhayader. "Come and settle these two slaughterers," and he caught Abel by the shoulder as he lumbered over. "No, leave it, man – no time now. Private fights after. Come on, lads, do not look pitiful.

Just the same as Efail-wen, we are bound to get tempers. It's a dirty old business, mind, the boy is right."

"But what about these people?" I was up now, gripping him.

He smacked my hands away. "All arranged," and he turned, shouting:

"Down to Kidwelly, lads – down to the squire. He has a snug little barn he is going to hand over or risk a visit from Mother Rebecca – she will see people housed. Away now, the gate is down!"

The flames were dying as we mounted the horses. Randy took a belt at me as I caught his bridle but I did not fight back – too weary, too sickened by the violence and savagery of men.

"You give me a lift again?" Matthew Luke John, standing below me and I leaned and hooked him up. Jogging on the horses now, eyes drooping for sleep, we marched on Kidwelly itself and the house of the squire; smashing the bar at the village entrance, going right up his drive. He dared not come out but I saw him at a window, face parched in moonlight. Very tidy was his barn by the time we had finished with it, and we put the tollkeeper and his family in warm and snug with a notice on the door daring anyone to evict them. Off again under the eyes of the peakfaced servants to the farm of the Reverend John Jenkins two miles east. A tinder to his ricks and we left them blazing, worth at least a thousand Bibles, and a Bible was left on the doorstep of the labourer, not even waking him.

Home now came the wraiths, soot-stained, weary; little bands leaving us as we passed the villages, and we dispersed a mile or so short of Tom Rhayader's place.

Strange that Matthew Luke John should kiss me goodbye, disappearing into the frozen woods without a wave.

The house was dead silent when I got in. I stabled Randy silently, stripped to the waist and washed myself clean. To bed now, watched every board for a creak, and I slipped into the blankets and laid there staring at the flush of dawn. Nearly daylight. With the nails of the vixen throbbing on my face, I dreamed. And the last thing I saw was the door coming open inches and Morfydd's face peeping to see if I was in. Heard her sigh.

I slept.

CHAPTER 17

WENT BACK to Ponty a week after this, for the bottom had come out of farming and we were only keeping alive by the skin of our fingers. No trouble with Job Gower, though he grinned a knowing grin: labour would be easy the way things were going, skilled men especially. And I went back to Liam Muldooney in his two foot seam. Good to be with Morfydd again. We were closer than ever now on the morning walks to the pit. Good to be relieved of the strain of pinching, too, for our combined wages were now nineteen shillings. Good to be away from Mari, hell to be away from Mari.

Came Christmas with its white dresses and glaciers, its red log fires and goodwill to neighbours though we were still burning ricks and gates. I was out most weeks with Rhayader now, save when on night shift and somehow or other Mam did not get wind of it though she had played the devil about the state of my face, with a pinch round her mouth and her suspicions of Sixpenny Jane who had marked more than one in the village.

Sweet were the nights when the neighbours called to sit in a circle for Readings of Him. Most religious, our friends, chiefly Nonconformists, though we sported a few Church of England, making allowances for the misguided, being Christmas. Matrons I do love to call at the house best, for they are of the world and with kindness, women like Biddy Flannigan with breasts for weeping on, Abel's mam, though she'd have given him Abel if she'd known he was burning gates.

"Well, well! Biddy Flannigan!" Mam would cry. "Come you in, *fach*, get warm by the fire!" And in she would come, black as a tomb with her bulges and wheezings as a mother should be. She sits in fat comfort, then, the sweat lying bright in the folds of her chins, black bun, black brooch with its picture of Victoria, God bless her. Living to satisfy the appetite of Abel, this one; going to grease in the heat of her oven. But she had another at home besides Abel – the idiot offspring of a church-yard digger, second husband, now deceased. Head lolling, spit dribbling, her idiot floundered and grunted, wallowing at table, screaming in bed. My cross, said Biddy, every woman's got one, if it isn't the womb it's the offspring, and Cain is mine, God help him. Strange is the body of Woman, delivering a man one year and spewing a devil the next, though with Abel and Cain in the house it was hard to find the devil.

Christmas dinner eaten now and Black Boar tavern was going like something out of Hades, for the men of the northern industries were sweeping in proper, coming like an army, ragged, starving, desperate; running from the closed pits and blown-out furnaces of the industry. Men who had not seen Carmarthen for years came home, dragging themselves along the highways, sleeping in snow with their little scrags of women and children dragging behind them. But a few had money that Christmas, single ones mostly, and they crowded the taverns from morning till night, quarrelling and drinking to drown their desperation. In his element was Grandfer now, of course; beer-swilled, tub-thumping, laying down the law, and night after night I heard him stumble to his room with Mari's gentle voice to guide him. Amazing to me that he'd lasted so long – still more amazing where he got his money from for the drink-ing – must have salted a tidy bit away before the gates sprang up. And the second day after Christmas it lasted no longer.

The county blew up as Grandfer blew up.

The wooden horse was marching day and night now and the hatreds were rising in bitterness and threats. Burning hayricks dotted the countryside, the tollgates were blazing from Llan-deilo to Pembroke, and as fast as we burned them they were rebuilt by Bullin, the price of the damage put on the tolls, and burned again. Windows were smashed nightly, gentry salmon weirs blown up, magistrates burned in effigy, people ridiculed in public. The whole teeming countryside from coast to coast brawled and rioted into open revolution. Special constables were sworn in to protect the gates, special constables were dragged out and horsewhipped by the Rebeccas. The dragoons and marines were dashing around arresting people, the magistrates had special sittings, with public warnings and transportations; the prisons were crammed to their doors, workhouses bulging. From Whitland to Laugharne, Saundersfoot to Carmarthen, the yeoman farmers armed for the fight. The poor became poorer, the poorest starved under the new Poor Law. Spindle-legged children were wandering the villages and dying of fever on beds of straw. Mass meetings were held on Mynydd Sylen and the torchlight processions around Picton's Column, Carmarthen, became bolder and bolder. From the first Rebecca – Tom Rees of Efail-wen – there sprang up a host of new Rebeccas, men of education and most with deep religious beliefs, and the gates went down in scores. But the gates, as Rhayader had told us, were only the outward symbol of oppression. The reasons of discontent reached out to the very throne of England. One bitter complaint was the workhouse test, and people were starving rather than accept it. An evil exchange, Rebecca said; better auction the poor to the highest bidder as in the old days than drive them to the workhouse to be torn apart from their families and starved. Unmarried mothers were another indignity. The new Poor Law sent them straight to the workhouse, for the task of proving paternity was now placed on the woman, and the man usually got off scotfree. Good women, many of these unmarried mothers, said Rebecca – violated by deceit and the promise of marriage, and the Poor Law violated them again. To starve was a crime and thousands were starving rather than enter the workhouses. The industrial depression of the east had hooked our county flat, and the ironworkers poured in with their tales of poverty and dying – thirteen hundred deaths from cholera in a year in Merthyr and Dowlais alone. People were banding together and emigrating – single fare to America the land of justice – four pounds a head steerage. Better to die in steerage than starve in this winter of hell, they said. And in the turmoil of a land where there was plenty for all Rebecca stacked her barrels of gunpowder high, cupping her hands to the tinder, watchful, waiting for the chance of a bloody revolution. And in the new year the tinder struck. The flash of the explosion detonated into thunder.

And in the blaze of Rebecca, Grandfer died.

In the kitchen now, two days after Christmas, all the guests gone.

"What you say his name is?" asked Mam, spinning.

"Hugh Williams," I said.

"There's a lovely Welsh name," said Mari, smiling at her sewing.

"Aye," said Mam. "I know a good English one that led us to hell in Monmouthshire. John Frost, is it?"

"Frost had no chance," I said. "We shifted him before he was ready," and I gave Morfydd a glance.

"Should have had Vincent for the march on Newport. No Queen on the throne now if we'd had Vincent," said she.

"O, aye?" said Mam. "A finger on her and I would have a hand in it."

Spectacles on the end of her nose, she was, spinning away. Revolts came and went but Mam just went on spinning. "And what does he do for a living?" she asked.

"Hugh Williams?"

"That's who I'm after."

"Solicitor," I said.

"History repeating itself," said Mam. "Another with a tongue, it seems."

"Frost was a draper," said Morfydd.

"A cloth-cutter," I said. "Hugh Williams is a leader."

And Morfydd turned her eyes from the fire. "Like a damned parrot," said she. "Repeating the rumours. Where did you learn such nonsense?"

"Never mind," I said.

"Aye, never mind!" Disdainful now, she rose. "Half chit revolutionaries, the lot of them – they wouldn't have lived with Frost. But no discredit to Mr Hugh Williams, mind. Mam is right. He is a solicitor, nothing more. There is no single Rebecca, nor could there be one for he would dare not show his face in defiance of the law. Williams might defend Rebecca at the Assizes, but it ends at that – too much has happened to men like Frost – a life sentence in Van Diemen's Land, so don't talk nonsense."

I did not reply. Expert, Morfydd.

"Now that we've had a revolution do you think I might have a cup of tea," said Mam. "I've been promised one six times an hour back."

"I will get it, Mam," said Mari.

Mam sniffed. "Pray God the world could be governed by women," she said. "Women like that."

"Damned fine state we'd be in then," I said.

"And a damned fine job you've made of it to date," replied Morfydd.

"But not so much greed, mind," said Mari, fetching the kettle.

"Tongue-pie in Parliament," I said. "Morning till night."

With the kettle on the hook Mari went back to her needling and Richard, Morfydd's boy, climbed up on her knee, knowing it was bedtime. She kissed him and bent again to her darning. Socks most nights for Mari, very calm, serene, smiling over the potato holes, mine chiefly, fingers spread, examining her art.

"Prancing round Parliament with the latest in hats," I said.

"The country could only starve, though," replied Mam. "And the country is doing that now, God bless the Members. Hey, you," she stirred Richard with her foot. "Time for bed, nippy," and he clung to Mari.

"Up," said Morfydd, jerking her thumb at him.

"Before you start shooting Members of Parliament – we shouldn't be talking like this in front of the children," said Mam. "Bed."

"This minute," said Morfydd.

"Is somebody coming up?" Great were his eyes in his little man's face; six years old now, handsome, strong, and I loved him.

"O, God," said Morfydd. "No peace for the wicked, is there?"

"Them old ghosties be roaming, Mam," he said. "They are

153

always out and doing about Christmas. Another five minutes ?"

We wavered.

"Not much control, is there," said Mam, treadling. "Feet first they went in my day, mind – no argument."

"I will take you," said Mari, kissing him.

"Give him here," I said. "I am going up, anyway. Come on, Dick boy, we will give them old ghosties," and I hooked my arm under him and turned him in a circle for kissing.

"Richard, if you please," said Morfydd. "There are no Dicks here."

In the bed beside Jonathon I put him down and covered him.

"Uncle Jethro ?"

"Aye, Dick ?"

"Where do the old moons go when they sink over Carmarthen ?"

"Chopped up into stars and put over Tenby," I said at the window.

"O, aye ?" He fell to silence.

I stood looking through the window. The country was white and misted and the snow caps of the hills were spearing at the moon like hunters. Away to the east the clouds flashed in strickening brilliance and I heard the faint plopping of the powder-guns of Rebecca.

"Uncle Jethro ?"

I grunted.

"You out again tonight, Uncle Jethro ?"

"Never go out," I answered. "Too cold to be roaming."

"There's strange," said he. "I see you out there most time, for the slightest sound do wake me. A secret, is it ?"

"Sort of," I said. "Will you tell on me ?"

"Swear honest," said he. "Wait now before you tell me while I fetch out the china or I will wake my mam later and then there will be a palaver."

"Right," I said, "but hurry."

Down with him, under with him, heaving it out, kneeling now, nightshirt held up, eyeing me excited.

"Please turn away," I said. "It is not a public exhibition, Dick."

"To the wall, turn round, is it?"

I nodded.

At the wall he said, "You courting then, Uncle Jethro?"

"Aye, a lady, but keep it secret, remember."

"Cross my heart, man," and I toed the thing under as he climbed into bed.

"What lady, Uncle Jethro?" His eyes were as jewels in that light.

"You never tell the lady's name," I replied.

"Sixpenny Jane?"

"Who said that?" This turned me.

"Is she indecent, then?" He played with his fingers. "Old Grandfer said it – that telling? All you are worth, he said."

"Aye?"

"And my mam do tell him to shut his mouth, eh, the wicked old bastard."

"Do not say bastard," I answered. "Least of all about Grandfer."

Nodding now, the blankets up to his chin. "Do all men wear petticoats when they do the courting, man?"

Just looked at him.

"I see'd you, remember – night after night – sitting on old Randy, wearing the petticoat, and I told my mam and she said hairpins in the bed next, poor old Jethro."

"Mistaken," I said. "Pretty snowy lately, Dick. When I go courting with the lady I come back covered. It wasn't a petticoat."

."O, aye?"

I examined his eyes for disbelief, finding none. O, for the eyes of children – innocent, trustful, read as a book. I had settled him, but not myself.

Coming sick of it, fearful of the danger. God knows what would happen to them here if the dragoons tailed me one night. More than once I had galloped Randy to shake off the military, for the new Colonel just come in had a nose for Rebecca. Only last week I had laid in a hedge a hundred yards from Cae White waiting for a patrol to move off. Very interested in the house, it appeared, and I had sweated. Rhayader said somebody was informing – somebody among us but he did not know who. So we watched each other at the meetings now; took breaths while eyes switched, the sentences stopped half way. And now a child was tracking me – little hope if the dragoons got onto him, aged six. God help him if I find that tongue, said Justin Slaughterer. I will have the thing out bloody and dripping.

Terrible to be harbouring the ears of a Judas.

"Sleep now, Dick," I said. "Don't forget your prayers."

"Our Father, is it?"

"He will listen. Just pray. Good night, boy."

I was going down the stairs when Morfydd met me halfway.

"Is Grandfer in?" she asked.

Opening his bedroom door I looked in; shook my head.

"Little devil," said she. "We thought he was abed. He is worrying that girl into her grave."

"Leave the back door," I said. "I am off to bed."

"Early tonight?"

"Yes," I said, "I am tired to death."

She smiled. "You won't serve Job Gower and Rebecca, too, man. Bed with you. At least I will sleep tonight." She came up the stairs and kissed me.

"Goodnight."

The problems multiply in darkness, pressing in heat and sweat. Yet when morning comes, fortified, you wake and face the molehills that were mountains last night. But even this remembering does not bring you peace, and you toss and hump about, knees up one minute, six feet down in the bed the next. Distantly that night I heard the thumps and clanks of the dragoons and waited with pent breathing till their galloping drifted into silence, and sleep came, fitfully, with visions of Tramping Boy Joey parting the hedges for a journey to St Clears and the special constables. It was close to dawn when the door of my room rasped and I rose up in the bed.

Mari stood there in her nightdress, hair down over her shoulders, holding a candle like a wandering saint.

"Jethro!"

She came towards me, drifting. "Grandfer," she said. "I have been waiting and it is nearly dawn. He has rarely been as late as this."

I sank back, sweating, cruelly relieved. "He will come in soon."

"Jethro . . ." now she was standing above me, her face pale, her eyes moving in anguish. "I am worried."

"For God's sake go back to bed," I said. "Does he give a thought for you?"

She sat on the bed then, shifting my knees. Beautiful she looked. Her clenched hand was lying an inch from mine, and my fingers itched to be upon it. I looked at her, closed my eyes as the magnet drew me, gripping myself in the bed as I flew against her, cursing myself.

"Jethro, please," she said.

"Away, then, let me get up."

She gripped my hand at this, her eyes narrowing with some kind of love and her touch brought fire to me, with a longing greater than I had ever known before, to hold her, to be one with her.

"Poor old Jethro," she said, smiling down. "Loaded with women and kids and drunkards, worrying day and night, trying to make ends meet, pestered with women like me."

God, the stupidity of women. She was leaning above me. The white smoothness of her breast, I saw, neck and throat. And her womanhood flashed between us in the instant I moved towards her, and she drew away sharp, eyes startled. Unblinking, we looked, in the year of that second as the understanding flew into her, and she caught her breath, her fingers pulling together the neck of her nightdress.

"Damned woman," I whispered. "Do you think I am stone?"

"I . . . I did not know, Jethro," she said, and lowered her face.

"Now . . . now get out before it's two in the bed."

Faltering, she stood, eyes closed.

"Go on, get out," I said, and turned away from her.

I did not hear the door shut but knew she was still there, and turned. She was standing with the candle, a look of infinite kindness on her face, and pity.

I dressed in a daze to go out looking for Grandfer, and crossing the snow-covered shippon I looked back at the house. Mari was standing by the window of the landing where Morfydd had stood when I first went out with Rebecca; holding the candle, misty in white, beautiful, looking as a soul in search of God. She waved.

I did not wave back but ran, taking the track to Tarn.

Raw cold are the peat bogs when they dress themselves in shrouds. I kept to the track through the peat, knowing the way Grandfer took on his stumbling journeys home. An unholy place this, billowy and wraithy in the hour before dawn; a world of tinkling icicles shivering in sweeps of the wind, with the branches bare-black against the moon. Bending, I examined the new sprinkling of snow and found footsteps, Grandfer's most likely, but leading one way – to the tavern. There was no sound but faint wind-sigh and the creaking of trees. All yesterday a thaw had been upon us with the rivers running wild again and the little brooks shouting down to the Tywi. But at night had come frost, fisting them into silence, and they stood as glass now, ready for the footstep and the wallowing plunge. Nothing moved in the stink of the peat. Wiping sweat from my eyes, I turned. The mere at the end of the track was black, its rushes as spears, and beyond lay the pine end of Black Boar tavern with its mud and wattle chimney stark against the sky. Took a step towards it, and sank. Twisting sideways, I threw myself flat and the peat bog bubbled in splinters of ice as I rolled back to the track. Panic hit me then, for the bog was fishing for sober men now, never mind drunkards.

"Grandfer!" I called, and the woods flung it back.

On again, cursing myself for bringing no lantern.

And the hiss came from behind me, swinging me round.

In the place where I had fallen the Corpse Candle was rising, with the peat bog hissing and sighing. And the flame of it struck then, glowing into a brilliance. Gripping a tree I watched. Now the blaze died, leaving one straight candle, three feet high from the goblin of the peat. Red-topped, evil, it danced and swayed; yellow now, leaping high into incandescent fire, and I felt the warmth of it. Then it moved, rushing past me along the track, thrusting me back, hands to my face.

For I had seen him.

Grandfer, not two yards from the track, ten feet from me, frozen, and in the light of the Corpse Candle I saw his face, eyes bulging, jaw dropped for the scream.

Flat on my belly now, wriggling towards him, grasping the tuft-grasses, the hair of the peat bog, and I reached him in pistol shots of cracking ice.

"Grandfer!" I cried, but he gave no answer. Not a sound he made standing there to his waist in bog, with one hand gripping a bottle and the other hand pointing to Tarn.

The fingers I clutched were frozen solid.

Preserved all right was Grandfer but not in hops as he'd planned it.

Preserved by peat for Cae White's generations.

As I snatched at his belt he slipped from my sight and his soul flew up to Bronwen, his lover.

And the peat bog sighed and sucked in hunger.

CHAPTER 18

AMAZING HOW many friends one has when it comes to weddings and funerals. Reckon half the county was in Mam's kitchen, come to pay respects to Grandfer, although we had lost the body, with people sitting around bowed under the weight of the loss. Respectful, kind, generous, but I prefer the habits of the Irish, for a man is grown up when he understands that death is a joke. For instance, a whale of a time Biddy Flannigan gave Dick Churchyard, her man, when he went down, according to reports. Called in his Irish friends from ten miles round, did Biddy, and they boxed old Dick and set him up in a corner with a quart mug of ale in his hand and the feasting went on till dawn. Everyone to their beliefs, said Biddy Flannigan – the Welsh have their black funerals, the Shropshire's their sin-eating, the Indians their burnings and the Irish their Wakes. Gave my Dick what he requested, face down burial, too – no conscience.

"Buried face down?" whispered Morfydd. "Why?"

"Well, being a gravedigger my Dick wanted something out of the ordinary," said Biddy. "For he'd put down hundreds proper way up, see?"

"*Well!*" said my mother.

"But I might just as well have saved myself trouble," said Biddy, "for a variable man was my Dick and bound to change his mind. Just back home I was, tired to death, for wearing old things be funerals, and then he started. First he hit up the chimney in Dai Alltwen Preacher's place, then he rattled the pots and pans in by here, which was clever, for a haunted man was Grandfer at the best of times. . . ."

"Good grief," whispered Mam.

"And when gravel sprayed my window near midnight I knew it was Dick playing up, see. 'Abel Flannigan,' I shouted down. 'Turn out of bed this minute, your stepfather's changed his mind again,' and up got Abel cursing. Pouring cats, it was – I stayed in, mind. It was a four mile walk and a two hour dig to turn my Dick face up. But worth it, eh, son?"

"Aye," grunted Abel. "Good man was Dick."

"Lucky in some ways, Mrs Mortymer, if I might say," added Biddy, "having no body."

"And Grandfer that variable, too," said Morfydd. "Anything could happen."

"Hush," I said. "Mari is coming."

Prayers now, but wasting their time in respect of Grandfer. I sat, listening, my heart aching for the living, not the dead. Poor Mari.

"We are gathered here to pay our last respects to our friend," said Tom the Faith. "Grandfer Zephaniah, rest his soul."

"Amen," said Justin Slaughterer beside me. Close as twin nuts was Justin and Grandfer in ale, but I was surprised to see Justin there next to me.

"For a good man knoweth the light of Heaven, and his face shall shine," said Tom the Faith, and we clasped our hands and bowed our heads, doing our best for Grandfer who was about ten to one on my betting.

And Justin beside me wept for Grandfer's soul. One sob only, and the silence rang.

"Good God," said a calf in the terror of that silence. "Just look what Justin Slaughterer is doing to Joe."

And Justin wept louder while Mari sat dry-eyed. If I'd had my way I'd have straightened him with a right, for I could smell his hops from here.

"Amen," we intoned.

"Good grief," whispered the calf in my ear, high-pitched. "Just look at Justin Slaughterer weeping."

For getting it proper was little Joe Calf the last time I called on Justin Slaughterer – getting it good to Justin's song; a bawling blackguard of a song that spouted from the end of his bloodstained pipe and battered on the slaughterhouse walls. O's and Ah's from his friends as Joe Calf went down. Shivering is in them at the blood on Justin's hands, gasps as the belly hide rips to the upward casual stroke, calf one moment, dinner the next. "And I am next," whispers another as Justin reaches to drag. Powerful on his knees is Justin Slaughterer, bass in the chanting, right on the note, loving his God, grieving for his neighbour. Come to pay respects to Grandfer, newly slaughtered.

"And may the Lord have mercy on his soul," ends Tom the Faith in deep reverence.

"Amen," we said.

"Amen," boomed Justin Slaughterer, dabbing, snuffling.

"Amen," said Joe Calf, treble from the fields.

I clenched my hands and rose; went out into air.

Couldn't bloody stick it. The brother of hypocrisy is the blubbering of drunkards.

Biddy Flannigan, every time. Death is a joke.

Much better are the memories of my last spring at Cae White. The wind blew cool from the south, the country flowered, joyful with birdsong, with the blackbirds singing around our door and the young woodpeckers laughing and twittering in the alders of the Tywi. Sometimes I went down to watch them in their mating, thinking of Tessa, listening to the harsh shrilling of their lovers' quarrelling, following the tossing and tumbling of the peewits and their bright diamond flutterings in sunlight against a cloudless blue. Pale green were the buds of the willows, shy and waving in the winds of spring, breathless as children before adventure, the bursting ecstasy of their flowering. Foxes stole from lairs among the ripening heather, eyes slanting to the scent of hounds, nose high for the stamping panic of the rabbit. Old Grandfer Badger rolled from his earth down in Bully Hole Bottom and lumbered around the mantraps of Waldo's preserves, nose twitching for the stink of Jethro Mortymer the man. And at night the young, fresh moon made the circle of her eternal fullness, waning before the invisible Lord. Bill Stork was down on the estuary, one-legged in white purity, monumental against the patterned branches of yew where Hesperus watched. The corncrakes were crying masterful, the herons were singing doleful from Kidwelly. Feather and fur, leaf and branch, man and maiden were reaching up fingers, vital, reborn, for the tumbling, shouting torrent of spring.

Eighteen now, me; feeling the surge of manhood. Six-feet-one in socks, every inch alive, every pound bothering, feeling the rise of the sap in me, with the flicker of an eye for an incautious maiden, longing for Woman.

Tessa was but a dream now, as eggshell china standing behind glass. Even Mari faded in these spring-heat days; something apart and unattainable that washed and mended in her nunlike purity, dedicated to another. So enough of Tessa, I thought, enough of Mari.

Dilly Morgan, me.

Dilly Morgan aged seventeen, lately come from carrots for hair and one tooth missing. God help her since she crossed my path.

Come beautiful all of a sudden, had Dilly; tall and willowy, black-haired and with a beckoning eye and lashes slanted low with a spring come-hither; narrow in the waist and hips, most pleasant in other places to say the least of it. From childhood to womanhood I had watched this Dilly bud, flower and bloom. It is strange to me how the little scrags of females grow to such beauty – the muddy sticks of legs that lengthen to stately grace, the dribble-stained pinafores that peak to curved beauty, the tight-scragged tufted hair that flowers to grace the Helen; discoloured, aching teeth change to pearls and the cracked lips of winter come cupid bows for kissing. From little dumps of shapelessness grows Woman; desirable, desiring, the perfect animal for the mating of Man. And as such grew Dilly Morgan or very damned near it.

Met her one Sunday, resting that Sunday from underground at Ponty. I was wandering down the lanes near Ferry with the Devil sitting on my shoulder looking for idle hands. Bright was the sun, and the world in love with the newborn spring and the hedges all leafy and the azalea bushes golden.

"Good afternoon, Jethro Mortymer," said Dilly, looking glorious.

"Good afternoon, Dilly Morgan."

She was picking primroses, fingers dainty and plucking, showing a yard of black-stockinged leg as she leaned to the hedges, so I plucked a posy for her.

"For me?" said she delighted.

"For you," I said, and pinned it on her breast.

"O, my," said she. "Hell and damnation for us if that Polly Scandal do see us. Loose me quick, Jethro Mortymer."

"One kiss first?"

"There is damned forward."

"Just one for spring, Dilly."

Soft were her lips.

"Another for summer?"

"Good grief, man, you'll have me in the heather. One for summer, then, and no more seasons."

Wind whisper.

"Eh," she said. "Grown up lately, is it?"

"One for autumn," I said, "don't waste time."

"Damned brutal, you are," said she, pushing and shoving.

"Eh, and none of that here, Jethro Mortymer! Stop it this minute!" And she fetched me a swing with a fist that I just ducked in time.

"Right, you!" said she, furious. "Now you've done it. Tell me dad, I will. Front row chapel, mind, strict deacon. Virtue has its own reward and it don't include that. He'll be up to see your mam in under five minutes."

I went like something scalded.

Hettie Winetree next. Second best choice was Hettie, hardly the figure for courting, but you can't be choosey in spring. Where Hettie went out Dilly went in, but her mam was having trouble with her still, it seemed, yearning for the facts of life. Sitting on a barrel was Hettie Winetree with a straw in her mouth, dressed more for farming than Sunday, with a lace cap on her little black curls and her sleeves rolled to the elbow.

"Good afternoon, Hettie Winetree."

"O, God," said she, going crimson.

"Haven't seen much of you lately," I said. "You free for a walk?"

"Welcome, I must say," which was a step in the right direction, but she went pretty frigid when we got to the woods. Just peeps and shivers at this the target of her visions, this the torment of her dreams.

"Down by here," I said, patting grass.

"O, my," said she.

"Come on, come on," I said.

"And what will happen then, Jethro Mortymer?"

"One guess is as good as another, girl."

"You heard about Beth Shenkins?"

"No," I replied.

"Little Beth Shenkins sat on grass and she hasn't been the same girl since."

I eyed her.

"Down by here came poor little Beth – courting that Ianto Powell from Cefn, thought it was for kissing, see? But she came home at midnight short of a garment, was in child by that

164

Ianto three months later, beaten by her mam, cast out by her dad, all in under a week." She stopped for breath.

"Go on," I said.

"Ended in the workhouse, caught a chill scrubbing, child died at birth and her dead three days later, poor Beth Shenkins. Just thinking the same thing could happen to me. That likely?"

"More than likely," I said.

Skirts up and running, with looks over her shoulder to see if I was following.

Pretty good spring so far, but probably for the best, for I couldn't help thinking of Dilly.

Black Boar tavern now, leaning over a quart. All the men were strangers save Ezekiel Marner who eyed me, blue-faced, red-eyed, cranked over his mug. I grinned at my thoughts. Could be that special punishments were being handed out for spring fulfilments. And up came Sixpenny Jane, smiling, and leaned her arms on the counter opposite.

"What is your pleasure, Jethro Mortymer?"

"A mug," I said, looking away.

"Eh, hoity-toity tonight, is it?"

"No, just drinking."

"You seen Justin Slaughterer?"

I shook my head.

"Looking for you, mind," she said. She pushed the ale towards me and I blew off the froth and drank.

"Aye?"

"Breathing fire and brimstone, too. Drunk as a coot on ice, he is. Squaring accounts, he said. You mind."

Didn't really hear her. Strange is ale with strong light above it, the image of the face: the bulbous nose, the slits of eyes, the heaped cheekbones; all refracting and shimmering in the amber haze; the hop-flecked mouth, the mad dog froth of the lips, the sabre teeth of the tiger, all is flung back, warping the vision as it warps the wits.

"You listening, Jethro. Raging is Justin, out for blood."

"O, aye?"

And ale is like life, I thought, the gentry froth at the top, puffed up and pompous, the dregs of beggars at the bottom.

Lower the mug and leave the dregs. Fighting, fighting, I thought, and for what? For another master, a dreg of a master; beggar or gentry they are tuned to greed. One pig in exchange for another one uneducated. I looked past Jane, thinking.

"Gone down to your house just now, you see him?"

"Who, now?" I asked.

"Justin Slaughterer. What the devil is wrong with you tonight?"

"Morfydd's back home. She will give him slaughterer. Another mug." I tossed her a penny. "One for you," I said.

"You'll be drinking in good company," said Jane. "You heard about Betsi?"

"No."

"Courting strong, Waldo Bailiff."

"Good match," I said.

"Turned over a new leaf, has Betsi, mind. And when Betsi turns we both turn, Gipsy May and me. A house of virgins this, all we lack is lamps. Taking the cloth, the three of us, sackcloth and ashes henceforth. Respectable now, says Betsi, convents don't come into it. But my time is my own after closing, of course." She dimpled and smirked and fluffed her hair. "You free tonight, Jethro Mortymer?"

I looked at her. The youth of her was reaching over the counter; skidding over the wet teak between us as a clarion sail on a sea of ale. I blinked away the fumes, unused to drinking. She smiled, head on one side.

"Have to make your mind up quick," she said. "Here comes Justin."

The shouting of the room died to silence as I turned. The door slammed as Justin heeled it. Men muttered, their eyes switching from Justin to me. North country colliers, mostly; massive men, hardened to iron by the tools of their trade, sensing the vendetta.

"Away," whispered Jane, gripping the counter.

I turned on my elbow and faced him.

I knew Justin Slaughterer in this mood; the trash of manhood, this one – six fights a week and a woman thrown in. I may have had an inch on him but he was a full two stone the

166

heavier, deep-chested, with black hair sprouting round the ring of his collar. He smiled then, his white teeth showing in the tan of his face. Handsome devil.

"Right you, Mortymer," he said, and slipped off his coat.

"Better outside, Justin."

"Outside last time, boy. Better in here." Hands on hips he wandered towards me. Thought he was drunk at first, but his feet were steady; as sober as me. Jane came round the counter, elbowing aside the audience.

"This is Betsi's night off, Justin," said she. "Outside now, we want no fighting in here."

Justin swept her behind him with one arm, grinning.

"Rebecca, is it, Mortymer? Handy enough with fifty behind you."

"You fool, shut your mouth," I said.

"I am here to shut yours," said Justin, and leaped.

I got him with the ale as he blundered past me, worth the price of the quart, and he tripped in his plunge and went over a table, smashing it to matchwood. A man laughed, the men lined the walls. Justin knelt, wiped the beer from his eyes, and rose.

It was strange that I knew no fear. Not a nerve moved in me as he planted his feet for swinging. Calmness is the key to it when handling bruisers, my father had taught me; the watchful eye more important than the fist: left knee turned in to ward off kicks, up on tiptoe and ready to drop, never stand square to the swing. The eye switches to the handy bottle, to the broken table where the wooden spears stick up white; the eye sticks on Justin's chin – thick and bristled that chin, begging for the cross. The smack hit to stop, the slanted hit to cut. And the swing came wide as Justin rushed. Stepping inside it I hooked him square like Fair Day, and his chin went up as he closed and gripped me, and he went to one knee and lifted me high. Locked, I went over with him on top of me. Legs sprawling, we fought, and I rose first.

"Mind the furnishings!" Jane now, screaming. "Every stick you break you pay for, remember!"

Had to keep away from him, I knew, for he was twice as

strong as me. I took the middle of the floor now, tried to side-step him but hit the counter, and he wheeled and gripped me but I slung him off and stopped him dead with a left, and crossed him again as he roared back in. I thought of Mari as I fought, trying to anger myself into greater strength. Up against the counter again now with the thudding impact of his fifteen stone against me, my back arched over the rail as he fought for my throat. Slipping away I tried to cross him, missed and fell into his arms again. Again the counter; sliding along it now, hitting short. I got him away somehow but he rushed again, keeping close quarters while I wanted him away. And every time he rushed I caught him square. Like hitting trees, for his onward rush bore me backwards. Sickening the smack of that rail in my back. Panic came then, for my strength was ebbing. I saw his face flushed and brutal, eyes gleaming, mouth gaping, gasping at breath, and I swung for the first time and slammed the mouth shut, but still he came on, and I saw the fist rushing up as the counter stopped me. Big as a tub that fist as I tried to ride it, but it took me square in the body, doubling me up. The lamp reeled over the ceiling as he hit me left and right full strength, and I slid along the rail seeking escape, but still he thudded them home. Weary, in agony, I sought a hold, but he flung me off and hit out again. Through slits of eyes I saw Justin now. His face was bleeding, his hair on end, but he was calm as he held me with one hand and measured for the blow. I tried to duck it but it caught me flush, spinning me sideways. The lamplight exploded, and I sank down, gripping his legs. Just peace then, lying at his feet, with the lace of his hobnails in the corner of my eye. I tried to climb up him they said later, but he hit me down, thumping, thumping.

I remember nothing more till I woke in the arms of Jane.

"Eh, there's a damned mess," she whispered, and held me.

I blinked about me at the barn next to the tavern, at the oil lamp hanging on the gnarled beam above us, and the face of Jane smiled down. She was sitting in the hay with her back against a tub, and me across the legs of her, my head in her lap, and the flannel she was dabbing with was red. Pretty good, me.

Cuts over each eye, lips swollen as a Negro's, and split. Very handsome, said Jane, with my new humped cheekbones, one going black.

"Teeth?" said she, and her hair swept my face.

I tried them with my tongue. "All there," I said.

"I will have him, mind," she said then. "Bricks and bottles, but I will bloody have him," and I felt her body tense with its sudden fire. Thin, her dress.

"Leave him," I said. "At least he fought fair."

"With me hanging on to his hobnails and three men dragging him off?"

I didn't remember that.

"And opening the door and dumping you out like a sack?"

Too sick just then to realize the indignity.

"Fair?" she exclaimed, indignant. "The men back in there told him you'd have killed him in the open. Half his weight and no room to move in! Eh, I will have him for this. Justin Slaughterer, is it? I will do him in dripping lumps and still carving."

Pretty good lying there with her flushed face above me for I had never been so close to wickedness before. And youth is good – awake now I could feel the strength sweeping back, but I was far too interested in Jane just then to have thoughts of Justin. Her fingers were soft on my face and I saw the high curve of her cheek shadowed and beautiful in the lamplight. Harlot one moment, mother the next. Many and varied are the characters of women I have found since, but all are mothers. I rose, unsteady, my hands to my face, waiting for strength to grip me then. When I uncovered my eyes Jane was kneeling at my feet, smiling up.

"Jethro," she said.

I looked down.

"Jethro, do not go," she said, and opened her arms.

But something in the night called and turned me.

"Not yet," I said.

It was cold in the wind outside the bar. The water butt was near and I plunged my head into it and let the trickles of freeze run down to my waist to shock me into sense and feeling, and I stood there looking at the stars, drawing great breaths. For many minutes I stood in growing anger: something from my father this, a blind obstinacy that forbade any movement save back into the tavern.

"I will take you home," said Jane behind me, but I scarcely heard her. Instead I heard the hoarse laughter of men, the guffaws of Justin, the high-pitched shrieks of Gipsy May who had taken the counter in place of Jane.

Couldn't go home, to be thumped by Justin every time he saw me.

I looked at the tavern door, at the bar of light beneath it. Mugs were thumping the counter, money chinking.

"No," whispered Jane, pulling at me. "Jethro, no!"

I shook her off, remembering my father. First time a Mortymer had been dumped outside, I reckoned.

"Jethro!"

I walked up the steps, slipped the catch and shouldered the door. The light was blinding as I went inside, kicked the door shut and leaned against it. All faces swung, and Justin's swung last, and never will I forget the look he gave; jaw dropped, frowning, mug half raised.

"Right, you, Justin," I said, and walked towards him. And he laughed as I reached him, smacking the counter, head flung back, roaring.

"Well, give you credit!" he shouted in the second before I hooked him, and his mug went up and he reeled away, his stool clattering. After him now, hitting to go through him as I turned him to the counter and he screamed as an injured child as the rail caught him, bouncing him on to the next one. Raging was Justin, and I was cool, with a brain snatched from the head of my father; cool as ice, measuring distance, calculating. The place was bedlam now, tables being cleared, chairs hooked aside and men flat against the walls, with Gipsy up on the counter fisting and screaming and threatening damages. A rush from Justin nearly upended her as I stepped aside, and I pulled him off her and crossed him solid, bringing him down. It should have killed him, but he got up slowly, spat blood and ran, clawing for a hold. Things reversed now as I turned him to the counter, snapping back his head with lefts, and I saw the boot coming and caught it, lifting high. Off-balance, he teetered on one foot, and I saw the curve of his chin and took my time. This staggered him. His eyes were glazed as he came off the counter and I swung with all my strength. The blow took him full and Gipsy screamed. Up on the counter went Justin, and me after him, pitiless, for to be beaten is one thing but dumped is another. Shoulders slipping, legs waving, he lay across the counter. A hand under his heel, I helped him over. Ten pounds damages by the sound of the glass, but not a sound from Justin. Wiping sweat from my eyes, I peeped. Sleeping like a baby, standing on his head, so I went round after him and pulled Gipsy out of it, getting my shoulder under him. Jane had opened the door and I carried Justin over and threw him out to the cheers of the men. Spreadeagled he fell and laid there, as he had spreadeagled a score of men, and I went back to the counter and drank what was left of his ale, doing the custom.

Stupid is fighting.

"You did him pretty well," said Jane.

With the tavern door shut behind me I turned to the sound of her voice, for fighting and women go together, handed down from the age of the club.

I did not reply. Just stood watching her. Tombstone blackness just then, but the night came brilliant in sudden majesty, bringing her to flesh and shape, and I went to the door of the barn. Ghostly she looked, her hairpins out, hair tumbling down, as if she would fade with the first touch.

"Never seen one done better," she said. "The boy can't complain."

Just stood watching; watching her eyes narrowed with their laughter; getting the scent of her, the curve of her. The lamp was glowing behind her and the barn was golden with hay, and warm.

"Dear me," she said. "Is it frightened? And you fight with grown men?" Dimpling now, posturing, her hands round her waist. "Only little I am, mind. Nobody will kill you in here, least of all Jane."

What is it that leaps, banishing pain, tensing the muscles, throbbing in the head? A vision of Mari flashed then, her fingers spread, examining her darning, her feet crossed before the fire, but the vision fled as Jane's hand reached out.

"Come, Jethro," she said, and drew me within.

"Come, Jethro," said Morfydd beside me, and I swung, hit into reality, the fire exploding as doused with buckets. But the shock of her voice died in shame.

"Eh, now, here's a pickle," said Morfydd. "I guessed you'd be here when Justin called. Just saw him again, going like the wind . . ." and she peered at my face and gripped me, turning me. "God, there's a mess. Did Justin do that, or Jane?" and she pushed me aside and turned. White as a sheet was Jane, I noticed, though she flushed a bit under Morfydd's smile.

"Not with Jethro, Jane," said Morfydd. "A pretty little girl you are, mind, and a man could do worse. But this thing's no good to you, it's only half grown." She turned to me. "Home, you. Or I will start slaughtering."

Head and shoulders above her I went, being prodded.

But I was not leaving it at that. Even more determined when the clock from the village struck midnight. Down the stairs with me, boots in hand, through the kitchen, hushing Tara quiet, and out of the back with owls hooting their heads off as I went down to Tarn.

Black Boar was silent and in darkness save for a chink of light. The world of night was silent here, the barn as black as gravestones at the entrance, but the lamp still burned dimly in the feeding bars below the rafters, and I went in on tiptoe, knowing that Jane was somewhere around, soon to come to her bed of straw. Dry in the throat I crept inside, peering, wondering what I would do when she came; cursing myself for the coming, wondering why I was there. Shivering, I laid myself down in the darkness, hands clenched, waiting, and my heart beat faster as the straw rustled to footsteps; moved over a bit as she laid herself down.

"Jane," I whispered.

"Gipsy," whispered Waldo Bailiff.

And we put out hands and gripped each other. Up scalded, me – skidded through the door and into the night with Waldo Bailiff howling.

A damned good spring, so far. Enjoying every minute.

CHAPTER 19

QUEER PEOPLE were getting into the country just now – that is the trouble with a decent revolution, said Tom Rhayader. We take to arms with Genesis behind us, play fair, fight fair against oppression and for the word of God, and in comes scum. In comes the scum for easy pickings, the adventurers who fight for a shilling a time. Men like Dai'r Cantwr and Shoni Sgubor Fawr, there's a mouthful, said Rhayader.

Take the last one first, the polluted.

I first met Shoni the night after dusting Justin, and was resting with my feet up and watching people from slits, getting tender glances from Mari, digs from Morfydd and mouth from Mam, she being dead against pugilists.

"Shameful," she breathed, laying the table. "God knows I have done my best to bring you up decent, and the poor man is over at Bayleaves with the Hughes putting on beef to bring down his swellings."

"Two to make a fight, remember," said Morfydd, and whispered, "lucky I was there in time to stop another slaughter, too."

"Hush," I whispered back, my eyes on Mari who was stitching as usual.

"And you keep from this!" Mam swung to Morfydd. "Fight decent, then. Osian says someone has been into him with an axe. Damned mutilated, he is."

"Some of his own medicine," I said, rising. "And I am off from here."

"Somebody will be killed," said Mam. "That will be the end of it."

"A joyful death, mind," said Morfydd on one side.

I gave her a look to settle her. I had to go out with Morfydd talking in riddles. Mam might have been bad at hearing but Mari had ears like a bat.

"And where are you off to this time of night, pray?" asked Mam, hands full of cups. "Supper in ten minutes, trust you to be off."

"Back by supper time," I answered.

"Kiss her for me," said Morfydd, and I got her with my finger and thumb as I passed, pinching open her eyes.

"And keep from Black Boar tavern, mind," said Mam.

"And Jane's stable straw," murmured Morfydd, and I saw Mari glance up.

But the walk was an excuse for I'd heard something more above the chatter of the women. Never heard screech owls as near to our shippon before.

Toby Maudlin.

Toby Maudlin sure enough, standing clear of the light as I opened the door, with his hair on end and his eyes as saucers.

"What is wrong?" I asked him.

Gasping, he patted his chest. "Rhayader's been taken."

As the sickening bite of the bread knife.

"Taken," gasped Toby. "I am rounding them up – midnight up on the mountain. Flannigan's called a meeting. . . ."

"But Tom Rhayader!" I gripped him, and he was shivering.

"The St Clears dragoons," gasped Toby. "Six of them, and special constables. They came down to Tom's place at dusk, and took him. God, there's some wailing and gnashing of teeth down his place I can tell you, his woman's gone demented."

"But on what charge?"

"Burning Pwll-trap gate – papers they had, and signatures, all very official."

"And Tom just went?"

"Just as you please, they told him – come dead or alive. Got him coming from chapel."

"God," I breathed. "And we haven't been near Pwll-trap."

"But somebody has, that's what Flannigan says. And he says something more – an informer," and he shrank at the name.

"Who?"

"Don't ask me," said Toby. "That's for Flannigan to find out – midnight, at Pengam, to elect a new leader."

"Go," I said.

I stood against the wall as Toby scampered away. Cool to my face, that wall, for my head was thumping. It seemed impossible that Rhayader could be taken, and I bled for his wife. A pretty little thing was Mrs Rhayader, prim for chapel and with lovely children, and they worshipped Tom. I clenched my fist and hit the wall. Gates were one thing; dumb wooden things ready for tinder, but Tom was flesh and blood, and the tongue put a limit on the thumbscrew, the bawlings and kicks of drunken tormentors. Not the dragoons, for they were disciplined – not the serving constables under men like George Martin the Welsh-speaking Englishman. It was the special constables we feared, the hired thumpers; scum like Shoni Sgubor Fawr who would break a man's arm for the price of his silence. Yet deep in me I knew Tom would not talk. If they set him on fire he would spit in their faces. Tramping Boy Joey rose up like a vision. Joey would sell a man's soul for the price of a dinner, because Tom was leader, that was enough. I fisted the wall, wanting Morfydd. Lost, I wanted her. And she came as if called by the heat and sweat of me, slowly into the yard, peering into shadows.

"That you, Jethro?"

"Quick," I said, and she ran the last yards. "Tom Rhayader's been taken."

"O, God," she said, her hands to her face.

"Morfydd, go down to Mrs Rhayader."

"Now, directly. No. Supper first, or Mam will be suspicious. You too, boy – supper first." She paused, her eyes steady. "Who?" she said.

"Who informed? God knows. We are meeting tonight."

"Is Osian Hughes in this?"

I shook my head.

"Who do you think, then?"

"We've got Joey," I answered.

"Tramping Boy Joey?" she peered, horrified. "Give me

strength! Do not tell me you gave house room to Joey Scarlet!"

"Workhouse boy. Entitled. You try keeping him out."

She drew herself up. "Revolution, you call it, and you bring in Joey! Perhaps my revolt failed but at least we were organized – at least we had oaths and people tried and trusted. But you are throwing away your lives!" She snatched at my hand. "Jethro, do you know what this means? Joey's tongue is loose – a pint of ale it needs, no more. He will gabble Rebecca all over the county, to dragoons, constables, anyone handy. He is gabbling now, can you hear him? Spouting it in bars – Rhayader, Flannigan, Maudlin, Mortymer – shouting it in markets – little Joey Scarlet grown to six-feet-six. And he has spouted Tom Rhayader because he hates authority – Rebecca or magistrate, they are all in authority, so Joey brings them down, can't you see?"

"Flannigan brought Joey in, not me."

Morfydd sighed. Sweat was lying on her face and she wiped it into her hair.

"I am disgusted with Flannigan," she whispered. "He is begging for Botany Bay. Listen, Jethro. Find Joey Scarlet or you will not last the night."

"You seem damned sure it is him," I said.

"Lay my life on it," said she. "Find Joey Scarlet, quick."

"And Mrs Rhayader? You will go down?"

"I . . . I will wink at Mari and get Mam steered early to bed. Leave it to me." At the door she turned. "O, you fools," she said.

Dark was the night with a hint of sleet in him from rolling black clouds running before the bloom of spring. With Morfydd down with Mrs Rhayader I set out early for the mountain meeting in the disused quarry, but took the path through Waldo's preserves. Nothing stirred in the woods and beyond the Reach Squire's mansion stood gaunt and lonely, shuttered and barred. No gentry carriages came there now. Empty it stood save for Lloyd Parry and old Ben since Tessa died. Nothing stirred as I went past it to the lime kilns where the cauldron burned the builders' lime, and the bee-hive kilns were as camels' humps against a crescent moon. Beside the slaking-pit now I looked around. Here was Joey's bed of straw; a half eaten crust nearby, the peat scarred here by the thrust of a boot. No sound save the cry of a distant bird and the bubbling of the pit where steam wisped up. I stood alone, listening, then turned and ran down the bank to the trees that reared as hunchback skeletons, stripped bare by the Atlantic gales. Leaping the peaty places, handspringing boulders I got to the foothills of the mountain and began the climb. Far below me I saw a light in Rhayader's cottage and imagined Morfydd there with Mrs Rhayader. Strange it would be without Tom tonight. Flannigan was standing at the entrance to the quarry, a dog's leg entrance that obliterated light.

"You seen Toby?" he asked. Vicious looked Flannigan.

"Bringing in the men," I said.

"Don't be too sure, Mortymer, you can't trust your neighbour."

"Joey Scarlet here yet?" I asked.

"Get inside, we can all talk there."

Must have sworn a few in since I came last. Nigh two hundred there that night; squatting shoulder to shoulder, leaning against the rocks, and they were as statues, making no sound, their faces shadowed and intense in the moonlight, and they grumbled like cattle as Flannigan followed me in.

"Two missing," said Flannigan. "Maudlin and Scarlet. Now listen, all of you know that Rhayader's been taken. Somebody's played Judas and we reckon to find him. Who saw Joey Scarlet last?"

"Up in Carmarthen market this forenoon, Flannigan," said a man at the back.

"You are sure?"

"Saw him plain as my face."

"Who's that speaking?"

"Evan ap Rees. Saw him right enough."

"What doing?"

"Begging."

"Sober?"

"More sober'n me, then some," and the men laughed.

"What time did you see him?"

"Close on midday – walking round the horses, he was – telling the tale, hat in his hand – you know Joey."

"Do I?" asked Flannigan.

"Don't jump, don't jump, man," said someone at the front. "Just a kid he is and too bloody frightened to turn informer – what about losing his tongue to Justin – you there, Justin boy?"

"Right here with the knife," said Justin, and I saw him for the first time since our fight, his face humped and bruised like mine, but grinning.

"Somebody's been slaughtering you for a change, is it?" and men guffawed.

"And he got his share," said Justin, "eh, Jethro man?"

I grinned back. One thing about fighting; you do it with men, but I still did not trust him.

"You heard about the reward St Clears has put up?" asked Flannigan.

This put them quiet. Pipes came out and they shouldered and muttered.

"Fifty pounds a time for Rebeccas. A little bit more than they paid for the Lord. You heard they picked up four Rebeccas between here and Carmarthen at fifty pounds a time, Tom included?"

"A fortune to Joey, fifty pounds," said one.

"Could have been any one of us."

"Some queer old boys been coming in lately, remember."

"You think Rhayader will talk – he can hook the lot of us."

"Shut your mouth," I said.

"Or I will shut it," said Flannigan.

We sat then, uncertain, lacking a leader. Flannigan wavered. I watched him walking about, thumping his hands, and I longed for Rhayader.

"Where have they got Tom?" asked one.

"St Clears."

"What about fetching him out of it, then?"

"Talk sense," said Flannigan.

"Do we leave him to rot? He'll get transportation next assizes for sure."

"And him with a wife and little ones."

"It was the chance he took," said Flannigan.

"Wouldn't take a lot to winkle him out of it, you thought?"

"We are not having bloodshed," said Flannigan.

"Half past two for Sunday School, prompt, mind. What is this, an outing?"

"Just a little buckshot and a few little knives."

"Where's your stomach, man?"

"We are not going after Rhayader," shouted Flannigan. "That's final."

"Since when were you Rebecca, then?"

"Not even elected. I say Rhayader comes out."

And Flannigan wavered, walking about. This is the time when the new man is born, the leader to be clutched at, revered. Up he got. He was a stranger to me, and never have I seen the like of him for size and power.

"And you sit down, Shoni," said Flannigan, eyeing him.

"You try and sit me," said Shoni Sgubor Fawr, and he came to the front.

I drew my breath at the sight of his face. It was ravaged, with the flattened features of the mountain fighter. Bull-necked, mop-haired, grinning, this one, and his clothes were ragged, his shirt open to the waist despite the frosty night and his feet and legs were bare, his ragged gentry riding breeches tied at the knees. Shoni Sgubor Fawr. This was the trash that was hanging a stink on the name of Rebecca, the scum that gathers on the top of the brew. Emperor of China, this one – emperor of the hell's kitchen of Merthyr called China where huddled a pitiful humanity. Wanted by the police in more than one county, this man; a kick-fighter, gouge-fighter. The men murmured at the sight of him.

"We can do without this one," I said to Flannigan.

"You can't do without Shoni," replied the stranger. "Not now you lack a leader, and if you want the proof of me I will take any three men here." The smile left his face. "Informers, is it? And what are you doing about it – nothing. You've lost Rhayader, and you're leaving him to rot. I say find the informer and slit his throat, march on St Clears and release Rhayader.

Does the burning of the gates bring you respect – prancing round the countryside in turbans and petticoats? Where's the belly of the county, men? By God, you should come to Monmouthshire if you want rebellion – look at the Chartists!"

"Aye, look at them," I shouted back.

"At least they had the guts to fight it out. To arms, I say – take shot to your powder-guns, forge your pikes, build your cannon and blow the military off the face of the earth!"

"I am out for one," I said, shifting.

"Who follows little Shoni?" yelled Sgubor Fawr.

"Get out," said a man. "We work it Flannigan's way."

"And my way is Tom Rhayader's way," shouted Flannigan. "Which do you want?"

The men waved a forest of hands. "Flannigan, Flannigan!"

"Out," said Flannigan, and jerked his thumb at Shoni, "You will find ten Rebeccas between here and Pembroke and I wish you luck, you are not needed here."

"And your informer?" yelled Shoni.

"Yours if you can find him," replied Flannigan, laughing, and turned as Toby Maudlin ran in.

"Been searching for young Joey," gasped Toby. "High and low I have searched – no sign."

"You tried the lime kilns?" I asked, and could have bitten of my tongue.

"Why the kilns?" asked one.

"Just wondered," I said.

"Then wonder again," answered Flannigan.

"Starts sleeping there in spring, Abel," called Evan ap Rees. "Could be he's just started. Worth trying."

"You and young Joey were pretty thick one time, remember?" mumbled Justin.

All I felt was eyes.

"Years back," I swung to him. "And if Joey talks I go under same as you," I said.

"Go there tonight," said Flannigan. "Any likely place must be searched, and if we find him he gets a fair trial."

"Like the other two hundred here," I said.

"You try the kilns and do less talking."

"What about the notice?" asked Justin, holding up a paper.

"O, aye, the notice," said Flannigan. "Now listen all! It was George Martin who pulled in Tom Rhayader, for he is behind the military, every move. We owe him one back and by God he'll get it. We are taking his gates next, but first he'll have notice – much more difficult to explain London. You with me?"

Good humour, now, with the men nudging and loving every minute.

"So hearken," shouted Flannigan. "Justin by here is good at writing, so Justin turned this out," which put the men into stitches for Justin was no scholar. "We will post this up to-night," and he read from the paper:

" ' Take Notice. I wish to give especial notice to those who have sworn to be constable in order to grasp 'Becca and her children, but I can assure you it will be too hard a matter for Bullin to finish the job that he began. . . .' "

His voice boomed on, telling of the gates that were soon to come down, and ended:

" 'As for the constables and the policemen Rebecca and her children heeds no more of them than the grasshoppers that fly in the summer, for the gates will be burned to the ground. Faithful to death with the county, Rebecca and her daughters.' "

Muffled cheers at this, especially for the poetic bits about grasshoppers and summer, and Flannigan shouted. "George Martin will lose some sleep now that Justin's started writing him love letters. Matthew Luke John – have this pinned up in the town before dawn light," and the boy I had met on my first burning sprang up to take it. "Next meeting Wednesday," said Flannigan. "Come armed and disguised, and we will burn every gate to do honour to Tom Rhayader, our old Rebecca. Right, meeting closed. Jethro!"

I went to him.

"You will search the kilns for Joey Scarlet?"

"Yes, Abel," I said, sickened.

The men crept out of the quarry and over the mountain to their homes.

I took the path home through Waldo's preserves again. A wet bitch of a night now for spring with the wind owl-screeching like a lost soul, right old music when searching for informers. Black and spooky was the wood now with the branches rattling for skeletons as I skidded down to the limekiln humps. I walked much slower as I came in sight of the kilns, for if Joey had blabbed about Rhayader his mood would now be murderous with conscience and fear. So I came on tiptoe the last few yards, going on all fours in the peat at the first tang of the kiln fires, wiped rain from my eyes and peered.

Joey was lying face down on the slaking-rim with a shroud of canvas pulled up to his ears, his body black against the glow of the fires.

"Joey!" Behind the bole of a tree, kneeling, I called.

This brought him upright.

"Who's there?"

"Mortymer," I shouted back.

"What you want with me, Mortymer?"

"Didn't see you at the meeting tonight," I shouted.

"To hell with the meeting and to hell with Rebecca."

"And Tom Rhayader in particular, Joey? You heard about Tom?"

This brought him to his feet, standing on the rim, white as a ghost in his dusting of lime. Hair plastered, rags fluttering, he peered for me, but I had already seen the gleam of his powder-gun and kept under cover.

"You alone?" he called.

"Aye."

"Then why don't you come out, man?"

"Not likely," I shouted. "Not considering what you did to Tom Rhayader."

Stiff he stood, then his hands went to his face.

"O, God," he said.

"You sold a Christian man, Joey Scarlet, God help you. You know what will happen if Justin lays hands on you?"

Kneeling now, he wept, crying as a child cries. "Mortymer! Drunk, I was, I swear it!" he shouted. "I'd never have done it sober. O, help me, Mortymer – pretty tidy you was to me in the old days, remember?" He was wringing his hands now, giving peeps for listeners, standing above the slaking-pit as something in the steam of hell, his face wet with tears and rain.

"Joey!" I shouted. "Are you listening? Up and away with you – hoof it out of the county. Put as much room as you can between you and Rebecca – and never mention the name of Rhayader again, for if Justin Slaughterer don't land you another slaughterer will. Where's your mam?"

"Shropshire county, sin-eating," he whimpered.

"Right then, move. Away with you quick, for if I get a sight of you round here again I'll do what Justin's aching to do – rid the world of another Judas. Away!"

Gibbering now, biting at his hands, God-blessing me, scampering around the wall of the pit, gathering up his possessions and bundling them into the canvas.

And I saw quite clearly the hand that rose from behind and pushed him.

Joey teetered on the edge of the slaking-pit, and screamed. Slowly he turned, snatching at air, his bundles flying, and he wheeled towards me as he fell face down, arms and legs spreadeagled, screaming once more as he hit the boiling lime, and the end of his scream was scalded into silence. In horror I leaped from my hiding place, racing up the mound to the rim of the pit, turning away from the stew that was Joey. The undergrowth was crashing to the passage of the murderer. Sickened, I turned.

"Joey," I said.

The slaking lime bubbled his answer, speaking for his soul for the next million years.

CHAPTER 20

MAY WAS flooding into us now and the lanes were glorious with primroses and celandine. Golden my country now, the fields shimmering with buttercups and dandelions and the old burn was stoking up for a furnace of a summer. O, sweet is wet-a-bed days, with the taste of the gold in the milk and the chops of the cows all plastered with yellow petals as they peep through the hedges at strangers, grinning their joy of fat udders and milkmaids, dripping their beads of silver spit. And the whole rolling county was alive and shimmering breathless with the promise of a belly-full harvest by day and weeping in dew for the rusted ploughs at night. Few fields were ploughed near us for the levy on corn and the tolls were killing us. But up and down the country the gates were going up in flames, with scores of Rebeccas and hundreds of men riding every night, winning the race of building and burning. Magistrates were shivering in their beds, horses of the dragoons dropping dead in the fruitless gallops after Rebecca; lost in the maze of a country we knew backwards, redirected, misdirected, laughed to scorn, publicly insulted. The military heads were being recalled and replaced, the military stations were strengthened, all to no avail. Rebecca grew as an army in numbers. The Trusts were being defeated, and knew it.

I had been out burning most nights since Joey's death at the kilns. Down had come the special constables, of course; notebooks, pencils, all very official, but it was not worth risking to tell what had happened and a week or two after the inquiries ceased. We had hooked Joey out, what was left of him, and buried him decent in a pauper's grave, with Dai Alltwen embalming him with the biblical and talk of the All-Seeing Eye that watches the fall of the sparrow, and a day later Joey Scarlet had never existed. Reckon I know who got Joey but I never had the proof of it, for nobody was steadier than Justin Slaughterer on the day Joey went down in his wooden suit.

Tom Rhayader was still at St Clears awaiting justice and his woman and kids long gone to the workhouse, Carmarthen. Talk of a Rebecca attack on this workhouse was in the wind at the night meetings now, for our people were starving in it, said Flannigan. Something's got to be done, the Rebeccas said. How can we sleep while our kinfolk starve. Floggings were being talked about, too, though we had no proof of this. A pig of a Master at Carmarthen house especially, it was said. Starve to death or be beaten to death, were the rumours. Gather the evidence and we will raze the place, said Rebecca – we will burn it as we burned Narberth house, and bring out our people. Then for some floggings, we will show who is master.

The strain of the night meetings were taking toll of me – in just before dawn sometimes, going on shift with Morfydd at the pit after an hour of sleep. Coming pretty gaunt were most of the daughters of Rebecca, very severe this night courting on little growing maids, the men joked. I looked in the mirror one day and saw my face, lined, shadowed, and the haggard swellings beneath my eyes. Nigh eighteen, is it? said Morfydd, you look like forty, then some, there's a damned sight. Mam and Mari must have noticed this but they made no mention; just quick glances over the table with the buttoned-up air of women disapproving, Mam believing it was a misspent life. I often wonder if my mother knew the truth, for most women did. Even the parish was complaining about the drop in the birth rate, so the joke went, with the men out burning every night when they should have been back home loving. But things were coming a mite better, people said. Now the gates were coming less we were having whey and rye bread twice a day instead of once, thank God for mercy. But we were all right at Cae White with double money coming in from coaling though the farm had gone to pot. Do not mind me, said Morfydd – why should farming pay while I can crawl round Ponty like a bloody donkey, one eye cocked for Job Gower Foreman.

"It will not be for ever, Morfydd," I said.

"Damned right you are," said she. "Remember it. But do not hurry, man, I am loving every minute."

"Easy," I said. "It is not my fault."

"Perhaps not, but I am sick of it!"

I had been watching Morfydd lately. Touchy, to say the least of it; silent in our walks to Ponty, ready for the quarrel, eyebrows up, flushing over nothing. Change of life, said Mam. Treat her kindly, Jethro, or account for it to me.

"Be damned for a tale," I said. "She's only turned thirty."

"You are discussing something you do not understand," replied Mam. "Kindly cease this conversation directly."

"Change of life, indeed – she is good for years yet. There is Mrs Evan ap Rees over at Llansaint carrying for her sixth and she is over fifty."

"Mrs Evan ap Rees has not worked in the heat of iron," replied Mam "Neither has she towed trams, neither has she starved half her life by the size of her. Now cease, it is most embarrassing."

"She will have no more babies, is it?"

"If she does I will want to know why," said Mam. "Leave it now, I am coming to a flush again myself. Just treat her gentle."

"Just gently, Jethro," said Mari, smiling up from her corner. "It will pass."

Expect no kisses from the mouth of a vixen.

"How are you today now?" I asked, very pleasant.

"Go to the devil," said Morfydd.

"Asking after your health, I am. Anything wrong with that?"

"Ask about Towey's," she replied, staring. "Towey can't be bothered now."

We were alone in the kitchen that night – Mam out delivering somewhere, Mari with flowers down at church, the boys up in bed.

This set me quiet. I did not see Towey catch it, being down with Muldooney in Number Two gallery at the time, but I had heard of it from him. Tripped on the top ladder rungs, had Towey, and fallen the whole hundred feet, clothes round her ears, head-diving, with her basket of coal coming down after her, collecting the other carriers. And they followed Towey down, all five of them, with their coal pouring on top of them, giving them a decent burial. Two Welsh women, a couple of Irish, and a Spanish boy aged ten. A long way for a soul to travel to Spain. "These bloody old ladders," said Liam, the first time I had heard him swear in anger. "I will rig one on St Paul's for the aristocracy of England, though long before that it will be worn out by Welsh squireens."

"I am sorry about Towey," I said to Morfydd now.

"Missus, to you," said she, touchy.

"We will have you up from the pit directly."

"And scrape on your eleven shillings a week? You see to your own business and leave me to mine, Jethro. I was born to coal and I will die in coal – you just go on burning gates, the farm can go to hell, isn't it?"

"Morfydd, the farm will not pay. I tried it." She did not pull away when I took her from the sink and held her. "O, *fach*," I said. "What is wrong these days?"

And she bent her head, and wept.

"Old Mrs Towey, is it?"

"No, the boy. So little, he was. Got to love him. I saw his face when I lifted his chin, and thought of my Richard – could have been Richard, mind – only a few years older. O, God!" And she swung in my arms and gripped me. "Now, listen, Jethro, listen. I will kill someone if this farm goes flat and my boy goes into coal – I will hold you responsible." She lowered her hands. "Nothing left for me, I am finished – I am coal outside and in now; corns on my knees that do credit to a horse. Dyed in coal, I am, in my mouth, my chest, my heart," and she gripped her wrist making the veins stand out proud. "Look now, coal rivers I am, not normal flesh and blood, going to a prune with the towing, stinking of coal, coughing coal; dried of my womanhood and just over thirty. D'you hear me?" Her eyes were wide and strangely bright and I saw the lashes and brows still rimmed black after the washing.

"As a pillar of salt, I am," she said, "useless to a bed, and I have longed for more children – ten if I'd had my way. Now too late."

I turned to the window.

"Saw little Towey yesterday," she said. "I helped pull them off her and cart her out of it. God, there's a mess, and I am used to messes. It didn't worry me much, seeing Towey. But, O, God, that boy!" She covered her face.

Just useless standing there. I went to the window. The fields were ablaze beyond, all over golden with buttercups. Quietly, behind me, she began to cry again, and I went to her and touched her.

"Keep away from me," she said.

I longed for Mari to come in just then, for there are places in a woman not even a brother can invade.

"You are leaving the pit," I said. "Today."

"You starting farming again, then?" she asked. "Is Randy getting sick of it? Aye, I'll take on. One pair of shafts is as good as another and at least I'd be towing in daylight."

"That was cruel," I said.

I turned to her. Strange it did not seem like Morfydd standing there, and strange, too, that she was smiling. Terrible is coal, reaching out its fingers for those who carve it; drawing their souls into its seams, making them one with it though hating it; taking over the brain.

"Jethro."

I did not reply.

"I am sorry," she said, and went to the table and gripped the edge of it and bent, her eyes clenched. "Do not go, Jethro," she said as I reached the door, and she turned to me.

"Come here, boy."

I went to her and she straightened. "There now," said she. "It has passed. There is a swine of a sister for you, cursing and swearing, and not your fault. Don't tell Mam, is it?"

I shook my head.

"No living soul?"

"Nobody, but you are leaving the pit."

She did not hear me. "Jethro . . ." she whispered, smiling. "Hold me. Do not let me go."

I held her, and she was trembling.

"You listening, boy?" she whispered, and I nodded against her face.

"Jethro, I am going into coal – as Liam Muldooney, and Towey, and Gwallter – and Dada. . . ."

"O, for God's sake!" I said, and tried to throw her off but she clung as if sewn to me.

"I have seen the leaf," she said. "I saw it yesterday – down in Number Six, before old Towey came down with the others. O, clear as day was that leaf in every vein, with a million years engraved on the shine! You heard what the old ones say about Number Six? As the leaf is pressed in coal, so will I become part of coal. Terrible is that Number Six. Day after day the props go down, it will have us for sure. First leaf seen for ages, this one."

I held her off. "You will never see it again," I said. "Forget the leaf."

She smiled then, changed. Brilliant was that smile.

"Not bloody having me, is it?"

I looked at her.

"Not sharp enough by halves, eh?" And she whistled a note or two and snatched at her bonnet, tying the ribbons under her chin, turning her head at me, dimpling, changed. "You like this old hat, Jethro Mortymer?"

"Seen worse," I said. "You are leaving Gower today, understand?"

"Gracious, no. I am seeing out the year now I've started, I am having my wages. But never mind about Gower. What you say about this new bonnet?"

"Wonderful," I said to please her.

She put her hand to her waist and postured, swinging her hips. "Not bad for thirty-two, is it? Come on, boy, be honest. I still get the eye, mind, when I walk down the village. Very cosy, still drive the chaps demented. Reckon I might meet Willie O'Hara tonight; give the boy a treat, begging like a dog, poor soul."

"That is better," I said, relieved.

"Down on the Burrows. You ever gone courting on the Burrows down by the sea?"

"My business," I said.

"O, beautiful is summer! And the moon comes up over the sea very tidy, very romantic, and the air is warm and sweet. Gentleman is Willie O'Hara, remember. Don't let them tell you otherwise, Jethro. Might even marry little Willie, all two yards of him, you astonished?"

"No, Morfydd."

"Cowman over at Kidwelly, good job, and ambitious. Might do worse, come to think of it."

"Bring him home, then."

"Eh, steady," said she. "Mam would have him in bits. And I am trying him first, anyway, to see what stitches him together. Let you know later. Goodbye."

"Goodbye," I said.

"Give my love to Mam and Mari. Back before midnight, God willing."

As a young girl she went, bonnet tilted back, ribbons fluttering, and I stood by the door watching her as she went towards the Reach.

I covered my face.

As long as I live I will remember that May night, but not because of Morfydd. Strange it is how Fate strikes twice, sometimes within the hour; as if it brings its clenched fist to the face, crouched for the felling blow. With the house empty save for the boys asleep upstairs I was wandering about the kitchen lost, dying for Mam or Mari to come home, when a tap came on the door, and I opened it.

Effie Downpillow stood there.

Fresh from Monmouthshire was Effie; come back home to her county when the Top Town furnaces blew out, and scrubbing for Osian Hughes and his mam this past week, no more. Last Sunday at Chapel we all saw Effie, a little rag of a woman no older than Morfydd but belted by iron into skin and bone. She made spare money, she said, by selling her hair for wigs to gentry; sitting at home for weeks bald as a badger, rubbing in oils until the next harvest, but I never had the proof of it for she was pretty well shod when Osian took her in. Strange little woman this, and with dignity, though her legs and feet were bare. And at her first chapel Sunday I saw her eyeing me from the back pews, treating me important.

"You Jethro Mortymer?" she whispered now, hugging herself.

"Yes," I said.

"The man of the Mortymer family, is it?"

I nodded, wondering.

"You asking me in, man?"

"Aye, come on," I said.

Wandering in, hugging herself for winter, looking around with a vacant stare, and bags under her eyes like the fleshpots of Jerusalem.

"Over at Osian Hughes, I am," she said.

I nodded, watching.

"Sit down, is it?"

"Yes," I said. "Sit down." And she sat, perched as a bird, with her white hair hanging down either side of her face.

"You called to see my mam, Effie Downpillow?" I asked.

"Called to see you," she said, so I sat down opposite, wishing her to the devil. Her eyes drifted around the room.

"Used to scrub here once," she said. "For old Grandfer, before I took my two-room tumbledown up by Osian Hughes. Been away years, see – following the iron up to Monmouthshire, where you come from." And she smiled of a sudden, leaning towards me. "You heard about my man, Sam Miller – his dad being in flour?"

"No," I answered.

Strange, those eyes. In repose one moment, wild with their inner madness the next.

"Good grief, man. And my Sam foreman puddler over at Blaina – next place to yours – Nantyglo, isn't it?"

"Who told you that?" I asked, more interested.

"Never mind who told me. Strikes me I'm on the wrong chap – you've never seen the sky over Nanty and Blaina if you didn't know my Sam. Best puddler-man the county ever had, was Sam. Marched with the men of the Eastern Valley when

they went to hit up Newport. Reckon you know Abel Flannigan, Biddy's boy?"

"Aye, I know Abel."

"There's bright. My Sam could give him a good two inches
up and a foot sideways. Dear God, you never seen such a man
for looks and fortifying. Aye! Topped six feet naked and as
broad as a barrel, with a smell of caulking tar and tobacco about
him, being of ships. Up Whitland way, you understand."

"Look, Miss Effie," I said. "I will tell my mam you called
and you come back later, is it?"

"And me been waiting till the three women were out?
Damned days I have waited. A monkey-tail had Sam, you see.
Fine, fine, he looked – worked the big two-riggers down in
Saundersfoot till he heard the iron call and made for Blaina.
Eh, God!" She narrowed her eyes. "Shoulders on him like
two bull heifers, eyes as black as coal and the grip of his arm
could break a woman's back. You seen such a man, Jethro
Mortymer?"

"Not lately," I said, pitying her. "You've been waiting till
my women were out?"

"Never mind that now," she replied. "Will you hear about
Sam?"

"Aye," I answered, eyeing her, and her voice went low and
sweet:

"Well, outside my tumbledown I found him," said she.
"Nigh six years back, could be more. Drunk as a coot, he was –
his friends forced it on him, see – down in that stinky old Black
Boar tavern. So I came out with my barrow and wheeled him in
– never had a man under a roof before – and I stripped him and
washed him clean. Like a baby he was in that washing, my Sam,
but I covered him well, mind, keeping it decent."

"Go on," I said, kinder, for she was with purity.

"Well, then I got him in the sheets, hit out my last little hen,
made him hot broth and fed him like a mother – bellowing all
through it, of course – but I got it down him." She raised her
face, screwing at her hands. "But there was only the one bed,
see, and he was cold to shivering. So in with me quick beside
him for thawing, it being winter. Was that improper?"

"No, Effie," I said.

"Slept without a snore, he did, by here," and she held her breast. "On here, you understand, where a man's head should be? You ever slept that way, boy?"

"Not yet."

A silence fell between us then and she lowered her head, picking at her ragged dress. I longed for my mother to come then. Thank God she did not.

"But . . . but men get drunk by night and come sober by morning," she whispered. "And in dawn light Sam woke and parted my hair and looked me in the face. Just one look, mind, then up with him screaming – one jump to the door and through it streaming bedsheets, hollering blue murder down the village. Can you explain such behaviour, Jethro Mortymer?"

I shook my head, and she smiled wistful, head on one side. "Scared of females, perhaps – him being of ships and with men all his years, for these sailor men don't know much about women, you see." She smiled, straightening. "But he did not go for good, remember. I still have my Sam for lovering, remember. And at night I do know the heat and strength of him and his childer leaping within me, down by here," and she held herself, smiling.

"Gone for good, then?" I asked.

"Good God, no. Do you think us women give up so easy? I tracked him. He sailed from Saundersfoot to Newport and unloaded himself for the Monmouthshire iron and legged it down to Blaina. But he opened his mouth in Black Boar tavern before he went, and I followed him to Blaina on foot. Aye, to Blaina town I went – barefoot, and I nailed him. 'Sam Miller,' I said, 'you have shared a bed with this Effie. Would you put me to shame and leave me stranded? Make me decent, Sam Miller, lest you be judged for it.' " She grinned up at me with a naked mouth. "More than one way of hitting out hens, but it takes a woman to think of it. You interested?"

"And he married you?"

"Galloped to the altar, thinking me in child. Aye, decent! Damned good Welsh, that one; proud to lie with him. Pity such men die."

"He died?"

"Like a dog – going in the carts to Monmouth. He marched with the men of the Eastern Valley, to Newport. And they shot him down on the steps of the Westgate and tied him, and put him in the carts for Monmouth trials."

My heart was thumping now. Leaning, I gripped her wrist. "My brother was in those carts," I whispered.

"O, aye," said she. "That is why I am here. You got a sister-in-law here by the name of Mari?"

"Yes, yes!" I had hold of her now, drawing her up. "What of her?"

"And do you know a man called Idris Foreman, Blaenafon?"

"My father's foreman, my brother's friend. For God's sake, woman, what are you trying to tell me?"

"Just this," she said. "Iestyn, your brother, is dead."

I heard her but faintly, as through the veil of years.

"Aye, dead," she said. "He died with my Sam. Your brother, my Sam and Idris Foreman, Blaenafon. And a man called Shanco Mathews charged me to tell you. Four years I waited, starving in Nanty, and then the news came through, and Shanco told me. 'Go back home to your county, Effie girl,' he said. 'And if ever you happen on people called Mortymer, you tell Jethro, the son, that his brother is dead,' and he gave me two shillings to help on the journey. 'Tell Jethro the son, but keep it from his women, for all three will go mad. As mad as you, Effie Downpillow,' he said. You think me mad, Jethro Mortymer?"

"Sane as me," I said, weeping.

"And I happened by here and Osian Hughes took me in. Saw you last Sunday near Chapel – you and three women, and I asked who you were. It is the Mortymers, Osian told me, him being sweet on your Morfydd."

"Do you know how it happened?" I asked, broken.

"You know Griff and Owen Howells, the brothers?"

"Aye, I know them."

"Well, Griff died, too, though Owen got clear – over in transportation, mind, like I hoped for my Sam," and she sighed. "I knew the Howells boys – they were more than just twins –

they shared the same plate, sparked the same women, drew the same breath, hand in hand in the womb. . . ."

"Tell me," I said.

"Well, the redcoats crammed them in the carts for Monmouth, with Sam, your Iestyn and Idris in one and the Howells boys in the cart following – standing and singing along the road to Monmouth, but Griff Howells was silent, standing stone dead. It took half a mile of whispers and kisses, said Shanco, before Owen Howells screamed and went into bedlam for the death of his twin. Over the cart side he went, bringing down redcoats, and all twelve carts stopped because of the palaver, with muskets going and redcoats swiping at Owen who was mad losing Griff. And Idris Foreman slipped out in the commotion and dragged my Sam and your brother after him, and they dived like demons for the open country. But the soldiers came up and gave them a volley, and the only one who got clear was Shanco Mathews from a cart farther down."

"They killed him?"

"The three of them. Idris, my Sam, your brother Iestyn."

"And not so much as a word," I said, thumping the chair.

"O, God," said Effie. "Were they important?" She sighed. "If you happen on the Mortymers you tell the boy Jethro, said Shanco Mathews – leave it to young Jethro, for there's a woman in that three who will march on Victoria."

"Go now," I said.

"Eh, so early – with the evening to myself? Now, listen, little man – have you heard about Sam, my man, Sam Miller?"

I raised my eyes and she swam, distorting.

"Dear God," said she. "You've never seen a man like my Sam for looks. Topped six feet naked, he did, and as broad as a barrel, with a smell of caulking-tar about him, being of ships . . . Jethro Mortymer, you are not listening!"

Through the door I went, swinging it shut. I walked, walked, praying for Mari. And the world was dark in a blustering wind, not a glimmer of light.

CHAPTER 21

BACK FROM Ponty, coal-grimed, sweaty, I broke it to Mari that night, and the face of Fate changed. For days I had gripped it to myself with love and duty tearing different ways. And I bided my time. Mam was over at Flannigan's place for a tongue-pie with Biddy, Morfydd was out courting with Willie O'Hara. Out every night now, Morfydd – snatching at life, grasping every second in false laughter, and I longed to get her from Ponty. And Willie O'Hara was another worry with Morfydd in this mood. She had fallen before and she might fall again, and we had enough to contend with. And this Willie not so simple as he looked, according to Abel Flannigan – stretching more aprons in the northern shires than gentry ham teas and come down west to start it again.

Hot from labour I came to the back and leaned against the shed, wiping with a sweat rag, cooling off in the shade when I heard Mari singing. She was flapping around the kitchen with her pots and pans and Richard and her son Jonathon were hammering something out at the front, shouting and playing. I listened. I am not one for singing, but being Welsh I am in love with the throat and its wondrous noises, and I stood there in sadness listening to Mari. Beautifully she sang in the minor key, tuning in to the great Welsh hymns. Is there a voice in the world more lovely than that of a woman working, unsuspecting? Thin is the note, plaintive, trembling wobbly to the lifting of pans and stoopings, snatching at breath. Closing my eyes I leaned and listened, and Mari's voice drifted out to me on the heat-laden air with its message of the moors and mountains of Mother Wales and her muted sadness. In the knowledge of God we sing, with words that spring from the Books of the Testaments; rising from the great believers, from the organ lofts of those who have clutched at glory, in praise of Him. The voices of sopranos are of the alders where streams are leaping, each silver leaf rimmed with the autumn stain. Welsh tenors, to me, are the tree's upper branches, but the bole beneath gnarled as a fist, clenched for the singer's hook of manhood. Bass comes as roots to me; of grovelling limbs sapbound in darkness, splitting forth in thunder from the belted bellies of men defiant.

The soul of Wales is the throat of its people.

Mari now. Had to tell her somehow. And her song stopped dead at the sight of my shadow, flung into crippledom over the flags. Heard her step then, saw her eyes.

"Mari," I said.

Beautiful, those eyes.

"You frightened me."

"I am sorry," I said.

Just stood there watching her, and she smiled and shrugged and turned to go.

"No, Mari, wait," I said, and reached out, taking her hand and drawing her closer. My throat was dust-dry, the lump rising, and I took a deep breath.

Out with it, no other way. Better do it quick as a smack in the face.

"Iestyn is dead."

She smiled faintly. "I know," she said.

The hammering of the boys drifted between us in Jonathon's treble shrieks of joy as Richard got a hammer to something, thudding away, thudding . . . and sunlight flashed from the green of the fields, and the wind was sudden cool to my face.

"I know," she repeated. "O, poor Jethro."

I waited disbelieving, but knowing the truth of it in her eyes. And she looked past me towards the field, lips moving, then lowered her face.

"How did you learn, Jethro?"

"From Effie Downpillow three days back – come back from Monmouthshire, and told by a friend to bring me the news. But you . . . ? Who told you?"

She clasped her hands, her face was in repose.

"Tomos Traherne," she said. "When he called at Christmas years back."

"Tomos?"

197

"Came special to break the news."

"But Mam and Morfydd – do they know, too?"

"To tell you is my duty, said Tomos Traherne, let them live in the paradise of hope. So much can happen in a seven year transportation, people can die. And the wound comes shallow with the passing of time. No, Jethro, they do not know."

"But Tomos's duty was to them, too – to me, his brother!"

"Four years of your life you have not mourned him dead," she replied. "Most of the men in the carts got seven years transportation – I will run your poor mother to six and a half, said Tomos – no point in taking all she has left." She turned to me. "Who is the Effie woman?"

"A little iron-rag – been down here a week – saw her in Chapel last Sunday evening? She is living over at Osian Hughes Bayleaves."

"O, aye," she said, remembering. "Has Effie a tongue?"

"Two feet of it, and addled in the head."

"But she called here with you alone?"

"Three days back while the rest of the family were out."

"Addled, perhaps," she replied, "but I doubt if she will talk – she was brainy enough to pick her time. Still, I will speak to her."

"And you know how he died."

"Yes, I know. And I am proud. Hitting it out in the carts for Monmouth, that is how he died, and best that way. For men like Iestyn were not born for the cage. No lash would drive him, no cruelties break him. Men like Iestyn are victors, not beggars – better he should stand in the light of the Father than scratch out a living in this pig of a place, as we. Can you imagine him landed with the troubles of Rebecca? 'Becca and her children, one to each village?" and she laughed deep in memory, her eyes alive. "He would rally them together for a march on London, and die there instead. No, Jethro, better this way."

"Perhaps," I said.

"Perhaps? I know it. Fighters are the Mortymers, and I am glad the blood is in my son. But it do not make for peace, Jethro. Remember it. It only breaks hearts. You stopping fighting one day?"

"Soon," I said.

She sighed deep. "Well, I am not begging you like I begged of my Iestyn. God help your woman, that is all I say." She walked to the end of the wall and leaned against it, her back towards me.

"Poor Jethro," she said, and reached out her hand. "A little pig, I am, forgetting you. Is it sad with you to tears, now you have lost your brother?"

I did not reply. Later, ashamed, I remembered only that she was near to me, that she was free, that she could be mine. For the wind hit between us then in a sweep from the fields and my arms reached out and caught her against me and my lips sought her lips in the yard between us. Empty that yard, could have been miles.

"You love him still, don't you, Mari," I whispered.

"Yes, I love him," and she turned to me again. "Still decent people about, isn't it – with you loving me?"

"Aye, I love you. You guessed?"

"Years back, Jethro. Years. . . ." Her eyes moved over my face.

No heat in me, as for Jane at Black Boar; no longing that springs from the surge of manhood, no aches, no fires I felt. Just empty for her as a cask is emptied of wine. Desolate as I turned away to the wall. Eyes closed, not trusting myself, I thought she had gone, but I heard her breathing beside me.

"Jethro, not yet," she said.

I kept the yard between us, because of her eyes, and she gripped my hand, smiled, and went from me, closing the kitchen door.

I do not know how long I stood there. The boys came scampering round the back and they gripped my legs, swinging themselves around me and Jonathon leaped against me till I lifted him, kissing his face, setting him quiet, for I had not kissed him before. A joy rose high in me when I should have been grieving, and I kissed him again. Great the strength in me as I reached down and hooked Richard up beside him, and stood there holding the pair of them, one in each arm to the wideflung door.

"Jethro!" said Mari.

CHAPTER 22

Tomos Traherne came back to Cae White in June.

No Tom the Faith, this one, creeping in as a mouse. He came demanding, in a trap with a little brown pony, all polish and jingles, trotting down the road from Carmarthen, sending satans belly-sliding over the hedges at the sight of him sitting there with the reins in his hand and his big Bible beside him. Coffin black, enormous he sat, gowned and collared, his spade beard trembling in the fervour of his love, but not with the love of God. He came for the love of Mam.

"Tomos!"

Mam shoved pretty fast for the creaking joints of middle age – arms out, skirts billowing, thumping down the path to the trap and not even giving him time to get down. Up on the step she went and straight into his hug. And they sat, the pair of them, motionless in the clear summer air, and then he kissed her face.

"One less in the family or I'm mistaken," said Morfydd. "And her bouncing me about Willie O'Hara."

"God bless him for coming back," whispered Mari.

"She has always loved him – even when Dada was alive," I said.

"No doubt," said Morfydd. "This will settle Tom Griffiths and Waldo Bailiff. Hairpins falling, lovers calling – eh, just look at that!"

"Inside quick, it is not decent watching," said Mari, and swept us all in with her skirts. But I went to the window and watched them from there: speaking no words by the look of them, with Mam only up to his shoulder, gripping his arm down the path to the house, and Tomos smiling down. I will always remember how I saw them, walking down the path with the trap behind them, enwrapped in the love and respect that leaps from old friendship. We waited pent, the three of us, holding the boys steady from confusion as the door opened and they stood there hand in hand.

"He has come back," said Mam, her eyes bright. "The day he said he would, to the very hour."

"O, Tomos!" exclaimed Mari.

"To claim her," boomed Tomos. "Five minutes late for this one would make a man a fool."

"And not a word to the family, mind," I said. "Driving the men of the village demented, and pledged to another all the time!" I gripped his hand, drawing him in. "God bless you, Tomos. Mari, get the kettle on – Morfydd, lay the cloth. . . ."

"Eh, hark at the head of the family!"

"And am I not the head of the family – for who will give her away? Food first," I cried, "and then Mam will walk him twice round the village hand in hand to settle the suitors!"

"Suitors? What suitors?" rumbled Tomos, eyebrows bushing up.

"Now, hush!" cried Mam, going scarlet.

"Nothing to get bothered about, Tomos," said Morfydd, sitting him down. "Just a little trouble with the men, it is – always the same when attractive widows are loose, but we kept her on the right path."

"O, Morfydd, you vixen," said Mari.

And there was Mam beside him wriggling and blushing as a young girl, with protests, giggles and peeps at his face. It is at such times that you see the woman in the mother, I think, as an eye behind the white starched apron that prises at the secrets. And the heart you see is young again, beating fast; no longer a couch for your head, that breast, but soft to the touch of another, and the lips that have scolded and crooned at you are strange lips for kissing, and red. Strange is the bitterness; that another should lie in her bed, turning at midnight in the place I had moulded. So great her lover.

"Mind," said Tomos, getting the spirit of it. "If she has been tempted in my absence I will make inquiries, and heaven help her if she is found wanting. More than one suitor, is it?"

"Queueing at the door," I said.

"With flowers every Sunday," added Morfydd. "Wearing out knees with biddings and beggings. Another five minutes and you'd have been too damned late, man."

"Tomos, Tomos! Do not heed them!" begged Mari, pulling at him. "Indelicate, they are."

"Not very considerate to your mother, I must say," said Mam, sniffing.

"O, Mam!" we cried while Tomos guffawed.

"All very well," she answered, well into her dignity. "But anyone human is likely to take it wrong."

Up with us then, dancing around her, pulling at her and kissing her, with Mari taking swipes at us and the boys screaming with joy. And there was Tomos with his arms around her consoling and teasing her in turn till we got her back mellow. Tea then, everyone happy, sitting at the table well into dusk, with Tomos telling us of his journey down and the state of things back home in Nanty.

"And so," said he, "after these years I return to you, fulfilling the promise I made to your mother that, should she remain unwed, I would offer her marriage and a home. . . ." Deep and pure was his voice as we sat in respectful silence. "I come in humility," said he, "having little to offer save food and a bed, being of little money. Yet I offer her more than life itself if I offer her service in the way of the Lord. For did she not spring from the black cloth of the manse? And is it not true that service to His children is the true path to joy? Elianor . . ." and here he used her name the first time I had heard it since the days of my father. "Will you come back with me to Nantyglo, to the town you learned to hate because of your Hywel who died there, and give me the chance to teach you how to love it?"

I stayed just long enough to see her touch his hand. Golden, this tongue, deep and sincere his offer. I knew my mother would not refuse him, this friend of my father, though I could not bear to see her accept a continuation of the poverty she had borne so long. Tomos would set her soul in diamonds, leaving her body to fend with sackcloth, yet this, I knew, was the way she would prefer it; this was how she was raised; as a flower pressed in the leaves of the Book of God, ending her life on the arm of Tomos, loving my father in the bed of his friend.

Dusk and bats had dropped over Cae White as I stood there

at the back listening to the laughter of Morfydd inside, the excited chatter of Mari, the protests of Richard and Jonathon as they were hooked up to bed. Silence was about me save for wind-whisper and the flea-scratching of crickets. The hens were still loose in the shippon, walking the path in their spiked, measured tread, the cockerel standing in his petrified confusion, mouthing unholy thoughts. I remembered the old days of Blaenafon where I was born and the care my mother took over her chickens; as a young girl she was then with her unbridled laughter; her childlike joy at finding an egg, her tears when my father brought in the lifeless body of a hen knocked off for the pot. The business of living had ground out the joy now, leaving her empty. Only in her God would she find solace, and Tomos had plenty of God. Heard the door click behind me as I moved to pen the chickens against the fox, and I turned. The mountain of Tomos drew beside me, and he gripped my shoulder, smiling down.

"To you I come, Jethro, not to your sisters, for you are the man of the Mortymers now. To you I come for blessing."

"You have it in full," I answered.

"From your heart now?"

"From my heart," I said. "My father would have wanted it."

He leaned on the rail beside me, frowning into the dusk, and the rail creaked at him and I sensed the power of him, and some of the soul.

"You will be good to her, Tomos."

He nodded.

"And gentle, as my father was gentle."

"As my Father do hear me, I love her," he whispered. "As He is witness, I have loved her from the day we met, Jethro, never coveting that which was my friend's, but loving, nevertheless, and I seek no forgiveness since Man is twopenny clay. This I tell you now, as man to man, that I have not sought her with my body as I have sought other women in the days of my youth, and found them wanting. For I met her when the soul enmeshed the body, draining it of fire." He chuckled deep, and grunted. "Just now you left too early for decency, and your mother, I could see, wondered why. But there are looks between men that need no explanation, so I came to tell you something to remember. In the bed of our marriage your mother will hold me when I am dispirited or fierce to the injustices. This and her presence is all I seek of her, asking nothing more, save that she keeps me fed. Aye, the fire has died, Jethro, and it is peaceful, and she is in love with your father."

"You know this, then?"

"She has never been short of a tongue. She made that clear four years back when I called at Christmas."

"Best you should know, Tomos."

"Aye." He sighed. "A man such as Hywel do take some shifting."

"We will miss her. Could you not live here?"

"No, my place is back with my people who need me. But there is a bed for any one of you, remember it. You will be welcome since I will be your father."

"Thank you," I said.

"Jethro." The tone of his voice turned me. "Jethro, another thing. Just now, on the stairs I spoke to Mari. You know about your brother?"

"Yes."

He nodded. "When I heard of Iestyn's death I hurried to tell Mari, for it was my duty. I owe the same duty to Morfydd and your mother, but I will not tell them. I stopped my mouth to them four years back, and I will not tell them now. Mari had to know because she was young and with her life before her, that is why I came that Christmas. But I will never tell your mother. Better for her to live in hope – already I have saved her years of grief. She believes he is in transportation for seven years. A lot can happen in three more years. You agree?"

I shrugged.

"And Mari?" he said.

"What of Mari?"

"She is in love with you, do you know?"

I swung to him, searching for his eyes shadowed under the bushy brows.

"She told you?" I whispered.

"Aye." He lit his pipe and played with the tinderbox. "Just now. And you love her, I hear it in your voice. Take her then, when you can afford it, but tread wary for youth is fire. Gently with her remember, until you are sure that Iestyn has gone. Hell it can be sitting in a kitchen with another man opposite."

I pitied him.

"Two in one boat," he said, grinning. "Though mine is but a ten year marriage, perhaps a little longer. Yours is for life."

He straightened then.

"I am going back in now," he said. "For women are as wary as cats at times like this. You coming?"

"Yes," I said. "But first I will lock the hens. Tomos. . . ."

He turned, black in the coming of night, smiling.

"Tomos, will you send Mari to me?"

"God bless the loyalty and love in this house," he said. "I will send her. She will help you catch the waywards hens, is it?"

I waited until he was back in the kitchen then went into the shippon and gathered the hens. There by the henhouse I waited. I saw the door come open again; heard Mari's footsteps.

"Over by here," I said, and she came.

"The old cockerel again, is it?" she asked, peering about her.

"They are all safe in bed," I answered. "Mari . . ." and I took her hand.

For the first time in my life I felt her near me.

"Mari, Mari!" I whispered, and drew her into my arms.

"Jethro!" she said as I kissed her.

And her arms went about me hard and strong as I bent above her, kissing her, kissing her, and I knew the trembling of her. Warm were her lips, snatching at breath.

"Jethro," she said, but I heard no sound, just saw her lips. As rock were we to the pressure of mountains; locked; beating as one, together.

Summer warm was the wind of the estuary, and the night was silver and rimming the clouds, the full moon shafting the sea with a broadsword of light. Wave-thunder came from the beach still heaped and despoiled from the low tide hunting of cockle-women, its forehead fringed with dark lines of weed. In my arbour of rocks above the beach I waited and great was the excitement within me, my heart thumping to the turn of the stones, waiting. Waiting for Mari at the end of the sheep track that led from Squire's Reach.

Eerie is the Burrows in moonlight, this place of rabbits and honeycombed with lairs; a refuge of steepled ears and screams: home of the fox, the bared teeth of vixens, the prancing death dances of stoats, the madbrained leapings of the March hares. And ghosts walk here, it is said. Here float the faces of murdered seamen, the souls of the sea, victims of plunder, walking out of the waves with seaweed for shrouds, in search of decent graves. Sitting alone I stared at the sea, seeing again the storm-tossed barques plunging to the swinging beacons of the criminal wreckers, wallowing, their decks awash, streaming to their doom on the outcrop rocks. And I saw again the falling cudgels, heard the screams of ancient crews as they staggered half drowned to the butchery of their brothers.

But this place of wraiths is the arbour of lovers, for ghosts are forgotten in the heat of kisses, and because of its name the Burrows were free of peepers. One pair of eyes was enough to have us round the village. So I waited, dry in the mouth and trembling, for Mari to come.

I fell to wondering, then, how many kisses had been given and taken in this haven clear of the sea, and new visions rose on the crested waves. Flying pennants I saw then; the curved bows of foreign invaders came driving in on the surf. Lance and mace flashed in fierce sunlight, swords were raised high. Invading banners I saw, strange tongues I heard, naked legs splashed to the shores as the horde drove in to lock in battle with the fur-clad ancients. Flung spears I saw, the skull-splitting hatchets, the new tide bloodstained to the wallowing dead. And then the conquest, the drunken goblets of the conquerors, the chained oars of the conquered creaking on the road to Rome.

But then I thought of lovers, the giving and taking of foreign kisses in this place where I was waiting to make love to Mari.

Roman warrior and Saxon maiden, conquering Greek and Celtic matron; mouth on mouth, breast against breast on this same sand while the same moon as mine, hooded and broody as a Benedictine monk, pulled up his skirts to shield his eyes as two became one. By here, just where I was sitting. Plaited hair I saw, the Nordic breast, the armour flung aside. I touched the rock beside me, feeling under my fingers its dumb eternity. O, that it had eyes and a mouth with which to speak that it might tell of my people from the time of the club; talk of the tears, the sighs, the laughter of children, the riven steel of the armour, the crumpled skirt. Here the invader, pining in his dreams of columned cities, has leaped to the arms of the humble cottager and buried his longing in the tumult of her breathing.

"Jethro!"
And the visions were banished in the shock of reality. Leaping up, I swung to her voice.

Mari, standing above me, her hands clasped, smiling down.
"You came!" I gasped.
"But not for long, mind – Mam will soon miss me."

Joyful that we were together I reached up and lifted her down beside me, and we stood clasped, shivering at the sudden nearness after the barren years of standing apart.

"Anyone see you?"
"Good grief, I saw to that. Came on all fours round the edge of the Reach!" Holding my hands she looked about her, then up at the moon, her eyes coming wide and bright as if startled. "O, Jethro, what a lovely place!"

"Secret," I whispered, holding her. I felt her heart thumping, thumping.

"And you behave," she whispered back.
"I've been doing that years," I said. "O, Mari!"
"Then another half an hour won't do you any harm," and she kissed my face. "What happens now?"

"Down by here," I said, squatting at her feet, patting sand.
"O, aye?"

The wind had her hair, whirling it about in a sudden warm gust from the sea, and she stood above me, tying it back, patting it, smoothing it, with downward flashes of smile, knowing her mastery.

"Down here," I said, dragging at her skirt.

"Safer up standing. I know you Mortymers."

Gave her ten seconds to enjoy her mastery, then I rolled towards her snatching at her ankle and pulled her kneeling in a cry of laughter. Whirling like a sand-crab I was there beside her, and I lay there holding her helpless while she shivered and giggled. Young again, girlish again . . . the years of sitting and darning over, the barrier crumbling. I was just content to lie there holding her, my face above her, her lips an inch from mine, waiting. Waiting for the final crash of the barrier, the rolling dust of its storm to drift to the sea. And there was no sound but breathing and wavelap to the incoming tide. Eyes shut tight, her face was turned away; as Morfydd lying there; the same deep shadows of her cheek; black her lips in that misty light. Smoothing her hair, I lay, watching, contented at last, whole for the first time in my life, since she was near. Strange is love in these moments of quiet, this the proof of love; to lie without demanding. No jangle in this loving, no sweeping hands, no hotness then. I lowered my face to hers, and we lay, just breathing, listening to heartbeat, at peace. Wind-murmur was in the cave, and the sand beneath us thumping to the fist of the breakers, and I raised my head, seeing beyond the tangle of her hair an emblazoned sea of moonlight with the solitary sails of a lonely ship, three-masted, standing against a line of silver. And farther beyond were the wastes of the Atlantic, thousands of miles of nothingness to the seagull cries of the shores of Newfoundland, and farther still to Philadelphia where the ovens of iron flash at the sky. This my industry, the call of the iron; calling again as it forever called me. Strange the call at a time like this, crying to a man on the breast of a woman. *Pittsburgh!* The magic name where the molten stream flashes to a thousand moulds, and its red brick chimneys flame to the sky. Calling to the Welsh for its experts of iron, for the crafts-men who can set the curve of the furnace-arch, for the men who know the colour of the pilot flame before the cauldron is turned, the length of the firing-iron, the time to rake, to coal, the ore to burn, the grade of limestone and thickness of layer; for the men who are tuned to the clang of the bar and chalk the cross that guarantees perfection. In the stink of coal and tollgate farming the call leaped high to start a new life.

"What you thinking?" said Mari.

I stirred, suddenly aware of her, ringing her waist with my arm, drawing her against me.

"I am taking you away," I said.

"Aye?" she said.

"Because I love you. Because I am sick of fighting." I drew from her, and knelt, and she turned, cupping her chin on her elbow, following my finger.

"Nothing between us and America. Look. Nothing but sea and more sea, ships and gulls and sky. Go as an arrow and you crawl out on sand, Mari – to a new land, to a new life. Cae White is finished, Mari. There is nothing left here except hunger and labour; no chance for your Jonathon, no promise for my children," and I caught her hand, kissing it.

"Next Sunday," she said. "To travel costs money, sovereigns, mind, not shillings."

"Five pounds a head steerage, that is all," I answered.

"A fortune," she said.

"I will find it, somehow."

"What is this old steerage thing, then?" she asked.

"Working the passage, girl. Scrubbing and waiting, rope-coiling, tarring and labouring – cheaper steerage, see."

"Eh, more labour, is it? Whee, I would rather go cabins."

"Gentry, is it? Peacock feathers and parasols, is it? You be content with steerage."

"You go steerage, then. I will go cabins."

"Then near thirty pounds between us if we tie Jonathon to the yard-arm – where the hell do you think I am getting thirty pounds from, woman?"

"Got fifty," said she, "all but two shillings."

"How many toes has a pig got?"

"Take off your boots and count them," said she. "Fifty pounds be mine all but two shillings."

"O, aye? Not that much money in the county of Carmarthen. Addled, you."

"So addled that I will give you every penny, man, if you kiss me proper. O, *Jethro!* Do I come down here for the town of Philadelphia, or for loving?"

The way she looked, then, the way she smiled, her mouth reaching for kissing.

How can a man know the heart of a woman. Frigid to freeze one minute, the flash in the mould the next.

"Mari," I whispered.

As a mirage she was in the faint blue light, to be snatched at and lost in the parched desert of my longing. In the years of waiting I had been denied her, and now she was against me she still seemed a part of my dreaming; that the ghost of her would fade to the opening eyes. Yet the arms I held now were tensed and strong; no visions these arms; no mirage the eyes that lowered to the kiss, and her breathing no sighing of some distant wind. Sudden the tumult between us, as if the night had exploded in brilliance, leaving blackness that enveloped us, obliterating all save its gusty breath. Once she opened her eyes and looked at me with the look I have seen in the eyes of things trapped and shrinking to the grip of the iron jaw.

"Jethro!" she said, just once.

And I kissed her to silence, hearing nothing, reasoning nothing as the wall went down, thundering in the breast. Great is a man then with the shout of the Unborn thrusting within him, strident, demanding as the falcon's cry; leaping to heights of power and beauty, denying the kiss as breath snatches breath in a perfumed fire; this, the song of the honeyed middle, the quenchless song, the chord that leaps from the fountain of life, that chains the singer and sung as one, and, chaining, transcends them as one, in joy.

I kissed her, and her cheek was wet.

"Mari," I said.

A nightbird sang in the troubled light. Wave-thump I heard, the wind of the Burrows and blackness came as the moon fainted; gave him a glance above her head, and hated him. Generations of this and still he was virginal. But the stars still shone as if approving, with Orion beaming silver and Venus still waving at her latticed window her lamp that brought out Mars.

"Mari. . . ."

And she wept.

Something shrieked from the woods of the Reach and branches snapped in the clattering panic of wings, then all was stillness save for the sobbing restrictions of her breast, and she turned away her face as I bent to kiss her again. Three of us lying in sand, I knew; not one.

"Mari!" I said, and pulled her against me, forcing her to face me. "It is me, Jethro. It is Jethro who is loving you. Iestyn is dead."

She stared at me, then closed her eyes again and her lips trembled to the inward breath.

"My woman now," I said. "The past is past."

I knelt as she sat up, head turned away, fingers working in a frenzy, straightening, tidying: brush away sand, straighten the lace; then flew to her hair, smoothing, patting and there's a damned mess. Strange, these women.

"All over the place," I said.

"O, no! Is it?"

"Through a hedge backwards, then over the haystack," I said.

"And that Morfydd with eyes for a lynx," she said. "Hairpins, see. That is the trouble," and she went round on all fours, feeling and patting.

Never looked for hairpins in sand before. Please God I never do it again.

Like sea-urchins, the pair of us then; going in circles, holding up seaweed and shells, and excuse me, please, there's one behind you, sweeping and smoothing half an acre. We were yards apart when Mari smiled. As a prowling dog I saw that smile. Then she put her hands to her face and laughed. God was wise when He invented sense of humour. As baying hounds we knelt, laughing, pealing it to the sky, then I rose and leaped the distance between us and gripped her waist and bent, kissing her. Her hair was down now, waving to her waist. Beautiful the kiss, joyful the reunion.

"O, Jethro, I love you, love you!" she said.

I did not answer, having loved so long.

Two of us went home, and no Iestyn.

Should not tell of it really, too secret to tell; too hot the fire of that week when Tomos stayed at Cae White and kept Mam occupied. Night after night, come in from shift at Ponty, strip to the bare and wash the body clean, then down to the kitchen for the evening meal with secret glances over the table at Mari; the raised eyebrow of the evening question, the narrowed promise in her eyes for reply. Easy, too, with Morfydd out courting with Willie O'Hara; no prowling eyes, no listening ears.

"Think I'll go out, Mam."

Only too pleased to be rid of me, the pair of them, for it is only right that courting couples like Mam and Tomos wanted to be alone. And they made no complaints when Mari went for her summer night strolls, either ... summer night strolls down to the estuary where I lay waiting.

"Jethro, you there?"

And the sound of her voice set my heart leaping.

Too secret to tell of the summer lovering; of the unbridled passion of our kisses, lying in sand. Rebecca and her burnings were forgotten in the newfound fire of possession. No blaze of ricks or tollgates invaded this mating, no eyes save the eyes of ghosts watched our kisses snatched in the roll of the breakers. As primaeval beings we were, diving together from rocks into the warm sea of moonlight, splashing demented in the surf, laughing, joyful, naked and unashamed, echoing the laughter of distant lovers on this same sand a thousand years before. Beautiful this new Mari in the shroud of her long, dark hair, resisting no more: and I would have the tongue of those who call it hateful, denouncing as obscene the purity of our love-making, making that which is noble into a thing satanic; twisting the beauty of God's present to lovers by darkened minds and crippled words. Three days before Tomos was due to leave Cae White we lay together, Mari and me, in our haven of rocks.

"And Jonathon?" she said.

"Jonathon is mine," I answered.

"You will love him, too, Jethro?"

"As my own son," I said.

"Time was you were jealous, mind."

I laughed, remembering. "That time has passed, Mari. The three of us it is from now on. Nothing will come between us now, nothing," and even as I said it the face of Grandfer seemed to rise before me in some strange trick of moonlight. Clear as living that face, toothless, goat-bearded, grinning as he grinned on the night he told me of his Bronwen. I shut my eyes and lowered my head to the sand.

"Jethro," Mari whispered, but I scarcely heard her.

'With Cae White as your Eden and your brother's wife for a lover, the fingers of Cain shall reach up from the dust, and seek you . . .'

Years, it seemed, since Grandfer died yet I heard his words again like yesterday; saw the face of my brother then, square and strong, unravaged by the blood and screams of the Westgate, yet Iestyn was smiling.

"Jethro, is it sad with you?" Mari now, turning on her elbow, brushing the water from her face, smoothing back her wet hair.

"No," I said, and rose and left her, going to the outcrop of the haven where the sea was cresting silver to the breakers. Warm the night, but I was shivering.

'For she bore my child and then she vanished, went down to the river for the shame of it, in the place where we loved. And they found her three weeks later on the reaches of Laugharne . . . with mud in her mouth and her eyes taken by gulls . . .'

Grandfer now, whispering again, words I had long forgotten; whispering in the rocks, but a trumpet of sound. I swung as Mari approached, fearing she would hear it.

"Jethro, for God's sake, what is the matter?" she said, arms out.

Leaned against the rocks and looked. This, my brother's wife, naked as me; beautiful this woman, the wife of Iestyn.

"Mari!" I took her against me, kissing her face, but she

fought herself free and pushed me away, staring, eyes wild.

"Jethro, what is wrong?"

I could not face her.

"Iestyn, is it?" she said, cold.

I nodded.

Strange that the Father with His one great eye Who has in His face the weight of the moon can suffer His children to know contemplation; stopping the lover's words in the mouth, turning joy to fear by the cold light of Reason.

"Sorry now, is it?" she whispered, frightened. I held her, but the night was between us.

"Mari, you will never leave me?"

She shook her head. "Jethro, listen. Iestyn is dead. You told me that but for years I have known it. I loved him as you, mind, do not forget it. Dead. And even if he is alive we cannot go back. . . ."

"Now I will say it, Mari. Listen, you will hear me. Iestyn is dead – there is only the two of us, you and me, Mari and Jethro."

"And Jonathon," she said.

"Aye, and Jonathon. Dress now, quick, or Mam will have babies."

"Rather Mam than me," she said.

CHAPTER 23

JUST THREE days more I had my mother before Tomos Traherne hooked her away.

Fully-fledged minister now, was Tomos, a man with his hand in God's and in love with His people, preaching His goodness; a man with a chapel of his own and a little stone manse. Rising in the world, we Mortymers, and I was proud. So pretty Mam looked as Tomos led her out to the trap that Sunday; as a young girl going for marriage; dressed in her chapel black with starched white frills at her wrists and throat and well pulled in at the waist; hair in a bun, the temples streaked with grey. Wished I was marrying her so she would not go away.

Half the county was out on the road; Biddy Flannigan to the front, as usual, wheezing and dabbing with a little lace handkerchief, for she loved my mam as a sister. Toby and Mrs Maudlin, the long and the short of it, the Parcybrains who were new neighbours down at Tarn; Tom the Faith, too, give him credit, though Waldo Bailiff was absent, and Polly Scandal knew why. I was out in the barn grooming Randy when Polly looked over the top of the door.

"There's a fine big man that Mr Traherne, isn't it?" said she, horse teeth shining. "Lucky, she is, mind, marrying the cloth, and Tom the Faith that miserable, you seen him, Jethro Mortymer?"

"Leave Tom be, Polly. At least he is here," and I went on brushing.

"But not Waldo Bailiff, I'll be bound."

I grunted.

"You heard about Waldo?"

I had heard but I was not telling Polly.

"Bound to happen sooner or later, mind – couldn't go on. And Tom the Faith standing up to his neck in the mere last night praying for his soul with the Lord slipping in ice-bags. Eh, it's a scandal!"

"No proof about Waldo Bailiff," I said. "You get on, Polly."

"No proof, is it? One arm round Gipsy May and another round Betsi, and poor little Gipsy outraged."

"Not before time."

"Waldo's child, nevertheless, and Waldo and Betsi have sent her on her way – back up to Cardie to her gipsy tribe, and crossed her palm with silver to shift her. Better things crawl from holes than that man Waldo Bailiff, says my mam."

"Your mam's right," I said.

"Isn't decent, mind. Isn't proper, not in a religious county. Leave him to Rebecca, is it? Leave him to the women, my mam says, they will see to him – they will give him Waldo Bailiff."

"Excuse me," I said, wiping away sweat, and pushed her aside as Mari ran up.

"Jethro, for heaven's sake!" she cried. "Tomos is ready for off."

"I have said goodbye once, Mari."

"And you will say it again. O, Jethro, you are not even dressed!" Pouting now, beautiful as summer, hands outspread as she eyed me. "Just come as you are, then, but come you must, for Mam is asking. Do not spoil her day."

I dreaded it, not trusting myself. I had hoped to hide and not be missed.

The trap was out on the road now with the crowd standing about it and Mam and Tomos already up in front and the little brown pony itching to get going. Backslapping and laughter from some, tears from others, though Morfydd, I noticed, was dry-eyed and pale, preferring her weeping at night. Willie O'Hara was standing beside her, fair-haired and handsome. Knew how to pick her men, this one, though I did not trust him. Old Uncle Silas was other side of her, teetering on his ploughing corns, wizened face turned up at her, begging for a smile. Abel Flannigan was there; Elias the Shop come down from Kidwelly; even Justin Slaughterer – eying Mari, I noticed. Got the size of Justin now; take him with one hand if he got within a foot of her, and he knew it. Everybody chattering and making conversation in that dreaded moment before the parting, and a silence fell upon us as my mother looked down.

"Jethro," she said.

Me, Jethro Mortymer, the last man left.

"Now, now," whispered Morfydd as I went slowly past her. I mounted the trap and Mam opened her arms to me.

Is there a face as beautiful as a mother's before her goodbye? The narrowing of the eyes before the kiss, the gasp before the miles divide. And the frail thing you hold in strength is the body from whence you sprung; the breast against you is the breast you fisted and suckled. No tongue will charm like this, or scold: she who gave life: one becoming two. I kissed her,

216

screwing up my fist. Better this purity than two becoming one. . . .

"Watch for Morfydd, Jethro?"

I nodded against her.

"And Mari. Be a good boy, now. Decent, remember."

I closed my eyes. She knew.

"Yes, Mam."

And she, the stronger, pushed me off.

"Go now," she said.

I pushed a path through their forest of arms and shouldered my way to the rail behind the shippon. Head bowed, I gripped it, listening to the hooves of the pony beating on the road to Carmarthen.

CHAPTER 24

WE DID the gates proud under the leadership of Flannigan; got two down and in flames and heading for the third. If Tom Rhayader had coolness Flannigan had dash and he led us headlong down the main street of the town, galloping wraiths with a thunder of hoofbeats – all sixty of us that night and mounted, more on foot. Caught a glimpse of wizened faces at windows, heard the screaming of a frightened child. Curtains were going over, doors being bolted, windows slamming to the galloping Rebeccas. Powder-guns raised we clattered down the cobbles past the Black Lion to the end of the town and wheeled, Randy sitting back on his haunches, pawing the air at the obstructing gate.

"Down with it, down with it!" roared Flannigan, dismounting, and men fell to the task with the hatchets going up and the powder-guns crashing. I saw Matthew Luke John again, well to the front, ramming his powder-gun, shouting with joy, and he swung it to the window of the tollhouse as I was spitting on my hands to swing an axe at the bar. A window came open and out popped a head, weeping, protesting, begging for life.

"Leave the house!" cried Flannigan. "No time for the house, get the gate – just heard the dragoons are two miles off. By God, we will finish the job we started."

"Out sentries!" yelled a man, and the outriders wheeled and galloped up the road. Men were working like things gone mad, cursing, bringing down the hatchets, splinters of timber flying in all directions. Spitting on my hands I took a fresh grip on my axe, bringing it down. Joyful it is to feel the bite of steel into something you hate. Over your head with the shaft, open the shoulders and hear it whistling, slide up the left hand to join the right and the muscles of the back arch and tighten to the biting thump, high rise the splinters. These the hateful things that represent government, these the bleeding things that starve.

"Down, down!" yelled Flannigan, up on his horse, petticoat streaming, the hooves prancing. "Down, down, my daughters, work like demons, every second counts. Splinter it, carve it. Up beacons! Who the hell has the tinder? Fire, man, fire!"

And the tinderman knelt and the torch came up, circling in the darkness before the wreckage caught alight. But I was looking past him to the road through the town where a single horseman in shrouds was coming headlong, hooves sparking, shouting, waving.

"Leave the tollhouse!" yelled Flannigan. "A few minutes are left – who says we try for Tom Rhayader? Who says we free the old Rebecca? He must be somewhere in the town!" Bellows and cheers at this with Toby Maudlin doing an Irish jig on the cobbles with the flames leaping up behind him and the men going mad with thoughts of Rhayader.

"No time!" I yelled at Flannigan, and dragged at his stirrup. "Look, the sentry!" Justin Slaughterer it was, coming straight at us like a man possessed, full gallop, and the daughters parted to let him through. Waving a scarf was Justin, bawling his head off, skidding to a stop.

"Out of it, Flannigan. Everybody out of it. Dragoons!"

We went like saints after satans, scrambling on horses, slipping, cursing, with hooves clattering and skidding on the cobbles, turbans coming off, axes dropping. Made a dive at

Randy and went clean over him and he gave me a look to kill as I snatched at his rein to steady him. The men on foot were going helterskelter, running for the cover of the woods, crashing through undergrowth, hanging on to stirrups, bellyflopping over the hedgerows head first, yelling dragoons. Bastards these dragoons if they got you cornered; sabres out, slashing, thrusting – dead men first, prisoners after, it was said – up in front of the magistrates at first light, down to Carmarthen gaol by breakfast and in Botany Bay for dinner. Trained men, these. We didn't stand a chance with them and they knew it. Spreadeagled on Randy I was fighting for a stirrup as they came down the street of the town. Heard the windows coming up now, saw white faces popping out in the blaze of the tollgate. Reckon I was the last one left then, for as I wheeled Randy away I saw them clearly, no more than a hundred yards off, coming four abreast, sabres out and flashing in the red light; heard their hoarse shouts as I got my heels into Randy and went like the wind towards Laugharne. I knew I was the wrong side of the estuary but I had no option. The woods and open fields were my only chance. Give it to Randy. Perhaps he expected to die under torture at the hooves of the dragoon stallions, for he set down his flanks and went like a whippet with me hanging on. Leaping a hedge we took to the fields now, hooves thumping dully on the rich red earth, but I reined him at the edge of a wood and we stood in the shadows, watching, listening. Evil is the feel of eyes when you are hunted; every twig stirring to snap the head round, every tree whispering. Strange was that rest, lonely as the grave, with Randy standing there sweating and shining in the sudden, cursed moonlight and breathing for something to be heard ten miles. He snorted as I wheeled him and took him into the wood. God knows where the others had got to, never been so lonely before. The wood was eerie, shafting moonlight, with the overhanging branches snatching to bring me off. Thicker now, so I got off and walked, gripping Randy's head, hushing him quiet. Had to get east of the town, I knew it – would have to swim the river somewhere, but Randy liked a swim to cool him down. South first to get clear of the town, then east before the river got too broad. On, on, standing square to the swinging smack of branches, plunging knee deep in peaty places, scrambling out on all fours with Randy making the worst of it, wallowing and rearing and rolling his eyes at me for the outrage. Lost, I checked him and looked through the pattern of branches above. Brilliant were the stars though the moon was hiding, thank God, and the billowing clouds were going like hammer for the rim of the sky. The wind rose, buffeting and whining in the wood, sweeping up leaves in clouds and scraping his violins in the high rook tops that waved demented. Never been alone in such woods before, and now the panic of the dragoons had died dryness came with the cooling sweat. Things on legs I do not fear, upright or crawling; but horror comes to me in the face in the tree that smiles, the grotesque branches that clutch and hold too long, the whispers of things that should be dead. Through the wood now and I mounted and galloped towards Whitehill, with Randy taking the hedges in his stride, dying for his head and the barn at Cae White. Reaching the road just short of the Taf I reined him, approaching slowly for fear of a patrol, but the road was deserted. Crossing it at a canter, we went into the undergrowth again and down to the bank of the river, and, as if awaiting me, the moon came out. Darkness one moment, bright as day the next and I cursed it as Randy waded in, forelegs feeling for the plunge. Icy the water that rose to my knees and Randy was steaming as something afire and snorting and tossing. For days now the river had been in flood and it carried us downstream towards the estuary. Scrambling out on a sandy bed we struck out again for the open country and the upper reaches of the Tywi at Llangain. Randy was drooping a bit by now so I turned him to a tiny wood, entered it, dismounted and tethered him. And as I stood there light flared behind me and the pistol ball carved the bole of the tree a foot above my head. Went flat, squirming for cover, eyes peering, heart thumping, and Randy flung up his head and neighed with shock. One in the belly to quieten him as I went back on elbows and knees deeper into the wood.

The soldier rode up, dismounted, tied his horse and approached the wood. Cool customer, this one, though few

Rebeccas were armed save with useless powder-guns. He took his time; a big man, over six feet, with the pistol lying in his palm. Castlemartin Yeomanry by the look of him, a long way from home and dying for the skin of the hatred Rebecca. His every action was casual as he stood there reloading, unconcerned, it seemed, that he was outlined against the stars. I heard the metallic click of his powder flask, the snap of the hammer as he thumbed it back and secretly cursed myself that I had given him time to reload. It seemed he knew he had me, for he jumped the ditch and parted the branches, took a look at Randy and came in stooping, pistol held out. Held my breath, watching, then lowered my face as he turned my way, and my heart nearly stopped. Trailing from Randy's stirrup was Morfydd's old petticoat that I had torn off riding five miles back and thought I had flung away. This the reason for the shot without so much as a question. The wind was blustering still, drowning my retreat as I eased my body backwards, feeling for stones. A brook was behind me, gurgling and splashing, and I slid down the little bank and into it in a little shower of stones and plops. Saw the soldier wheel, and he came at a trot, swerving to branches, leaping lithely, the pistol rigid. Only one chance for me – to empty the pistol; best to empty it while he was running and I rose with a yell and flung stones, going flat. God knows how he missed me; heard the ball strike inches from me and go whining away and clattering through branches. His rush took him on me, swinging with the pistol, catching me on the shoulder and spinning me round, and next moment we were locked. Other side of the ditch now, arms and legs entangled, gasping, grunting; a farmer by the sound of him and as strong as Abel Flannigan. We were clasped as lovers as we went down the bank again, and into the brook, me uppermost. Splashing, threshing, we fought like cats, no rules, no honour. I had him by the throat now, holding him down while the water flooded over him and he gasped to breathe, but he brought up a knee and took me over his head, and we floundered and slipped, scrambling for the bank. Drenched, mud-covered, I clawed out first and stood awaiting him, eyes measuring him, switching to his hands for a knife.

"Right, you bloody swine Rebecca," he gasped, and dived at my legs, but I leaped away and he went past sprawling, and waited for next time. Big as a horse he looked in that moonlight, confident, trained to a hair with his yeomanry service; not much older than me by the look of him; farmer probably, I remember thinking – farmer fighting farmer, gentry against the people. Armlocks, headlocks, everything in his armoury, no doubt, and he came head on now, hands clenched for the swing. More my line. I ducked it and hooked him solid and I saw the shine of his eyes and his teeth bared white as his head went back and I caught him with another as he skidded against a tree. No use to him this. Every time he came in diving I hit to drop him, but he still kept coming, and I saw him more clearly as he circled for an opening. More like thirty he looked then, curly-haired and handsome; a bad age to quarrel with; full strength, full stamina, and I would have to finish him quick in case there were others. Diving, he got me, pinning me against a tree, and we slipped down the bole, punching short, rolling around the roots, but I was up first, swinging blindly and the fool ran into them. I felt the pain leap to my elbow and my hand went numb as the blow took him square. Feet up soldier now, landing on his shoulders, legs waving, rolling in leaves, and I leaned against the tree gasping, praying he would lie still and put an end to it, but not this one. Face elbowed against boots, he got to a knee, staggered upright and swayed towards me swinging blind. I ducked the first easily, the second grazed my chin and crashed against the tree with every pound of his weight behind it. In a flash of the moon I saw his face, one eye shut tight, blood from his mouth, black stains on his tunic and he opened his mouth and screamed like a girl to the agony of his broken hand. No honour in this. Fighting for life. I measured him, sighted the chin and hit it crisply, and he clutched at the tree and went down it slowly, rolled over once and lay still at my feet. With my hands to my face I swayed above him. I do not remember him catching me square, but there was blood on my fingers when I drew them clear. Gasping, I leaned against the tree above him with the world of moonlight spinning above me, with no sound but the bluster of

222

wind and the gasping breaths of the soldier below me. I got to the brook and knelt in the water, letting the coldness flood over me, bringing back life. The soldier was stirring as I left him for Randy, his buttocks arching to the fighting spirit within him, his hands clutching as he rolled in the leaves.

Had to get going. With this one not knowing what a beating is he would start the same business within seconds of consciousness. Blinded with weariness, my shoulder like fire from the thump of his pistol, I spreadeagled myself on Randy, snatched up the petticoat and stuffed it in my pocket. By the time I reached the Tywi my strength was coming back. No more dragoons between Kidwelly and Cae White, thank God, and when I reached home we were into a gallop again. Opening the barn I shoved Randy in. Damned near dawn. Cocks were crowing from Bayleaves Farm as I rubbed myself dry and got into the bed, awaking an instant later, it seemed, in bright sunlight.

No mam to contend with, just dull looks from Morfydd and Mari. Not so bad in the mirror, really; nose, that was all, half way over my face, and skinned.

"Justin Slaughterer again by the look of it," said Mari, banging down the plate. Only the three of us now not counting Richard and Jonathon.

"More like the yeomanry – good beak-busters, them – the colonel himself, was it?" Morfydd now, acid curious, frightened. I saw her trembling hands.

"Second-in-command," I said.

"Good grief," she replied, "we are coming down the scale," and turned to Mari. "Make the most of your brother-in-law," she said. "We will not have him long."

Inclined to agree with her at this rate.

CHAPTER 25

WALDO BAILIFF caught it that June, got it proper from Flannigan's daughters, though I had no hand in it, more the pity.

"Terrible, disgusting," whispered Mari at breakfast next day.

"Waldo Bailiff you speaking of, or Rebecca?" asked Morfydd.

For the first time since Cae White their eyes met in challenge over the table.

"Took him through on the pole, saw it myself," said Richard, his eyes like saucers. Growing fast, this one, regular man.

"Hush," said Mari. "It is too indecent to think about."

"Ask Gipsy May," said Morfydd, chewing. "Indecent all right. Things are coming improper indeed when a man pays a shilling for a child, though I hold no grief for Gipsy. Cross her palm with silver, turn her out. Do you call that justice?"

"A public exhibition. Better horsewhip him in private – never have I seen the like of it," said Mari. "It has a bad effect on the children."

A bad effect on Waldo, too.

The rumours varied but I knew the truth of it. Flannigan and ten of the daughters went up to the Reach and caught Waldo sprucing himself for his Saturday outing with Betsi Ramrod. Heading for marriage these two, arm in arm, large as life, peas in a pod in their treatment of Gipsy. Lucky for Betsi she wasn't carried, too. Trial, sentence and punishment, all within the hour, and they brought him through the village on the pole near midnight; staghung, naked but for his trews, screaming for a pigsticking, begging for mercy, while windows went up and doors came open and Betsi Ramrod weeping and tearing out her hair when they dumped him in the taproom of Black Boar tavern. Six pounds savings they found under the bed, six pounds for Gipsy May, said Flannigan to me later, though the trouble was getting it to her. Wonderful to see Flannigan in Chapel next day with Dai Alltwen Preacher roasting Rebecca up in the pulpit for dastardly attacks on God-fearing people; not a hair out of place had Abel Flannigan, and Toby Maudlin sitting next to him beating his breast for the sins of the village and Justin Slaughterer giving his bass Amen. That was a week back and not a daughter recognized: recognized, no doubt, but nobody dared breathe a name, and not a soul had seen Waldo since. Still going, said Flannigan. Thank God, said Morfydd.

"You ready?" she asked me now.

"Aye," I said, rising from table.

It was three days or so since I had tangled with the soldier and my bruises were going down and my nose coming normal. I had been lying low of late though every Rebecca and daughter in the county were out doing overtime on burning ricks and gates, and the victory was practically gained. The Trusts had lost all heart for rebuilding and the splintered remains of gates littered the highways, the charred timbers of the tollhouse rafters grinning at the summer sky. Due on shift at Gower's pit that morning, Morfydd and I took the endless road to coal. Strangely, she was looking better since Mam had left; as if the constant suppressing hand of my mother had lifted, leaving her free of criticism, but I knew the truth of it when we were half way to Ponty on that bright June day.

"I am bringing Willie O'Hara home tonight, Jethro. D'you mind?"

She glanced at me sideways and I winked.

"None of that," she said. "Respectable is Willie, never mind the tales – a woman could do worse."

"Handsome devil, I'll say that for him."

"Knows how to treat a woman," and she smiled. "Opening doors, closing gates, and he wants me."

"Are you in love with him?" I asked.

"Take me out of coal, mind."

"I am doing that," I said. "The end of this month. I asked if you loved him."

"I will only ever love one," she said. "I am thinking of my

225

son. His father for the next world, if there is one. Willie O'Hara will do for this."

"He wants to marry you, this Willie?"

She did not reply. Still beautiful she looked with her shawl over her shoulders and the wind catching her hair, still young enough to be loved.

"Bring him home, girl," I said. "We will make him welcome."

We walked on, leaping the brooks, taking the short cuts over the fields on the paths we knew so well. Years it seemed since we first came to Cae White. Willie O'Hara had come into her life at a time I feared for her sanity, and I was grateful to him, and relieved. For Morfydd was the one reason why I stayed on at Cae White. Much as I longed to get to America there seemed no chance with Morfydd around, and I knew that Mari would never leave her alone to fend for Richard.

"The trouble is you and Mari," said Morfydd. "Hardly fair, is it, to walk out of the place with Willie and Richard and leave the pair of you alone – not fair on Iestyn, come to that."

"No," I answered.

"Queer old life, isn't it?"

I nodded, taking her hand over a stream. Brilliant that early morning sunshine with the mist billowing down the river and the rooks screaming in the tops of the trees. Every detail of that last walk together to the pit is impressed on my mind, cut in deep grooves as with the knife of the woodcutter; every second of that morning I hear: the gurgling rush of water over stones, the coloured darts of the kingfishers I see, as if it was yesterday instead of through the mist of years.

"Mari and me will be all right," I said.

"O, aye?"

"You go and make a home with Willie, do not study us."

"No, Jethro," she said. "Not till Iestyn comes back."

"Three years," I said, watching her, wondering. . . . But I knew she thought him still alive when I saw her smile.

"God, I know how Mari feels," she said. "Three years more, that is all, and then I will see him."

Less than three hours.

I knew of a ship at Saundersfoot; a three-masted barque that was lying at the quay; waiting for the flood of immigrants from the north – people coming down on foot, it was said. Two weeks or longer she had laid at Saundersfoot with her sails trimmed down and smoke drifting from her galleys, and her captain was taking the fares at the gangplank, five pounds a head steerage, fifteen pounds a head cabins. Bound for the port of Philadelphia: a leap from there to the town of Pittsburgh and the flaming ovens of the iron. White in the deck, black-tarred her hull, a leviathan of a ship of two hundred tons, stalwart, braced in the bows for ploughing Atlantics, with pigtailed Plymouth men manning her and her captain with the face of Neptune himself, bearded and sideboarded and a gold-buttoned tunic. God, how I longed for that fifteen pounds, for Mari, Jonathon and me. Saving every penny now in the black box under the bed. No more quarts in Black Boar tavern, skimping on this and that, coming the Welsh Jew, longing for the feel of the deck beneath me, with Mari one side of me and Jonathon on the other, turning my back on the labour I hated. Last fall I had ploughed and sown Cae White, doing it spare time after a full Ponty shift, and the corn was standing high now, begging for the reapers – full price and profit for corn now the gates were nearly down. Like a longing for Mari it grew within me, this yearning for the land of promise, to make a decent life. This very morning Rebecca was marching on Carmarthen city, but I was sick of fighting. Led by Rebecca John Harries of Talog Mill thousands of the daughters were marching on the city to burn the workhouse down, they said; burn it to the ground and succour the starving, and God help the man who stands in our path. Flannigan would be there, Toby and Justin, Matthew Luke John and even Tom the Faith – scores of others I knew, fighting for justice. For this was Rebecca triumphant, showing her strength now the gates were down; pitting her numbers against the sabres of the yeomanry, spitting on dragoons, constables and magistrates. Fighting, fighting – four years of it, me – and for what? Not for gates. Fighting for Mari and the ship that was lying at Saundersfoot Quay. I would hang in her rigging, unfurl her sails, tar her from bow to stern while she rode at sea, scrub her white, labour in the galleys, bow and scrape to the dining gentry – just to hear the song of her, feel the roll of her, the buck and toss of the swell beneath her and listen to the whine of the Atlantic gales that drove her west to Philadelphia. Fifteen pounds between me and freedom – saving it now at two shillings a week – take me three years at this rate. And in three years time Iestyn would come back – tiptoeing over the waves from Botany Bay, his fingers clutching for Mari, invading her life.

I had to get away.

Lying in the seam in Number Three now, coal-grimed, sweating in inches of water, with the pick reaching in to the two foot roof. Liam Muldooney beside me mouthing the Bible, intoning deep about Kabzeel; his grandpa; grumbling and grunting about lions in snow. Worse than ever was Liam these days, what brain the coal left him was deserting him fast now: stupifying his body with unending labour, and God knows for what for he didn't need the money. The tram-towers and basketers were labouring behind us, coming in a queue from the ladders to the seams where fifty men or more lay side by side with us. I stopped for a breather and turned on my back, arms behind my head. Saw Morfydd next one up with a tram and an Irish girl shovelling it full like a man, singing above the bedlam of wheels and chinks some plaintive song of home. Pretty it sounded to its backcloth of thumps, the grunting of men, grumbling shovels, the wounding picks that echoed in the gallery to the shaft of the pit where Gower was bellowing. Pretty little Irish woman, too, come to that, coming upright now, leaning on her shovel and giving me a wink.

"Right, girl," she said to Morfydd. "Switch road, this one – through Number Six," and Morfydd nodded and crawled down to hitch up.

I got Liam Muldooney with an elbow. "Since when has Gower been using the switch road through Six?" I asked.

"Every fourth tram – Foreman's orders."

"To hell with Foreman," I said. "It isn't even propped." I sat up, hitting my head on the roof and cursing.

"Sit down, sit down, man," said Liam. "There's enough props by there to hold up government – they got them all in on last night's shift. Would I let a little woman go where I wouldn't go myself. Firm as Moses' rock that roof."

"That roof was dropping plugs not a week back," I said.

"And they fetched the plugs down, you satisfied? You start looking to your own business, little man, and leave me to mine. Shall I tell you of my grandpa now, and put your mind at ease?"

"To hell with your grandpa."

"Then would you rather have a chapter from Galatians?"

"O, for God's sake!" I said, for I was watching the end of Morfydd's tram, watching the glint of the backboard steel as it curved down the line to the switch road on Six, smaller and smaller in the lights of the tallow lamps.

"Sharp enough to cut yourself this morning," said Liam. "Rest you in God, little man, He will care for your Morfydd. No satan shall snatch at her in the presence of the Lord. Now give proof of your faith in Him, *bach* – tell Him what you know of the Book of the King, just to please Liam and take your mind from fear. How many books in the Old Testament, for instance?"

"Thirty-nine," I said. "Liam, I am afraid. . . ."

"And the New Testament, little man?"

"Twenty-seven. Liam. . . ."

"Hush you," said he. "It is not fear but the Devil wreaking his vengeance for the burning of the gates. And eight hundred and thirty-eight thousand three hundred and eighty letters in the New Testament all told, and do not argue, man, for I have taken the trouble to count them. Man, be calm."

"I am away to see Gower," I said, crawling, but he caught my wrist and twisted me back.

"Peace! The shortest sentence in His Book, if you please. . . .?"

"Jesus wept," I murmured.

"Aye, aye, for the likes of you and me, Jethro. Would you take a fist to me and sweep me aside when I tell you your girl will be safe?"

229

Just looked at him. This the saint of faith; such men as this have prayed to their God with their bodies alight.

Liam was smiling.

"Trust you in Him," he whispered. "Do not put your trust in props, for I have prayed and the golden Lord has answered. On, now. What is the middle verse of the Book of our God, boy? Think now, shiver up the herring-roes. Shall I tell, is it? The eighth verse of the hundred and eighteenth Psalm. And how many times does the word *Lord* occur? Forty-six thousand two hundred and twenty-seven, and there is no word therein more than six syllables, and the word *Reverend* occurs only once, as if the Lord just remembered to slip the thing in. How now do I stand in the knowledge of my God?" He gripped my hand. "Forsake all wickedness. Stand you firm in the countenance of the Father, and He will protect you and those whom you love."

"As Towey." I raised my face.

"Is she not with happiness now, man? And the boy from Spain?"

"I want Morfydd living, not dead."

"So you put your faith in a four-inch prop when He can shift a mountain with His finger? O, Jethro, *bach*, do you listen to old Liam. Battered and addled I am, my body despoiled, but my soul is with glory and yours with dust. Conflict with the kings of the earth is conflict with God, for did He not teach humility to men? And the servants of the earthly queen is asking questions, you heard?"

This raised me again.

"What do you mean?"

"In search of Rebeccas, looking for daughters to break the march on Carmarthen – and searching for a man with broken hands – yours are not so tidy."

I heard his words but I did not care. Looking for the one who had flattened their dragoon, no doubt. I would do it again with half a chance, but quicker.

"God help him if they find him, mind," said Liam.

I heard his words as an echo, for I was trundling with Morfydd down Number Six gallery, the new shaft opened in a forest of props; couldn't rest till she got back to the seam, couldn't work, couldn't think.

"The Lord says turn the other cheek, Jethro."

"Aye? Well I am not turning mine."

"God forgive you," said Liam.

"Nothing to forgive."

"God help you, then," said he, and as he said it Number Six went down.

A dull thump first, then thunder, rocking us as with an earthquake, turning us, felling those standing, burying those lying. One moment light, next moment blackness. Props were going like twigs, bending, snapping, driving into the ground. Lying as I was, the drop took me square across the thighs, pinning me, and I fought to breathe as the pressure came greater; pinned as if nailed there, coal against my face, my chest, stretching as a mantle down to my ankles. Couldn't even gasp; lying solid in a tomb of coal, twisting, thighs bucking, screaming for breath, and the hand that clawed at my face was Liam's, groping for my mouth, knuckles arched for my first inward breath. Heard him scratching, someone screaming; trickles in my mouth as the dust filled it solid. This, the press, the shudder of a county. Liam was tearing the dust from my face now; somebody on my ankles heaving tons, and they drew me out as a thumb from a thumbscrew before the roof arch bellied and dropped flat. The place was in torment as I staggered up, half naked men and women rushing, screaming, tripping, falling, and children shrieking for lost parents. Gower was at the entrance to the gallery, his voice booming for order, but the mob that rushed the ladders rolled him down, passing over him. Leaning against the wall, spitting out coal, digging out my eyes, I looked at Liam Muldooney. He was sitting as a man dazed, gaping to the shock, mouthing some incantation, his face grimed against the white roll of his eyes, and then I remembered Morfydd.

The gallery was coming empty now, few tallow lamps were burning, but the colliers were still yelling down at the ladders, and I heard from there the cries of children, the bawling shouts of overmen trying to get order. Only fire was needed to turn it into Hell. Took one look at Liam and staggered to the entrance to Number Six, snatching at a tallow lamp and holding it before me as I went down the incline. Terror was in me, sweat flooding over me. Reckoning by time she was half way through the switch road when the roof came down. A forest of pitprops here and I stumbled and hit myself against them in my swaying run down the line. Queer how you pray when you fear such loss – strange how God is neglected till the testing time, and there is no other with ears. The shouts and bedlam was dying behind me now as I plunged on, following the shimmer of the rails in the faltering light of the candle. The air was fetid here, heavy with dust. The roof was lower now, the walls with jutting biceps of rocks; ankle deep in water now. Stopping, I listened. No sound but the thumping of my heart and the trickling of water from above. I looked at the roof. Wide fissures were crazing it from wall to wall, dust cascading in sudden spurts from the pressure building up. Gaunt the shadows of the candle, only an inch or so of it left, the flame spluttering to the heavy air. Dank the smell that wafted then from some devil's hole, and I knew that I was holding in my hand the flame of detonation. Fear struck, thumping as a fist, putting me against the wall, and I dropped to my knees, staring at the blackness ahead.

"Morfydd!"

Flung back in my face in countless echoes, reverberating down the gallery, bouncing off the drop. The roof cracked like a shot behind me, the pressure begging for the least vibration to bring it roaring down. Couldn't even shout without reprisal. Spitting out dust, I lurched on.

Narrow here. The gallery was tapering. This is the hardest rock, its walls as filed from the body of the mountain, the roof still lower. Had to bend here, now go on all fours, with the candle held out, one hand gripping a line, and this was the beginning of the fall. Boulders of rock and coal were strewn over the narrow floor, coming thicker as I crept onward, stumbling, cursing as my knees pressed the flints. Had to rest, for my head was thumping with the hammer of my heart and each breath was drawn against the iron band of my chest. As a dog, I rested, tongue lolling, panting, hearing as if in dreams a dull roll of thunder far behind me, and the floor beneath me trembled to the new drop. As alive the rail sprang under my hand, transmitting its message of entombment for someone. Perhaps me. I did not really give it a thought. Past caring now: had to find Morfydd. The candle was spilling its tallow now, the wick hooked and black for the last minutes of flame, guttering, sparking. On again, the boulders coming thicker till the line disappeared. Crying aloud, I wept as a child weeps in all its tuneless sounds as I set the lamp down and clawed a path up the drop. It seemed a mountain but it was only three feet, for my head struck the roof, knocking me back. This was the end of it, this was the fall.

Turning on my back I lay against the heap with the floor at my heels and the roof against my forehead, eyes closed to the scald of the tears, hands clenched to the loss. This is the end of it then, as she had said, engrained as the leaf; becoming part of the living earth, buried alive in the filth of coal for the profits of industry and the greed of men. The candle was chittering, opening my eyes to its incandescent fire in the blackness of the pit. Didn't care now if I lived or died. Hope sprang then, shivering me awake in brief excitement, weighing the chances that she was beyond the fall, but I knew she was not. A gallery fall this, running as the drop of a stick; no isolated plug that she might have missed. I knew she was lost. And I saw in the seconds before the candle spat out a silver strand of shining braid, hanging from the splintered tip of a wooden prop, and stretched towards it and caught it in my fingers, pulling it down.

Blackness.

I put it against my face.

Gower came in for me, led by Muldooney, they said after, but I do not remember; with a twenty foot burrow through the drop I had heard, up by the start of the switch; hewing like madman, stark naked, some of them, sweating, bleeding, dropping with exhaustion to rise and hew again. God, these colliers!

Came in for me, ten men risking their lives for one, the most important man in their earth. A day and a night it took them, but they came crawling, with a tram rolling behind them – in like ants, out like things scalded. And ten hours later the whole of Number Six went down with a rumble they heard in Kidwelly, but I do not remember. Just a day and a night of dreaming for me; lying against the fall where Morfydd slept; hearing her voice raised in rebellion, hearing the whisper of her in a Willie O'Hara love-making; seeing her frown, the brilliance of her smile. A day and a night I lay with her, walking in summer with her over the green of the Coity mountain back home; standing beside her black starchness in chapel, hearing her sing. Sitting at home now, feeding her Richard, drawing up her bodice to the shift of my eyes: scolding now, going round the bedroom, swinging her fists like a man at me: innocent as a child under my mother's stare. Sister and lover.

I opened my eyes and saw Mari then; stars were about the curve of her shawl as she knelt by the hurdle and put her arms around me.

"O, Jethro," she said, and kissed me. "Jethro!"

Men turning away to bury the dead.

CHAPTER 26

THEY GOT Abel Flannigan in bed, said Mari, on the night after the march on Carmarthen city: clanking horses and sabres drawn in his shippon, she said, heaving down the door and bursting up the stairs with Biddy screaming murder and heaving pans at them, yelling like a mad thing at Abel to hoof it through the window, but she yelled too late. Back to the wall in his nightshirt went Abel Flannigan, with a dragoon on his back and a constable on his legs, hitting off helmets with one hand and smacking them out with the other; five on the floor at one time, said Biddy, bleeding, ragged, tormented as a Spanish bull, was Abel, roaring to Biddy to saddle his mare while he settled all fifteen. They could have shot him, cut him down, but they didn't, to their credit. But they thumped him to his knees and tied his wrists behind him and booted him out on the end of a rope, haltered as a wife being sold at market. Biddy's screams could be heard from here, said Mari.

"And then?" I asked, flat.

"Then they went for Toby Maudlin."

Toby went easy, Mari said, thumped black and blue by his misery missus at the first clank of the sabres; kicked out through the door into the arms of the constables, his face still blackened, still wearing her nightdress, for he had taken a gate in his stride on the way back from Carmarthen.

"Justin Slaughterer was taken in Carmarthen workhouse," she said now. "He forced his way in there a yard behind John Harries Rebecca and two hundred following them, overturned the tables, smashed down the doors to free the inmates so they could put the place to flames. But the dragoons came galloping in and slammed the gates behind them."

"Got the lot," I said.

"Rebecca John Harries made back home," she answered, "but not poor Justin."

"A damned fine way to end a page of history," I said.

"Then they came here," said Mari, kneeling by the bed.

This raised me on the pillow.

"Six dragoons and a captain, Jethro. Looking for a man with broken hands, a man who had murdered one of their soldiers."

I stared at her.

"Found drowned in a brook in the woods near St Clears – beaten, and left to die, left to roll about, and drown."

"O, God," I said, sweating.

So small and unequal she looked standing there in profile, one hand gripping the sill. Hard on women, this business. She had lost one man to rebellion. She looked like losing another. Murder now. Sick, I felt.

"What ... what did you tell them?" I whispered.

"What Gower told me – that you and Morfydd were dead. O, God," she said.

I thought of the ship, tranquil on the calm sea, waiting, waiting.

She said, "Then they went to the pit to get the truth of it and Liam Muldooney told them the same."

I covered my face with my hands.

"Jethro, you must get away," she said. "Every man under sixty in the village has been taken. Special magistrates are being sworn in to try them – hundreds and hundreds have been taken – even men who have never seen a Rebecca just in case. They will come back for you, you cannot stay here."

"Yes."

This was the Chartists all over again. With victory coming closer they had bungled it by moving too soon – men like my brother who had listened to John Frost; men like Flannigan who had followed the hothead John Harries. And now murder.

"Thank God Mam isn't here," she said.

"And if I go . . . what of you?"

"I will manage," she said.

"Cae White, on your own?"

"I have Richard and Jonathon for help. I will manage."

"You will starve, the three of you. You first," I replied.

"Perhaps for the good," she said, empty. "Not much of a life as things stand, is it?"

"Mari," I said, and put out my hand to her and she came obediently and stood above me, looking down, before she went on her knees beside the bed and into my arms. Just held her for a bit. I knew she was sobbing for Morfydd; that the grief was cutting as a knife. Then the door came open silently and the faces of Jonathon and Richard peeped round. Jonathon as Mari, dark as Richard was fair. And I saw in Richard's eyes the unspoken question as Mari rose like lightning and went to Jonathon. I glanced at Mari, my eyebrows raised and she shook her head and hurried Jonathon through the door.

"The soldiers came, Uncle Jethro," Richard said by the bed. "You heard one of them's been killed?"

"Yes."

"And Aunt Mari did say that you didn't do it and that you and my mam be dead, anyway, then they went away."

"Yes," I said.

Seven years old now, ten by the bite of his teeth on his lip

236

and he looked at me, his eyes large and blue, misted with tears.

"Where's my mam, Uncle Jethro?"

"Richard, come to me," I said.

Quite still he stood, hands clenched by his sides, his hair alight in a shaft of the window sun, then he lowered his face, weeping without sound.

"Richard," I said, and reached out and drew him against me.

Just held him, pressing him hard against me, feeling useless, cursing coal, the county, the country; cursing the world. No need to tell this one, no explanations begged. Just held him while he wept, thinking of the soldier.

"Aunt Mari now," I said. "Richard . . ." and I held him away, smiling. "With Jonathon for your brother, and Aunt Mari and me for your mam and dad."

"Took by the coal, is it?" Lips trembling, he faced me.

"Yes."

"Eh, the bloody old coal," he said, eyes slanting away from me. "Mam did say the coal would be the end of it, one night in prayers."

I nodded.

He said, hands screwing, "Staying with you, is it? Not going to the workhouse or the Hirings like Ianto Vaughan when his mam passed on?"

"No, Richard. We would not allow it."

"Tea now, is it?"

The simplicity of the grief of childhood.

"Yes," I said.

"Then I will help Aunt Mari bring it up."

"I am coming down," I said, getting out. "Would you have me lying for days like a lazy old lump?"

"Head bumps, is it?" he asked, feeling.

"Aye, but most of them going down. Away like a good boy while I dress, Dick."

He got to the door, turned and flashed me a smile, but I heard the stuttering breath of his sobbing as he went down the stairs.

"Jethro," said Mari when the boys were in bed, "you have got to get away. The soldiers will come back."

"Yes," I said.

Agitated, walking the kitchen for the last two hours, she was pulling at her fingers, encircling the finger that had once held her wedding ring, out of habit, for the ring was there no more. Face strained and pale she walked and turned, head switching to the slightest sound of the night.

"I have written to Mam and Tomos – Osian Hughes got it on the mail coach," she said. "Had to say both of you had gone, in case it was opened. Policemen are opening all letters, they say. When she hears of the pair of you Mam will go mad."

"But you were wise," I said.

She was wandering from window to window, pulling the curtains tighter, hands trembling, her lips dead white, and I longed to hold and comfort her.

"Mari," I said, and she turned as if struck.

"O, God," she whispered, and wept.

Up then, pulling her against me. She did not fight free as I expected but clung to me, her fingers as claws on my back. Cold her face when I kissed it and she twisted away when I tried for her lips.

"You have got to get away, do you understand? There is no time for this. O, but a damned child you are, Jethro! They will drag you off as they dragged off Flannigan and the others. Transportation, that will be the end of it."

Death, I thought.

"Talk sense," I said, pushing her off. "I have less than a pound saved – how far will I get without money? Best to wait here till things cool down."

"I have money," she said.

"You will need every penny you've got."

"I have fifty pounds all but two shillings. Fifty pounds. I told you before."

Me staring now.

"Grandfer's money," she said.

I sighed. "You kept it pretty dark."

"I told you down on the Burrows but you wouldn't believe me."

"Yes," I said, "I remember."

I sat down, sweating, trying to get the size of it. Me setting three years aside to save fifteen pounds and her standing here with fifty.

I rose. "Then come away with me, Mari. We will take the boys and leave this damned place. There is a ship lying at Saundersfoot. . . ."

"Not with you, Jethro," she said.

And she came nearer, standing above me as I sat down before her. Soft her voice now, every word as measured, her eyes unflinching on mine. "Time was when I would have gone to the ends of the earth with you, but not now. The women of you Mortymers are solid gold, Jethro, but they bring forth sons of solid iron – fighters all – one word and the blow, the fist before the word always, seeing but one side of the argument. Up workers, down gentry, isn't it – and there are gentry folk in America as well as in Wales. And where you find gentry you will find the Mortymers to stand against them to take that which is theirs by right." Her voice rose now, her eyes grew large and she swept her arm to the window. "Some damned good gentry people live in this county – not the puffed up little magistrates who have thieved ten fields – these are the people who have raised your gates, the absentee landlords who jump in to buy and jump back to London to live on their rents – these are the enemies." She folded her arms and smiled down at me. "But there are other kinds of gentry, boy – gentlefolk whose ancestors have made their roots here – who were great in this county and decent to their workers before you damned Mortymers turned an eye to light. And that is your trouble, you Mortymers. You tar and feather every gentleman in sight, never choosing, never dividing the black from the white – everything with a foot of lace or a carriage is branded by the Mortymers as enemies of the people, but you are blind. Look towards Squire's Reach – hasn't Lloyd Parry treated us decent – did you not give your love to a gentry girl ? Look North and West to the great mansions that were built by the Welsh as the beating hearts of the people – this is the true aristocracy who think like you, Jethro – not the jumped-up little pit-owners who have raced into Wales to drive a shaft for quick profits – hating the evil little magistrates, these gentry, aye, and taking them to law." She paused, bending above me, one hand clenched. "These people are one with you, Jethro, with all their birth and nobility, and you will never make me think otherwise, for I am one of them."

New, this Mari, as tempered by fire, commanding. I stared up at her.

"I have had too much," she said, her voice dying. "I have been hit too hard by you Mortymers, the people I love. I have a son to consider now, and Morfydd's boy now she has gone. It is a load. And the fight of the Mortymers is in these boys, I know it, but I will drive it out. I will teach them peace, not war; to love and not to hate; to make light of the injustices that is the lot of the poor and triumph over them with the help of God – Church or Chapel, makes no difference – God just the same." She knelt then, smiling in tears, and bowed her head, her fingers smoothing the knuckles of my hands. Skinned and swollen, these hands. I drew them away, and she raised her eyes to mine.

"The soldier is dead, Jethro," she said. "Do you remember?"

The sweat sprang to my face and I rose, turning from her.

"You?" she whispered, instantly beside me.

Cool the glass of the window on my forehead. I bowed my head.

"My God," she said, and wrung her hands. "This is the end of it, then – murder."

I had lost her. The knowledge was enough to silence me, obliterating remorse. I could hear her pacing the floor behind me. Her steps ended.

"And you killed him in cold blood."

"Him or me," I said, flat. "It was a fair fight. I did not seek it. He must have rolled and drowned in the brook after I left. I did not kill him."

"And do you expect them to believe that?" She caught my

arm and swung me round. "They will search the county. They will never give up. When they learn you did not die with Morfydd they will come back. O, what are we doing talking, wasting time. Quick, you must get away!"

Agitation gripped her again. Her face was stark white. "Quick, now – how much the fare for the ship at Saundersfoot?"

"Five pounds."

"You shall have twenty-five – half what is in the box."

This turned me. "It is one way of getting me out of your sight, isn't it? Give me five and you will have back every penny."

"O, God," she said, empty. "It has come to that? O, Jethro, can't you see that I love you? It is not the dirty old money – you can have all fifty. It is because I love you that I could not bear you to be taken."

"But you will not come with me?"

She lowered her hands as if slapped in the face. Eyes closed, she stood.

"And after I am gone – what then?" I said.

She emptied her hands at me.

"Back to Nanty with Tomos, is it, and labour in bloody coal?"

She opened large, rebellious eyes at me. "Do not swear at me," she said. Beautiful, she looked.

"Humping and heaving fourteen hours a day, ending the same way as Morfydd, and you shout to me about gentry," I said.

"Did it once before, Jethro," she replied. "Two children now, and I can do it again."

"So you will not come with me?"

"Not to America, not anywhere, to start the same fighting all over again."

"Because of the soldier, isn't it?"

"Because I want *peace* – nothing to do with the soldier!"

"Mari, I beg of you," I said.

"Jethro, for God's sake go."

"Better to stay and be taken. I have loved you for years, and yet but once. What kind of a life with three thousand miles between us?" Cold her lips when I kissed her, with no response, as if I had drained her of youth and fire. Strange the excitement seizing me at her nearness, the sudden torrent of my breathing drowning the chance of footsteps, the knock. So I held her, unable to leave her, unable to go.

"O, that Tomos was here!" she said as a whisper.

Just sweated and held her, ears tingling, fearful to move.

"Ask Tomos," I said, gripping her. "Tomos will know what to do. You are of me now, Mari, I am of you. Ask Tomos!"

She held me away, smiling sad. "Jethro, Iestyn – both the same. Loved them both the same. Queer, isn't it, they cannot do without me. He brought me home in rags, clothed and fed me, and left me for you. And while you hold me here I am dying inside, until you go."

"But you will speak to Tomos? Mari, I beg you!"

She said softly, her eyes closed: "I will tell him that I am afraid. And I will tell of the soldier, because you have killed. I have my God, Jethro, you have yours – that is the difference. Now you will swear to me that you did not leave him dead?"

"I swear it," I said.

"Now go. Wait at the ship. I do not promise to come, but if it is his wish Tomos will bring me, for Tomos and me have the same God. We will leave it to Him, is it?" She turned from my arms and set her back to me. "Do not kiss me again, Jethro. I could not bear it. Just go."

I stood there, hands clenched, hearing the rustle of her dress as she went past me to the stairs, catching the scent of her. Barren of her, I died in seconds at the click of the door; listened to the creak of the stairs.

Empty that room in the dim light of the lamp. I stood looking at it, at my mother's empty chair by the fireplace, the place where Morfydd sat. And I saw, standing there, the shine of the table grow to life again, the snow of its cloth, the gleam of knives, and heard the tinkle of cups and plates. Blinding the lamp, its wick turned low; shimmering, dancing to the chatter and laughter. Morfydd's high shrieks, Mam's sharp replies, Mari's soft voice, Grandfer's snores. This the mood of the table, the centre of the family, the servant of life. Laughter, joy one minute, heads bent low to the plates the next; sidelong glances at someone in disgrace, nudges and winks. Cursed is the mind that it brings such visions, cursed the table. Swung away from it, cursing, and took five pounds from the box on the dresser and shouldered the door to the back, but turned.

"Goodbye," I said.

I could not see the table.

Out in the night now, the shippon was steaming. I ran over to the barn and whistled for Tara and she came out wriggling.

"Up," I said, and she leaped into my arms.

Randy turned and snorted hate at me as I closed the door and dropped the stick. Lonely it was, standing in the shippon with Tara against me, looking up at the blind windows, seeking a hand. Nothing. I turned.

Grandfer was right. My mind went back years. Fifty feet down, spreadeagled in the peat bog on the track to Tarn, head lolling, suspended in mud, I reckon he smiled.

CHAPTER 27

No STARS that night, not even a moon, thank God. The world was as black as a witch's gown, the air velvet and warm coming over the estuary. I walked fast at first, eager to get north to cross the barriers of the Tywi and Taf rivers, reckoning for a journey of thirty miles to Saundersfoot though it was twenty as the crow flies. I was heading for Llangain, taking the same route as I had done when we last burned the gates, striking north first, then south-west, keeping to the low ground, trotting at times with Tara running at my heels. Good to have Tara with me. Funny how a little dog can make up for humans; there always with her excited grinning, tongue seeking your fingers, in love with you, her eyes adoring though you are less than muck to your race, unloved by those you love, criticized and rejected. And I knelt at times in the darkness and held her to me. Queer little woman.

With the face of Mari sweeping back I stopped once before dropping to the Gwendraeth and turned, looking back. Distantly I saw Cae White, hooded and bewitched by night, one chink of light beaming from a curtain Mari had forgotten to pull, its gables and twisted chimneys outlined starkly against white, rolling clouds, and the standing corn beyond sweeping into blackness. Turned my back on it, whistled at Tara and hurried on, keeping to the tracks, seeking the safety of woods and thickets. Midnight was tolling from a blind clock as I reached the Tywi opposite Llangain, and I went down the bank to the water and stripped naked while Tara, squatting, shivered and looked appalled at me. Not fancying to travel soaked, I tied my clothes into a bundle and hung them round my neck, then waded in while Tara whined delighted. Gave her a whistle and struck out. Muzzle sweeping the calm water she swam beside me, one eye cocked at an otter that barked and dived at our approach. Out now, streaming, shivering, and I rolled in the river grass to dry myself, Tara copying, leaping to this new adventure after the years of neglect. Dressing, I started off again at a trot to warm myself, eyes skinned for every rustle of a thicket, going for St Clears and the narrow reaches of the Taf. Treating it likewise at Whitehill Down I reached the high ground above Newton, and lay there in the stubbled grass with Tara in the crook of my arm, shivering at the sky where the first grey streak of dawn was flushing up from the east. I slept, awaking in bright sunlight with Tara licking my face, encircled by rabbits, five all told. A man with a dog can conquer the universe. Kissing and scolding her, I picked up a rabbit and stuffed it into my coat, rose and ran down the hillock, leaping the boulders, alive to the joy of the newfound day of sun and warmth, until I remembered Cae White and Mari. In the shelter of jutting rocks now, a disused quarry, I gutted and skinned the rabbit, rubbed for a flame and hung him from sticks for roasting. God must have a special heaven for rabbits in return for the sacrifice of their bodies to Man. Never smelled the like of this one after a sleep in the open, and between us we put him well down with Tara running in circles sniffing and whining for more.

We stayed in the quarry all that day and crept out at dusk to the evening star. Brilliant this night with the full moon showing me across country to Windleways and Amroth, leading me south to the sea. Deserted country this, a few miles from Saundersfoot and I reached the bay at midnight and lay on the short grass looking at the stars. There, with the sea beneath me, I watched the procession of the worlds; helmeted Mars beaming at the molten Jupiter, Saturn spinning in his rings of white satin, the white-dusted Heavens of worlds beyond worlds. Uranus and his servant moons, I saw, Venus making her crucifix sign; Little Bear, Great Bear, the Plough in all its regal majesty; stars and constellation dripping white light in the obliterated eye of the Mother Sun. I dreamed, eyes half closed to the beauty of night. Strange, I thought in a moment of wakefulness, that this same earth upon which I was lying was the tissue and bones of men long dead; holding the cinders of tongues long silent in the billion years of time and space, warm under the belly of the panting Tara. Just the two of us, Tara and me, man and dog linked in friendship, lying on a cliff that had echoed the wolfhound, the screamed commands of primaeval man. How small the ambitions and the loves compared to the greatness of earth and sky, the unmeasured wastes of the sea, how pitiful, I thought. One man running, and loving; seeking the new in exchange for the old. So trivial this seventy years of living and dying; all ambitions ending the same, in earth.

After more than a week of hiding in sea caves, poaching and trapping to keep alive, I reached the hills dominating the harbour. The sea was flat calm and misted as I crested a rise and looked down to the quay. Yellow sands flashed brilliant light, fishing-boats dotted the bay. And the black hulk of the *Cestria* stretched its great length against the jetty where coal trams were rumbling from the nearby mine to a waiting schooner. Already the ship had unfurled her sails, jerseyed seamen were running her decks and the air was filled with hoarse cries; merchants' stalls were end to end along the sea wall, their vendors screaming their wares as I went down the main street to the quay. Market day by the look of it, the place thronged with coalmen, limemen, and labourers from the mine, coal-grimed, weary. Women bent under loads too heavy for men, barefooted children ran in the gutters, screaming a Welsh I did not understand. Beggars flung up skinny arms as I went down to the ship, fishermen lounged by their boats or needled at nets. Excitement grew within me at the sight of the ship, but I knew that I must not raise suspicion. Too many fugitives were travelling these days for eagerness. With Tara gripped against me I turned into a tavern. The room was crowded to the doors with men, seamen chiefly, roaring, bantering, thumping the counter, the mugs going down, mugs upturned in shafts of the morning sun. Welsh here, chiefly; men of the sea, barrel-chested, brown-faced, with the blue slits of eyes for scanning horizons. They parted good natured as I elbowed my way to the counter.

"A quart ale," I said, slapping down money, and got the mug and steered it through the sailors to a corner, and set it down.

"God," said a voice.

Matthew Luke John, his corn-coloured hair standing on end.

"Lord," he breathed. "You on the same do as me, boy?"

His eyes were shadowed with the sleeping out, his face pinched and pale with hunger.

"The *Cestria*, evening tide," I said. "You leaving your mam to fend alone, then?"

"The old man passed on," said he. "So she sold up and got out of farming – other ways to starve, she said. You hop out of it, man, she said, and take the chance I missed, and she gave me five pounds for steerage if I brought back a fortune."

"America, is it?"

"Couldn't be worse than this bitch of a place though it ought to be God's country. Lucky my mam was poorly or I'd have been on the march for Carmarthen. You heard about Flannigan?"

"Yes," I answered.

"And Toby Maudlin, Tom the Faith, and . . ."

"Tom's not taken?" I asked, straightening.

"Taken like the rest of them. John Penry, Howell Jones, Will

246

Raven, Ifor Walker – could go on for weeks. The dragoons were knocking on my door within two hours of the Carmarthen business. Justin did us well."

"Justin?" I stared at him.

"You haven't heard? Turned Queen's Evidence. They booted him twice in the workhouse yard and he couldn't gabble the names quick enough."

"God Almighty," I said.

He raised his sad eyes to mine. "You reckon he's Welsh?"

"Doubtful," I said.

"Nothing you can put your tongue to, eh? Forget him. The dragoons booted him harder after it and now he's explaining to St Peter. Found dead in a well within two miles of Carmarthen."

"Do they know who?" I asked.

"Rebecca. She didn't leave notes. The world's well rid of him." He sighed. "You signed on yet?"

"The *Cestria*? Not yet."

"Nor me. These boys say the dragoons will search her any minute. I've been waiting days for them to clear her. But the captain isn't choosey, thank God. Saints or convicts, he says, five pounds steerage. I got away from the house with ten minutes to spare – saw my mam giving hell to those dragoons – so I'm not rushing things now." He drank and gasped, wiping with his sleeve. "Been mooching round here for the last ten days."

"We sail together then?"

"Wacko!" said he. "We'll give them America. Do you reckon they starve out there?"

"Not if you work, they say."

"I drink to that," said he. "You heard about Tom Rhayader?"

I saw a vision of the beloved Rhayader; square-faced, tanned, his eyes of steel, and shook my head.

"Hit out two of them and tried to escape, but they got him in ten yards. He didn't come out of it."

I closed my eyes. "And his wife and kids?"

"Carmarthen workhouse last time I heard. God knows now. You leaving that woman, Jethro?"

I looked at him.

"The nightgown woman," said he. "The one who filled that was worth while bringing," and he winked at Tara. "Poor exchange with that old bitch. She bedded?"

"Not that woman," I said.

"Has she gone fripperty with another Welsh chap, then?"

"Leave it, Matthew."

"Only asking, mind. No offence."

"Leave it," I said.

Commotion on the cobbles outside now; hoofbeats, clanks, the angry cries of vendors, shouted commands. We rose. The sailors were pressing to the windows, jugs dangling, fists clenched as the horsemen drew sabres to clear a path to the *Cestria*. With a captain leading they forced their way along the quay to the gangplank where the skipper stood, hands on his hips. Three soldiers pushed past him and went aboard. We watched, tense, but they came back in five minutes.

"Routine check," I said. "Their hearts are not in it."

"Give them an hour," said Matthew. "Wait for the evening tide. They might come back."

The nightshift colliers had started when we left the tavern primed with enough ale to make us cheeky, and I thought of the Gower pit as I passed the black-faced labourers; the dull-eyed Welsh and Irish women hauling and singing to the clank of the wheels. But one was young, vital, alive. Irish by her looks, this girl, with the same bright beauty as my Morfydd, black-haired, one eye closing at me as I passed. Morfydd this, this the shade of another, I thought; one who was lying a hundred feet down in the press and smashed props of Number Six, one in the seam, one inch thick. Was Willie O'Hara weeping? I wondered, or seeking the breast of another Morfydd now she had left him for Richard, her lover? Strange the wish to snatch at this Irish, strange the wish to grip her, and I went back slowly to the gangplank where the captain was waiting. Matthew was doing the talking, fist thumping, bargaining. Money chinked and I was elbowed for mine, but I was not really there. I was down in Cae White with the dinner coming out, with the treadling of Mam's wheel in my ears, listening to the swish of the shuttle, Jonathon's high shrieks to Mari, her soft voice. And I heard again the sigh of the scythe and saw the wheat falling obliquely in sunfire; heard the herons crying doleful from Kidwelly, the curlews shouting at dawn, the barking of otters from the Reach, the whispers of Tessa. Other things I heard: Mari's shout to go to Chapel, the crackling hiss of the blazing gates, Mam's contralto in *Sanctus*. Dashing into the pitprops now, screaming for Morfydd; making love to Mari down on the shore. I put my hand into my pocket and gripped my earth, the handful I had brought from the fields of Cae White.

"Not that, you fool," said Matthew, eyeing me. "The man wants his money."

"O, aye," I said, and fished it out.

Snow-white deck now, pigtailed seamen, the smell of tar.

I stood by the rail with my hand in my pocket and gripped the earth.

"What the hell is wrong with you, man?" said Matthew.

But I did not answer him. Just staring at Wales. Sails were billowing above me, oceans of white as they dropped and unfurled. Feet stamped the deck. Dimly I heard the creaks, the commands, the shrieking of capstans.

"Damned pixilated, you," said Matthew. "I'm going below."

I gripped it in my hand, this Wales, and bowed my head. Gripped this plot for which men died; for which my kin had stood square to invaders, mocking the whip, spitting in the faces of kings. For such small muck and pebbles men have laboured and suffered – for this proud land of the Celts, Iberians, Moors and Spaniards, Angles, Jutes, Bretons, *Welsh!* For this blessed race whose mongrel blood is stirred with the blood of nobles and princes, this land of song and greenness that has flung an empire of invaders into the sea. The ship shuddered and rocked to the swell and I raised my head. Relations and friends were thronging the quay now; weepy matrons, stalwart fathers, ancient grandfers pinned on sticks, and the dying red sun was shining on the bare heads of children. Screamed goodbyes now, sobs and laughter as the exiles jostled beside me.

"For God's sake what is wrong with you, man?" Matthew again, turning me.

Wind in the rigging now, sails slapping; ropes were curling against the evening sun. The *Cestria* heaved and bucked beneath me. Hawsers tightened and sprayed water, drooped slack and tightened again as she fought to be free. Hands clenched, I stood there holding Tara.

What is it that enters the blood and chains a man's soul to the soul of his country? What is it that pierces as a barb and cannot be drawn? O, this beloved country that has raised its sword to the fire of its persecutors and reddened its soil with beloved sons! *Wales!* What lies in your possession that you bite at the throats of those who leave you? You of the mountainous crags of Dinas, of Snowden, Pembrey and Capel Pass – you of the valleys, heaths and pastures, the roaring rivers, the village brooks – what is your golden key that turns in the hearts of your patriots; what flame sears their souls in the last goodbye?

The gap was widening. The *Cestria* strained to the bridling hawsers. Heard the captain then; saw his arms outstretched to the quay where the crowd was gathering into an informal choir, and the labouring Welsh and Irish rushed to join them – any excuse for a song; barefooted, ragged, come to sing.

"A song for the exiles, then?" roared the captain.

"*Sanctus, Sanctus!*" a woman shrieked.

"Right, you, *Sanctus!*" And he stood conducting.

The ship vibrated to the voices, the crew stopped work and sang; faces turned up, they sang, and it was glorious, but I could not sing.

The crowd was thicker now, pouring down to the harbour, emptying from the hovels and taverns. Vendors screamed their wares at us, bullying a path for their carts, elbowing at tipsy sailors. Bull-chested colliers shouldered in from the mine, bantering, quarrelling, forming a circle of stamping hobnails, clapping to the time as a skinny Irish woman did a jig on the quay, skirts up, scarf waving, her black sticks of legs raising the dust, and the child-labour, drooping in their rags, watched her with dejected eyes. A drunken foreigner now, bottle waving, screaming insults, bristling for a fight; a black-gowned priest, hand up in blessing, telling his beads. All the bedlam of it grew about us in a thundering of sails, and above all was *Sanctus* in power and majesty, pulling in the crowd until it jammed them solid before the gangplank. Only one stood alone. Bending at the stern rail, I watched her. This, the image of Morfydd I had seen earlier, cheeky with her harlot come-hitherings, lounging impish on a bollard, smoothing back her long dark hair. Hands on her hips, brazen, she smiled at me. Rags fluttering, she waved, and I smiled back. Dimly I heard the captain's voice:

"We leave in joy, good people, so do not weep. For the exile takes but his body to the sister land, leaving his heart in Wales. Last verse of *Sanctus* again, and sing it to the sky! Sing!"

The tide had got us proper, swinging us to the stern ropes. The wind was rising, the pennant standing as stiff as a bar. Impatient, the *Cestria* bucked to the swell. Screamed goodbyes now, people weeping aloud, ropes splashing silver as they were hooked from bollards. Halyards stiffening, sails billowing, the ship heeled and rolled in the wind, thumping in the waves. I looked again at the Irish Morfydd, and saw through her breast the winding road that led to Amroth where Mari might be coming, and far beyond it to Llangain and Carmarthen, Llandeilo and Senny, and I laboured up the Clydach Valley road to home. Cae White I saw, ruined, deserted, the golden sweeps of its rejected corn; the empty kitchen, the cold, dead hob. And then came a vision of Mari, sitting in Tomos's trap with Richard and Jonathon either side, dominated by the black mass of Tomos, trotting east towards Nanty, and Mari was weeping. Aye, weeping – but for me, or her Iestyn? Strange and cruel are the laws of God, that a woman cannot marry her dead husband's brother. And this, I knew, was why she had not come. Stranger, too, are the laws of women. The road to Amroth danced in my eyes, and the road was empty. The crowd was as solid as a heading of coal now, arms raised as a forest as the gap between us widened, and I smiled again at the Irish Morfydd; she who had risen, it seemed, from the smashed props of Number Six and walked the galleries through a thousand tons of rock, sent by my Welsh Morfydd, to say goodbye.

Matthew Luke John at my elbow now, hooking me to face him.

"For God's sake, man," said he, "you are weeping."

"Go to hell," I said.

"For the petticoat woman? For that one there? O, aye!" and he narrowed his eyes. "Well, there's a waste, but never you mind, for we'll tar and feather a few in the town of Pittsburgh. Eh, dry it up, Jethro. They come better in silk than rags."

He spoke again, but I did not hear him, for in turning I had seen the crimson sky. The sun was setting, blazing and red as a Dutch cheese with him, one half steaming the sea and the other half in Hades, flaring at the clouds with his furnace glow, taking my mind back to childhood and the flashes of Blaenafon. It was as if the ovens of Pittsburgh had crashed back on hinges, striking at the world with their incinerating glare, and Mari's face grew dim in that light as the sea divided us. Creaking, clanking, shuddering, the *Cestria* was lumbering before the wind, and in the magnificence of her bedlam I heard the call of the iron as men had heard it for a thousand years before me. O, brilliant was this sky! Brilliant is the flaring when the cauldron is turned and the molten streams run wild, hissing and firing in the moulds! I put out my arm and thrust Matthew behind me, hearing again the clang of the loading bays, the thump of hammers, the whine of the mills. Bedlam in the rigging now as the *Cestria* got going, with the wind singing as a puddler's hammer and the spray hissing as water in the steaming-pit. This, the cold kiss of the firing-iron, the scald of the ladle, the heat and stink and sweat and call of it in all its hobnail stamping, this the iron that no woman understands. With Tara held against me I shouldered my way through the exiles huddled in their tears, staring at home; lace-trimmed gentry, half naked beggars, half starved Welsh and starving Irish. Reaching the prow I stared at the western sky where the iron was pouring, turning but once to wave.

Standing erect, she was, and alone, her shawl held high.

Morfydd no longer now, but Mari standing there.

"Mari," I said. "*Goodbye.*"

If you have enjoyed this Coronet book,
you may like to choose your next book from
the titles listed on the following pages

RAPE OF THE FAIR COUNTRY –
ALEXANDER CORDELL

RAPE OF THE FAIR COUNTRY is the first in Alexander Cordell's superb trilogy of mid-nineteenth century Wales, which continues with HOSTS OF REBECCA

Set in the grim valley of the Welsh Iron country, this turbulent, unforgettable novel begins the saga of the Mortymer family. A family of hard men and beautiful women, all forced into bitter struggle with their harsh environment, as they slave and starve for the cruel English iron-masters.

But adversity could never still the free spirit of Wales, or quiet its soaring voice, and the Mortymers fight and sing and make love even as the iron foundries ravish their homeland and cripple their people.

'Ribald, bawdy, exciting, tragically violent'
New York Times

'A tremendously lusty story ... a splendid novel'
Sunday Express

CORONET BOOKS

SONG OF THE EARTH –
ALEXANDER CORDELL

The final title in Alexander Cordell's unforgettable trilogy of mid-nineteenth century Wales which began with RAPE OF THE FAIR COUNTRY

Mostyn Evan and family, miners turned bargees wage a glorious but hopeless struggle against rapacious coal-masters, Irish navvies, the ravages of cholera, and the bullying illegal Unions.

As they ply their trade between the furnaces of Cyfarthfa and the lush beauty of the Neath Valley, they pray and fight, and sing and love and face each obstacle undaunted with all the stubborness and exuberance of Wales itself.

'Absorbing ... fascinating ... compelling'
Illustrated London News

'Memorably touching ... a brilliant degree of tenderness ... tragic power'
New Yorker

CORONET BOOKS

ALSO AVAILABLE FROM CORONET BOOKS

ALEXANDER CORDELL

☐ 20515 6	Rape Of The Fair Country	£2.50
☐ 17403 X	The Fire People	£2.25
☐ 23224 2	This Sweet And Bitter Earth	£2.25
☐ 20516 4	Song Of The Earth	£2.25

R. F. DELDERFIELD

☐ 23840 2	Diana	£2.95
☐ 16225 2	Theirs Was The Kingdom	£2.95

MALCOLM MACDONALD

☐ 22330 8	The Rich Are With You Always	£2.50
☐ 20010 3	World From The Rough Stones	£2.50
☐ 24170 5	Sons Of Fortune	£2.50

All these books are available at your local bookshop or newsagent, or can be ordered direct from the publisher. Just tick the titles you want and fill in the form below.

Prices and availability subject to change without notice.